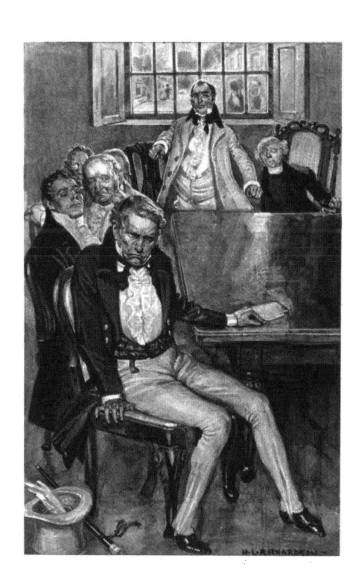

All eyes in the room were turned upon Mr. Bulstrode"
MIDDLEMARCH. *Page* 733

MIDDLEMARCH

BY

GEORGE ELIOT

IN THREE VOLUMES
VOLUME THREE

ILLUSTRATED

LITTLE, BROWN, AND COMPANY
BOSTON

CONTENTS

VOLUME THREE

BOOK VI.—THE WIDOW AND THE WIFE.

CHAPTER LIV.

"Negli occhi porta la mia donna Amore;
Per che si fa gentil ciò ch'ella mira:
Ov'ella passa, ogni uom ver lei si gira,
E cui saluta fa tremar lo core.
Sicchè, bassando il viso, tutto smore,
E d'ogni suo difetto allor sospira:
Fuggon dinanzi a lei Superbia ed Ira:
Aiutatemi, donne, a farle onore.
Ogni dolcezza, ogni pensiero umile
Nasce nel core a chi parlar la sente;
Ond' è beato chi prima la vide.
Quel ch'ella par quand' un poco sorride,
Non si può dicer, nè tener a mente,
Si è nuovo miracolo gentile."

—DANTE: *La Vita Nuova.*

By that delightful morning, when the hayricks at Stone Court were scenting the air quite impartially, as if Mr. Raffles had been a guest worthy of finest incense, Dorothea had again taken up her abode at Lowick Manor. After three months Freshitt had become rather oppressive: to sit like a model for St. Catherine looking rapturously at Celia's baby would not do for many hours in the day, and to remain in that momentous babe's presence with persistent disregard was a course that could not have been tolerated in a childless sister. Dorothea would have been capable of carrying baby joyfully for a mile if there had been need, and of loving it the more tenderly for that labor; but to an aunt who does not recognize her infant nephew as Bouddha, and has nothing to do for him but to admire, his behavior is apt to appear monotonous, and the interest of watching him exhaustible.

This possibility was quite hidden from Celia, who felt that Dorothea's childless widowhood fell in quite prettily with the birth of little Arthur (baby was named after Mr. Brooke).

"Dodo is just the creature not to mind about having any-

thing of her own—children or anything!" said Celia to her
husband. "And if she had had a baby, it never could have
been such a dear as Arthur. Could it, James?"

"Not if it had been like Casaubon," said Sir James, conscious of some indirectness in his answer, and of holding a
strictly private opinion as to the perfections of his first-born.

"No! just imagine! Really, it was a mercy," said Celia;
"and I think it very nice for Dodo to be a widow. She can
be just as fond of our baby as if it were her own, and she can
have as many notions of her own as she likes."

"It is a pity she was not a queen," said the devout Sir
James.

"But what should we have been then? We must have been
something else," said Celia, objecting to so laborious a flight
of imagination. "I like her better as she is."

Hence, when she found that Dorothea was making arrangements for her final departure to Lowick, Celia raised her eyebrows with disappointment, and in her quiet, unemphatic way
shot a needle-arrow of sarcasm.

"What will you do at Lowick, Dodo? You say yourself
there is nothing to be done there: everybody is so clean and
well off, it makes you quite melancholy. And here you have
been so happy going all about Tipton with Mr. Garth into the
worst back yards. And, now uncle is abroad, you and Mr.
Garth can have it all your own way; and I am sure James
does everything you tell him."

"I shall often come here, and I shall see how baby grows
all the better," said Dorothea.

"But you will never see him washed," said Celia; "and
that is quite the best part of the day." She was almost pouting: it did seem to her very hard in Dodo to go away from the
baby when she might stay.

"Dear Kitty, I will come and stay all night on purpose,"
said Dorothea; "but I want to be alone now, and in my own
home. I wish to know the Farebrothers better, and to talk to
Mr. Farebrother about what there is to be done in Middlemarch."

Dorothea's native strength of will was no longer all converted
into resolute submission. She had a great yearning to be at

Lowick, and was simply determined to go, not feeling bound
to tell all her reasons. But every one around her disapproved.
Sir James was much pained, and offered that they should all
migrate to Cheltenham for a few months with the sacred ark,
otherwise called a cradle: at that period a man could hardly
know what to propose if Cheltenham were rejected.

The Dowager Lady Chettam, just returned from a visit to
her daughter in town, wished, at least, that Mrs. Vigo should
be written to, and invited to accept the office of companion to
Mrs. Casaubon: it was not credible that Dorothea as a young
widow would think of living alone in the house at Lowick.
Mrs. Vigo had been reader and secretary to royal personages,
and in point of knowledge and sentiments even Dorothea could
have nothing to object to her.

Mrs. Cadwallader said, privately: "You will certainly go
mad in that house alone, my dear. You will see visions. We
have all got to exert ourselves a little to keep sane, and call
things by the same names as other people call them by. To
be sure, for younger sons and women who have no money, it
is a sort of provision to go mad: they are taken care of then.
But you must not run into that. I dare say you are a little
bored here with our good dowager; but think what a bore you
might become yourself to your fellow-creatures if you were
always playing tragedy queen and taking things sublimely.
Sitting alone in that library at Lowick you may fancy yourself
ruling the weather; you must get a few people round you who
wouldn't believe you if you told them. That is a good lowering medicine."

"I never called everything by the same name that all the
people about me did," said Dorothea, stoutly.

"But I suppose you have found out your mistake, my dear,"
said Mrs. Cadwallader, "and that is a proof of sanity."

Dorothea was aware of the sting, but it did not hurt her.
"No," she said; "I still think that the greater part of the
world is mistaken about many things. Surely one may be
sane and yet think so, since the greater part of the world has
often had to come round from its opinion."

Mrs. Cadwallader said no more on that point to Dorothea,
but to her husband she remarked: "It will be well for her to

marry again as soon as it is proper, if one could get her among the right people. Of course the Chettams would not wish it. But I see clearly a husband is the best thing to keep her in order. If we were not so poor, I would invite Lord Triton. He will be marquis some day, and there is no denying that she would make a good marchioness: she looks handsomer than ever in her mourning."

"My dear Elinor, do let the poor woman alone. Such contrivances are of no use," said the easy rector.

"No use? How are matches made, except by bringing men and women together? And it is a shame that her uncle should have run away and shut up the Grange just now. There ought to be plenty of eligible matches invited to Freshitt and the Grange. Lord Triton is precisely the man: full of plans for making the people happy in a soft-headed sort of way. That would just suit Mrs. Casaubon."

"Let Mrs. Casaubon choose for herself, Elinor."

"That is the nonsense you wise men talk! How can she choose if she has no variety to choose from? A woman's choice usually means taking the only man she can get. Mark my words, Humphrey—if her friends don't exert themselves, there will be a worse business than the Casaubon business yet."

"For Heaven's sake don't touch on that topic, Elinor! It is a very sore point with Sir James. He would be deeply offended if you entered on it to him unnecessarily."

"I have never entered on it," said Mrs. Cadwallader, opening her hands. "Celia told me all about the will at the beginning, without any asking of mine."

"Yes, yes; but they want the thing hushed up, and I understand that the young fellow is going out of the neighborhood."

Mrs. Cadwallader said nothing, but gave her husband three significant nods, with a very sarcastic expression in her dark eyes.

Dorothea quietly persisted in spite of remonstrance and persuasion. So by the end of June the shutters were all opened at Lowick Manor, and the morning gazed calmly into the library, shining on the rows of note-books, as it shines on the weary waste planted with huge stones, the mute memorial of a forgotten faith; and the evening, laden with roses, entered silently into the blue-green boudoir where Dorothea chose oftenest to sit. At first she walked into every room, questioning the eighteen months of her married life, and carrying on her thoughts as if they were a speech to be heard by her husband. Then she lingered in the library, and could not be at rest till she had carefully ranged all the note-books as she imagined that he would wish to see them, in orderly sequence. The pity which had been the restraining compelling motive in her life with him still clung about his image, even while she remonstrated with him in indignant thought and told him that he was unjust. One little act of hers may perhaps be smiled at as superstitious. The *Synoptical Tabulation for the use of Mrs. Casaubon*, she carefully enclosed and sealed, writing within the envelope: "*I could not use it. Do you not see now that I could not submit my soul to yours, by working hopelessly at what I have no belief in?—Dorothea.*" Then she deposited the paper in her own desk.

That silent colloquy was perhaps only the more earnest, because underneath and through it all there was always the deep longing which had really determined her to come to Lowick. The longing was to see Will Ladislaw. She did not know any good that could come of their meeting: she was helpless; her hands had been tied from making up to him for any unfairness in his lot. But her soul thirsted to see him. How could it be otherwise? If a princess in the days of enchantment had seen a four-footed creature, from among those which live in herds, come to her once and again with a human gaze which rested upon her with choice and beseeching, what would she think of in her journeying, what would she look for when the herds passed her? Surely for the gaze which had found her, and which she would know again. Life would be no better than candle-light tinsel and daylight rubbish if our spirits were not touched by what has been, to issues of longing and constancy. It was true that Dorothea wanted to know the Farebrothers better, and especially to talk to the new rector, but also true that, remembering what Lydgate had told her about Will Ladislaw and little Miss Noble, she counted on Will's coming to Lowick to see the Farebrother family. The very first Sunday, *before* she entered the church, she saw him as she had seen him the last time she was there, alone in the clergyman's pew; but *when* she entered his figure was gone.

In the week days when she went to see the ladies at the Rectory, she listened in vain for some word that they might let fall about Will; but it seemed to her that Mrs. Farebrother talked of everyone else in the neighborhood and out of it.

"Probably some of Mr. Farebrother's Middlemarch hearers may follow him to Lowick sometimes. Do you not think so?" said Dorothea, rather despising herself for having a secret motive in asking the question.

"If they are wise, they will, Mrs. Casaubon," said the old lady. "I see that you set a right value on my son's preaching. His grandfather on my side was an excellent clergyman, but his father was in the law: most exemplary and honest nevertheless, which is a reason for our never being rich. They say Fortune is a woman, and capricious. But sometimes she is a good woman, and gives to those who merit, which has been the case with you, Mrs. Casaubon, who have given a living to my son."

Mrs. Farebrother recurred to her knitting with a dignified satisfaction in her neat little effort at oratory, but this was not what Dorothea wanted to hear. Poor thing! she did not even know whether Will Ladislaw was still at Middlemarch, and there was no one whom she dared to ask, unless it were Lydgate. But just now she could not see Lydgate without sending for him or going to seek him. Perhaps Will Ladislaw, having heard of that strange ban against him left by Mr. Casaubon, had felt it better that he and she should not meet again, and perhaps she was wrong to wish for a meeting that others might find many good reasons against. Still "I do wish it" came at the end of those wise reflections as naturally as a sob after holding the breath. And the meeting did happen, but in a formal way quite unexpected by her.

One morning, about eleven, Dorothea was seated in her boudoir with a map of the land attached to the manor and other papers before her, which were to help her in making an exact statement for herself of her income and affairs. She had not yet applied herself to her work, but was seated with her hands folded on her lap, looking out along the avenue of limes to the distant fields.   Every leaf was at rest in the sunshine, the familiar scene was changeless, and seemed to represent the prospect of her life, full of motiveless ease—motiveless, if her own energy could not seek out reasons for ardent action.   The widow's cap of those times made an oval frame for the face, and had a crown standing up; the dress was an experiment in the utmost laying on of crape; but this heavy solemnity of clothing made her face look all the younger, with its recovered bloom, and the sweet, inquiring candor of her eyes.

Her reverie was broken by Tantripp, who came to say that Mr. Ladislaw was below, and begged permission to see madam if it were not too early.

"I will see him," said Dorothea, rising immediately.   "Let him be shown into the drawing-room."

The drawing-room was the most neutral room in the house to her—the one least associated with the trials of her married life: the damask matched the woodwork, which was all white and gold; there were two tall mirrors, and tables with nothing on them—in brief, it was a room where you had no reason for sitting in one place rather than in another.   It was below the boudoir, and had also a bow-window looking out on the avenue. But when Pratt showed Will Ladislaw into it the window was open; and a winged visitor, buzzing in and out now and then without minding the furniture, made the room look less formal and uninhabited.

"Glad to see you here again, sir," said Pratt, lingering to adjust a blind.

"I am only come to say good-bye, Pratt," said Will, who wished even the butler to know that he was too proud to hang about Mrs. Casaubon, now she was a rich widow.

"Very sorry to hear it, sir," said Pratt, retiring.   Of course, as a servant who was to be told nothing, he knew the fact of which Ladislaw was still ignorant, and had drawn his inferences; indeed, had not differed from his betrothed Tantripp when she said: " *Your* master was as jealous as a fiend —and no reason.   Madam would look higher than Mr. Ladislaw, else I don't know her.   Mrs. Cadwallader's maid says there's a lord coming who is to marry her when the mourning's over."

There were not many moments for Will to walk about with his hat in his hand before Dorothea entered. The meeting was very different from that first meeting in Rome when Will had been embarrassed and Dorothea calm. This time he felt miserable but determined, while she was in a state of agitation which could not be hidden. Just outside the door she had felt that this longed-for meeting was, after all, too difficult; and when she saw Will advancing toward her, the deep blush which was rare in her came with painful suddenness. Neither of them knew how it was, but neither of them spoke. She gave her hand for a moment, and they went to sit down near the window, she on one settee, and he on another opposite. Will was peculiarly uneasy: it seemed to him not like Dorothea that the mere fact of her being a widow should cause such a change in her manner of receiving him; and he knew of no other condition which could have affected their previous relation to each other—except that, as his imagination at once told him, her friends might have been poisoning her mind with their suspicions of him.

"I hope I have not presumed too much in calling," said Will; "I could not bear to leave the neighborhood and begin a new life without seeing you to say good-bye."

"Presumed? Surely not. I should have thought it unkind of you not to wish to see me," said Dorothea, her habit of speaking with perfect genuineness asserting itself through all her uncertainty and agitation. "Are you going away immediately?"

"Very soon, I think. I intend to go to town and eat my dinners as a barrister, since, they say, that is the preparation for all public business. There will be a great deal of political work to be done by and by, and I mean to try and do some of it. Other men have managed to win an honorable position for themselves without family or money."

"And that will make it all the more honorable," said Dorothea, ardently. "Besides, you have so many talents. I have heard from my uncle how well you speak in public, so that every one is sorry when you leave off, and how clearly you can explain things. And you care that justice should be done to every one. I am so glad. When we were in Rome, I thought you only cared for poetry and art, and the things that adorn life for us who are well off. But now I know you think about the rest of the world."

While she was speaking, Dorothea had lost her personal embarrassment, and had become like her former self. She looked at Will with a direct glance, full of delighted confidence.

"You approve of my going away for years, then, and never coming here again till I have made myself of some mark in the world?" said Will, trying hard to reconcile the utmost pride with the utmost effort to get an expression of strong feeling from Dorothea.

She was not aware how long it was before she answered. She had turned her head and was looking out of the window on the rose-bushes, which seemed to have in them the summers of all the years when Will would be away. This was not judicious behavior. But Dorothea never thought of studying her manners: she thought only of bowing to a sad necessity which divided her from Will. Those first words of his about his intentions had seemed to make everything clear to her: he knew, she supposed, all about Mr. Casaubon's final conduct in relation to him, and it had come to him with the same sort of shock as to herself. He had never felt more than friendship for her—had never had anything in his mind to justify what she felt to be her husband's outrage on the feelings of both; and that friendship he still felt. Something which may be called an inward, silent sob had gone on in Dorothea before she said, with a pure voice, just trembling in the last words as if only from its liquid flexibility:

"Yes, it must be right for you to do as you say. I shall be very happy when I hear that you have made your value felt. But you must have patience: it will perhaps be a long while."

Will never quite knew how it was that he saved himself from falling down at her feet, when the "long while" came forth with its gentle tremor. He used to say that the horrible hue and surface of her crape dress was most likely the sufficient controlling force. He sat still, however, and only said:

35

"I shall never hear from you. And you will forget all about me."

"No," said Dorothea, "I shall never forget you. I have never forgotten any one whom I once knew. My life has never been crowded, and seems not likely to be so. And I have a great deal of space for memory at Lowick, haven't I?" She smiled.

"Good God!" Will burst out passionately, rising, with his hat still in his hand, and walking away to a marble table, where he suddenly turned and leaned his back against it. The blood had mounted to his face and neck, and he looked almost angry. It had seemed to him as if they were like two creatures slowly turning to marble in each other's presence, while their hearts were conscious and their eyes were yearning. But there was no help for it. It should never be true of him that in this meeting to which he had come with bitter resolution, he had ended by a confession which might be interpreted into asking for her fortune. Moreover, it was actually true that he was fearful of the effect which such confessions might have on Dorothea herself.

She looked at him from that distance in some trouble, imagining that there might have been an offence in her words. But all the while there was a current of thought in her about his probable want of money, and the impossibility of her helping him. If her uncle had been at home, something might have been done through him! It was this preoccupation with the hardship of Will's wanting money, while she had what ought to have been his share, which led her to say, seeing that he remained silent and looked away from her:

"I wonder whether you would like to have that miniature which hangs upstairs—I mean that beautiful miniature of your grandmother. I think it is not right for me to keep it, if you would wish to have it. It is wonderfully like you."

"You are very good," said Will, irritably. "No; I don't mind about it. It is not very consoling to have one's own likeness. It would be more consoling if others wanted to have it."

"I thought you would like to cherish her memory—I thought——" Dorothea broke off an instant, her imagination suddenly warning her away from Aunt Julia's history—"you would surely like to have the miniature as a family memorial."

"Why should I have that, when I have nothing else? A man with only a portmanteau for his stowage must keep his memorials in his head."

Will spoke at random: he was merely venting his petulance; it was a little too exasperating to have his grandmother's portrait offered him at that moment. But to Dorothea's feelings his words had a peculiar sting. She rose, and said, with a touch of indignation as well as hauteur:

"You are much the happier of us two, Mr. Ladislaw, to have nothing."

Will was startled. Whatever the words might be, the tone seemed like a dismissal; and quitting his leaning posture, he walked a little way toward her. Their eyes met, but with a strange questioning gravity. Something was keeping their minds aloof, and each was left to conjecture what was in the other. Will had really never thought of himself as having a claim of inheritance on the property which was held by Dorothea, and would have required a narrative to make him understand her present feeling.

"I never felt it a misfortune to have nothing till now," he said. "But poverty may be as bad as leprosy, if it divides us from what we most care for."

The words cut Dorothea to the heart, and made her relent. She answered, in a tone of sad fellowship:

"Sorrow comes in so many ways. Two years ago I had no notion of that—I mean of the unexpected way in which trouble comes, and ties our hands, and makes us silent when we long to speak. I used to despise women a little for not shaping their lives more, and doing better things. I was very fond of doing as I liked, but I have almost given it up," she ended, smiling playfully.

"I have not given up doing as I like, but I can very seldom do it," said Will. He was standing two yards from her, with his mind full of contradictory desires and resolves—desiring some unmistakable proof that she loved him, and yet dreading the position into which such a proof might bring him. "The thing one most longs for may be surrounded with conditions that would be intolerable."

At this moment Pratt entered and said: "Sir James Chettam is in the library, madam."

"Ask Sir James to come in here," said Dorothea, immediately. It was as if the same electric shock had passed through her and Will. Each of them felt proudly resistant, and neither looked at the other, while they awaited Sir James's entrance.

After shaking hands with Dorothea, he bowed as slightly as possible to Ladislaw, who repaid the slightness exactly, and then, going toward Dorothea, said:

"I must say good-by, Mrs. Casaubon; and probably for a long while."

Dorothea put out her hand and said her good-by cordially. The sense that Sir James was depreciating Will, and behaving rudely to him, roused her resolution and dignity; there was no touch of confusion in her manner. And when Will had left the room, she looked with such calm self-possession at Sir James, saying, "How is Celia?" that he was obliged to behave as if nothing had annoyed him. And what would be the use of behaving otherwise? Indeed, Sir James shrank with so much dislike from the association, even in thought, of Dorothea with Ladislaw as her possible lover, that he would himself have wished to avoid an outward show of displeasure which would have recognized the disagreeable possibility. If any one had asked him why he shrank in that way, I am not sure that he would at first have said anything fuller or more precise than "*that* Ladislaw!"—though, on reflection, he might have urged that Mr. Casaubon's codicil, barring Dorothea's marriage with Will, except under penalty, was enough to cast unfitness over any relation at all between them. His aversion was all the stronger because he felt himself unable to interfere.

But Sir James was a power in a way unguessed by himself. Entering at that moment, he was an incorporation of the strongest reasons through which Will's pride became a repellent force, keeping him asunder from Dorothea.

CHAPTER LV.

"Hath she her faults? I would you had them too.
They are the fruity must of soundest wine;
Or say, they are regenerating fire
Such as hath turned the dense black element
Into a crystal pathway for the sun."

IF youth is the season of hope, it is often so only in the sense that our elders are hopeful about us; for no age is so apt as youth to think its emotions, partings, and resolves are the last of their kind. Each crisis seems final, simply because it is new. We are told that the oldest inhabitants in Peru do not cease to be agitated by the earthquakes, but they probably see beyond each shock, and reflect that there are plenty more to come.

To Dorothea, still in that time of youth when the eyes with their long full lashes look out after their rain of tears unsoiled and unwearied as a freshly-opened passion-flower, that morning's parting with Will Ladislaw seemed to be the close of their personal relations. He was going away into the distance of unknown years, and if ever he came back he would be another man. The actual state of his mind—his proud resolve to give the lie beforehand to any suspicion that he would play the needy adventurer seeking a rich woman—lay quite out of her imagination, and she had interpreted all his behavior easily enough by her supposition that Mr. Casaubon's codicil seemed to him, as it did to her, a gross and cruel interdict on any active friendship between them. Their young delight in speaking to each other, and saying what no one else would care to hear, was forever ended, and become a treasure of the past. For this very reason she dwelt upon it without inward check. That unique happiness, too, was dead, and in its shadowed silent chamber she might vent the passionate grief which she herself wondered at. For the first time she took down the miniature from the wall and kept it before her, liking to blend the woman who had been too hardly judged with the grandson whom her own heart and judgment defended. Can any one who has rejoiced in woman's tenderness think it

a reproach to her that she took the little oval picture in her
palm and made a bed for it there, and leaned her cheek upon
it, as if that would soothe the creatures who had suffered
unjust condemnation? She did not know then that it was
Love who had come to her briefly, as in a dream before awak-
ing, with the hues of morning on his wings—that it was Love
to whom she was sobbing her farewell as his image was
banished by the blameless rigor of irresistible day. She only
felt that there was something irrevocably amiss and lost in
her lot, and her thoughts about the future were the more
readily shapen into resolve. Ardent souls, ready to construct
their coming lives, are apt to commit themselves to the fulfilment of their own visions.

One day that she went to Freshitt to fulfil her promise of
staying all night and seeing baby washed, Mrs. Cadwallader
came to dine, the rector being gone on a fishing excursion. It
was a warm evening, and even in the delightful drawing-room,
where the fine old turf sloped from the open window toward
a lilied pool and well-planted mounds, the heat was enough to
make Celia, in her white muslin and light curls, reflect with
pity on what Dodo must feel, in her black dress and close cap.
But this was not until some episodes with baby were over, and
had left her mind at leisure. She had seated herself and
taken up a fan for some time before she said, in her quiet
guttural:

"Dear Dodo, do throw off that cap. I am sure your dress
must make you feel ill."

"I am so used to the cap, it has become a sort of shell,"
said Dorothea, smiling. "I feel rather bare and exposed when
it is off."

"I *must* see you without it; it makes us all warm," said
Celia, throwing down her fan, and going to Dorothea. It
was a pretty picture to see this little lady in white muslin
unfastening the widow's cap from her more majestic sister,
and tossing it on to a chair. Just as the coils and braids of
dark-brown hair had been set free, Sir James entered the
room. He looked at the released head, and said, "Ah!" in a
tone of satisfaction.

"It was I who did it, James," said Celia. "Dodo need not

make such a slavery of her mourning; she need not wear that cap any more among her friends."

"My dear Celia," said Lady Chettam, "a widow must wear her mourning at least a year."

"Not if she marries again before the end of it," said Mrs. Cadwallader, who had some pleasure in startling her good friend the dowager. Sir James was annoyed, and leaned forward to play with Celia's Maltese dog.

"That is very rare, I hope," said Lady Chettam, in a tone intended to guard against such events. "No friend of ours .ever committed herself in that way except Mrs. Beevor, and it was very painful to Lord Grinsell when she did so. Her first husband was objectionable, which made it the greater wonder. And severely she was punished for it. They said Captain Beevor dragged her about by the hair, and held up loaded pistols at her."

"Oh, if she took the wrong man!" said Mrs. Cadwallader, who was in a decidedly wicked mood. "Marriage is always bad then, first or second. Priority is a poor recommendation in a husband, if he has got no other. I would rather have a good second husband than an indifferent first."

"My dear, your clever tongue runs away with you," said Lady Chettam. "I am sure you would be the last woman to marry again prematurely, if our dear rector were taken away."

"Oh, I make no vows; it might be a necessary economy. It is lawful to marry again, I suppose; else we might as well be Hindoos instead of Christians. Of course, if a woman accepts the wrong man, she must take the consequences, and one who does it twice over deserves her fate. But if she can marry blood, beauty, and bravery—the sooner the better."

"I think the subject of our conversation is very ill-chosen," said Sir James, with a look of disgust. "Suppose we change it."

"Not on my account, Sir James," said Dorothea, determined not to lose the opportunity of freeing herself from certain oblique references to excellent matches. "If you are speaking on my behalf, I can assure you that no question can be more indifferent and impersonal to me than second marriage. It is no more to me than if you talk of women going fox-hunting:

whether it is admirable in them or not, I shall not follow them. Pray let Mrs. Cadwallader amuse herself on that subject as much as on any other."

"My dear Mrs. Casaubon," said Lady Chettam, in her stateliest way, "you do not, I hope, think there was any allusion to you in my mentioning Mrs. Beevor. It was only an instance that occurred to me. She was stepdaughter to Lord Grinsell: he married Mrs. Teveroy for his second wife. There could be no possible allusion to you."

"Oh, no," said Celia. "Nobody chose the subject; it all came out of Dodo's cap. Mrs. Cadwallader only said what was quite true. A woman could not be married in a widow's cap, James."

"Hush, my dear!" said Mrs. Cadwallader. "I will not offend again. I will not even refer to Dido or Zenobia. Only what are we to talk about? I, for my part, object to the discussion of human nature, because that is the nature of rectors' wives."

Later in the evening, after Mrs. Cadwallader was gone, Celia said privately to Dorothea: "Really, Dodo, taking your cap off made you like yourself again in more ways than one. You spoke up just as you used to do, when anything was said to displease you. But I could hardly make out whether it was James that you thought wrong, or Mrs. Cadwallader."

"Neither," said Dorothea. "James spoke out of delicacy to me, but he was mistaken in supposing that I minded what Mrs. Cadwallader said. I should only mind if there were a law obliging me to take any piece of blood and beauty that she or anybody else recommended."

"But you know, Dodo, if you ever did marry, it would be all the better to have blood and beauty," said Celia, reflecting that Mr. Casaubon had not been richly endowed with those gifts, and that it would be well to caution Dorothea in time.

"Don't be anxious, Kitty; I have quite other thoughts about my life. I shall never marry again," said Dorothea, touching her sister's chin, and looking at her with indulgent affection. Celia was nursing her baby, and Dorothea had come to say good-night to her.

"Really—quite?" said Celia. "Not anybody at all—if he were very wonderful indeed?"

Dorothea shook her head slowly. "Not anybody at all. I have delightful plans. I should like to take a great deal of land, and drain it, and make a little colony, where everybody should work, and all the work should be done well. I should know every one of the people, and be their friend. I am going to have great consultations with Mr. Garth: he can tell me almost everything I want to know."

"Then you *will* be happy if you have a plan, Dodo," said Celia. "Perhaps little Arthur will like plans when he grows up, and then he can help you."

Sir James was informed that same night that Dorothea was really quite set against marrying anybody at all, and was going to take to "all sorts of plans," just like what she used to have. Sir James made no remark. To his secret feeling there was something repulsive in a woman's second marriage, and no match would prevent him from feeling it a sort of desecration for Dorothea. He was aware that the world would regard such a sentiment as preposterous, especially in relation to a woman of one-and-twenty; the practice of "the world" being to treat of a young widow's second marriage as certain and probably near, and to smile with meaning if the widow acts accordingly. But if Dorothea did choose to espouse her solitude, he felt that the resolution would well become her.

CHAPTER LVI.

" How happy is he born and taught
That serveth not another's will :
Whose armor is his honest thought,
And simple truth his only skill !
*   *   *   *   *   *   *
This man is freed from servile bands
Of hope to rise, or fear to fall ;
Lord of himself, though not of lands ;
And having nothing, yet hath all. "
—SIR HENRY WOTTON.

DOROTHEA'S confidence in Caleb Garth's knowledge, which had begun on her hearing that he approved of her cottages, had grown fast during her stay at Freshitt, Sir James having induced her to take rides over the two estates in company with himself and Caleb, who quite returned her admiration, and told his wife that Mrs. Casaubon had a head for business most uncommon in a woman. It must be remembered that by "business" Caleb never meant money transactions, but the skilful application of labor.

"Most uncommon!" repeated Caleb. "She said a thing I often used to think myself when I was a lad: 'Mr. Garth, I should like to feel, if I lived to be old, that I had improved a great piece of land and built a great many good cottages, because the work is of a healthy kind while it is being done, and after it is done, men are the better for it.' Those were the very words: she sees into things in that way."

"But womanly, I hope," said Mrs. Garth, half suspecting that Mrs. Casaubon might not hold the true principle of subordination.

"Oh, you can't think," said Caleb, shaking his head. "You would like to hear her speak, Susan. She speaks in such plain words, and a voice like music. Bless me! it reminds me of bits in the 'Messiah'—'and straightway there appeared a multitude of the heavenly host, praising God and saying'; it has a tone with it that satisfies your ear."

Caleb was very fond of music, and when he could afford it, went to hear an oratorio that came within his reach, returning from it with a profound reverence for this mighty structure of tones, which made him sit meditatively looking on the floor and throwing much unutterable language into his outstretched hands.

With this good understanding between them, it was natural that Dorothea asked Mr. Garth to undertake any business connected with the three farms and the numerous tenements attached to Lowick Manor; indeed, his expectation of getting work for two was being fast fulfilled. As he said, "Business breeds." And one form of business which was beginning to breed just then was the construction of railways. A projected line was to run through Lowick parish, where the cattle had hitherto grazed in a peace unbroken by astonishment; and thus it happened that the infant struggles of the railway system entered into the affairs of Caleb Garth, and determined the course of this history with regard to two persons who were dear to him.

The submarine railway may have its difficulties; but the bed of the sea is not divided among various landed proprietors with claims for damages not only measurable but sentimental. In the hundred to which Middlemarch belonged, railways were as exciting a topic as the Reform Bill or the imminent horrors of cholera, and those who held the most decided views on the subject were women and landholders. Women, both old and young, regarded travelling by steam as presumptuous and dangerous, and argued against it by saying that nothing should induce them to get into a railway carriage; while proprietors, differing from each other in their arguments as much as Mr. Solomon Featherstone differed from Lord Medlicote, were yet unanimous in the opinion that in selling land, whether to the Enemy of mankind or to a company obliged to purchase, these pernicious agencies must be made to pay a very high price to landowners for permission to injure mankind.

But the slower wits, such as Mr. Solomon and Mrs. Waule, who both occupied land of their own, took a long time to arrive at this conclusion, their minds halting at the vivid conception of what it would be to cut the Big Pasture in two, and turn it into three-cornered bits, which would be "nohow"; while accommodation-bridges and high payments were remote and incredible.

"The cows will all cast their calves, brother," said Mrs. Waule, in a tone of deep melancholy, "if the railway comes across the Near Close; and I shouldn't wonder at the mare too, if she was in foal. It's a poor tale if a widow's property is to be spaded away, and the law say nothing to it. What's to hinder 'em from cutting right and left if they begin? It's well known, *I* can't fight?

"The best way would be to say nothing, and set somebody on to send 'em away with a flea in their ear, when they came spying and measuring," said Solomon. "Folks did that about Brassing, by what I can understand. It's all a pretense, if the truth was known, about their being forced to take one way. Let 'em go cutting in another parish. And I don't believe in any pay to make amends for bringing a

lot of ruffians to trample your crops. Where's a company's
pocket?"

"Brother Peter, God forgive him, got money out of a company," said Mrs. Waule. "But that was for the manganese.
That wasn't for railways to blow you to pieces right and
left."

"Well, there's this to be said, Jane," Mr. Solomon concluded, lowering his voice in a cautious manner—"the more
spokes we put in their wheel, the more they'll pay us to let
'em go on, if they must come whether or not."

This reasoning of Mr. Solomon's was perhaps less thorough
than he imagined, his cunning bearing about the same relation
to the course of railways as the cunning of a diplomatist bears
to the general chill of catarrh of the solar system. But he
set about acting on his views in a thoroughly diplomatic manner, by stimulating suspicion. His side of Lowick was the
most remote from the village, and the houses of the laboring
people were either lone cottages or were collected in a hamlet
called Frick, where a water-mill and some stone-pits made a
little centre of slow, heavy-shouldered industry.

In the absence of any precise idea as to what railways were,
public opinion in Frick was against them; for the human
mind in that grassy corner had not the proverbial tendency to
admire the unknown, holding rather that it was likely to be
against the poor man, and that suspicion was the only wise
attitude with regard to it. Even the rumor of reform had
not yet excited any millennial expectations in Frick, there
being no definite promise in it, as of gratuitous grains to fat-
ten Hiram Ford's pig, or of a publican at the "Weights and
Scales" who would brew beer for nothing, or of an offer on
the part of the three neighboring farmers to raise wages during the winter. And without distinct good of this kind in its
promises, reform seemed on a footing with the bragging of
peddlers, which was a hint for distrust to every knowing person. The men of Frick were not ill-fed, and were less given
to fanaticism than to a strong muscular suspicion; less inclined
to believe that they were peculiarly cared for by Heaven, than
to regard Heaven itself as rather disposed to take them in—a
disposition observable in the weather.

Thus the mind of Frick was exactly of the sort for Mr. Solomon Featherstone to work upon, he having more plenteous ideas of the same order, with a suspicion of heaven and earth which was better fed and more entirely at leisure. Solomon was overseer of the roads at that time, and on his slow-paced cob often took his rounds by Frick to look at the workmen getting the stones there, pausing with a mysterious deliberation, which might have misled you into supposing that he had some other reason for staying than the mere want of impulse to move. After looking for a long while at any work that was going on, he would raise his eyes a little and look at the horizon; finally he would shake his bridle, touch his horse with the whip, and get it to move slowly onward. The hour-hand of the clock was quick by comparison with Mr. Solomon, who had an agreeable sense that he could afford to be slow. He was in the habit of pausing for a cautious, vaguely designing chat with every hedger or ditcher on his way, and was especially willing to listen even to news which he had heard before, feeling himself at an advantage over all narrators in partially disbelieving them. One day, however, he got into a dialogue with Hiram Ford, a wagoner, in which he himself contributed information. He wished to know whether Hiram had seen fellows with staves and instruments spying about: they called themselves railroad people, but there was no telling what they were, or what they meant to do. The least they pretended was that they were going to cut Lowick Parish into sixes and sevens.

"Why, there'll be no stirrin', from one pla-ace to another," said Hiram, thinking of his wagon and horses.

"Not a bit," said Mr. Solomon. "And cutting up fine land such as this parish! Let 'em go into Tipton, say I. But there's no knowing what there is at the bottom of it. Traffic is what they put for'ard; but it's to do harm to the land and the poor man in the long run."

"Why, they're Lunnon chaps, I reckon," said Hiram, who had a dim notion of London as a centre of hostility to the country.

"Ay, to be sure. And in some parts against Brassing, by what I've heard say. the folks fell on 'em when they were spying, and broke their peep-holes as they carry, and drove 'em away, so as they knew better than come again."

"It war good foon, I'd be bound," said Hiram, whose fun was much restricted by circumstances.

"Well, I wouldn't meddle with 'em myself," said Solomon. "But some say this country's seen its best days, and the sign is, as it's being overrun with these fellows trampling right and left, and wanting to cut it up into railways; and all for the big traffic to swallow up the little, so as there sha'n't be a team left on the land, nor a whip to crack."

"I'll crack *my* whip about their ear'n, afore they bring it to that, though," said Hiram, while Mr. Solomon, shaking his bridle, moved onward.

Nettle-seed needs no digging. The ruin of this country-side by railroads was discussed, not only at the "Weights and Scales," but in the hay-field, where the muster of working-hands gave opportunities for talk such as were rarely had through the rural year.

One morning, not long after that interview between Mr. Farebrother and Mary Garth, in which she confessed to him her feeling for Fred Vincy, it happened that her father had some business which took him to Yoddrell's farm in the direction of Frick: it was to measure and value an outlying piece of land belonging to Lowick Manor, which Caleb expected to dispose of advantageously for Dorothea (it must be confessed that his bias was toward getting the best possible terms from railroad companies). He put up his gig at Yoddrell's, and in walking with his assistant and measuring-chain to the scene of his work, he encountered the party of the company's agents, who were adjusting their spirit-level. After a little chat he left them, observing that by-and-by they would reach him again where he was going to measure. It was one of those gray mornings after light rains, which become delicious about twelve o'clock, when the clouds part a little, and the scent of the earth is sweet along the lanes and by the hedge-rows.

The scent would have been sweeter to Fred Vincy, who was coming along the lanes on horseback, if his mind had not been worried by unsuccessful efforts to imagine what he was

to do, with his father on one side expecting him straightway
to enter the Church, with Mary on the other threatening to
forsake him if he did enter it, and with the working-day
world showing no eager need whatever of a young gentleman
without capital and generally unskilled. It was the harder
to Fred's disposition, because his father, satisfied that he was
no longer rebellious, was in good humor with him, and had
sent him on this pleasant ride to see after some greyhounds.
Even when he had fixed on what he should do, there would
be the task of telling his father. But it must be admitted
that the fixing, which had to come first, was the more difficult
task:—what secular avocation on earth was there for a young
man (whose friends could not get him an "appointment")
which was at once gentlemanly, lucrative, and to be followed
without special knowledge? Riding along the lanes by Frick
in this mood, and slackening his pace while he reflected
whether he should venture to go around by Lowick Parsonage
to call on Mary, he could see over the hedges from one field
to another. Suddenly a noise roused his attention, and on
the far side of a field on his left hand he could see six or
seven men in smock-frocks, with hay-forks in their hands, making an offensive approach toward the four railway agents who
were facing them, while Caleb Garth and his assistant were
hastening across the field to join the threatened group. Fred,
delayed a few moments by having to find the gate, could not
gallop up to the spot before the party in smock-frocks, whose
work of turning the hay had not been too pressing after swal-
lowing their mid-day beer, were driving the men in coats before them with their hay-forks: while Caleb Garth's assistant, a lad of seventeen, who had snatched up the spirit-level
at Caleb's order, had been knocked down, and seemed to be
lying helpless. The coated men had the advantage as runners,
and Fred covered their retreat by getting in front of the
smock-frocks and charging them suddenly enough to throw
their chase into confusion. "What do you confounded fools
mean?" shouted Fred, pursuing the divided group in a zig-
zag, and cutting right and left with his whip. "I'll swear to
every one of you before the magistrate. You've knocked the
lad down and killed him, for what I know. You'll every one

of you be hanged at the next assizes, if you don't mind," said
Fred, who afterward laughed heartily as he remembered his
own phrases.

The laborers had been driven through the gateway into their
hay-field, and Fred had checked his horse, when Hiram Ford,
observing himself at a safe challenging distance, turned back
and shouted a defiance which he did not know to be Homeric.

"Yo're a coward, yo are. Yo git off your horse, young
measter, and I'll have a round wi' ye, I wull. Yo daredn't
come on wi'out your hoss an' whip. I'd soon knock the breath
out on ye, I would."

"Wait a minute, and I'll come back presently, and have a
round with you all in turn, if you like," said Fred, who felt
confidence in his power of boxing with his dearly beloved
brethren. But just now he wanted to hasten back to Caleb
and the prostrate youth.

The lad's ankle was strained, and he was in much pain
from it, but he was no further hurt, and Fred placed him on
the horse that he might ride to Yoddrell's and be taken care
of there.

"Let them put the horse in the stable, and tell the survey-
ors they can come back for their traps," said Fred. "The
ground is clear now."

"No, no," said Caleb, "here's a breakage. They'll have
to give up for to-day, and it will be as well. Here, take the
things before you on the horse, Tom. They'll see you coming, and they'll turn back."

"I'm glad I happened to be here at the right moment, Mr.
Garth," said Fred, as Tom rode away. "No knowing what
might have happened if the cavalry had not come up in
time."

"Ay, ay, it was lucky," said Caleb, speaking rather absently, and looking toward the spot where he had been at
work at the moment of interruption. "But—deuce take it—
this is what comes of men being fools—I'm hindered of my
day's work. I can't get along without somebody to help me
with the measuring-chain. However!" He was beginning
to move toward the spot with a look of vexation, as if he had
forgotten Fred's presence, but suddenly he turned round and

said quickly, "What have you got to do to-day, young
fellow?"

"Nothing, Mr. Garth. I'll help you with pleasure—can
I?" said Fred, with a sense that he should be courting Mary
when he was helping her father.

"Well, you mustn't mind stooping and getting hot."

"I don't mind anything. Only I want to go first and have
a round with that hulky fellow who turned to challenge me.
It would be a good lesson for him. I shall not be five
minutes."

"Nonsense!" said Caleb, with his most peremptory intona-
tion. "I shall go and speak to the men myself. It's all
ignorance. Somebody has been telling them lies. The poor
fools don't know any better."

"I shall go with you, then," said Fred.

"No, no; stay where you are. I don't want your young
blood. I can take care of myself."

Caleb was a powerful man, and knew little of any fear
except the fear of hurting others and the fear of having to
speechify. But he felt it his duty at this moment to try
and give a little harangue. There was a striking mixture in
him—which came from his having always been a hard-work-
ing man himself—of rigorous notions about workmen and
practical indulgence toward them. To do a good day's work
and to do it well, he held to be a part of their welfare, as it
was the chief part of his own happiness; but he had a strong
sense of fellowship with them. When he advanced toward
the laborers they had not gone to work again, but were standing in that form of rural grouping which consists in each turning a shoulder toward the other, at a distance of two or three
yards. They looked rather sulkily at Caleb, who walked
quickly, with one hand in his pocket and the other thrust between the buttons of his waistcoat, and had his every-day mild
air when he paused among them.

"Why, my lads, how's this?" he began, taking as usual
to brief phrases, which seemed pregnant to himself, because
he had many thoughts lying under them, like the abundant roots
of a plant that just manages to peep above the water. "How
came you to make such a mistake as this? Somebody has

36

been telling you lies. You thought those men up there wanted
to do mischief."

"Aw!" was the answer, dropped at intervals by each according to his degree of unreadiness.

"Nonsense! No such thing! They're looking out to see
which way the railroad is to take. Now, my lads, you can't
hinder the railroad: it will be made whether you like it or
not. And if you go fighting against it, you'll get yourselves
into trouble. The law gives those men leave to come here on
the land. The owner has nothing to say against it, and if
you meddle with them you'll have to do with the constable
and Justice Blakesley, and with the handcuffs and Middlemarch jail. And you might be in for it now, if anybody
informed against you."

Caleb paused here, and perhaps the greatest orator could
not have chosen his pause or his images better for the occasion.

"But come, you didn't mean any harm. Somebody told
you the railroad was a bad thing. That was a lie. It may
do a bit of harm here and there, to this and to that; and so
does the sun in heaven. But the railway's a good thing."

"Aw! good for the big folks to make money out on," said
old Timothy Cooper, who had stayed behind turning his hay
while the others had been gone on their spree: "I'n seen lots
o' things turn up sin' I war a young un—the war an' the
peace, and the canells, an' the oald King George, an' the
Regen', an' the new King George, an' the new un as has got
a new ne-ame—an' it's been all aloike to the poor mon.
What's the canells been t' him? They'n brought him ney-
ther me-at nor be-acon, nor wage to lay by, if he didn't save
it wi' clemmin' his own inside. Times ha' got wusser for him
sin' I war a young un. An' so it'll be wi' the railroads.
They'll only leave the poor mon furder behind. But them are
fools as meddle, and so I told the chaps here. This is the big
folks's world, this is. But you're for the big folks, Muster
Garth, yo are."

Timothy was a wiry old laborer, of a type lingering in those
times—who had his savings in a stocking-foot, lived in a lone
cottage, and was not to be wrought on by any oratory, having
as little of the feudal spirit, and believing as little, as if he

had not been totally unacquainted with the Age of Reason
and the Rights of Man.   Caleb was in a difficulty known to
any person attempting in dark times, and unassisted by miracle, to reason with rustics who are in possession of an undeniable truth which they know through a hard process of feeling, and can let it fall like a giant's club on your neatly carved
argument for a social benefit which they do *not* feel.   Caleb
had no cant at command, even if he could have chosen to use
it; and he had been accustomed to meet all such difficulties
in no other way then by doing his "business" faithfully.
He answered:

"If you don't think well of me, Tim, never mind; that's
neither here nor there now.   Things may be bad for the poor
man—bad they are; but I want the lads here not to do what
will make things worse for themselves.   The cattle may have
a heavy load, but it won't help 'em to throw it over into the
roadside pit, when it's partly their own fodder."

"We war on'y for a bit o' foon," said Hiram, who was beginning to see consequences.   "That war all we war arter."

"Well, promise me not to meddle again, and I'll see that
nobody informs against you."

"I'n ne'er meddled an' I'n no call to promise," said Timothy.

"No, but the rest.   Come, I'm as hard at work as any of
you to-day, and I can't spare much time.   Say you'll be quiet
without the constable."

"Aw, we wooant meddle—they may do as they loike for
oos"—were the forms in which Caleb got his pledges; and
then he hastened back to Fred, who had followed him, and
watched him in the gateway.

They went to work, and Fred helped vigorously.   His spirits
had risen, and he heartily enjoyed a good slip in the moist
earth under the hedgerow, which soiled his perfect summer
trousers.   Was it his successful onset which had elated him,
or the satisfaction of helping Mary's father?   Something
more.   The accidents of the morning had helped his frustrated
imagination to shape an employment for himself which had
several attractions.   I am not sure that certain fibres in Mr.
Garth's mind had not resumed their old vibration toward the
very end which now revealed itself to Fred.   For the effec-

tive accident is but the touch of fire where there is oil and tow; and it always appeared to Fred that the railway brought the needed touch. But they went on in silence, except when their business demanded speech. At last, when they had finished, and were walking away, Mr. Garth said:

"A young fellow needn't be a B.A. to do this sort of work, eh, Fred?"

"I wish I had taken to it before I had thought of being a B.A.," said Fred. He paused a moment, and then added, more hesitatingly, "Do you think I am too old to learn your business, Mr. Garth?"

"My business is of many sorts, my boy," said Mr. Garth, smiling. "A good deal of what I know can only come from experience: you can't learn it off as you learn things out of a book. But you are young enough to lay a foundation yet." Caleb pronounced the last sentence emphatically, but paused in some uncertainty. He had been under the impression lately that Fred had made up his mind to enter the Church.

"You do think I could do some good at it, if I were to try?" said Fred, more eagerly.

"That depends," said Caleb, turning his head on one side, and lowering his voice, with the air of a man who felt himself to be saying something deeply religious. "You must be sure of two things: you must love your work, and not be always looking over the edge of it, wanting your play to begin. And the other is, you must not be ashamed of your work, and think it would be more honorable to you to be doing something else. You must have a pride in your own work and in learning to do it well, and not be always saying, There's this and there's that —if I had this or that to do, I might make something of it. No matter what a man is—I wouldn't give twopence for him" —here Caleb's mouth looked bitter, and he snapped his fingers —"whether he was the prime minister or the rick-thatcher, if he didn't do well what he undertook to do."

"I can never feel that I should do that in being a clergy-man," said Fred, meaning to take a step in argument.

"Then let it alone, my boy," said Caleb, abruptly, "else you'll never be easy. Or, if you *are* easy, you'll be a poor stick."

"That is very nearly what Mary thinks about it," said Fred, coloring. "I think you must know what I feel for Mary, Mr. Garth: I hope it does not displease you that I have always loved her better than any one else, and that I shall never love any one as I love her."

The expression of Caleb's face was visibly softening while Fred spoke. But he swung his head with a solemn slowness, and said:

"That makes things more serious, Fred, if you want to take Mary's happiness into your keeping."

"I know that, Mr. Garth," said Fred, eagerly, "and I would do anything for *her*. She says she will never have me if I go into the Church; and I shall be the most miserable devil in the world if I lose all hope of Mary. Really, if I could get some other profession, business—anything that I am at all fit for—I would work hard, I would deserve your good opinion. I should like to have to do with outdoor things. I know a good deal about land and cattle already. I used to believe, you know—though you will think me rather foolish for it—that I should have land of my own. I am sure knowledge of that sort would come easily to me, especially if I could be under you in any way."

"Softly, my boy," said Caleb, having the image of " Susan " before his eyes. "What have you said to your father about all this?"

"Nothing yet; but I must tell him. I am only waiting to know what I can do instead of entering the Church. I am very sorry to disappoint him, but a man ought to be allowed to judge for himself when he is four-and-twenty. How could I know, when I was fifteen, what it would be right for me to do now? My education was a mistake."

"But hearken to this, Fred," said Caleb. "Are you sure Mary is fond of you, or would ever have you?"

"I asked Mr. Farebrother to talk to her, because she had forbidden me—I didn't know what else to do," said Fred, apologetically. "And he says that I have every reason to hope, if I can put myself in an honorable position—I mean, out of the Church. I dare say you think it unwarrantable in me, Mr. Garth, to be troubling you and obtruding my own wishes about Mary, before I have done anything at all for myself. Of course I have not the least claim—indeed, I have already a debt to you which will never be discharged, even when I have been able to pay it in the shape of money."

"Yes, my boy, you have a claim," said Caleb, with much feeling in his voice. "The young ones have always a claim on the old to help them forward. I was young myself once, and had to do without much help; but help would have been welcome to me, if it had been only for the fellow-feeling's sake. But I must consider. Come to me to-morrow at the office, at nine o'clock. At the office, mind."

Mr. Garth would take no important step without consulting Susan, but it must be confessed that before he reached home he had taken his resolution. With regard to a large number of matters about which other men are decided or obstinate, he was the most easily manageable man in the world. He never knew what meat he would choose; and if Susan had said that they ought to live in a four-roomed cottage, in order to save, he would have said, "Let us go," without inquiring into details. But where Caleb's feeling and judgment strongly pronounced, he was a ruler; and in spite of his mildness and timidity in reproving, every one about him knew that on the exceptional occasions, when he chose, he was absolute. He never, indeed, chose to be absolute except on some one else's behalf. On ninety-nine points Mrs. Garth decided, but on the hundredth she was often aware that she would have to perform the singularly difficult task of carrying out her own principle, and to make herself subordinate.

"It is come round as I thought, Susan," said Caleb, when they were seated alone in the evening. He had already narrated the adventure which had brought about Fred's sharing in his work, but had kept back the further result. "The children *are* fond of each other—I mean, Fred and Mary."

Mrs. Garth laid her work on her knee, and fixed her penetrating eyes anxiously on her husband.

"After we'd done our work, Fred poured it all out to me. He can't bear to be a clergyman, and Mary says she won't have him if he is one; and the lad would like to be under me, and give his mind to business. And I've determined to take him and make a man of him."

"Caleb!" said Mrs. Garth, in a deep contralto, expressive of resigned astonishment.

"It's a fine thing to do," said Mr. Garth, settling himself firmly against the back of his chair, and grasping the elbows. "I shall have trouble with him, but I think I shall carry it through. The lad loves Mary, and a true love for a good woman is a great thing, Susan. It shapes many a rough fellow."

"Has Mary spoken to you on the subject?" said Mrs. Garth, secretly a little hurt that she had to be informed on it herself.

"Not a word. I asked her about Fred once; I gave her a bit of warning. But she assured me she would never marry an idle, self-indulgent man—nothing since. But it seems Fred set on Mr. Farebrother to talk to her, because she had forbidden him to speak himself, and Mr. Farebrother has found out that she is fond of Fred, but says he must not be a clergyman. Fred's heart is fixed on Mary, that I can see; it gives me a good opinion of the lad—and we always liked him, Susan."

"It is a pity for Mary, I think," said Mrs. Garth.

"Why—a pity?"

"Because, Caleb, she might have had a man who is worth twenty Fred Vincys."

"Ah?" said Caleb, with surprise.

"I firmly believe that Mr. Farebrother is attached to her, and meant to make her an offer; but of course, now that Fred has used him as an envoy, there is an end to that better prospect." There was a severe precision in Mrs. Garth's utterance. She was vexed and disappointed, but she was bent on abstaining from useless words.

Caleb was silent a few moments under a conflict of feelings. He looked at the floor, and moved his head and hands in accompaniment to some inward argumentation. At last he said:

"That would have made me very proud and happy, Susan, and I should have been glad for your sake. I've always felt that your belongings have never been on a level with you. But you took me, though I was a plain man."

"I took the best and cleverest man I had ever known," said Mrs. Garth, convinced that *she* would never have loved any one who came short of that mark.

"Well, perhaps others thought you might have done better. But it would have been worse for me. And that is what touches me close about Fred. The lad is good at bottom, and clever enough to do, if he's put.in the right way; and he loves and honors my daughter beyond anything, and she has given him a sort of promise according to what he turns out. I say, that young man's soul is in my hand; and I'll do the best I can for him, so help me God! It's my duty, Susan."

Mrs. Garth was not given to tears, but there was a large one rolling down her face before her husband had finished. It came from the pressure of various feelings, in which there was much affection and some vexation. She wiped it away quickly, saying—-

"Few men besides you would think it a duty to add to their anxieties in that way, Caleb."

"That signifies nothing—what other men would think. I've got a clear feeling inside me, and that I shall follow; and I hope your heart will go with me, Susan, in making everything as light as can be to Mary, poor child."

Caleb, leaning back in his chair, looked with anxious appeal toward his wife. She rose and kissed him, saying, "God bless you, Caleb! Our children have a good father."

But she went out and had a hearty cry, to make up for the suppression of her words. She felt sure that her husband's conduct would be misunderstood, and about Fred she was rational and unhopeful. Which would turn out to have the more foresight in it—her rationality or Caleb's ardent generosity?

When Fred went to the office the next morning, there was a test to be gone through which he was not prepared for.

"Now, Fred," said Caleb, "you will have some desk-work. I have always done a good deal of writing myself, but I can't do without help; and as I want you to understand the accounts and get the values into your head, I mean to do without another clerk. So you must buckle to. How are you at writing and arithmetic?"

Fred felt an awkward movement of the heart; he had not thought of desk-work; but he was in a resolute mood, and not going to shrink. "I'm not afraid of arithmetic, Mr. Garth: it always came easily to me. I think you know my writing."

"Let us see," said Caleb, taking up a pen, examining it carefully, and handing it, well dipped, to Fred with a sheet of ruled paper. "Copy me a line or two of that valuation, with the figures at the end."

At that time the opinion existed that it was beneath a gentleman to write legibly, or with a hand in the least suitable to a clerk. Fred wrote the lines demanded in a hand as gentlemanly as that of any viscount or bishop of the day: the vowels were all alike, and the consonants only distinguishable as turning up or down; the strokes had a blotted solidity, and the letters disdained to keep the line—in short, it was a manuscript of that venerable kind easy to interpret when you know beforehand what the writer means.

As Caleb looked on, his visage showed a growing depression, but when Fred handed him the paper he gave something like a snarl, and rapped the paper passionately with the back of his hand. Bad work like this dispelled all Caleb's mildness.

"The deuce!" he exclaimed, snarlingly. "To think that this is a country where a man's education may cost hundreds and hundreds, and it turns you out this!" Then, in a more pathetic tone, pushing up his spectacles and looking at the unfortunate scribe, "The Lord have mercy on us, Fred, I can't put up with this!"

"What can I do, Mr. Garth?" said Fred, whose spirits had sunk very low, not only at the estimate of his handwriting, but at the vision of himself as liable to be ranked with office-clerks.

"Do? Why, you must learn to form your letters and keep the line. What's the use of writing at all if nobody can understand it?" asked Caleb, energetically, quite preoccupied with the bad quality of the work. "Is there so little business in the world that you must be sending puzzles over the country? But that's the way people are brought up. I should lose no end of time with the letters some people send

me, if Susan did not make them out for me.   It's disgusting."
Here Caleb tossed the paper from him.

Any stranger peeping into the office at that moment might
have wondered what was the drama between the indignant
man of business, and the fine-looking young fellow whose
blonde complexion was getting rather patchy as he bit his lip
with mortification.   Fred was struggling with many thoughts.
Mr. Garth had been so kind and encouraging at the beginning
of their interview, that gratitude and hopefulness had been at
a high pitch, and the downfall was proportionate.   He had
not thought of desk-work—in fact, like the majority of young
gentlemen, he wanted an occupation which should be free from
disagreeables.   I cannot tell what might have been the consequences if he had not distinctly promised himself that he
would go to Lowick to see Mary and tell her that he was engaged to work under her father.   He did not like to disappoint himself there.

"I am very sorry," were all the words that he could muster.
But Mr. Garth was already relenting.

"We must make the best of it, Fred," he began, with a return to his usual quiet tone.   "Every man can learn to write.
I taught myself.   Go at it with a will, and sit up at night, if
the daytime isn't enough.   We'll be patient, my boy.   Callum
shall go on with the books for a bit, while you are learning.
But now I must be off," said Caleb, rising.   "You must let
your father know our agreement.   You'll save me Callum's
salary, you know, when you can write; and I can afford to
give you eighty pounds for the first year, and more after."

When Fred made the necessary disclosure to his parents,
the relative effect on the two was a surprise which entered
very deeply into his memory.   He went straight from Mr.
Garth's office to the warehouse, rightly feeling that the most
respectful way in which he could behave to his father was to
make the painful communication as gravely and formally as
possible.   Moreover, the decision would be more certainly
understood to be final, if the interview took place in his
father's gravest hours, which were always those spent in his
private room at the warehouse.

Fred entered on the subject directly, and declared briefly

what he had done and was resolved to do, expressing at the
end his regret that he should be the cause of disappointment
to his father, and taking the blame on his own deficiencies.
The regret was genuine, and inspired Fred with strong, simple
words.

Mr. Vincy listened in profound surprise, without uttering
even an exclamation—a silence which, in his impatient temperament, was a sign of unusual emotion.   He had not been in
good spirits about trade that morning, and the slight bitterness in his lips grew intense as he listened.   When Fred had
ended, there was a pause of nearly a minute, during which
Mr. Vincy replaced a book in his desk and turned the key emphatically.   Then he looked at his son steadily, and said—

"So you've made up your mind at last, sir?"

"Yes, father."

"Very well; stick to it.   I've no more to say.   You've
thrown away your education, and gone down a step in life,
when I had given you the means of rising, that's all."

"I am very sorry that we differ, father.   I think I can be
quite as much of a gentleman at the work I have undertaken
as if I had been a curate.   But I am grateful to you for wishing to do the best for me."

"Very well; I have no more to say.   I wash my hands of
you.   I only hope, when you have a son of your own, he will
make a better return for the pains you spend on him."

This was very cutting to Fred.   His father was using that
unfair advantage possessed by us all when we are in a pathetic
situation, and see our own past as if it were simply part of the
pathos.   In reality, Mr. Vincy's wishes about his son had had
a great deal of pride, inconsiderateness, and egoistic folly in
them.   But still the disappointed father held a strong lever,
and Fred felt as if he were being banished with a malediction.

"I hope you will not object to my remaining at home, sir?"
he said, after rising to go; "I shall have a sufficient salary to
pay for my board, as of course I should wish to do."

"Board, be hanged!" said Mr. Vincy, recovering himself
in his disgust at the notion that Fred's keep would be missed
at his table.   "Of course your mother will want you to stay.
But I shall keep no horse for you, you understand; and you

will pay your own tailor.   You will do with a suit or two less, I fancy, when you have to pay for 'em."

Fred lingered; there was still something to be said.   At last it came.

"I hope you will shake hands with me, father, and forgive me the vexation I have caused you."

Mr. Vincy from his chair threw a quick glance upward at his son, who had advanced near to him, and then gave his hand, saying hurriedly, "Yes, yes, let us say no more."

Fred went through much more narrative and explanation with his mother, but she was inconsolable, having before her eyes what perhaps her husband had never thought of, the certainty that Fred would marry Mary Garth, that her life would henceforth be spoiled by a perpetual infusion of Garths and their ways, and that her darling boy, with his beautiful face and stylish air, "beyond anybody else's son in Middlemarch," would be sure to get like that family in plainness of appearance and carelessness about his clothes.   To her it seemed that there was a Garth conspiracy to get possession of the desirable Fred; but she dared not enlarge on this opinion, because a slight hint of it had made him "fly out" at her as he had never done before.   Her temper was too sweet for her to show any anger; but she felt that her happiness had received a bruise, and for several days merely to look at Fred made her cry a little, as if he were the subject of some baleful prophecy.   Perhaps she was the slower to recover her usual cheerfulness because Fred had warned her that she must not reopen the sore question with his father, who had accepted his decision and forgiven him.   If her husband had been vehement against Fred, she would have been urged into defence of her darling.   It was the end of the fourth day when Mr. Vincy said to her:

"Come, Lucy, my dear, don't be so down-hearted.   You always have spoiled the boy, and you must go on spoiling him."

"Nothing ever did cut me so before, Vincy," said the wife, her fair throat and chin beginning to tremble again, "only his illness."

"Pooh, pooh, never mind!   We must expect to have trouble

with our children. Don't make it worse by letting me see you out of spirits."

"Well, I won't," said Mrs. Vincy, roused by this appeal, and adjusting herself with a little shake, as of a bird which lays down its ruffled plumage.

"It won't do to begin making a fuss about one," said Mr. Vincy, wishing to combine a little grumbling with domestic cheerfulness. "There's Rosamond as well as Fred."

"Yes, poor thing. I'm sure I felt for her being disappointed of her baby; but she got over it nicely."

"Baby, pooh! I can see Lydgate is making a mess of his practice, and getting into debt too, by what I hear. I shall have Rosamond coming to me with a pretty tale one of these days. But they'll get no money from me, I know. Let *his* family help him. I never did like that marriage. But it's no use talking. Ring the bell for lemons, and don't look dull any more, Lucy. I'll drive you and Louisa to Riverston to-morrow."

CHAPTER LVII.

They numbered scarce eight summers, when a name
  Rose on their souls, and stirred such motions there
As thrill the buds and shape their hidden frame
  At penetration of the quickening air:
His name who told of loyal Evan Dhu,
  Of quaint Bradwardine, and Vich Ian Vor,
Making the little world their childhood knew
  Large with a land of mountain, lake, and scaur,
And larger yet with wonder, love, belief
  Toward Walter Scott, who, living far away,
Sent them this wealth of joy and noble grief.
  The book and they must part, but day by day,
  In lines that thwart like portly spiders ran,
  They wrote the tale, from Tully Veolan.

THE evening that Fred Vincy walked to Lowick Parsonage (he had begun to see that this was a world in which even a spirited young man must sometimes walk for want of a horse to carry him) he set out at five o'clock, and called on Mrs. Garth by the way, wishing to assure himself that she accepted their new relations willingly.

He found the family group, dogs and cats included, under the great apple-tree in the orchard. It was a festival with

Mrs. Garth, for her eldest son, Christy, her peculiar joy and pride, had come home for a short holiday—Christy, who held it the most desirable thing in the world to be a tutor, to study all literatures and be a regenerate Porson, and who was an incorporate criticism on poor Fred, a sort of object-lesson given to him by the educational mother. Christy himself, a square-browed, broad-shouldered masculine edition of his mother not much higher than Fred's shoulder—which made it the harder that he should be held superior—was always as simple as possible, and thought no more of Fred's disinclination to scholarship than of a giraffe's, wishing that he himself were more of the same height. He was lying on the ground now by his mother's chair, with his straw hat laid flat over his eyes, while Jim on the other side was reading aloud from that beloved writer who has made a chief part in the happiness of many young lives. The volume was "Ivanhoe," and Jim was in the great archery scene at the tournament, but suffered much interruption from Ben, who had fetched his own old bow and arrows, and was making himself dreadfully disagreeable, Letty thought, by begging all present to observe his random shots, which no one wished to do except Brownie, the active-minded but probably shallow mongrel, while the grizzled Newfoundland lying in the sun looked on with the dull-eyed neutrality of extreme old age. Letty herself, showing as to her mouth and pinafore some slight signs that she had been assisting at the gathering of the cherries which stood on a coral-heap on the tea-table, was now seated on the grass, listening open-eyed to the reading.

But the centre of interest was changed for all by the arrival of Fred Vincy. When, seating himself on a garden-stool, he said that he was on his way to Lowick Parsonage, Ben, who had thrown down his bow, and snatched up a reluctant half-grown kitten instead, strode across Fred's outstretched leg, and said, "Take me!"

"And me too," said Letty.

"You can't keep up with Fred and me," said Ben.

"Yes, I can. Mother, please say that I am to go," urged Letty, whose life was much checkered by resistance to her depreciation as a girl.

"*I* shall stay with Christy," observed Jim; as much as to say that he had the advantage of those simpletons; whereupon Letty put her hand up to her head and looked with jealous indecision from the one to the other.

"Let us all go and see Mary," said Christy, opening his arms.

"No, my dear child, we must not go in a swarm to the parsonage. And that old Glasgow suit of yours would never do. Besides, your father will come home. We must let Fred go alone. He can tell Mary that you are here, and she will come back to-morrow."

Christy glanced at his own threadbare knees, and then at Fred's beautiful white trousers. Certainly Fred's tailoring suggested the advantages of an English university, and he had a graceful way even of looking warm and of pushing his hair back with his handkerchief.

"Children, run away," said Mrs. Garth, "it is too warm to hang about your friends. Take your brother and show him the rabbits."

The eldest understood, and led off the children immediately. Fred felt that Mrs. Garth wished to give him an opportunity of saying anything he had to say; but he could only begin by observing—

"How glad you must be to have Christy here!"

"Yes; he has come sooner than I expected. He got down from the coach at nine o'clock, just after his father went out. I am longing for Caleb to come and hear what wonderful progress Christy is making. He has paid his expenses for the last year by giving lessons, carrying on hard study at the same time. He hopes soon to get a private tutorship and go abroad."

"He is a great fellow," said Fred, to whom these cheerful truths had a medicinal taste, "and no trouble to anybody." After a slight pause, he added, "But I fear you will think that I am going to be a great deal of trouble to Mr. Garth."

"Caleb likes taking trouble: he is one of those men who always do more than any one would have thought of asking them to do," answered Mrs. Garth. She was knitting, and could either look at Fred or not, as she chose—always an advantage when one is bent on loading speech with salutary meaning: and though Mrs. Garth intended to be duly reserved, she did wish to say something that Fred might be the better for.

"I know you think me very undeserving, Mrs. Garth, and with good reason," said Fred, his spirit rising a little at the perception of something like a disposition to lecture him. "I happen to have behaved just the worst to the people I can't help wishing for the most from. But while two men like Mr. Garth and Mr. Farebrother have not given me up, I don't see why I should give myself up." Fred thought it might be well to suggest these masculine examples to Mrs. Garth.

"Assuredly," said she, with gathering emphasis. "A young man for whom two such elders have devoted themselves would indeed be culpable if he threw himself away and made their sacrifices vain."

Fred wondered a little at this strong language, but only said, "I hope it will not be so with me, Mrs. Garth, since I have some encouragement to believe that I may win Mary. Mr. Garth has told you about that? You were not surprised, I dare say?" Fred ended innocently, referring only to his own love as probably evident enough.

"Not surprised that Mary has given you encouragement?" returned Mrs. Garth, who thought it would be well for Fred to be more alive to the fact that Mary's friends could not possibly have wished this beforehand, whatever the Vincys might suppose. "Yes, I confess I *was* surprised."

"She never did give me any—not the least in the world, when I talked to her myself," said Fred, eager to vindicate Mary. "But when I asked Mr. Farebrother to speak for me, she allowed him to tell me there was a hope."

The power of admonition which had begun to stir in Mrs. Garth had not yet discharged itself. It was a little too provoking even for *her* self-control that this blooming youngster should flourish on the disappointments of sadder and wiser people—making a meal of a nightingale and never knowing it —and that all the while his family should suppose that hers was in eager need of this sprig; and her vexation had fermented the more actively because of its total repression toward her husband. Exemplary wives will sometimes find scapegoats in this way. She now said with energetic decision, "You made a great mistake, Fred, in asking Mr. Farebrother to speak for you."

"Did I?" said Fred, reddening instantaneously. He was alarmed, but at a loss to know what Mrs. Garth meant, and added, in an apologetic tone, "Mr. Farebrother has always been such a friend of ours; and Mary, I knew, would listen to him gravely; and he took it on himself quite readily."

"Yes, young people are usually blind to everything but their own wishes, and seldom imagine how much those wishes cost others," said Mrs. Garth. She did not mean to go beyond this salutary general doctrine, and threw her indignation into a needless unwinding of her worsted, knitting her brow at it with a grand air.

"I cannot conceive how it could be any pain to Mr. Farebrother," said Fred, who, nevertheless, felt that surprising conceptions were beginning to form themselves.

"Precisely; you cannot conceive," said Mrs. Garth, cutting her words as neatly as possible.

For a moment Fred looked at the horizon with a dismayed anxiety, and then turning with a quick movement, said almost sharply:

"Do you mean to say, Mrs. Garth, that Mr. Farebrother is in love with Mary?"

"And if it were so, Fred, I think you are the last person who ought to be surprised," returned Mrs. Garth, laying her knitting down beside her and folding her arms. It was an unwonted sign of emotion in her that she should put her work out of her hands. In fact, her feelings were divided between the satisfaction of giving Fred his discipline and the sense of having gone a little too far. Fred took his hat and stick and rose quickly.

"Then you think I am standing in his way, and in Mary's, too?" he said, in a tone which seemed to demand an answer.

Mrs. Garth could not speak immediately. She had brought herself into the unpleasant position of being called on to say what she really felt, yet what she knew there were strong reasons for concealing. And to her the consciousness of having exceeded in words was peculiarly mortifying. Besides,

37

Fred had given out unexpected electricity, and he now added, "Mr. Garth seemed pleased that Mary should be attached to me. He could not have known anything of this."

Mrs. Garth felt a severe twinge at this mention of her husband, the fear that Caleb might think her in the wrong not being easily endurable. She answered, wanting to check unintended consequences:

"I spoke from inference only. I am not aware that Mary knows anything of the matter."

But she hesitated to beg that he would keep entire silence on a subject which she had herself unnecessarily mentioned, not being used to stoop in that way; and while she was hesitating there was already a rush of unintended consequences under the apple-tree where the tea-things stood. Ben, bouncing across the grass with Brownie at his heels, and seeing the kitten dragging the knitting by a lengthening line of wool, shouted and clapped his hands; Brownie barked, the kitten, desperate, jumped on the tea-table and upset the milk, then jumped down again and swept half the cherries with it; and Ben, snatching up the half-knitted sock top, fitted it over the kitten's head as a new source of madness, while Letty arriving cried out to her mother against this cruelty—it was a history as full of sensation as "This is the house that Jack built." Mrs. Garth was obliged to interfere, the other young ones came up, and the tête-à-tête with Fred was ended. He got away as soon as he could, and Mrs. Garth could only imply some retractation of her severity by saying "God bless you" when she shook hands with him.

She was unpleasantly conscious that she had been on the verge of speaking as "one of the foolish women speaketh"—telling first and entreating silence after. But she had not entreated silence, and to prevent Caleb's blame she determined to blame herself, and confess all to him that very night. It was curious what an awful tribunal the mild Caleb's was to her whenever he set it up. But she meant to point out to him that the revelation might do Fred Vincy a great deal of good.

No doubt it was having a strong effect on him as he walked to Lowick. Fred's light, hopeful nature had, perhaps, never had so much of a bruise as from this suggestion, that if he had been out of the way Mary might have made a thoroughly good match. Also he was piqued that he had been what he called such a stupid lout as to ask that intervention from Mr. Farebrother. But it was not in a lover's nature—it was not in Fred's, that the new anxiety raised about Mary's feeling should not surmount every other. Notwithstanding his trust in Mr. Farebrother's generosity, notwithstanding what Mary had said to him, Fred could not help feeling that he had a rival; it was a new consciousness, and he objected to it extremely, not being in the least ready to give up Mary for her good, being ready rather to fight for her with any man whatsoever. But the fighting with Mr. Farebrother must be of a metaphorical kind, which was much more difficult to Fred than the muscular. Certainly this experience was a discipline for Fred hardly less sharp than his disappointment about his uncle's will. The iron had not entered into his soul, but he had begun to imagine what the sharp edge would be. It did not occur once to Fred that Mrs. Garth might be mistaken about Mr. Farebrother, but he suspected that she might be wrong about Mary. Mary had been staying at the parsonage lately, and her mother might know very little of what had been passing in her mind.

He did not feel easier when he found her looking cheerful with the three ladies in the drawing-room. They were in animated discussion on some subject which was dropped when he entered, and Mary was copying the labels from a heap of shallow cabinet drawers, in a minute handwriting which she was skilled in. Mr. Farebrother was somewhere in the village, and the three ladies knew nothing of Fred's peculiar relation to Mary. It was impossible for either of them to propose that they should walk round the garden, and Fred predicted to himself that he should have to go away without saying a word to her in private. He told her first of Christy's arrival and then of his own engagement with her father, and he was comforted by seeing that this latter news touched her keenly. She said hurriedly, "I am so glad," and then bent over her writing to hinder any one from noticing her face. But here was a subject which Mrs. Farebrother could not let pass.

"You don't mean, my dear Miss Garth, that you are glad to hear of a young man giving up the Church for which he was educated; you only mean that things being so, you are glad that he should be under an excellent man like your father."

"No, really, Mrs. Farebrother, I am glad of both, I fear," said Mary, cleverly getting rid of one rebellious tear. "I have a dreadfully secular mind. I never liked any clergyman except the Vicar of Wakefield and Mr. Farebrother."

"Now why, my dear?" said Mrs. Farebrother, pausing on her large wooden knitting-needles and looking at Mary. "You have always a good reason for your opinions, but this astonishes me. Of course I put out of the question those who preach new doctrine. But why should you dislike clergymen?"

"Oh, dear," said Mary, her face breaking into merriment as she seemed to consider a moment, "I don't like their neck-cloths."

"Why, you don't like Camden's, then," said Miss Winifred, in some anxiety.

"Yes, I do," said Mary. "I don't like the other clergymen's neckcloths, because it is they who wear them."

"How very puzzling!" said Miss Noble, feeling that her own intellect was probably deficient.

"My dear, you are joking. You would have better reasons than these for slighting so respectable a class of men," said Mrs. Farebrother, majestically.

"Miss Garth has such severe notions of what people should be that it is difficult to satisfy her," said Fred.

"Well, I am glad at least that she makes an exception in favor of my son," said the old lady.

Mary was wondering at Fred's piqued tone, when Mr. Farebrother came in and had to hear the news about the engagement under Mr. Garth. At the end he said with quiet satisfaction, "*That* is right," and then bent to look at Mary's labels and praise her handwriting. Fred felt horribly jealous —was glad, of course, that Mr. Farebrother was so estimable, but wished that he had been ugly and fat as men at forty sometimes are. It was clear what the end would be, since Mary openly placed Farebrother above everybody, and these women were all evidently encouraging the affair. He was feeling sure that he should have no chance of speaking to Mary, when Mr. Farebrother said:

"Fred, help me to carry these drawers back into my study
—you have never seen my fine new study. Pray come too,
Miss Garth. I want you to see a stupendous spider I found
this morning."

Mary at once saw the vicar's intention. He had never since
the memorable evening deviated from his old pastoral kindness
toward her, and her momentary wonder and doubt had quite
gone to sleep. Mary was accustomed to think rather rigor-
ously of what was probable, and if a belief flattered her vanity
she felt warned to dismiss it as ridiculous, having early had
much exercise in such dismissals. It was as she had foreseen;
when Fred had been asked to admire the fittings of the study,
and she had been asked to admire the spider, Mr. Farebrother
said:

"Wait here a minute or two. I am going to look out an
engraving which Fred is tall enough to hang for me. I shall
be back in a few minutes." And then he went out. Nevertheless, the first word Fred said to Mary was:

"It is of no use, whatever I do, Mary. You are sure to
marry Farebrother at last." There was some rage in his tone.

"What do you mean, Fred?" Mary exclaimed indignantly,
blushing deeply, and surprised out of all her readiness in
reply.

"It is impossible that you should not see it all clearly
enough—you who see everything."

"I only see that you are behaving very ill, Fred, in speaking so of Mr. Farebrother after he has pleaded your cause in
every way. How can you have taken up such an idea?"

Fred was rather deep, in spite of his irritation. If Mary
had really been unsuspicious, there was no good in telling her
what Mrs. Garth had said.

"It follows as a matter of course," he replied. "When you
are continually seeing a man who beats me in everything, and
whom you set up above everybody, I can have no fair chance."

"You are very ungrateful, Fred," said Mary. "I wish I
had never told Mr. Farebrother that I cared for you in the
least."

"No, I am not ungrateful; I should be the happiest fellow
in the world if it were not for this. I told your father every-

thing, and he was very kind; he treated me as if I were his son. I could go at the work with a will, writing and everything, if it were not for this."

"For this? for what?" said Mary, imagining now that something specific must have been said or done.

"This dreadful certainty that I shall be bowled out by Farebrother." Mary was appeased by her inclination to laugh.

"Fred," she said, peeping round to catch his eyes, which were sulkily turned away from her, "you are too delightfully ridiculous. If you were not such a charming simpleton, what a temptation this would be to play the wicked coquette, and let you suppose that somebody besides you had made love to me."

"Do you really like me best, Mary?" said Fred, turning eyes full of affection on her, and trying to take her hand.

"I don't like you at all at this moment," said Mary, retreating and putting her hands behind her. "I only said that no mortal ever made love to me besides you. And that is no argument that a very wise man ever will," she ended, merrily.

"I wish you would tell me that you could not possibly ever think of him," said Fred.

"Never dare to mention this any more to me, Fred," said Mary, getting serious again. "I don't know whether it is more stupid or ungenerous in you not to see that Mr. Farebrother has left us together on purpose that we might speak freely. I am disappointed that you should be so blind to his delicate feeling."

There was no time to say any more before Mr. Farebrother came back with the engraving; and Fred had to return to the drawing-room still with a jealous dread in his heart, but yet with comforting arguments from Mary's words and manner. The result of the conversation was on the whole more painful to Mary: inevitably her attention had taken a new attitude, and she saw the possibility of new interpretations. She was in a position in which she seemed to herself to be slighting Mr. Farebrother, and this, in relation to a man who is much honored, is always dangerous to the firmness of a grateful woman. To have a reason for going home the next day was a relief, for Mary earnestly desired to be always clear that she loved Fred best. When a tender affection has been storing itself in us through many of our years, the idea that we could accept any exchange for it seems to be a cheapening of our lives. And we can set a watch over our affections and our constancy as we can over other treasures.

"Fred has lost all his other expectations; he must keep this," Mary said to herself, with a smile curling her lips. It was impossible to help fleeting visions of another kind—new dignities and an acknowledged value, of which she had often felt the absence. But these things with Fred outside them, Fred forsaken and looking sad for the want of her, could never tempt her deliberate thought.

———————◆———————

CHAPTER LVIII.

" For there can live no hatred in thine eye,
Therefore in that I cannot know thy change:
In many's looks the false heart's history
Is writ in moods and frowns and wrinkles strange;
But Heaven in thy creation did decree
That in thy face sweet love should ever dwell;
Whate'er thy thoughts or thy heart's workings be,
Thy looks should nothing thence but sweetness tell. "
—SHAKESPEARE: *Sonnets.*

AT the time when Mr. Vincy uttered that presentiment about Rosamond, she herself had never had the idea that she should be driven to make the sort of appeal which he foresaw. She had not yet had any anxiety about ways and means, although her domestic life had been expensive as well as eventful. Her baby had been born prematurely, and all the embroidered robes and caps had to be laid by in darkness. This misfortune was attributed entirely to her having persisted in going out on horseback one day when her husband had desired her not to do so; but it must not be supposed that she had shown temper on the occasion, or rudely told him that she would do as she liked.

What led her particularly to desire horse-exercise was a visit from Captain Lydgate, the baronet's third son, who, I am sorry to say, was detested by our Tertius of that name as a vapid fop, "parting his hair from the brow to nape in a despicable fashion" (not followed by Tertius himself), and showing an ignorant security that he knew the proper thing to say on every topic. Lydgate inwardly cursed his own folly that he had drawn down this visit by consenting to go to his uncle's on the wedding-tour, and he made himself rather disagreeable to Rosamond by saying so in private. For to Rosamond this visit was a source of unprecedented but gracefully concealed exultation. She was so intensely conscious of having a cousin who was a baronet's son staying in the house, that she imagined the knowledge of what was implied by his presence to be diffused through all other minds; and when she introduced Captain Lydgate to her guests, she had a placid sense that his rank penetrated them as if it had been an odor. The satisfaction was enough for the time to melt away some disappointment in the conditions of marriage with a medical man even of good birth: it seemed now that her marriage was visibly as well as ideally floating her above the Middlemarch level, and the future looked bright with letters and visits to and from Quallingham, and vague advancement in consequence for Tertius. Especially as, probably at the Captain's suggestion, his married sister, Mrs. Mengan, had come with her maid, and stayed two nights on her way from town. Hence it was clearly worth while for Rosamond to take pains with her music and the careful selection of her lace.

As to Captain Lydgate himself, his low brow, his aquiline nose bent on one side, and his rather heavy utterance, might have been disadvantageous in any young gentleman who had not a military bearing and mustache to give him what is doted on by some flower-like blonde heads as "style." He had, moreover, that sort of high-breeding which consists in being free from the petty solicitudes of middle-class gentility, and he was a great critic of feminine charms. Rosamond delighted in his admiration now even more than she had done at Quallingham, and he found it easy to spend several hours of the day in flirting with her. The visit altogether was one of the pleasantest larks he had ever had, not the less so, perhaps, because he suspected that his queer cousin Tertius wished him away: though Lydgate, who would rather (hyperbolically speaking) have died than have failed in polite hospitality, suppressed

his dislike, and only pretended generally not to hear what the
gallant officer said, consigning the task of answering him to
Rosamond. For he was not at all a jealous husband, and
preferred leaving a feather-headed young gentleman alone with
his wife to bearing him company.

"I wish you would talk more to the Captain at dinner, Tertius," said Rosamond one evening when the important guest
was gone to Loamford to see some brother officers stationed
there. "You really look so absent sometimes—you seem to
be seeing through his head into something behind it, instead
of looking at him."

"My dear Rosy, you don't expect me to talk much to such
a conceited ass as that, I hope," said Lydgate, brusquely.
"If he got his head broken, I might look at it with interest,
not before."

"I cannot conceive why you should speak of your cousin so
contemptuously," said Rosamond, her fingers moving at her
work while she spoke with a mild gravity which had a touch
of disdain in it.

"Ask Ladislaw if he doesn't think your Captain the greatest
bore he ever met 'with. Ladislaw has almost forsaken the
house since he came."

Rosamond thought she knew perfectly well why Mr. Ladislaw disliked the Captain: he was jealous, and she liked his
being jealous.

"It is impossible to say what will suit eccentric persons,"
she answered, "but in my opinion Captain Lydgate is a thorough gentleman, and I think you ought not, out of respect to
Sir Godwin, to treat him with neglect."

"No, dear; but we have had dinners for him. And he
comes in and goes out as he likes. He doesn't want me."

"Still, when he is in the room you might show him more
attention. He may not be a phœnix of cleverness in your
sense; his profession is different; but it will be all the better
for you to talk a little on his subjects. I think his conversation is quite agreeable. And he is anything but an unprinci-
pled man."

"The fact is, you would wish me to be a little more like
him, Rosy," said Lydgate, in a sort of resigned murmur,

with a smile which was not exactly tender, and certainly not
merry. Rosamond was silent and did not smile again; but
the lovely curves of her face looked good-tempered enough
without smiling.

Those words of Lydgate's were like a sad mile-stone marking how far he had travelled from his old dreamland, in which
Rosamond Vincy appeared to be that perfect piece of womanhood who would reverence her husband's mind after the fashion of an accomplished mermaid, using her comb and looking-
glass and singing her song for the relaxation of his adored
wisdom alone. He had begun to distinguish between that
imagined adoration and the attraction toward a man's talent
because it gives him prestige, and is like an order in his
buttonhole or an Honorable before his name.

It might have been supposed that Rosamond had travelled
too, since she had found the pointless conversation of Mr.
Ned Plymdale perfectly wearisome; but to most mortals there
is a stupidity which is unendurable and a stupidity which is
altogether acceptable—else, indeed, what would become of
social bonds? Captain Lydgate's stupidity was delicately
scented, carried itself with "style," talked with a good accent,
and was closely related to Sir Godwin. Rosamond found it
quite agreeable, and caught many of its phrases.

Therefore since Rosamond, as we know, was fond of horseback, there were plenty of reasons why she should be tempted
to resume her riding when Captain Lydgate, who had ordered
his man with two horses to follow him and put up at the
"Green Dragon," begged her to go out on the gray, which he
warranted to be gentle and trained to carry a lady—indeed, he
had bought it for his sister, and was taking it to Quallingham.
Rosamond went out the first time without telling her husband,
and came back before his return; but the ride had been so
thorough a success, and she declared herself so much the better in consequence, that he was informed of it with full reli-
ance on his consent that she should go riding again.

On the contrary, Lydgate was more than hurt—he was utterly confounded that she had risked herself on a strange horse
without referring the matter to his wish. After the first
almost thundering exclamations of astonishment, which suffi-

ciently warned Rosamond of what was coming, he was silent
for some moments.

"However, you have come back safely," he said at last, in a
decisive tone. "You will not go again, Rosy; that is understood. If it were the quietest, most familiar horse in the
world, there would always be the chance of accident. And
you know very well that I wished you to give up riding the
roan on that account."

"But there is the chance of accident indoors, Tertius."

"My darling, don't talk nonsense," said Lydgate, in an
imploring tone; "surely I am the person to judge for you. I
think it is enough that I say you are not to go again."

Rosamond was arranging her hair before dinner, and the
reflection of her head in the glass showed no change in its
loveliness except a little turning aside of the long neck. Lydgate had been moving about with his hands in his pockets,
and now paused near her, as if he waited some assurance.

"I wish you would fasten up my plaits, dear," said Rosamond, letting her arms fall with a little sigh, so as to make
a husband ashamed of standing there like a brute. Lydgate
had often fastened the plaits before, being among the deftest
of men with his large, finely formed fingers. He swept up
the soft festoons of plaits and fastened in the tall comb (to
such uses do men come!); and what could he do then but kiss
the exquisite nape which was shown in all its delicate curves?
But when we do what we have done before, it is often with a
difference. Lydgate was still angry, and had not forgotten his
point.

"I shall tell the Captain that he ought to have known better than offer you his horse," he said as he moved away.

"I beg you will not do anything of the kind, Tertius," said
Rosamond, looking at him with something more marked than
usual in her speech. "It will be treating me as if I were a
child. Promise that you will leave the subject to me."

There did seem to be some truth in her objection. Lydgate
said, "Very well," with a surly obedience, and. thus the discussion ended with his promising Rosamond, and not with her
promising him.

In fact, she had been determined not to promise. Rosamond

had that victorious obstinacy which never wastes its energy in
impetuous resistance. What she liked to do was to her the
right thing, and all her cleverness was directed to getting the
means of doing it. She meant to go out riding again on
the gray, and she did go on the next opportunity of her husband's absence, not intending he should know until it was late
enough not to signify to her. The temptation was certainly
great: she was very fond of the exercise, and the gratification
of riding on a fine horse, with Captain Lydgate, Sir Godwin's
son, on another fine horse by her side, and of being met in
this position by any one but her husband, was something as
good as her dreams before marriage; moreover, she was rivet-
ing the connection with the family at Quallingham, which
must be a wise thing to do.

But the gentle gray, unprepared for the crash of a tree that
was being felled on the edge of Halsell wood, took fright,
and caused a worse fright to Rosamond, leading finally to the
loss of her baby. Lydgate could not show his anger toward
her, but he was rather bearish to the Captain, whose visit
naturally soon came to an end.

In all future conversations on the subject, Rosamond was
mildly certain that the ride had made no difference, and that
if she had stayed at home the same symptoms would have
come on and would have ended the same way, because she had
felt something like them before.

Lydgate could only say, "Poor, poor darling!"—but he
secretly wondered over the terrible tenacity of this mild creature. There was gathering within him an amazed sense of
his powerlessness over Rosamond. His superior knowledge
and mental force, instead of being, as he had imagined, a
shrine to consult on all occasions, was simply set aside on
every practical question. He had regarded Rosamond's cleverness as precisely of the receptive kind which became a woman.
He was now beginning to find out what that cleverness was
—what was the shape into which it had run as into a close
network aloof and independent. No one quicker than Rosamond to see causes and effects which lay within the track of
her own tastes and interests: she had seen clearly Lydgate's
pre-eminence in Middlemarch society, and could go on imagi-

natively tracing still more agreeable social effects when his talent should have advanced him; but for her, his professional and scientific ambition had no other relation to these desirable effects than if they had been the fortunate discovery of an ill-smelling oil. And that oil apart, with which she had nothing to do, of course she believed in her own opinion more than she did in his. Lydgate was astounded to find in numberless trifling matters, as well as in this last serious case of the riding, that affection did not make her compliant. He had no doubt that the affection was there, and had no presentiment that he had done anything to repel it. For his own part, he said to himself that he loved her as tenderly as ever, and could make up his mind to her negations; but—well! Lydgate was much worried, and conscious of new elements in his life as noxious to him as an inlet of mud to a creature that has been used to breathe and bathe and dart after its illuminated prey in the clearest of waters.

Rosamond was soon looking lovelier than ever at her work-table, enjoying drives in her father's phaeton and thinking it likely that she might be invited to Quallingham. She knew that she was a much more exquisite ornament to the drawing-room there than any daughter of the family, and in reflecting that the gentlemen were aware of that, did not perhaps sufficiently consider whether the ladies would be eager to see themselves surpassed.

Lydgate, relieved from anxiety about her, relapsed into what she inwardly called his moodiness—a name which to her covered his thoughtful preoccupation with other subjects than herself, as well as that uneasy look of the brow and distaste for all ordinary things as if they were mixed with bitter herbs, which really made a sort of weather-glass to his vexation and foreboding. These latter states of mind had one cause, among others, which he had generously but mistakenly avoided mentioning to Rosamond, lest it should affect her health and spirits. Between him and her, indeed, there was that total missing of each other's mental track, which is too evidently possible even between persons who are continually thinking of each other. To Lydgate it seemed that he had been spending month after month in sacrificing more than half of his best

intent and best power to his tenderness for Rosamond; bearing her little claims and interruptions without impatience,
and, above all, bearing without betrayal of bitterness to look
through less and less of interfering illusion at the blank, unreflecting surface her mind presented to his ardor for the more
impersonal ends of his profession and his scientific study, an
ardor which he had fancied that the ideal wife must somehow
worship as sublime, though not in the least knowing why.
But his endurance was mingled with a self-discontent which,
if we know how to be candid, we shall confess to make more
than half our bitterness under grievances, wife or husband
included.   It always remains true that if we had been greater,
circumstance would have been less strong against us.   Lydgate
was aware that his concessions to Rosamond were often little
more than the lapse of slackening resolution, the creeping
paralysis apt to seize an enthusiasm which is out of adjustment to a constant portion of our lives.   And on Lydgate's
enthusiasm there was constantly pressing not a simple weight
of sorrow, but the biting presence of a petty degrading care,
such as casts the blight of irony over all higher effort.

This was the care which he had hitherto abstained from
mentioning to Rosamond; and he believed, with some wonder,
that it had never entered her mind, though certainly no difficulty could be less mysterious.   It was an inference with a
conspicuous handle to it, and had been easily drawn by indifferent observers, that Lydgate was in debt; and he could not
succeed in keeping out of his mind for long together that he
was every day getting deeper into that swamp, which tempts
men toward it with such a pretty covering of flowers and ver-
dure.   It is wonderful how soon a man gets up to his chin
there—in a condition in which, spite of himself, he is forced
to think chiefly of release, though he had a scheme of the universe in his soul.

Eighteen months ago Lydgate was poor, but had never
known the eager want of small sums, and felt rather a burning
contempt for any one who descended a step in order to gain
them.   He was now experiencing something worse than a simple deficit; he was assailed by the vulgar hateful trial of a
man who has bought and used a great many things which

might have been done without, and which he is unable to pay for, though the demand for payment has become pressing.

How this came about may be easily seen without much arithmetic or knowledge of prices. When a man in setting up a house and preparing for marriage finds that his furniture and other initial expenses come to between four and five hundred pounds more than he has capital to pay for; when at the end of a year it appears that his household expenses, horses, and et ceteras, amount to nearly a thousand, while the proceeds of the practice reckoned from the old books to be worth eight hundred per annum have sunk like a summer pond and make hardly five hundred, chiefly in unpaid entries, the plain inference is that, whether he minds it or not, he is in debt. Those were less expensive times than our own, and provincial life was comparatively modest; but the ease with which a medical man who had lately bought a practice, who thought that he was obliged to keep two horses, whose table was supplied without stint, and who paid an insurance on his life and a high rent for house and garden, might find his expenses doubling his receipts, can be conceived by any one who does not think these details beneath his consideration. Rosamond, accustomed from her childhood to an extravagant household, thought that good housekeeping consisted simply in ordering the best of everything—nothing else "answered"; and Lydgate supposed that "if things were done at all, they must be done properly"—he did not see how they were to live otherwise. If each head of household expenditure had been mentioned to him beforehand, he would have probably observed that "it could hardly come to much," and if any one had suggested a saving on a particular article—for example, the substitution of cheap fish for dear—it would have appeared to him simply a penny-wise, mean notion. Rosamond, even without such an occasion as Captain Lydgate's visit, was fond of giving invitations, and Lydgate, though he often thought the guests tiresome, did not interfere. This sociability seemed a necessary part of professional prudence, and the entertainment must be suitable. It is true Lydgate was constantly visiting the homes of the poor and adjusting his prescriptions of diet to their small means; but, dear me! has it not by this time ceased to be remarkable—is it not rather what we expect in men, that they should have numerous strands of experience lying side by side and never compare them with each other? Expenditure—like ugliness and errors—becomes a totally new thing when we attach our own personality to it, and measure it by that wide difference which is manifest (in our own sensations) between ourselves and others. Lydgate believed himself to be careless about his dress, and he despised a man who calculated the effects of his costume; it seemed to him only a matter of course that he had abundance of fresh garments—such things were naturally ordered in sheaves. It must be remembered that he had never hitherto felt the check of importunate debt, and he walked by habit, not by self-criticism. But the check had come.

Its novelty made it the more irritating. He was amazed, disgusted that conditions so foreign to all his purposes, so hatefully disconnected with the objects he cared to occupy himself with, should have lain in ambush and clutched him when he was unaware. And there was not only the actual debt; there was the certainty that in his present position he must go on deepening it. Two furnishing tradesmen at Brassing, whose bills had been incurred before his marriage, and whom uncalculated current expenses had ever since prevented him from paying, had repeatedly sent him unpleasant letters which had forced themselves on his attention. This could hardly have been more galling to any disposition than to Lydgate's, with his intense pride—his dislike of asking a favor or being under an obligation to any one. He had scorned even to form conjectures about Mr. Vincy's intentions on money matters, and nothing but extremity could have induced him to apply to his father-in-law, even if he had not been made aware in various indirect ways since his marriage that Mr. Vincy's own affairs were not flourishing, and that the expectation of help from him would be resented. Some men easily trust in the readiness of friends; it had never in the former part of his life occurred to Lydgate that he should need to do so: he had never thought what borrowing would be to him; but now that the idea had entered his mind, he felt that he would rather incur any other hardship. In the meantime he had no money or prospects of money; and his practice was not getting more lucrative.

No wonder that Lydgate had been unable to suppress all signs of inward trouble during the last few months; and now that Rosamond was regaining brilliant health, he meditated taking her entirely into confidence on his difficulties. New conversance with tradesmen's bills had forced his reasoning into a new channel of comparison: he had begun to consider from a new point of view what was necessary and unnecessary in goods ordered, and to see that there must be some change of habits. How could such a change be made without Rosamond's concurrence? The immediate occasion of opening the disagreeable fact to her was forced upon him.

Having no money, and having privately sought advice as to what security could possibly be given by a man in his position, Lydgate had offered the one good security in his power to the less peremptory creditor, who was a silversmith and jeweller, and who consented to take on himself the upholsterer's credit also, accepting interest for a given term. The security necessary was a bill of sale on the furniture of his house, which might make a creditor easy for a reasonable time about a debt amounting to less than four hundred pounds; and the silversmith, Mr. Dover, was willing to reduce it by taking back a portion of the plate and any other article which was as good as new. "Any other article" was a phrase delicately implying jewelry, and more particularly some purple amethysts costing thirty pounds, which Lydgate had bought as a bridal present.

Opinions may be divided as to his wisdom in making this present: some may think that it was a graceful attention to be expected from a man like Lydgate, and that the fault of any troublesome consequences lay in the pinched narrowness of provincial life at that time, which offered no conveniences for professional people whose fortune was not proportioned to their tastes; also, in Lydgate's ridiculous fastidiousness about asking his friends for money.

However, it had seemed a question of no moment to him on that fine morning when he went to give a final order for plate: in the presence of other jewels enormously expensive,

38

and as an addition to orders of which the amount had not been exactly calculated, thirty pounds for ornaments so exquisitely suited to Rosamond's neck and arms could hardly appear excessive when there was no ready cash for it to exceed. But at this crisis Lydgate's imagination could not help dwelling on the possibility of letting the amethysts take their place again among Mr. Dover's stock, though he shrank from the idea of proposing this to Rosamond. Having been roused to discern consequences which he had never been in the habit of tracing, he was preparing to act on this discernment with some of the rigor (by no means all) that he would have applied in pursuing experiment. He was nerving himself to this rigor as he rode from Brassing, and meditated on the representations he must make to Rosamond.

It was evening when he got home. He was intensely miserable, this strong man of nine-and-twenty and of many gifts. He was not saying angrily within himself that he had made a profound mistake; but the mistake was at work in him like a recognized chronic disease, mingling its uneasy importunities with every prospect, and enfeebling every thought. As he went along the passage to the drawing-room, he heard the piano and singing.

Of course, Ladislaw was there. It was some weeks since Will had parted from Dorothea, yet he was still at the old post in Middlemarch. Lydgate had no objection in general to Ladislaw's coming, but just now he was annoyed that he could not find his hearth free. When he opened the door the two singers went on toward the key-note, raising their eyes and looking at him indeed, but not regarding his entrance as an interruption. To a man galled with his harness as poor Lydgate was, it is not soothing to see two people warbling at him, as he comes in with the sense that the painful day has still pains in store. His face, already paler than usual, took on a scowl as he walked across the room and flung himself into a chair.

The singers feeling themselves excused by the fact that they had only three bars to sing, now turned round.

"How are you, Lydgate?" said Will, coming forward to shake hands.

Lydgate took his hand, but did not think it necessary to speak.

"Have you dined, Tertius? I expected you much earlier," said Rosamond, who had already seen that her husband was in a "horrible humor." She seated herself in her usual place as she spoke.

"I have dined. I should like some tea, please," said Lydgate, curtly, still scowling and looking markedly at his legs stretched out before him.

Will was too quick to need more. "I shall be off," he said, reaching his hat.

"Tea is coming," said Rosamond; "pray don't go."

"Yes, Lydgate is bored," said Will, who had more comprehension of Lydgate than Rosamond had, and was not offended by his manner, easily imagining outdoor causes of annoyance.

"There is the more need for you to stay," said Rosamond, playfully, and in her lightest accent; "he will not speak to me all the evening."

"Yes, Rosamond, I shall," said Lydgate, in his strong baritone. "I have some serious business to speak to you about."

No introduction of the business could have been less like that which Lydgate had intended; but her indifferent manner had been too provoking.

"There! you see," said Will. "I'm going to the meeting about the Mechanics' Institute. Good-by," and he went quickly out of the room.

Rosamond did not look at her husband, but presently rose and took her place before the tea-tray. She was thinking that she had never seen him so disagreeable. Lydgate turned his dark eyes on her and watched her as she delicately handled the tea-service with her taper fingers, and looked at the objects immediately before her with no curve in her face disturbed, and yet with an ineffable protest in her air against all people with unpleasant manners. For the moment he lost the sense of his wound in a sudden speculation about this new form of feminine impassibility revealing itself in the sylph-like frame which he had once interpreted as the sign of a ready intelligent sensitiveness. His mind glancing back to Laure while he looked at Rosamond, he said inwardly, "Would *she* kill me

because I wearied her?" and then, "It is the way with all
women." But this power of generalizing which gives men so
much the superiority in mistake over the dumb animals, was
immediately thwarted by Lydgate's memory of wondering impressions from the behavior of another woman—from Dorothea's looks and tones of emotion about her husband when
Lydgate began to attend him—from her passionate cry to be
taught what would best comfort that man for whose sake it
seemed as if she must quell every impulse in her except the
yearnings of faithfulness and compassion. These revived
impressions succeeded each other quickly and dreamily in
Lydgate's mind while the tea was being brewed. He had
shut his eyes in the last instant of reverie while he heard
Dorothea saying: "Advise me—think what I can do—he has
been all his life laboring and looking forward. He minds
about nothing else—and I mind about nothing else."

That voice of deep-souled womanhood had remained within
him as the enkindling conceptions of dead and sceptred genius
had remained within him (is there not a genius for feeling
nobly which also reigns over human spirits and their conclusions?); the tones were a music from which he was falling
away—he had really fallen into a momentary doze, when
Rosamond said in her silvery neutral way, "Here is your tea,
Tertius," setting it on the small table by his side, and then
moved back to her place without looking at him. Lydgate
was too hasty in attributing insensibility to her; after her own
fashion, she was sensitive enough, and took lasting impressions. Her impression now was one of offence and repulsion.
But then, Rosamond had no scowls and had never raised her
voice; she was quite sure that no one could justly find fault
with her.

Perhaps Lydgate and she had never felt so far off each other
before; but there were strong reasons for not deferring his
revelation, even if he had not already begun it by that abrupt
announcement; indeed, some of the angry desire to rouse her
into more sensibility on his account which had prompted him
to speak prematurely, still mingled with his pain in the prospect of her pain. But he waited till the tray was gone, the
candles were lit, and the evening quiet might be counted on;

the interval had left time for repelled tenderness to return into the old course. He spoke kindly:

"Dear Rosy, lay down your work and come to sit by me," he said, gently, pushing away the table, and stretching out his arm to draw a chair near his own.

Rosamond obeyed. As she came toward him in her drapery of transparent, faintly tinted muslin, her slim yet round figure never looked more graceful; as she sat down by him and laid one hand on the elbow of his chair, at last looking at him and meeting his eyes, her delicate neck and cheek and purely cut lips never had more of that untarnished beauty which touches us in springtime and infancy and all sweet freshness. It touched Lydgate now, and mingled the early moments of his love for her with all the other memories which were stirred in this crisis of deep trouble. He laid his ample hand softly on hers, saying:

"Dear!" with the lingering utterance which affection gives to the word. Rosamond, too, was still under the power of that same past, and her husband was still in part the Lydgate whose approval had stirred delight. She put his hair lightly away from his forehead, then laid her other hand on his, and was conscious of forgiving him.

"I am obliged to tell you what will hurt you, Rosy. But there are things which husband and wife must think of together. I dare say it has occurred to you already that I am short of money."

Lydgate paused; but Rosamond turned her neck and looked at a vase on the mantelpiece.

"I was not able to pay for all the things we had to get before we were married, and there have been expenses since which I have been obliged to meet. The consequence is, there is a large debt at Brassing—three hundred and eighty pounds—which has been pressing on me a good while, and in fact we are getting deeper every day, for people don't pay me the faster because others want the money. I took pains to keep it from you while you were not well; but now we must think together about it, and you must help me."

"What can I do, Tertius?" said Rosamond, turning her eyes on him again. That little speech of four words, like so many

others in all languages, is capable by varied vocal inflections
of expressing all states of mind from helpless dimness to ex-
haustive argumentative perception, from the completest self-
devoting fellowship to the most neutral aloofness.   Rosamond's thin utterance threw into the words "What can *I*
do?" as much neutrality as they could hold.   They fell like a
mortal chill on Lydgate's roused tenderness.   He did not
storm in indignation—he felt too sad a sinking of the heart.
And when he spoke again it was more in the tone of a man
who forces himself to fulfil a task.

"It is necessary for you to know, because I have to give
security for a time, and a man must come to make an inventory of the furniture."

Rosamond colored deeply.   "Have you not asked papa for
money?" she said, as soon as she could speak.

"No."

"Then I must ask him!" she said, releasing her hands from
Lydgate's, and rising to stand at two yards' distance from him.

"No, Rosy," said Lydgate, decisively.   "It is too late to
do that.   The inventory will be begun to-morrow.   Remember it is a mere security; it will make no difference; it is a
temporary affair.   I insist upon it that your father shall not
know, unless I choose to tell him," added Lydgate, with a
more peremptory emphasis.

This certainly was unkind, but Rosamond had thrown him
back on evil expectation as to what she would do in the way
of quiet steady disobedience.   The unkindness seemed unpar-
donable to her: she was not given to weeping, and disliked it,
but now her chin and lips began to tremble and the tears welled
up.   Perhaps it was not possible for Lydgate, under the double stress of outward material difficulty and of his own proud
resistance to humiliating consequences, to imagine fully what
this sudden trial was to a young creature who had known
nothing but indulgence, and whose dreams had all been of new
indulgence, more exactly to her taste.   But he did wish to spare
her as much as he could, and her tears cut him to the heart.
He could not speak again immediately; but Rosamond did not
go on sobbing; she tried to conquer her agitation, and wiped
away her tears, continuing to look before her at the mantelpiece.

"Try not to grieve, darling," said Lydgate, turning his eyes up toward her. That she had chosen to move away from him in this moment of her trouble made everything harder to say, but he must absolutely go on. "We must brace ourselves to do what is necessary. It is I who have been in fault: I ought to have seen that I could not afford to live in this way. But many things have told against me in my practice, and it really just now has ebbed to a low point. I may recover it, but in the meantime we must pull up—we must change our way of living. We shall weather it. When I have given this security I shall have time to look about me; and you are so clever that if you turn your mind to managing you will school me into carefulness. I have been a thoughtless rascal about squaring prices—but come, dear, sit down and forgive me."

Lydgate was bowing his neck under the yoke like a creature who had talons, but who had reason, too, which often reduces us to meekness. When he had spoken the last words in an imploring tone, Rosamond returned to the chair by his side. His self-blame gave her some hope that he would attend to her opinion, and she said:

"Why can you not put off having the inventory made? you can send the men away to-morrow when they come."

"I shall not send them away," said Lydgate, the peremptoriness rising again. Was it of any use to explain?

"If we left Middlemarch, there would of course be a sale, and that would do as well."

"But we are not going to leave Middlemarch."

"I am sure, Tertius, it would be much better to do so. Why can we not go to London? Or near Durham where your family is known?"

"We can go nowhere without money, Rosamond."

"Your friends would not wish you to be without money. And surely these odious tradesmen might be made to understand that and to wait, if you would make proper representations to them."

"This is idle, Rosamond," said Lydgate, angrily. "You must learn to take my judgment on questions you don't understand. I have made necessary arrangements, and they must

be carried out. As to friends, I have no expectations whatever from them, and shall not ask them for anything."

Rosamond sat perfectly still. The thought in her mind was
that if she had known how Lydgate would behave, she would
never have married him.

"We have no time to waste now on unnecessary words,
dear," said Lydgate, trying to be gentle again. "There are
some details that I want to consider with you. Dover says
he will take a good deal of the plate back again, and any of
the jewelry we like. He really behaves very well."

"Are we to go without spoons and forks, then?" said Rosamond, whose very lips seemed to get thinner with the thinness
of her utterance. She was determined to make no further
resistance or suggestions.

"Oh, no, dear!" said Lydgate. "But look here," he continued, drawing a paper from his pocket and opening it;
"here is Dover's account. See, I have marked a number of
articles, which if we returned them would reduce the amount
by thirty pounds and more. I have not marked any of the
jewelry." Lydgate had really felt this point of the jewelry
very bitter to himself; but he had overcome the feeling by
severe argument. He could not propose to Rosamond that she
should return any particular present of his, but he had told
himself that he was bound to put Dover's offer before her,
and her inward prompting might make the affair easy.

"It is useless for me to look, Tertius," said Rosamond,
calmly; "you will return what you please." She would not
turn her eyes on the paper, and Lydgate, flushing up to the
roots of his hair, drew it back and let it fall on his knee.
Meanwhile Rosamond quietly went out of the room, leaving
Lydgate helpless and wondering. Was she not coming back?
It seemed that she had no more identified herself with him
than if they had been creatures of different species and opposing interests. He tossed his head and thrust his hands deep
into his pockets with a sort of vengeance. There was still
science—there was still good objects to work for. He must
give a tug still—all the stronger because other satisfactions
were going.

But the door opened and Rosamond re-entered. She carried the leather box containing the amethysts, and a tiny ornamental basket which contained other boxes, and laying them on the chair where she had been sitting, she said, with perfect propriety in her air:

"This is all the jewelry you ever gave me. You can return what you like of it, and of the plate also. You will not, of course, expect me to stay at home to-morrow. I shall go to papa's."

To many women the look Lydgate cast at her would have been more terrible than one of anger: it had in it a despairing acceptance of the distance she was placing between them.

"And when shall you come back again?" he said, with a bitter edge on his accent.

"Oh, in the evening. Of course I shall not mention the subject to mamma." Rosamond was convinced that no woman could behave more irreproachably than she was behaving; and she went to sit down at her work-table. Lydgate sat meditating a minute or two, and the result was that he said, with some of the old emotion in his tone:

"Now we have been united, Rosy, you should not leave me to myself in the first trouble that has come."

"Certainly not," said Rosamond; "I shall do everything it becomes me to do."

"It is not right that the thing should be left to servants, or that I should have to speak to them about it. And I shall be obliged to go out—I don't know how early. I understand your shrinking from the humiliation of these money affairs. But, my dear Rosamond, as a question of pride, which I feel just as much as you can, it is surely better to manage the thing ourselves, and let the servants see as little of it as possible; and since you are my wife, there is no hindering your share in my disgraces—if there were disgraces."

Rosamond did not answer immediately, but at last she said, "Very well, I will stay at home."

"I shall not touch these jewels, Rosy. Take them away again. But I will write out a list of plate that we may return, and that can be packed up and sent at once."

"The servants will know *that*," said Rosamond, with the slightest touch of sarcasm.

"Well, we must meet some disagreeables as necessities. Where is the ink, I wonder?" said Lydgate, rising and throwing the account on the larger table where he meant to write.

Rosamond went to reach the inkstand, and after setting it on the table was going to turn away, when Lydgate, who was standing close by, put his arm round her and drew her toward him, saying:

"Come, darling, let us make the best of things. It will only be for a time, I hope, that we shall have to be stingy and particular. Kiss me."

His native warm-heartedness took a great deal of quenching, and it is a part of manliness for a husband to feel keenly the fact that an inexperienced girl has got into trouble by marrying him. She received his kiss and returned it faintly, and in this way an appearance of accord was recovered for the time. But Lydgate could not help looking forward with dread to the inevitable future discussions about expenditure and the necessity for a complete change in their way of living.

CHAPTER LIX.

They said of old the Soul had human shape,
But smaller, subtler than the fleshy self,
So wandered forth for airing when it pleased.
And see! beside her cherub-face there floats
A pale-lipped form aerial whispering
Its promptings in that little shell, her ear.

NEWS is often dispersed as thoughtlessly and effectively as that pollen which the bees carry off (having no idea how powdery they are) when they are buzzing in search of their particular nectar. This fine comparison has reference to Fred Vincy, who on that evening at Lowick Parsonage heard a lively discussion among the ladies on the news which their old servant had got from Tantripp concerning Mr. Casaubon's strange mention of Mr. Ladislaw in a codicil to his will made not long before his death. Miss Winifred was astounded to find that her brother had known the fact before, and observed that Camden was the most wonderful man for knowing things and not telling them; whereupon Mary Garth said that the codicil had perhaps got mixed up with the habits of spiders, which Miss Winifred would never listen to.   Mrs. Farebrother considered that the news had something to do with their having only once seen Mr. Ladislaw at Lowick, and Miss Noble made many small, compassionate mewings.

Fred knew little and cared less about Ladislaw and the Casaubons, and his mind never recurred to that discussion till one day calling on Rosamond at his mother's request to deliver a message as he passed, he happened to see Ladislaw going away.   Fred and Rosamond had little to say to each other now that marriage had removed her from collision with the unpleasantness of brothers, and especially now that he had taken what she held the stupid and even reprehensible step of giving up the Church to take to such a business as Mr. Garth's.   Hence Fred talked by preference of what he considered indifferent news, and " à propos of that young Ladislaw," mentioned what he had heard at Lowick Parsonage.

Now Lydgate, like Mr. Farebrother, knew a great deal more than he told; and when he had once been set thinking about the relation between Will and Dorothea, his conjectures had gone beyond the fact.   He imagined that there was a passionate attachment on both sides, and this struck him as much too serious to gossip about.   He remembered Will's irritability when he had mentioned Mrs. Casaubon, and was the more circumspect.   On the whole his surmises, in addition to what he knew of the fact, increased his friendliness and tolerance toward Ladislaw, and made him understand the vacillation which kept him at Middlemarch after he had said that he should go away.   It was significant of the separateness between Lydgate's mind and Rosamond's that he had no impulse to speak to her on the subject; indeed, he did not quite trust her reticence toward Will.   And he was right there; though he had no vision of the way in which her mind would act in urging her to speak.

When she repeated Fred's news to Lydgate, he said: " Take care you don't drop the faintest hint to Ladislaw, Rosy. He is likely to fly out as if you insulted him.   Of course it is a painful affair."

Rosamond turned her neck and patted her hair, looking the

image of placid indifference. But the next time Will came when Lydgate was away, she spoke archly about his not going to London as he had threatened.

"I know all about it. I have a confidential little bird," said she, showing very pretty airs of her head over the bit of work held high between her active fingers. "There is a powerful magnet in this neighborhood."

"To be sure there is. Nobody knows that better than you," said Will, with light gallantry, but inwardly prepared to be angry.

"It is really the most charming romance: Mr. Casaubon jealous, and foreseeing that there was no one else whom Mrs. Casaubon would so much like to marry, and no one who would so much like to marry her as a certain gentleman; and then laying a plan to spoil all by making her forfeit her property if she did marry that gentleman—and then—and then—and then —oh, I have no doubt the end will be thoroughly romantic."

"Great God! what do you mean?" said Will, flushing over face and ears, his features seeming to change as if he had had a violent shake. "Don't joke; tell me what you mean."

"You don't really know?" said Rosamond, no longer playful, and desiring nothing better than to tell, in order that she might evoke effects.

"No!" he returned impatiently.

"Don't know that Mr. Casaubon has left it in his will that if Mrs. Casaubon marries you she is to forfeit all her property?"

"How do you know that it is true?" said Will, eagerly.

"My brother Fred heard it from the Farebrothers."

Will started up from his chair and reached his hat.

"I dare say she likes you better than the property," said Rosamond, looking at him from a distance.

"Pray don't say any more about it," said Will, in a hoarse undertone extremely unlike his usual light voice. "It is a foul insult to her and to me." Then he sat down absently, looking before him, but seeing nothing.

"Now you are angry with *me*," said Rosamond. "It is too bad to bear *me* malice. You ought to be obliged to me for telling you."

"So I am," said Will abruptly, speaking with that kind of

double soul which belongs to dreamers who answer questions.

"I expect to hear of the marriage," said Rosamond, playfully.

"Never! You will never hear of the marriage!"

With those words uttered impetuously, Will rose, put out his hand to Rosamond, still with the air of a somnambulist, and went away.

When he was gone, Rosamond left her chair and walked to the other end of the room, leaning, when she got there, against a *chiffonière*, and looking out of the window wearily. She was oppressed by ennui, and by that dissatisfaction which in women's minds is continually turning into a trivial jealousy, referring to no real claims, springing from no deeper passion than the vague exactingness of egoism, and yet capable of impelling action as well as speech. "There really is nothing to care for much," said poor Rosamond inwardly, thinking of the family at Quallingham, who did not write to her; and that perhaps Tertius, when he came home, would tease her about expenses. She had already secretly disobeyed him by asking her father to help them, and he had ended decisively by saying, "I am more likely to want help myself."

CHAPTER LX.

"Good phrases are surely, and ever were, very commendable."
—*Justice Shallow.*

A FEW days afterward—it was already the end of August—there was an occasion which caused some excitement in Middlemarch: the public, if it chose, was to have the advantage of buying, under the distinguished auspices of Mr. Borthrop Trumbull, the furniture, books, and pictures, which anybody might see by the handbills to be the best in every kind, belonging to Edwin Larcher, Esq. This was not one of the sales indicating the depression of trade; on the contrary, it was due to Mr. Larcher's great success in carrying business, which warranted his purchase of a mansion near Riverston, already furnished in high style by an illustrious Spa physician—furnished, indeed, with such large framefuls of expensive flesh-painting in the dining-room, that Mrs. Larcher was nervous, until reassured by finding the subjects to be scriptural. Hence the fine opportunity to purchasers, which was well pointed out in the handbills of Mr. Borthrop Trumbull, whose acquaintance with the history of art enabled him to state that the hall fruniture, to be sold without reserve, comprised a piece of carving by a contemporary of Gibbons.

At Middlemarch, in those times, a large sale was regarded as a kind of festival. There was a table spread with the best cold eatables, as at a superior funeral; and facilities were offered for that generous drinking of cheerful glasses which might lead to generous and cheerful bidding for undesirable articles. Mr. Larcher's sale was the more attractive in the fine weather because the house stood just at the end of the town, with a garden and stables attached, in that pleasant issue from Middlemarch called the London Road, which was also the road to the New Hospital and to Mr. Bulstrode's retired residence, known as the Shrubs. In short, the auction was as good as a fair, and drew all classes with leisure at command: to some, who risked making bids in order simply to raise prices, it was almost equal to betting at the races. The second day, when the best furniture was to be sold, "everybody" was there; even Mr. Thesiger, the rector of St. Peter's, had looked in for a short time, wishing to buy the carved table, and had rubbed elbows with Mr. Bambridge and Mr. Horrock. There was a wreath of Middlemarch ladies accommodated with seats round the large table in the dining-room, where Mr. Borthrop Trumbull was mounted with desk and hammer; but the rows chiefly of masculine faces behind were often varied by incomings and outgoings, both from the door and the large bow-window opening on to the lawn.

"Everybody" that day did not include Mr. Bulstrode, whose health could not well endure crowds and draughts. But Mrs. Bulstrode had particularly wished to have a certain picture—a Supper at Emmaus, attributed in the catalogue to Guido; and at the last moment before the day of the sale Mr. Bulstrode had called at the office of the *Pioneer*, of which he

was now one of the proprietors, to beg of Mr. Ladislaw, as a
great favor, that he would obligingly use his remarkable knowledge of pictures on behalf of Mrs. Bulstrode, and judge of the
value of this particular painting—"if," added the scrupulously
polite banker, "attendance at the sale would not interfere
with the arrangements for your departure, which I know is
imminent."

This proviso might have sounded rather satirically in Will's
ear if he had been in the mood to care about such satire.   It
referred to an understanding entered into many weeks before
with the proprietors of the paper, that he should be at liberty
any day he pleased to hand over the management to the sub-
editor whom he had been training; since he wished finally to
quit Middlemarch.   But indefinite visions of ambition are
weak against the ease of doing what is habitual or beguilingly
agreeable; and we all know the difficulty of carrying out a
resolve when we secretly long that it may turn out to be
unnecessary.   In such states of mind the most incredulous
person has a private leaning toward miracle: impossible to
conceive how our wish could be fulfilled, still—very wonderful things have happened!   Will did not confess this weakness to himself, but he lingered.   What was the use of going
to London at that time of the year?   The Rugby men who
would remember him were not there; and so far as political
writing was concerned, he would rather for a few weeks go on
with the *Pioneer*.   At the present moment, however, when
Mr. Bulstrode was speaking to him, he had both a strength-
ened resolve to go, and an equally strong resolve not to go, till
he had once more seen Dorothea.   Hence he replied that he
had reasons for deferring his departure a little, and would be
happy to go to the sale.

Will was in a defiant mood, his consciousness being deeply
stung with the thought that the people who looked at him
probably knew a fact tantamount to an accusation against
him as a fellow with low designs, which were to be frustrated
by a disposal of property.   Like most people who assert their
freedom with regard to conventional distinction, he was prepared to be sudden and quick at quarrel with any one who
might hint that he had personal reasons for that assertion—

that there was anything in his blood, his bearing, or his character to which he gave the mask of an opinion. When he was under an irritating impression of this kind, he would go about for days with a defiant look, the color changing in his transparent skin as if he were on the *qui vive*, watching for something which he had to dart upon.

This expression was peculiarly noticeable in him at the sale, and those who had only seen him in his moods of gentle oddity or of bright enjoyment would have been struck with a contrast. He was not sorry to have this occasion for appearing in public before the Middlemarch tribes of Toller, Hackbutt, and the rest, who looked down on him as an adventurer, and were in a state of brutal ignorance about Dante—who sneered at his Polish blood, and were themselves of a breed very much in need of crossing. He stood in a conspicuous place not far from the auctioneer, with a forefinger in each side pocket and his head thrown backward, not caring to speak to anybody, though he had been cordially welcomed as a connoiss*ure* by Mr. Trumbull, who was enjoying the utmost activity of his great faculties.

And surely among all men whose vocation requires them to exhibit their powers of speech, the happiest is a prosperous provincial auctioneer keenly alive to his own jokes and sensible of his encyclopædic knowledge. Some saturnine, sour-blooded persons might object to be constantly insisting on the merits of all articles from boot-jacks to "Berghems"; but Mr. Borthrop Trumbull had a kindly liquid in his veins; he was an admirer by nature, and would have liked to have the universe under his hammer; feeling that it would go at a higher figure for his recommendation.

Meanwhile Mrs. Larcher's drawing-room furniture was enough for him. When Will Ladislaw had come in, a second fender, said to have been forgotten in its right place, suddenly claimed the auctioneer's enthusiasm, which he distributed on the equitable principle of praising those things most which were most in need of praise. The fender was of polished steel, with much lancet-shaped open-work and a sharp edge.

"Now, ladies," said he, "I shall appeal to you. Here is a fender which at any other sale would hardly be offered without reserve, being, as I may say, for quality of steel and quaintness of design, a kind of thing"—here Mr. Trumbull dropped his voice and became slightly nasal, trimming his outlines with his left finger—"that might not fall in with ordinary tastes. Allow me to tell you that by and by this style of workmanship will be the only one in vogue—half-a-crown, you said? thank you—going at half-a-crown, this characteristic fender; and I have particular information that the antique style is very much sought after in high quarters. Three shillings—three-and-sixpence—hold it well up, Joseph! Look, ladies, at the chastity of the design—I have no doubt myself that it was turned out in the last century! Four shillings, Mr. Mawmsey?—four shillings."

"It's not a thing I would put in *my* drawing-room," said Mrs. Mawmsey, audibly, for the warning of the rash husband. "I wonder *at* Mrs. Larcher. Every blessed child's head that fell against it would be cut in two. The edge is like a knife."

"Quite true," rejoined Mr. Trumbull, quickly, "and most uncommonly useful to have a fender at hand that will cut, if you have a leather shoe-tie or a bit of string that wants cutting and no knife at hand: many a man has been left hanging because there was no knife to cut him down. Gentlemen, here's a fender that if you had the misfortune to hang yourselves would cut you down in no time—with astonishing celerity—four-and-sixpence—five—five-and-sixpence—an appropriate thing for a spare bedroom where there was a four-poster and a guest a little out of his mind—six shillings—thank you, Mr. Clintup—going at six shillings—going—gone!" The auctioneer's glance, which had been searching round him with a preternatural susceptibility to all signs of bidding, here dropped on the paper before him, and his voice, too, dropped into a tone of indifferent dispatch as he said, "Mr. Clintup. Be handy, Joseph."

"It was worth six shillings to have a fender you could always tell that joke on," said Mr. Clintup, laughing low and apologetically to his next neighbor. He was a diffident though distinguished nurseryman, and feared that the audience might regard his bid as a foolish one.

Meanwhile Joseph had brought a trayful of small articles.
39

"Now, ladies," said Mr. Trumbull, taking up one of the articles, "this tray contains a very recherchy lot—a collection of trifles for the drawing-room table—and trifles make the sum of human things—nothing more important than trifles—(yes, Mr. Ladislaw, yes, by and by)—but pass the tray round, Joseph—these bijoux must be examined, ladies. This I have in my hand is an ingenious contrivance—a sort of practical rebus, I may call it: here, you see, it looks like an elegant heart-shaped box, portable—for the pocket ; there, again, it becomes like a splendid double flower—an ornament for the table; and now "—Mr. Trumbull allowed the flower to fall alarmingly into strings of heart-shaped leaves—"a book of riddles! No less than five hundred printed in a beautiful red. Gentlemen, if I had less of a conscience, I should not wish you to bid high for this lot—I have a longing for it myself. What can promote innocent mirth, and I may say virtue, more than a good riddle?—it hinders profane language, and attaches a man to the society of refined females. This ingenious article itself, without the elegant domino-box, card-basket, etc., ought alone to give a high price to the lot. Carried in the pocket it might make an individual welcome in any society. Four shillings, sir?—four shillings for this remarkable collection of riddles with the et ceteras. Here is a sample: 'How must you spell honey to make it catch lady-birds? Answer—money.' You hear?—lady-birds—honey—money. This is an amusement to sharpen the intellect; it has a sting—it has what we call satire, and wit without indecency. Four-and-sixpence—five shillings."

The bidding ran on with warming rivalry. Mr. Bowyer was a bidder, and this was too exasperating. Bowyer couldn't afford it, and only wanted to hinder every other man from making a figure. The current carried even Mr. Horrock with it, but this committal of himself to an opinion fell from him with so little sacrifice of his neutral expression, that the bid might not have been detected as his but for the friendly oaths of Mr. Bambridge, who wanted to know what Horrock would do with blasted stuff only fit for haberdashers given over to that state of perdition which the horse-dealer so cordially recognized in the majority of earthly existences. The lot was

finally knocked down at a guinea to Mr. Spilkins, a young
Slender of the neighborhood, who was reckless with his
pocket-money and felt his want of memory for riddles.

"Come, Trumbull, this is too bad; you have been putting
some old maid's rubbish into the sale," murmured Mr. Toller,
getting close to the auctioneer. "I want to see how the prints
go, and I must be off soon."

"*Immediately*, Mr. Toller. It was only an act of benevolence which your noble heart would approve. Joseph! quick
with the prints—Lot 235. Now, gentlemen, you who are
connoiss*ures*, you are going to have a treat. Here is an engraving of the Duke of Wellington surrounded by his staff on
the Field of Waterloo; and notwithstanding recent events
which have, as it were, enveloped our great hero in a cloud, I
will be bold to say—for a man in my line must not be blown
about by political winds—that a finer subject of the modern
order belonging to our own time and epoch, the understanding of man could hardly conceive; angels might perhaps, but
not men, sirs, not men."

"Who painted it?" said Mr. Powderell, much impressed.

"It is a proof before the letter, Mr. Powderell—the painter
is not known," answered Trumbull, with a certain gaspingness
in his last words, after which he pursed up his lips and stared
round him.

"I'll bid a pound!" said Mr. Powderell in a tone of resolved
emotion, as of a man ready to put himself in the breach.
Whether from awe or pity, nobody raised the price on him.

Next came two Dutch prints which Mr. Toller had been
eager for, and after he had secured them he went away.
Other prints, and afterward some paintings, were sold to leading Middlemarchers who had come with a special desire for
them, and there was a more active movement of the audience
in and out; some who had bought what they wanted going
away, others coming in either quite newly or from a temporary
visit to the refreshments which were spread under the marquee
on the lawn. It was this marquee that Mr. Bambridge was
bent on buying, and he appeared to like looking inside it frequently as a foretaste of its possession. On the last occasion
of his return from it he was observed to bring with him a new

companion, a stranger to Mr. Trumbull and every one else,
whose appearance, however, led to the supposition that he
might be a relative of the horse-dealer's—also "given to indulgence." His large whiskers, imposing swagger, and swing of
the leg, made him a striking figure; but his suit of black,
rather shabby at the edges, caused the prejudicial inference
that he was not able to afford himself as much indulgence as
he liked.

"Who is it you've picked up, Bam?" said Mr. Horrock,
aside.

"Ask him yourself," returned Mr. Bambridge.   "He said
he'd just turned in from the road."

Mr. Horrock eyed the stranger, who was leaning back
against his stick with one hand, using his toothpick with the
other, and looking about him with a certain restlessness apparently under the silence imposed on him by circumstances.

At length the Supper at Emmaus was brought forward, to
Will's immense relief, for he was getting so tired of the proceedings that he had drawn back a little and leaned his shoulder against the wall just behind the auctioneer.   He now
came forward again, and his eye caught the conspicuous stranger, who, rather to his surprise, was staring at him markedly.
But Will was immediately appealed to by Mr. Trumbull.

"Yes, Mr. Ladislaw, yes; this interests you as a connoissure,
I think.   It is some pleasure," the auctioneer went on with a
rising fervor, "to have a picture like this to show to a company of ladies and gentlemen—a picture worth any sum to an
individual whose means were on a level with his judgment.
It is a painting of the Italian school—by the celebrated *Guydo*,
the greatest painter in the world, the chief of the old masters,
as they are called—I take it, because they were up to a thing
or two beyond most of us—in possession of secrets now lost to
the bulk of mankind.   Let me tell you, gentlemen, I have
seen a great many pictures by the old masters, and they are
not all up to this mark—some of them are darker than you
might like, and not family subjects.   But here is a *Guydo*—the
frame alone is worth pounds—which any lady might be proud
to hang up—a suitable thing for what we call a refectory in a
charitable institution, if any gentleman of the corporation

wished to show his munifi*cence*.   Turn it a little, sir? yes.
Joseph, turn it a little toward Mr. Ladislaw—Mr. Ladislaw,
having been abroad, understands the merit of these things, you
observe."

All eyes were for a moment turned toward Will, who said,
coolly, "Five pounds."   The auctioneer burst out in deep
remonstrance.

"Ah! Mr. Ladislaw! the frame alone is worth that.
Ladies and gentlemen, for the credit of the town!   Suppose it
should be discovered hereafter that a gem of art has been among
us in this town, and nobody in Middlemarch awake to it.   Five
guineas—five seven-six—five ten.   Still, ladies, still!   It is a
gem, and ' Full many a gem,' as the poet says, has been allowed
to go at a nominal price because the public knew no better,
because it was offered in circles where there was—I was going
to say a low feeling, but no!—Six pounds—six guineas—a
Guydo of the first order going at six guineas—it is an insult
to religion, ladies; it touches us all as Christians, gentlemen,
that a subject like this should go at such a low figure—six
pounds ten—seven——"

The bidding was brisk, and Will continued to share in it,
remembering that Mrs. Bulstrode had a strong wish for the
picture, and thinking that he might stretch the price to twelve
pounds.   But it was knocked down to him at ten guineas,
whereupon he pushed his way toward the bow-window and
went out.   He chose to go under the marquee to get a glass
of water, being hot and thirsty: it was empty of other visitors, and he asked the woman in attendance to fetch him
some fresh water; but before she was well gone he was annoyed to see entering the florid stranger who had stared at
him.   It struck Will at this moment that the man might be
one of those political parasitic insects of the bloated kind who
had once or twice claimed acquaintance with him as having
heard him speak on the reform question, and who might think
of getting a shilling by news.   In this light his person, already
rather heating to behold on a summer's day, appeared the more
disagreeable; and Will, half-seated on the elbow of a garden-
chair, turned his eyes carefully away from the comer.   But
this signified little to our acquaintance, Mr. Raffles, who never

hesitated to thrust himself on unwilling observation, if it suited his purpose to do so. He moved a step or two till he was in front of Will, and said with full-mouthed haste, "Excuse me, Mr. Ladislaw—was your mother's name Sarah Dunkirk?"

Will, starting to his feet, moved backward a step, frowning, and saying with some fierceness: "Yes, sir, it was. And what is that to you?"

It was in Will's nature that the first spark it threw out was a direct answer of the question and a challenge of the consequences. To have said, "What is that to you?" in the first instance, would have seemed like shuffling—as if he minded who knew anything about his origin!

Raffles on his side had not the same eagerness for a collision which was implied in Ladislaw's threatening air. The slim young fellow with his girl's complexion looked like a tiger-cat ready to spring on him. Under such circumstances, Mr. Raffles's pleasure in annoying his company was kept in abeyance.

"No offence, my good sir, no offence! I only remember your mother—knew her when she was a girl. But it is your father that you feature, sir. I had the pleasure of seeing your father, too. Parents alive, Mr. Ladislaw?"

"No!" thundered Will, in the same attitude as before.

"Should be glad to do you a service, Mr. Ladislaw—by Jove, I should. Hope to meet again."

Hereupon Raffles, who had lifted his hat with the last words, turned himself round with a swing of his leg and walked away. Will looked after him a moment, and could see that he did not re-enter the auction-room, but appeared to be walking toward the road. For an instant he thought that he had been foolish not to let the man go on talking; but no! on the whole he preferred doing without knowledge from that source.

Later in the evening, however, Raffles overtook him in the street, and appearing either to have forgotten the roughness of his former reception or to intend avenging it by a forgiving familiarity, greeted him jovially and walked by his side, remarking at first on the pleasantness of the town and neighborhood. Will suspected that the man had been drinking, and was considering how to shake him off, when Raffles said:

"I've been abroad myself, Mr. Ladislaw—I've seen the world—used to parley-vous a little. It was at Boulogne I saw your father—a most uncommon likeness you are of him, by Jove! mouth—nose—eyes—hair turned off your brow just like his—a little in the foreign style. John Bull doesn't do much of that. But your father was very ill when I saw him. Lord, Lord! hands you might see through. You were a small youngster then. Did he get well?"

"No," said Will, curtly.

"Ah! Well! I've often wondered what became of your mother. She ran away from her friends when she was a young lass—a proud-spirited lass, and pretty, by Jove! *I* knew the reason why she ran away," said Raffles, winking slowly as he looked sideways at Will.

"You know nothing dishonorable of her, sir," said Will, turning on him rather savagely. But Mr. Raffles just now was not sensitive to shades of manner.

"Not a bit!" said he, tossing his head decisively. "She was a little too honorable to like her friends—that was it!" Here Raffles again winked slowly. "Lord bless you, I knew all about 'em—a little in what you may call the respectable thieving line—the high style of receiving-house—none of your holes and corners—first-rate. Slap-up shop, high profits and no mistake. But Lord! Sarah would have known nothing about it—a dashing young lady she was—fine boarding-school —fit for a lord's wife—only Archie Duncan threw it at her out of spite, because she would have nothing to do with him. And so she ran away from the whole concern. I travelled for 'em, sir, in a gentlemanly way—at a high salary. They didn't mind her running away at first—godly folks, sir, very godly—and she was for the stage. The son was alive then, and the daughter was at a discount. Hallo! here we are at the Blue Bull. What do you say, Mr. Ladislaw, shall we turn in and have a glass?"

"No, I must say good evening," said Will, dashing up a passage which led into Lowick Gate, and almost running to get out of Raffles's reach.

He walked a long while on the Lowick Road away from the town, glad of the starlit darkness when it came. He felt as if he had had dirt cast on him amid shouts of scorn. There was this to confirm the fellow's statement—that his mother never would tell him the reason why she had run away from her family.

Well! what was he, Will Ladislaw, the worse, supposing the truth about that family to be the ugliest? His mother had braved hardship in order to separate herself from it. But if Dorothea's friends had known this story—if the Chettams had known it—they would have had a fine color to give their suspicions a welcome ground for thinking him unfit to come near her. However, let them suspect what they pleased, they would find themselves in the wrong. They would find out that the blood in his veins was as free from the taint of meanness as theirs.

CHAPTER LXI.

"'Inconsistencies,' answered Imlac, 'cannot both be right, but imputed to man they may both be true.'"—RASSELAS.

THE same night, when Mr. Bulstrode returned from a journey to Brassing on business, his good wife met him in the entrance-hall and drew him into his private sitting-room.

"Nicholas," she said, fixing her honest eyes upon him anxiously, "there has been such a disagreeable man here asking for you—it has made me quite uncomfortable."

"What kind of man, my dear?" said Mr. Bulstrode, dreadfully certain of the answer.

"A red-faced man with large whiskers, and most impudent in his manner. He declared he was an old friend of yours, and said you would be sorry not to see him. He wanted to wait for you here, but I told him he could see you at the bank to-morrow morning. Most impudent he was—stared at me, and said his friend Nick had luck in wives. I don't believe he would have gone away, if Blucher had not happened to break his chain and come running round on the gravel—for I was in the garden; so I said, ' You'd better go away—the dog

is very fierce, and I can't hold him.' Do you really know
anything of such a man?"

"I believe I know who he is, my dear," said Mr. Bulstrode,
in his usual subdued voice, "an unfortunate dissolute wretch,
whom I helped too much in days gone by. However, I presume you will not be troubled by him again. He will probably come to the bank—to beg, doubtless."

No more was said on the subject until the next day, when
Mr. Bulstrode had returned from the town and was dressing
for dinner. His wife, not sure that he was come home, looked
into his dressing-room and saw him with his coat and cravat
off, leaning one arm on a chest of drawers and staring absently
at the ground. He started nervously and looked up as she
entered.

"You look very ill, Nicholas. Is there anything the matter?"

"I have a good deal of pain in my head," said Mr. Bulstrode, who was so frequently ailing that his wife was always
ready to believe in this cause of depression.

"Sit down and let me sponge it with vinegar."

Physically Mr. Bulstrode did not want the vinegar, but
morally the affectionate attention soothed him. Though
always polite, it was his habit to receive such services with
marital coolness, as his wife's duty. But to-day, while she
was bending over him, he said, "You are very good, Harriet,"
in a tone which had something new in it to her ear; she did
not know exactly what the novelty was, but her woman's
solicitude shaped itself into a darting thought that he might
be going to have an illness.

"Has anything worried you?" she said. "Did that man
come to you at the bank?"

"Yes; it was as I had supposed. He is a man who at one
time might have done better. But he has sunk into a drunken,
debauched creature."

"Is he quite gone away?" said Mrs. Bulstrode anxiously;
but for certain reasons she refrained from adding, "It was
very disagreeable to hear him calling himself a friend of
yours." At that moment she would not have liked to say
anything which implied her habitual consciousness that her

husband's earlier connections were not quite on a level with her own. Not that she knew much about them. That her husband had at first been employed in a bank, that he had afterward entered into what he called city business and gained a fortune before he was three-and-thirty, that he had married a widow who was much older than himself—a Dissenter, and in other ways probably of that disadvantageous quality usually perceptible in a first wife if inquired into with the dispassionate judgment of a second—was almost as much as she had cared to learn beyond the glimpses which Mr. Bulstrode's narrative occasionally gave of his early bent toward religion, his inclination to be a preacher, and his association with missionary and philanthropic efforts. She believed in him as an excellent man whose piety carried a peculiar eminence in belonging to a layman, whose influence had turned her own mind toward seriousness, and whose share of perishable good had been the means of raising her own position. But she also liked to think that it was well in every sense for Mr. Bulstrode to have won the hand of Harriet Vincy; whose family was undeniable in a Middlemarch light—a better light surely than any thrown in London thoroughfares or dissenting chapel-yards. The unreformed provincial mind distrusted London; and while true religion was everywhere saving, honest Mrs. Bulstrode was convinced that to be saved in the Church was more respectable. She so much wished to ignore toward others that her husband had ever been a London Dissenter, that she liked to keep it out of sight even in talking to him. He was quite aware of this; indeed, in some respects he was rather afraid of this ingenuous wife, whose imitative piety and native worldliness were equally sincere, who had nothing to be ashamed of, and whom he had married out of a thorough inclination still subsisting. But his fears were such as belong to a man who cares to maintain his recognized supremacy; the loss of high consideration from his wife, as from every one else who did not clearly hate him out of enmity to the truth, would be as the beginning of death to him. When she said:

"Is he quite gone away?"

"Oh, I trust so," he answered with an effort to throw as much sober unconcern into his tone as possible.

But in truth Mr. Bulstrode was very far from a state of quiet trust. In the interview at the bank, Raffles had made it evident that his eagerness to torment was almost as strong in him as any other greed. He had frankly said that he had turned out of the way to come to Middlemarch, just to look about him and see whether the neighborhood would suit him to live in. He had certainly had a few debts to pay more than he expected, but the two hundred pounds were not gone yet; a cool five-and-twenty would suffice him to go away with for the present. What he had wanted chiefly was to see his friend Nick and family, and know all about the prosperity of a man to whom he was so much attached. By and by he might come back for a longer stay. This time Raffles declined to be "seen off the premises," as he expressed it—declined to quit Middlemarch under Bulstrode's eyes. He meant to go by coach the next day—if he chose.

Bulstrode felt himself helpless. Neither threats nor coaxing could avail: he could not count on any persistent fear nor on any promise. On the contrary, he felt a cold certainty at his heart that Raffles—unless providence sent death to hinder him—would come back to Middlemarch before long. And that certainly was a terror.

It was not that he was in danger of legal punishment or of beggary: he was in danger only of seeing disclosed to the judgment of his neighbors and the mournful perception of his wife, certain facts of his past life which would render him an object of scorn and an opprobrium of the religion with which he had diligently associated himself. The terror of being judged sharpens the memory: it sends an inevitable glare over the long-unvisited past which has been habitually recalled only in general phrases. Even without memory, the life is bound into one by a zone of dependence in growth and decay; but intense memory forces a man to own his blameworthy past. With memory set smarting like a reopened wound, a man's past is not simply a dead history, an outworn preparation of the present: it is not a repented error shaken loose from the life: it is a still quivering part of himself, bringing shudders and bitter flavors and the tinglings of a merited shame.

Into this second life Bulstrode's past had now risen, only

the pleasures of it seeming to have lost their quality. Night and day, without interruption save of brief sleep, which only wove retrospect and fear into a fantastic present, he felt the scenes of his earlier life coming between him and everything else, as obstinately as, when we look through the window from a lighted room, the objects we turn our backs on are still before us, instead of the grass and the trees. The successive events inward and outward were there in one view: though each might be dwelt on in turn, the rest still kept their hold in the consciousness.

Once more he saw himself the young banker's clerk, with an agreeable person, as clever in figures as he was fluent in speech and fond of theological definition: an eminent though young member of a Calvinistic dissenting church at Highbury, having had striking experience in conviction of sin and sense of pardon. Again he heard himself called for as Brother Bulstrode in prayer-meetings, speaking on religious platforms, preaching in private houses. Again he felt himself thinking of the ministry as possibly his vocation, and inclined toward missionary labor. That was the happiest time of his life: that was the spot he would have chosen now to awake in and find the rest a dream. The people among whom Brother Bulstrode was distinguished were very few, but they were very near to him, and stirred his satisfaction the more: his power stretched through a narrow space, but he felt its effect the more intensely. He believed without effort in the peculiar work of grace within him, and in the signs that God intended him for special instrumentality.

Then came the moment of transition: it was with the sense of promotion he had when he, an orphan educated at a commercial charity-school, was invited to a fine villa belonging to Mr. Dunkirk, the richest man in the congregation. Soon he became an intimate there, honored for his piety by the wife, marked out for his ability by the husband, whose wealth was due to a flourishing city and West End trade. That was the setting in of a new current for his ambition, directing his prospects of "instrumentality" toward the uniting of distinguished religious gifts with successful business.

By and by came a decided external leading: a confidential

subordinate partner died, and nobody seemed to the principal
so well fitted to fill the severely felt vacancy as his young
friend Bulstrode, if he would become confidential accountant.
The offer was accepted. The business was a pawnbroker's,
of the most magnificent sort both in extent and profits: and
on a short acquaintance with it Bulstrode became aware that
one source of magnificent profit was the easy reception of any
goods offered, without strict inquiry as to where they came
from. But there was a branch house at the West End, and
no pettiness or dinginess to give suggestions of shame.

He remembered his first moments of shrinking. They were
private, and were filled with arguments—some of these taking
the form of prayer. The business was established and had
old roots: is it not one thing to set up a new gin-palace, and
another to accept an investment in an old one? The profits
made out of lost souls—where can the line be drawn at which
they begin in human transactions? Was it not even God's
way of saving His chosen? "Thou knowest,"—the young
Bulstrode had said then, as the older Bulstrode was saying
now— "thou knowest how loose my soul sits from these
things—how I view them all as implements for tilling Thy
garden rescued here and there from the wilderness."

Metaphors and precedents were not wanting; peculiar spiritual experiences were not wanting, which at last made the
retention of his position seem a service demanded of him:
the vista of a fortune had already opened itself, and Bulstrode's shrinking remained private. Mr. Dunkirk had never
expected that there would be any shrinking at all: he had
never conceived that trade had anything to do with the scheme
of salvation. And it was true that Bulstrode found himself
carrying on two distinct lives; his religious activity could not
be incompatible with his business as soon as he had argued
himself into not feeling it incompatible.

Mentally surrounded with that past again, Bulstrode had
the same pleas—indeed, the years had been perpetually spin-
ning them into intricate thickness, like masses of spider-web,
padding the moral sensibility; nay, as age made egoism more
eager but less enjoying, his soul had become more saturated
with the belief that he did everything for God's sake, being

indifferent to it for his own. And yet—if he could be back
in that far-off spot with his youthful poverty—why, then he
would choose to be a missionary.

But the train of causes in which he had locked himself went
on. There was trouble in the fine villa at Highbury. Years
before, the only daughter had run away, defied her parents,
and gone on the stage; and now the only boy died, and after
a short time Mr. Dunkirk died also. The wife, a simple,
pious woman, left with all the wealth in and out of the magnificent trade, of which she never knew the precise nature, had
come to believe in Bulstrode, and innocently adore him as
women often adore their priest or "man-made" minister. It
was natural that after a time marriage should have been
thought of between them. But Mrs. Dunkirk had qualms
and yearnings about her daughter, who had long been regarded
as lost both to God and her parents. It was known that the
daughter had married, but she was utterly gone out of sight.
The mother, having lost her boy, imagined a grandson, and
wished in a double sense to reclaim her daughter. If she
were found, there would be a channel for property—perhaps a
wide one, in the provision for several grandchildren. Efforts
to find her must be made before Mrs. Dunkirk would marry
again. Bulstrode concurred; but after advertisement as well
as other modes of inquiry had been tried, the mother believed
that her daughter was not to be found, and consented to marry
without reservation of property.

The daughter had been found; but only one man besides
Bulstrode knew it, and he was paid for keeping silence and
carrying himself away.

That was the bare fact which Bulstrode was now forced to
see in the rigid outline with which acts present themselves
to onlookers. But for himself at that distant time, and even
now in burning memory, the fact was broken into little sequences, each justified as it came by reasonings which seemed
to prove it righteous. Bulstrode's course up to that time had,
he thought, been sanctioned by remarkable providences, appearing to point the way for him to be the agent in making
the best use of a large property and withdrawing it from perversion. Death and other striking dispositions, such as femi-

nine trustfulness, had come; and Bulstrode would have adopted
Cromwell's words: "Do you call these bare events? The
Lord pity you!" The events were comparatively small, but
the essential condition was there—namely, that they were in
favor of his own ends. It was easy for him to settle what
was due from him to others by inquiring what were God's
intentions with regard to himself. Could it be for God's service that this fortune should in any considerable proportion go
to a young woman and her husband who were given up to the
lightest pursuits, and might scatter it abroad in triviality—people who seemed to lie outside the path of remarkable providences? Bulstrode had never said to himself beforehand,
"The daughter shall not be found"—nevertheless when the
moment came he kept her existence hidden; and when other
moments followed, he soothed the mother with consolation in
the probability that the unhappy young woman might be no
more.

There were hours in which Bulstrode felt that his action
was unrighteous; but how could he go back? He had mental
exercises, called himself nought, laid hold on redemption, and
went on in his course of instrumentality. And after five years
Death again came to widen his path, by taking away his wife.
He did gradually withdraw his capital, but he did not make
the sacrifices requisite to put an end to the business, which
was carried on for thirteen years afterward before it finally
collapsed. Meanwhile Nicholas Bulstrode had used his hundred thousand discreetly, and was become provincially, solidly
important—a banker, a Churchman, a public benefactor; also
a sleeping partner in trading concerns, in which his ability
was directed to economy in the raw material, as in the case of
the dyes which rotted Mr. Vincy's silk. And now, when this
respectability had lasted undisturbed for nearly thirty years—
when all that preceded it had long lain benumbed in the consciousness—that past had risen and immersed his thought as
if with the terrible eruption of a new sense overburdening the
feeble being.

Meanwhile, in his conversation with Raffles, he had learned
something momentous, something which entered actively into
the struggle of his longings and terrors. There, he thought,

lay an opening toward spiritual, perhaps toward material, rescue.

The spiritual kind of rescue was a genuine need with him. There may be coarse hypocrites who consciously affect beliefs and emotions for the sake of gulling the world, but Bulstrode was not one of them. He was simply a man whose desires had been stronger than his theoretic beliefs, and who had gradually explained the gratification of his desires into satisfactory agreement with those beliefs. If this be hypocrisy, it is a process which shows itself occasionally in us all, to whatever confession we belong, and whatever we believe in the future perfection of our race or in the nearest date fixed for the end of the world; whether we regard the earth as a putrefying nidus for a saved remnant, including ourselves, or have a passionate belief in the solidarity of mankind.

The service he could do to the cause of religion had been through life the ground he alleged to himself for his choice of action: it had been the motive which he had poured out in his prayers. Who would use money and position better than he meant to use them? Who could surpass him in self-abhorrence and exaltation of God's cause? And to Mr. Bulstrode God's cause was something distinct from his own rectitude of conduct: it enforced a discrimination of God's enemies, who were to be used merely as instruments, and whom it would be as well, if possible, to keep out of money and consequent influence. Also, profitable investments in trades where the power of the prince of this world showed its most active devices, became sanctified by a right application of the profits in the hands of God's servant.

This implicit reasoning is essentially no more peculiar to evangelical belief than the use of wide phrases for narrow motives is peculiar to Englishmen. There is no general doctrine which is not capable of eating out our morality if unchecked by the deep-seated habit of direct fellow-feeling with individual fellow-men.

But a man who believes in something else than his own greed, has necessarily a conscience or standard to which he more or less adapts himself. Bulstrode's standard had been his serviceableness to God's cause: "I am sinful and nought

—a vessel to be consecrated by use—but use me!"—had been the mould into which he had constrained his immense need of being something important and predominating. And now had come a moment in which that mould seemed in danger of being broken and utterly cast away.

What, if the acts he had reconciled himself to because they made him a stronger instrument of the divine glory, were to become the pretext of the scoffer, and a darkening of that glory? If this were to be the ruling of Providence, he was cast out from the temple as one who had brought unclean offerings.

He had long poured out utterances of repentance. But to-day a repentance had come which was of a bitterer flavor, and a threatening Providence urged him to a kind of propitiation which was not simply a doctrinal transaction. The divine tribunal had changed its aspect for him; self-prostration was no longer enough, and he must bring restitution in his hand. It was really before his God that Bulstrode was about to attempt such restitution as seemed possible: a great dread had seized his susceptible frame, and the scorching approach of shame wrought in him a new spiritual need. Night and day, while the resurgent threatening past was making a conscience within him, he was thinking by what means he could recover peace and trust—by what sacrifice he could stay the rod. His belief in these moments of dread was, that if he spontaneously did something right, God would save him from the consequences of wrong-doing. For religion can only change when the emotions which fill it are changed; and the religion of personal fear remains nearly at the level of the savage.

He had seen Raffles actually going away on the Brassing coach, and this was a temporary relief; it removed the pressure of an immediate dread, but did not put an end to the spiritual conflict and the need to win protection. At last he came to a difficult resolve, and wrote a letter to Will Ladislaw, begging him to be at the Shrubs that evening for a private interview at nine o'clock. Will had felt no particular surprise at the request, and connected it with some new notions about the *Pioneer;* but when he was shown into Mr. Bulstrode's private room, he was struck with the painfully worn look on the

40

banker's face, and was going to say, "Are you ill?" when, checking himself in that abruptness, he only inquired after Mrs. Bulstrode, and her satisfaction with the picture bought for her.

"Thank you, she is quite satisfied; she has gone out with her daughters this evening. I begged you to come, Mr. Ladislaw, because I have a communication of a very private—indeed, I will say, of a sacredly confidential—nature, which I desire to make to you. Nothing, I dare say, has been farther from your thoughts than that there had been important ties in the past which could connect your history with mine."

Will felt something like an electric shock. He was already in a state of keen sensitiveness and hardly allayed agitation on the subject of ties in the past, and his presentiments were not agreeable. It seemed like the fluctuations of a dream—as if the action begun by that loud bloated stranger were being carried on by this pale-eyed, sickly looking piece of respectability, whose subdued tone and glib formality of speech were at this moment almost as repulsive to him as their remembered contrast. He answered, with a marked change of color:

"No, indeed, nothing."

"You see before you, Mr. Ladislaw, a man who is deeply stricken. But for the urgency of conscience and the knowledge that I am before the bar of One who seeth not as man seeth, I should be under no compulsion to make the disclosure which has been my object in asking you to come here to-night. So far as human laws go, you have no claim on me whatever."

Will was even more uncomfortable than wondering. Mr. Bulstrode had paused, leaning his head on his hand, and looking at the floor. But he now fixed his examining glance on Will and said:

"I am told that your mother's name was Sarah Dunkirk, and that she ran away from her friends to go on the stage. Also, that your father was at one time much emaciated by illness. May I ask if you can confirm these statements?"

"Yes, they are all true," said Will, struck with the order in which an inquiry had come, that might have been expected to be preliminary to the banker's previous hints. But Mr. Bulstrode had to-night followed the order of his emotions; he entertained no doubt that the opportunity for restitution had come, and he had an overpowering impulse toward the penitential expression by which he was deprecating chastisement.

"Do you know any particulars of your mother's family?" he continued.

"No; she never liked to speak of them. She was a very generous, honorable woman," said Will, almost angrily.

"I do not wish to allege anything against her. Did she never mention her mother to you at all?"

"I have heard her say that she thought her mother did not know the reason of her running away. She said 'Poor mother' in a pitying tone."

"That mother became my wife," said Bulstrode, and then paused a moment before he added, "you have a claim on me, Mr. Ladislaw: as I said before, not a legal claim, but one which my conscience recognizes. I was enriched by that marriage—a result which would probably not have taken place—certainly not to the same extent—if your grandmother could have discovered her daughter. That daughter, I gather, is no longer living?"

"No," said Will, feeling suspicion and repugnance rising so strongly within him, that without quite knowing what he did, he took his hat from the floor and stood up. The impulse within him was to reject the disclosed connection.

"Pray be seated, Mr. Ladislaw," said Bulstrode, anxiously. "Doubtless you are startled by the suddenness of this discovery. But I entreat your patience with one who is already bowed down by inward trial."

Will reseated himself, feeling some pity which was half contempt for this voluntary self-abasement of an elderly man.

"It is my wish, Mr. Ladislaw, to make amends for the deprivation which befell your mother. I know that you are without fortune, and I wish to supply you adequately from a store which would have probably already been yours had your grandmother been certain of your mother's existence and been able to find her."

Mr. Bulstrode paused. He felt that he was performing a striking piece of scrupulosity in the judgment of his auditor, and a penitential act in the eyes of God. He had no clue to

the state of Will Ladislaw's mind, smarting as it was from
the clear hints of Raffles, and with its natural quickness in
construction stimulated by the expectation of discoveries which
he would have been glad to conjure back into darkness.   Will
made no answer for several moments, till Mr. Bulstrode, who
at the end of his speech had cast his eyes on the floor, now
raised them with an examining glance, which Will met fully,
saying:

"I suppose you did know of my mother's existence, and
knew where she might have been found."

Bulstrode shrank—there was a visible quivering in his face
and hands.   He was totally unprepared to have his advances
met in this way, or to find himself urged into more revelation
than he had beforehand set down as needful.   But at that
moment he dared not tell a lie, and he felt suddenly uncertain
of his ground which he had trodden with some confidence
before.

"I will not deny that you conjecture rightly," he answered,
with a faltering in his tone.   "And I wish to make atonement
to you as the one still remaining who has suffered a loss
through me.   You enter, I trust, into my purpose, Mr. Ladislaw, which has reference to higher than merely human
claims, and, as I have already said, is entirely independent of
any legal compulsion.   I am ready to narrow my own resources
and the prospects of my family by binding myself to allow
you five hundred pounds yearly during my life, and to leave
you a proportional capital at my death—nay, to do still more,
if more should be definitely necessary to any laudable project
on your part."   Mr. Bulstrode had gone on to particulars in
the expectation that these would work strongly on Ladislaw,
and merge other feelings in grateful acceptance.

But Will was looking as stubborn as possible, with his lip
pouting and his fingers in his side pockets.   He was not in the
least touched, and said firmly:

"Before I make any reply to your proposition, Mr. Bulstrode, I must beg you to answer a question or two.   Were
you connected with the business by which that fortune you
speak of was originally made?"

Mr. Bulstrode's thought was, "Raffles has told him."   How

could he refuse to answer when he had volunteered what drew
forth the question? He answered, "Yes."

"And was that business—or was it not—a thoroughly dishonorable one—nay, one that, if its nature had been made
public, might have ranked those concerned in it with thieves
and convicts?"

Will's tone had a cutting bitterness: he was moved to put
his questions as nakedly as he could.

Bulstrode reddened with irrepressible anger. He had been
prepared for a scene of self-abasement, but his intense pride
and his habit of supremacy overpowered penitence, and even
dread, when this young man, whom he had meant to benefit,
turned on him with the air of a judge.

"The business was established before I became connected
with it, sir; nor is it for you to institute an inquiry of that
kind," he answered, not raising his voice, but speaking with
quick defiantness.

"Yes, it is," said Will, starting up again, with his hat in
his hand. "It is eminently mine to ask such questions, when
I have to decide whether I will have transactions with you and
accept your money. My unblemished honor is important to
me. It is important to me to have no stain on my birth and
connections. And now I find there is a stain which I can't
help. My mother felt it, and tried to keep as clear of it as
she could, and so will I. You shall keep your ill-gotten
money. If I had any fortune of my own, I would willingly
pay it to any one who could disprove what you have told me.
What I have to thank you for is that you kept the money till
now, when I can refuse it. It ought to lie with a man's self
that he is a gentleman. Good-night, sir."

Bulstrode was going to speak, but Will, with determined
quickness, was out of the room in an instant, and in another
the hall door had closed behind him. He was too strongly
possessed with passionate rebellion against this inherited blot
which had been thrust on his knowledge to reflect at present
whether he had not been too hard on Bulstrode—too arrogantly
merciless toward a man of sixty, who was making efforts at
retrieval when time had rendered them vain.

No third person listening could have thoroughly understood

the impetuosity of Will's repulse or the bitterness of his words. No one but himself then knew how everything connected with the sentiment of his own dignity had an immediate bearing for him on his relation to Dorothea and to Mr. Casaubon's treat- ment of him.   And in the rush of impulses by which he flung back that offer of Bulstrode's there was mingled the sense that it would have been impossible for him ever to tell Dorothea that he had accepted it.

As for Bulstrode—when Will was gone he suffered a violent reaction, and wept like a woman.   It was the first time he had encountered an open expression of scorn from any man higher than Raffles; and with that scorn hurrying like venom through his system, there was no sensibility left to consola- tions.   But the relief of weeping had to be checked.   His wife and daughters soon came home from hearing the address of an Oriental missionary, and were full of regret that papa had not heard, in the first instance, the interesting things which they tried to repeat to him.

Perhaps, through all other hidden thoughts, the one that breathed most comfort was, that Will Ladislaw at least was not likely to publish what had taken place that evening.

CHAPTER LXII.

"He was a squyer of lowe degre,
That loved the king's daughter of Hungrie. "
—Old Romance.

WILL LADISLAW's mind was now wholly bent on seeing Dorothea again, and forthwith quitting Middlemarch.   The morning after his agitating scene with Bulstrode he wrote a brief letter to her, saying that various causes had detained him in the neighborhood longer than he had expected, and asking her permission to call again at Lowick at some hour which she would mention on the earliest possible day, he being anxious to depart, but unwilling to do so until she had granted him an interview.   He left the letter at the office, ordering the messenger to carry it to Lowick Manor, and wait for an answer.

Ladislaw felt the awkwardness of asking for more last words. His former farewell had been made in the hearing of Sir James Chettam, and had been announced as final even to the butler. It is certainly trying to a man's dignity to reappear when he is not expected to do so: a first farewell has pathos in it, but to come back for a second lends an opening to comedy, and it was possible even that there might be bitter sneers afloat about Will's motives for lingering. Still it was on the whole more satisfactory to his feeling to take the directest means of seeing Dorothea, than to use any device which might give an air of chance to a meeting of which he wished her to understand that it was what he earnestly sought. When he had parted from her before, he had been in ignorance of facts which gave a new aspect to the relation between them, and made a more absolute severance than he had then believed in. He knew nothing of Dorothea's private fortune, and being little used to reflect on such matters, took it for granted that according to Mr. Casaubon's arrangement, marriage to him, Will Ladislaw, would mean that she consented to be penniless. That was not what he could wish for even in his secret heart, or even if she had been ready to meet such hard contrast for his sake. And then, too, there was the fresh smart of that disclosure about his mother's family, which if known would be an added reason why Dorothea's friends should look down upon him as utterly below her. The secret hope that after some years he might come back with the sense that he had at least a personal value equal to her wealth, seemed now the dreamy continuation of a dream. This change would surely justify him in asking Dorothea to receive him once more.

But Dorothea on that morning was not at home to receive Will's note. In consequence of a letter from her uncle announcing his intention to be at home in a week, she had driven first to Freshitt to carry the news, meaning to go on to the Grange to deliver some orders with which her uncle had intrusted her—thinking, as he said, "a little mental occupation of this sort good for a widow."

If Will Ladislaw could have overheard some of the talk at Freshitt that morning, he would have felt all his suppositions confirmed as to the readiness of certain people to sneer at his lingering in the neighborhood. Sir James, indeed, though much relieved concerning Dorothea, had been on the watch to learn Ladislaw's movements, and had an instructed informant in Mr. Standish, who was necessarily in his confidence on this matter. That Ladislaw had stayed in Middlemarch nearly two months after he had declared that he was going immediately, was a fact to embitter Sir James's suspicions, or at least to justify his aversion to a "young fellow" whom he represented to himself as slight, volatile, and likely enough to show such recklessness as naturally went along with a position unriveted bv family ties or a strict profession. But he had just heard something from Standish which, while it justified these surmises about Will, offered a means of nullifying all danger with regard to Dorothea.

Unwonted circumstances may make us all rather unlike ourselves: there are conditions under which the most majestic person is obliged to sneeze, and our emotions are liable to be acted on in the same incongruous manner. Good Sir James was this morning so far unlike himself that he was irritably anxious to say something to Dorothea on the subject which he usually avoided as if it had been a matter of shame to them both. He could not use Celia as a medium, because he did not choose that she should know the kind of gossip he had in his mind; and before Dorothea happened to arrive he had been trying to imagine how, with his shyness and unready tongue, he could ever manage to introduce his communication. Her unexpected presence brought him to utter hopelessness in his own power of saying anything unpleasant; but desperation suggested a resource; he sent the groom on an unsaddled horse across the park, with a pencilled note to Mrs. Cadwallader, who already knew the gossip, and would think it no compromise of herself to repeat it as often as required.

Dorothea was detained on the good pretext that Mr. Garth, whom she wanted to see, was expected at the Hall within the hour, and she was still talking to Caleb on the gravel when Sir James, on the watch for the rector's wife, saw her coming and met her with the needful hints.

"Enough! I understand," said Mrs. Cadwallader. "You

shall be innocent. I am such a blackamoor that I cannot smirch myself."

"I don't mean that it's of any consequence," said Sir James, disliking that Mrs. Cadwallader should understand too much. "Only it is desirable that Dorothea should know there are reasons why she should not receive him again; and I really can't say so to her. It will come lightly from you."

It came very lightly indeed. When Dorothea quitted Caleb and turned to meet them, it appeared that Mrs. Cadwallader had stepped across the park by the merest chance in the world, just to chat with Celia in a matronly way about the baby. And so Mr. Brooke was coming back? Delightful!—coming back, it was to be hoped, quite cured of Parliamentary fever and pioneering. *Apropos* of the *Pioneer*—somebody had prophesied that it would soon be like a dying dolphin, and turn all colors for want of knowing how to help itself, because Mr. Brooke's *protégé*, the brilliant young Ladislaw, was gone or going. Had Sir James heard that?

The three were walking along the gravel slowly, and Sir James, turning aside to whip a shrub, said he had heard something of that sort.

"All false!" said Mrs. Cadwallader. "He is not gone, or going, apparently; the *Pioneer* keeps its color, and Mr. Orlando Ladislaw is making a sad dark-blue scandal by warbling continually with your Mr. Lydgate's wife, who they tell me is as pretty as pretty can be. It seems nobody ever goes into the house without finding this young gentleman lying on the rug or warbling at the piano. But the people in manufacturing towns are always disreputable."

"You began by saying that one report was false, Mrs. Cadwallader, and I believe this is false too," said Dorothea, with indignant energy; "at least I feel sure it is a misrepresentation. I will not hear any evil spoken of Mr. Ladislaw; he has already suffered too much injustice."

Dorothea, when thoroughly moved, cared little what any one thought of her feelings; and even if she had been able to reflect, she would have held it petty to keep silence at injurious words about Will from fear of being herself misunderstood. Her face was flushed and her lip trembled.

Sir James, glancing at her, repented of his stratagem; but Mrs. Cadwallader, equal to all occasions, spread the palms of her hands outward and said: "Heaven grant it, my dear!—I mean that all bad tales about anybody may be false. But it is a pity that young Lydgate should have married one of these Middlemarch girls. Considering he's a son of somebody, he might have got a woman with good blood in her veins, and not too young, who would have put up with his profession. There's Clara Harfager, for instance, whose friends don't know what to do with her; and she has a portion. Then we might have had her among us. However!—it's no use being wise for other people. Where is Celia? Pray let us go in."

"I am going on immediately to Tipton," said Dorothea, rather haughtily. "Good-by."

Sir James could say nothing as he accompanied her to the carriage. He was altogether discontented with the result of a contrivance which had cost him some secret humiliation beforehand.

Dorothea drove along between the berried hedgerows and the shorn corn-fields, not seeing or hearing anything around. The tears came and rolled down her cheeks, but she did not know it. The world, it seemed, was turning ugly and hateful, and there was no place for her trustfulness. "It is not true—it is not true!" was the voice within her that she listened to; but all the while a remembrance to which there had always clung a vague uneasiness would thrust itself on her attention—the remembrance of that day when she had found Will Ladislaw with Mrs. Lydgate, and had heard his voice accompanied by the piano.

"He said he would never do anything I disapproved—I wish I could have told him that I disapproved of that," said poor Dorothea, inwardly, feeling a strange alternation between anger with Will and the passionate defence of him. "They all try to blacken him before me; but I will care for no pain, if he is not to blame. I always believed he was good." These were her last thoughts before she felt that the carriage was passing under the archway of the lodge-gate at the Grange, when she hurriedly pressed her handkerchief to her face and began to think of her errands. The coachman begged leave to

take out the horses for half an hour, as there was something
wrong with a shoe; and Dorothea, having the sense that she
was going to rest, took off her gloves and bonnet, while she was
leaning against a statue in the entrance hall, and talking to the
housekeeper. At last she said:

"I must stay here a little, Mrs. Kell. I will go into the
library and write you some memoranda from my uncle's letter,
if you will open the shutters for me."

"The shutters are open, madam," said Mrs. Kell, following
Dorothea, who had walked along as she spoke. "Mr. Ladislaw is there, looking for something."

(Will had come to fetch a portfolio of his own sketches
which he had missed in the act of packing his movables, and
did not choose to leave behind.)

Dorothea's heart seemed to turn over as if it had had a
blow, but she was not perceptibly checked. In truth, the
sense that Will was there was for the moment all-satisfying to
her, like the sight of something precious that one has lost.
When she reached the door she said to Mrs. Kell:

"Go in first, and tell him that I am here."

Will had found his portfolio, and had laid it on the table at
the far end of the room, to turn over the sketches and please
himself by looking at the memorable piece of art which had a
relation to nature too mysterious for Dorothea. He was smiling at it still, and shaking the sketches into order with the
thought that he might find a letter from her awaiting him at
Middlemarch, when Mrs. Kell, close to his elbow, said:

"Mrs. Casaubon is coming in, sir."

Will turned round quickly, and the next moment Dorothea
was entering. As Mrs. Kell closed the door behind her,
they met; each was looking at the other, and consciousness
was overflowed by something that suppressed utterance. It
was not confusion that kept them silent, for they both felt
that parting was near, and there is no shamefacedness in a sad
parting.

She moved automatically toward her uncle's chair against
the writing-table, and Will, after drawing it out a little for
her, went a few paces off and stood opposite to her.

"Pray sit down," said Dorothea, crossing her hands on her

lap; "I am very glad you were here." Will thought that her face looked just as it did when she first shook hands with him in Rome; for her widow's cap, fixed in her bonnet, had gone off with it, and he could see that she had lately been shedding tears.   But the mixture of anger in her agitation had vanished at the sight of him; she had been used, when they were face to face, always to feel confidence and the happy freedom which comes with mutual understanding, and how could other people's words hinder that effect on a sudden?   Let the music which can take possession of our frame and fill the air with joy for us, sound once more—what does it signify that we heard it found fault with in its absence?

"I have sent a letter to Lowick Manor to-day, asking leave to see you," said Will, seating himself opposite to her.   "I am going away immediately, and I could not go without speaking to you again."

"I thought we had parted when you came to Lowick many weeks ago—you thought you were going then," said Dorothea, her voice trembling a little.

"Yes, but I was in ignorance then of things which I know now—things which have altered my feelings about the future. When I saw you before, I was dreaming that I might come back some day.   I don't think I ever shall—now."   Will paused here.

"You wished me to know the reasons?" said Dorothea, timidly.

"Yes," said Will, impetuously, shaking his head backward, and looking away from her with irritation in his face.   "Of course I must wish it.   I have been grossly insulted, in your eyes and in the eyes of others.   There has been a mean implication against my character.   I wish you to know that under no circumstances would I have lowered myself by—under no circumstances would I have given men the chance of saying that I sought money under the pretext of seeking—something else.   There was no need of other safeguard against me—the safeguard of wealth was enough."

Will rose from his chair with the last word, and went— he hardly knew where; but it was to the projecting window nearest him, which had been open as now about the same sea-

son a year ago, when he and Dorothea had stood within it
and talked together. Her whole heart was going out at this
moment in sympathy with Will's indignation : she only wanted
to convince him that she had never done him injustice, and he
seemed to have turned away from her as if she, too, had been
part of the unfriendly world.

"It would be very unkind of you to suppose that I ever
attributed any meanness to you," she began. Then in her
ardent way, wanting to plead with him, she moved from
her chair and went in front of him to her old place in the
window, saying, "Do you suppose that I ever disbelieved in
you?"

When Will saw her there, he gave a start, and moved backward out of the window, without meeting her glance. Dorothea was hurt by this movement, following up the previous
anger of his tone. She was ready to say that it was as hard
on her as on him, and that she was helpless ; but those strange
particulars of their relation, which neither of them could ex-
plicitly mention, kept her always in dread of saying too much.
At this moment she had no belief that Will would in any case
have wanted to marry her, and she feared using words which
might imply such a belief. She only said earnestly, recurring
to his last word :

"I am sure no safeguard was ever needed against you."

Will did not answer. In the stormy fluctuation of his feelings these words of hers seemed to him cruelly neutral, and
he looked pale and miserable after his angry outburst. He
went to the table and fastened up his portfolio, while Dorothea looked at him from the distance. They were wasting
these last moments together in wretched silence. What could
he say, since what had got obstinately uppermost in his mind
was the passionate love for her which he forbade himself to
utter? What could she say, since she might offer him no help?
—since she was forced to keep the money that ought to have
been his?—since to-day he seemed not to respond as he used
to do to her thorough trust and liking?

But Will at last turned away from his portfolio, and approached the window again.

"I must go," he said, with that peculiar look of the eyes

which sometimes accompanies bitter feeling, as if they had been tired and burned with gazing too close at a light.

"What shall you do in life?" said Dorothea, timidly. "Have your intentions remained just the same as when we said good-by before?"

"Yes," said Will, in a tone that seemed to waive the subject as uninteresting. "I shall work away at the first thing that offers. I suppose one gets a habit of doing without happiness or hope."

"Oh, what sad words!" said Dorothea, with a dangerous tendency to sob. Then trying to smile, she added, "We used to agree that we were alike in speaking too strongly."

"I have not spoken too strongly now," said Will, leaning back against the angle of the wall. "There are certain things which a man can only go through once in his life; and he must know some time or other that the best is over with him. This experience has happened to me while I am very young—that is all. What I care more for than I can ever care for anything else is absolutely forbidden to me—I don't mean merely by being out of my reach, but forbidden me, even if it were within my reach, by my own pride and honor—by everything I respect myself for. Of course I shall go on living as a man might do who had seen heaven in a trance."

Will paused, imagining that it would be impossible for Dorothea to misunderstand this; indeed, he felt that he was contradicting himself and offending against his self-approval in speaking to her so plainly; but still—it could not be fairly called wooing a woman to tell her that he would never woo her. It must be admitted to be a ghostly kind of wooing.

But Dorothea's mind was rapidly going over the past with quite another vision than his. The thought that she herself might be what Will most cared for did throb through her an instant, but then came doubt: the memory of the little they had lived through together turned pale and shrank before the memory which suggested how much fuller might have been the intercourse between Will and some one else with whom he had had constant companionship. Everything he had said might refer to that other relation, and whatever had passed between him and herself was thoroughly explained by what she had always regarded as their simple friendship and the cruel obstruction thrust upon it by her husband's injurious act. Dorothea stood silent, with her eyes cast down dreamily, while images crowded upon her which left the sickening certainty that Will was referring to Mrs. Lydgate. But why sickening? He wanted her to know that here, too, his conduct should be above suspicion.

Will was not surprised at her silence. His mind also was tumultuously busy while he watched her, and he was feeling rather wildly that something must happen to hinder their parting—some miracle, clearly nothing in their own deliberate speech. Yet, after all, had she any love for him?—he could not pretend to himself that he would rather believe her to be without that pain. He could not deny that a secret longing for the assurance that she loved him was at the root of all his words.

Neither of them knew how long they stood in that way. Dorothea was raising her eyes, and was about to speak, when the door opened and her footman came to say:

"The horses are ready, madam, whenever you like to start."

"Presently," said Dorothea. Then, turning to Will, she said, "I have some memoranda to write for the house-keeper."

"I must go," said Will, when the door had closed again—advancing toward her. "The day after to-morrow I shall leave Middlemarch."

"You have acted in every way rightly," said Dorothea, in a low tone, feeling a pressure at her heart which made it difficult to speak.

She put out her hand, and Will took it for an instant, without speaking, for her words had seemed to him cruelly cold and unlike herself. Their eyes met, but there was discontent in his, and in hers there was only sadness. He turned away and took his portfolio under his arm.

"I have never done you injustice. Please remember me," said Dorothea, repressing a rising sob.

"Why should you say that?" said Will, with irritation.
"As if I were not in danger of forgetting everything else."

He had really a movement of anger against her at that moment, and it impelled him to go away without pause. It was
all one flash to Dorothea—his last words—his distant bow to
her as he reached the door—the sense that he was no longer
there. She sank into the chair, and for a few moments sat
like a statue, while images and emotions were hurrying upon
her. Joy came first, in spite of the threatening train behind
it—joy in the impression that it was really herself whom Will
loved and was renouncing, that there was really no other love
less permissible, more blameworthy, which honor was hurrying him away from. They were parted all the same, but—
Dorothea drew a deep breath and felt her strength return—she
could think of him unrestrainedly. At that moment the parting was easy to bear: the first sense of loving and being loved
excluded sorrow. It was as if some hard, icy pressure had
melted, and her consciousness had room to expand: her past
was come back to her with larger interpretation. The joy was
not the less—perhaps it was the more complete just then—
because of the irrevocable parting; for there was no reproach,
no contemptuous wonder to imagine in any eye or from any
lips. He had acted so as to defy reproach, and make wonder
respectful.

Any one watching her might have seen that there was a for-
tifying thought within her. Just as when inventive power is
working with glad ease, some small claim on the attention is
fully met as if it were only a cranny opened to the sunlight,
it was easy now for Dorothea to write her memoranda. She
spoke her last words to the housekeeper in cheerful tones, and
when she seated herself in the carriage her eyes were bright
and her cheeks blooming under the dismal bonnet. She threw
back the heavy "weepers," and looked before her, wondering
which road Will had taken. It was in her nature to be proud
that he was blameless, and through all her feelings there ran
this vein—"I was right to defend him."

The coachman was used to drive his grays at a good pace,
Mr. Casaubon being unenjoying and impatient in everything
away from his desk, and wanting to get to the end of all jour-

neys; and Dorothea was now bowled along quickly. Driving was pleasant, for rain in the night had laid the dust, and the blue sky looked far off, away from the region of the great clouds that sailed in masses. The earth looked like a happy place under the vast heavens, and Dorothea was wishing that she might overtake Will and see him once more.

After a turn of the road, there he was with the portfolio under his arm; but the next moment she was passing him while he raised his hat, and she felt a pang at being seated there in a sort of exaltation, leaving him behind. She could not look back at him. It was as if a crowd of indifferent objects had thrust them asunder, and forced them along different paths, taking them farther and farther away from each other, and making it useless to look back. She could no more make any sign that would seem to say, "Need we part?" than she could stop the carriage to wait for him. Nay, what a world of reasons crowded upon her against any movement of her thought toward a future that might reverse the decision of this day!

"I only wish I had known before—I wish he knew—then we could be quite happy in thinking of each other, though we are forever parted. And if I could but have given him the money, and made things easier for him!"—were the longings that came back the most persistently. And yet, so heavily did the world weigh on her, in spite of her independent energy, that with this idea of Will as in need of such help, and at a disadvantage with the world, there came always the vision of that unfittingness of any closer relation between them which lay in the opinion of every one connected with her. She felt to the full all the imperativeness of the motives which urged Will's conduct. How could he dream of her defying the barrier that her husband had placed between them?—how could she ever say to herself that she would defy it?

Will's certainty, as the carriage grew smaller in the distance, had much more bitterness in it. Very slight matters were enough to gall him in his sensitive mood, and the sight of Dorothea driving past him while he felt himself plodding along as a poor devil seeking a position in a world which, in his present temper, offered him little that he coveted, made

41

his conduct seem a mere matter of necessity, and took away
the sustainment of resolve. After all, he had no assurance
that she loved him: could any man pretend that he was simply glad in such a case to have the suffering all on his own
side?

That evening Will spent with the Lydgates; the next evening he was gone.

'

BOOK VII.—TWO TEMPTATIONS.

CHAPTER LXIII.

"These little things are great to little man."—GOLDSMITH.

"HAVE you seen much of your scientific phœnix, Lydgate, lately?" said Mr. Toller at one of his Christmas dinner-parties, speaking to Mr. Farebrother on his right hand.

"Not much, I am sorry to say," answered the vicar, accustomed to parry Mr. Toller's banter about his belief in the new medical light. "I am out of the way, and he is too busy."

"Is he? I am glad to hear it," said Dr. Minchin, with mingled suavity and surprise.

"He gives a great deal of time to the New Hospital," said Mr. Farebrother, who had his reasons for continuing the subject: "I hear of that from my neighbor, Mrs. Casaubon, who goes there often. She says Lydgate is indefatigable, and is making a fine thing of Bulstrode's institution. He is preparing a new ward in case of the cholera coming to us."

"And preparing theories of treatment to try on the patients, I suppose," said Mr. Toller.

"Come, Toller, be candid," said Mr. Farebrother. "You are too clever not to see the good of a bold fresh mind in medicine, as well as in everything else; and as to cholera, I fancy, none of you are very sure what you ought to do. If a man goes a little too far along a new road, it is usually himself that he harms more than any one else."

"I am sure you and Wrench ought to be obliged to him," said Dr. Minchin, looking toward Toller, "for he has sent you the cream of Peacock's patients."

"Lydgate has been living at a great rate for a young beginner," said Mr. Harry Toller, the brewer. "I suppose his relations in the North back him up."

"I hope so," said Mr. Chichely, "else he ought not to have married that nice girl we were all so fond of. Hang it, one has a grudge against a man who carries off the prettiest girl in the town."

"Ay, by God! and the best too," said Mr. Standish.

"My friend Vincy didn't half like the marriage, I know that," said Mr. Chichely. "*He* wouldn't do much. How the relations on the other side may have come down I can't say." There was an emphatic kind of reticence in Mr. Chichely's manner of speaking.

"Oh, I shouldn't think Lydgate ever looked to practice for a living," said Mr. Toller, with a slight touch of sarcasm; and there the subject was dropped.

This was not the first time that Mr. Farebrother had heard hints of Lydgate's expenses being obviously too great to be met by his practice, but he thought it not unlikely that there were resources or expectations which excused the large outlay at the time of Lydgate's marriage, and which might hinder any bad consequences from the disappointment in his practice. One evening, when he took the pains to go to Middlemarch on purpose to have a chat with Lydgate as of old, he noticed in him an air of excited effort quite unlike his usual easy way of keeping silence or breaking it with abrupt energy whenever he had anything to say. Lydgate talked persistently when they were in his work-room, putting arguments for and against the probability of certain biological views; but he had none of those definite things to say or to show which give the way-marks of a patient uninterrupted pursuit, such as he used himself to insist on, saying that "there must be a systole and diastole in all inquiry," and that "a man's mind must be continually expanding and shrinking between the whole human horizon and the horizon of an object-glass." That evening he seemed to be talking widely for the sake of resisting any personal bearing; and before long they went into the drawing-room, where Lydgate having asked Rosamond to give them music, sank back in his chair in silence, but with a strange light in his eyes. "He may have been taking an opiate," was a thought that crossed Mr. Farebrother's mind—"tic-douloureux perhaps—or medical worries."

It did not occur to him that Lydgate's marriage was not delightful: he believed, as the rest did, that Rosamond was an amiable, docile creature, though he had always thought her rather uninteresting—a little too much the pattern-card of the finishing-school: and his mother could not forgive Rosamond because she never seemed to see that Henrietta Noble was in the room. "However, Lydgate fell in love with her," said the vicar to himself, "and she must be to his taste."

Mr. Farebrother was aware that Lydgate was a proud man, but having very little corresponding fibre in himself, and perhaps too little care about personal dignity, except the dignity of not being mean or foolish, he could hardly allow enough for the way in which Lydgate shrank, as from a burn, from the utterance of any word about his private affairs. And soon after that conversation at Mr. Toller's, the vicar learned something which made him watch the more eagerly for an opportunity of indirectly letting Lydgate know that if he wanted to open himself about any difficulty there was a friendly ear ready.

The opportunity came at Mr. Vincy's, where, on New Year's Day, there was a party, to which Mr. Farebrother was irresistibly invited, on the plea that he must not forsake his old friends on the first new year of his being a greater man, and rector as well as vicar. And this party was thoroughly friendly: all the ladies of the Farebrother family were present; the Vincy children all dined at the table, and Fred had persuaded his mother that if she did not invite Mary Garth, the Farebrothers would regard it as a slight to themselves, Mary being their particular friend. Mary came, and Fred was in high spirits, though his enjoyment was of a checkered kind—triumph that his mother should see Mary's importance with the chief personages in the party being much streaked with jealousy when Mr. Farebrother sat down by her. Fred used to be much more easy about his own accomplishments in the days when he had not begun to dread being "bowled out by Farebrother," and this terror was still before him. Mrs. Vincy, in her fullest matronly bloom, looked at Mary's little figure, rough wavy hair, and visage quite without lilies and roses, and wondered; trying unsuccessfully to fancy herself caring

about Mary's appearance in wedding clothes, or feeling complacency in grandchildren who would "feature" the Garths.
However, the party was a merry one, and Mary was particularly bright; being glad, for Fred's sake, that his friends were
getting kinder to her, and being also quite willing that they
should see how much she was valued by others whom they
must admit to be judges.

Mr. Farebrother noticed that Lydgate seemed bored, and
that Mr. Vincy spoke as little as possible to his son-in-law.
Rosamond was perfectly graceful and calm, and only a subtle
observation such as the vicar had not been roused to bestow
on her would have perceived the total absence of that interest
in her husband's presence which a loving wife is sure to
betray, even if etiquette keeps her aloof from him. When
Lydgate was taking part in the conversation, she never looked
toward him any more than if she had been a sculptured Psyche
modeled to look another way : and when, after being called
out for an hour or two, he re-entered the room, she seemed
unconscious of the fact, which eighteen months before would
have had the effect of a numeral before ciphers. In reality,
however, she was intensely aware of Lydgate's voice and
movements; and her pretty good-tempered air of unconsciousness was a studied negation by which she satisfied her inward
opposition to him without compromise of propriety. When
the ladies were in the drawing-room after Lydgate had been
called away from the dessert, Mrs. Farebrother, when Rosamond happened to be near her, said, "You have to give up a
great deal of your husband's society, Mrs. Lydgate."

"Yes, the life of a medical man is very arduous: especially
when he is so devoted to his profession as Mr. Lydgate is,"
said Rosamond, who was standing, and moved easily away at
the end of this correct little speech.

"It is dreadfully dull for her when there is no company,"
said Mrs. Vincy, who was seated at the old lady's side. "I
am sure I thought so when Rosamond was ill, and I was staying
with her. You know, Mrs. Farebrother, ours is a cheerful
house. I am of a cheerful disposition myself, and Mr. Vincy
always likes something to be going on. That is what Rosamond has been used to. Very different from a husband out at

odd hours, and never knowing when he will come home, and of a close, proud disposition, *I* think "—indiscreet Mrs. Vincy did lower her tone slightly with this parenthesis. "But Rosamond always had an angel of a temper; her brothers used very often not to please her, but she was never the girl to show temper; from a baby she was always as good as good, and with a complexion beyond anything. But my children are all good-tempered, thank God."

This was easily credible to any one looking at Mrs. Vincy as she threw back her broad cap-strings, and smiled toward her three little girls, aged from seven to eleven. But in that smiling glance she was obliged to include Mary Garth, whom the three girls had got into a corner to make her tell them stories. Mary was just finishing the delicious tale of Rumpelstiltskin, which she had well by heart, because Letty was never tired of communicating it to her ignorant elders from a favorite red volume. Louisa, Mrs. Vincy's darling, now ran to her with wide-eyed serious excitement, crying, "Oh, mamma, mamma, the little man stamped so hard on the floor he couldn't get his leg out again!"

"Bless you, my cherub!" said mamma; "you shall tell me all about it to-morrow. Go and listen!" and then, as her eyes followed Louisa back toward the attractive corner, she thought that if Fred wished her to invite Mary again she would make no objection, the children being so pleased with her.

But presently the corner became still more animated, for Mr. Farebrother came in, and seating himself behind Louisa, took her on his lap; whereupon the girls all insisted that he must hear Rumpelstiltskin, and Mary must tell it over again. He insisted, too, and Mary, without fuss, began again in her neat fashion, with precisely the same words as before. Fred, who had also seated himself near, would have felt unmixed triumph in Mary's effectiveness if Mr. Farebrother had not been looking at her with evident admiration, while he dramatized an intense interest in the tale to please the children.

"You will never care any more about my one-eyed giant, Loo," said Fred at the end.

"Yes, I shall. Tell about him now," said Louisa.

"Oh, I dare say; I am quite cut out. Ask Mr. Farebrother."

"Yes," added Mary; "ask Mr. Farebrother to tell you about the ants whose beautiful house was knocked down by a giant named Tom, and he thought they didn't mind because he could not hear them cry, or see them use their pocket handkerchiefs."

"Please," said Louisa, looking up at the vicar.

"No, no, I am a grave old parson. If I try to draw a story out of my bag a sermon comes instead. Shall I preach you a sermon?" said he, putting on his short-sighted glasses, and pursing up his lips.

"Yes," said Louisa, falteringly.

"Let me see, then. Against cakes: how cakes are bad things, especially if they are sweet and have plums in them."

Louisa took the affair rather seriously, and got down from the vicar's knee to go to Fred.

"Ah, I see it will not do to preach on New Year's Day," said Mr. Farebrother, rising and walking away. He had discovered of late that Fred had become jealous of him, and also that he himself was not losing his preference for Mary above all other women.

"A delightful young person, is Miss Garth," said Mrs. Farebrother, who had been watching her son's movements.

"Yes," said Mrs. Vincy, obliged to reply, as the old lady turned to her expectantly. "It's a pity she is not better-looking."

"I cannot say that," said Mrs. Farebrother, decisively. "I like her countenance. We must not always ask for beauty, when a good God has seen fit to make an excellent young woman without it. I put good manners first, and Miss Garth will know how to conduct herself in any station."

The old lady was a little sharp in her tone, having a prospective reference to Mary's becoming her daughter-in-law; for there was this inconvenience in Mary's position with regard to Fred, that it was not suitable to be made public, and hence the three ladies at Lowick Parsonage were still hoping that Camden would choose Miss Garth.

New visitors entered, and the drawing-room was given up to music and games, while whist-tables were prepared in the quiet room on the other side of the hall. Mr. Farebrother played a rubber to satisfy his mother, who regarded her occasional whist as a protest against scandal and novelty of opinion, in which light even a revoke had its dignity. But at the end he got Mr. Chichely to take his place, and left the room. As he crossed the hall, Lydgate had just come in and was taking off his great-coat.

"You are the man I was going to look for," said the vicar; and instead of entering the drawing-room, they walked along the hall and stood against the fireplace, where the frosty air helped to make a glowing bank. "You see, I can leave the whist-table easy enough," he went on, smiling at Lydgate, "now I don't play for money. I owe that to you, Mrs. Casaubon says."

"How?" said Lydgate, coldly.

"Ah, you didn't mean me to know it; I call that ungenerous reticence. You should let a man have the pleasure of feeling that you have done him a good turn. I don't enter into some people's dislike of being under an obligation: upon my word, I prefer being under an obligation to everybody for behaving well to me."

"I can't tell what you mean," said Lydgate, "unless it is that I once spoke of you to Mrs. Casaubon. But I did not think that she would break her promise not to mention that I had done so," said Lydgate, leaning his back against the corner of the mantelpiece, and showing no radiance in his face.

"It was Brooke who let it out, only the other day. He paid me the compliment of saying that he was very glad I had the living, though you had come across his tactics, and had praised me up as a Ken and a Tillotson, and that sort of thing, till Mrs. Casaubon would hear of no one else."

"Oh, Brooke is such a leaky-minded fool," said Lydgate contemptuously.

"Well, I was glad of the leakiness then. I don't see why you shouldn't like me to know that you wished to do me a service, my dear fellow. And you certainly have done me one. It's rather a strong check to one's self-complacency to find how much of one's right doing depends on not being in want of money. A man will not be tempted to say the Lord's Prayer backward to please the devil, if he doesn't want the devil's services. I have no need to hang on the smiles of chance now."

"I don't see that there's any money-getting without chance," said Lydgate; "if a man gets it in a profession, it's pretty sure to come by chance."

Mr. Farebrother thought he could account for this speech, in striking contrast with Lydgate's former way of talking, as the perversity which will often spring from the moodiness of a man ill at ease in his affairs. He answered in a tone of good-humored admission:

"Ah, there's enormous patience wanted with the way of the world. But it is the easier for a man to wait patiently when he has friends who love him, and ask for nothing better than to help him through, so far as it lies in their power."

"Oh, yes," said Lydgate, in a careless tone, changing his attitude and looking at his watch. "People make much more of their difficulties than they need to do."

He knew as distinctly as possible that this was an offer of help to himself from Mr. Farebrother, and he could not bear it. So strangely determined are we mortals, that, after having been long gratified with the sense that he had privately done the vicar a service, the suggestion that the vicar discerned his need of a service in return made him shrink into unconquerable reticence. Besides, behind all making of such offers what else must come?—that he should "mention his case," imply that he wanted specific things. At that moment, suicide seemed easier.

Mr. Farebrother was too keen a man not to know the meaning of that reply, and there was a certain massiveness in Lydgate's manner and tone, corresponding with his physique, which if he repelled your advances in the first instance seemed to put persuasive devices out of question.

"What time are you?" said the vicar, devouring his wounded feeling.

"After eleven," said Lydgate. And they went into the drawing-room.

CHAPTER LXIV.

1st *Gent.* Where lies the power, there let the blame lie too.
2d *Gent.* Nay, power is relative; you cannot fright
The coming pest with border fortresses
Or catch your carp with subtle argument.
All force is twain in one; cause is not cause
Unless effect be there; and action's self
Must needs contain a passive. So command
Exists but with obedience.

Even if Lydgate had been inclined to be quite open about his affairs, he knew that it would have hardly been in Mr. Farebrother's power to give him the help he immediately wanted. With the year's bills coming in from his tradesmen, with Dover's threatening hold on his furniture, and with nothing to depend on but slow dribbling payments from the patients who must not be offended—for the handsome fees he had had from Freshitt Hall and Lowick Manor had been easily absorbed—nothing less than a thousand pounds would have freed him from actual embarrassment, and left a residue which, according to the favorite phrase of hopefulness in such circumstances, would have given him "time to look about him."

Naturally, the merry Christmas bringing the happy New Year, when fellow-citizens expect to be paid for the trouble and goods they have smilingly bestowed on their neighbors, had so tightened the pressure of sordid cares on Lydgate's mind that it was hardly possible for him to think unbrokenly of any other subject, even the most habitual and soliciting. He was not an ill-tempered man; his intellectual activity, the ardent kindness of his heart, as well as his strong frame, would always, under tolerably easy conditions, have kept him above the petty uncontrolled susceptibilities which make bad temper. But he was now a prey to that worst irritation which arises not simply from annoyances, but from the second consciousness underlying those annoyances, of wasted energy and a degrading preoccupation, which was the reverse of all his former purposes. " *This* is what I am thinking of; and *that* is what I might have been thinking of," was the bitter incessant murmur within him, making every difficulty a double goad to impatience.

Some gentlemen have made an amazing figure in literature by general discontent with the universe as a trap of dulness into which their great souls have fallen by mistake; but the sense of a stupendous self and an insignificant world may have its consolations. Lydgate's discontent was much harder to bear; it was the sense that there was a grand existence in thought and effective action lying around him, while his self was being narrowed into the miserable isolation of egotistic fears, and vulgar anxieties for events that might allay such fears. His troubles will perhaps appear miserably sordid, and beneath the attention of lofty persons who can know nothing of debt except on a magnificent scale. Doubtless they were sordid; and for the majority, who are not lofty, there is no escape from sordidness but by being free from money-craving, with all its base hopes and temptations, its watching for death, its hinted requests, its horse-dealer's desire to make bad work pass for good, its seeking for function which ought to be another's, its compulsion often to long for luck in the shape of a wide calamity.

It was because Lydgate writhed under the idea of getting his neck beneath this vile yoke that he had fallen into a bitter moody state which was continually widening Rosamond's alienation from him. After the first disclosure about the bill of sale, he had made many efforts to draw her into sympathy with him about possible measures for narrowing their expenses, and with the threatening approach of Christmas his propositions grew more and more definite. "We two can do with only one servant, and live on very little," he said, "and I shall manage with one horse." For Lydgate, as we have seen, had begun to reason, with a more distinct vision about the expenses of living, and any share of pride he had given to appearances of that sort was meagre compared with the pride which made him revolt from exposure as a debtor, or from asking men to help him with their money.

"Of course you can dismiss the other two servants if you like," said Rosamond, "but I should have thought it would be very injurious to your position for us to live in a poor way. You must expect your practice to be lowered."

"My dear Rosamond, it is not a question of choice. We

have begun too expensively. Peacock, you know, lived in a much smaller house than this. It is my fault; I ought to have known better, and I deserve a thrashing—if there were anybody who had a right to give it to me—for bringing you into the necessity of living in a poorer way than you have been used to. But we married because we loved each other, I suppose. And that may help us to pull along till things get better. Come, dear, put down that work and come to me."

He was really in chill gloom about her at that moment, but he dreaded a future without affection, and was determined to resist the oncoming of division between them. Rosamond obeyed him, and he took her on his knee, but in her secret soul she was utterly aloof from him. The poor thing saw only that the world was not ordered to her liking, and Lydgate was part of that world. But he held her waist with one hand and laid the other gently on both of hers; for this rather abrupt man had much tenderness in his manners toward women, seeming to have always present in his imagination the weakness of their frames and the delicate poise of their health both in body and mind. And he began again to speak persuasively.

"I find, now I look into things a little, Rosy, that it is wonderful what an amount of money slips away in our housekeeping. I suppose the servants are careless, and we have had a great many people coming. But there must be many in our rank who manage with much less: they must do with commoner things, I suppose, and look after the scraps. It seems money goes but a little way in these matters, for Wrench has everything as plain as possible, and he has a very large practice."

"Oh, if you think of living as the Wrenches do!" said Rosamond, with a little turn of her neck. "But I have heard you express your disgust at that way of living."

"Yes, they have bad taste in everything—they make economy look ugly. We needn't do that. I only meant that they avoid expenses, although Wrench has a capital practice."

"Why should not you have a good practice, Tertius? Mr. Peacock had. You should be more careful not to offend people, and you should send out·medicines as the others do. I am sure you began well, and you got several good houses. It cannot answer to be eccentric; you should think what will be generally liked," said Rosamond, in a decided little tone of admonition.

Lydgate's anger rose; he was prepared to be indulgent toward feminine weakness, but not toward feminine dictation. The shallowness of a waternixie's soul may have a charm until she becomes didactic. But he controlled himself, and only said, with a touch of despotic firmness:

"What I am to do in my practice, Rosy, it is for me to judge. That is not the question between us. It is enough for you to know that our income is likely to be a very narrow one—hardly four hundred, perhaps less, for a long time to come, and we must try to rearrange our lives in accordance with that fact."

Rosamond was silent for a moment or two, looking before her, and then said: "My uncle Bulstrode ought to allow you a salary for the time you give to the hospital: it is not right that you should work for nothing."

"It was understood from the beginning that my services would be gratuitous. That, again, need not enter into our discussion. I have pointed out what is the only probability," said Lydgate, impatiently. Then checking himself, he went on more quietly:

"I think I see one resource which would free us from a good deal of the present difficulty. I hear that young Ned Plymdale is going to be married to Miss Sophy Toller. They are rich, and it is not often that a good house is vacant in Middlemarch. I feel sure that they would be glad to take this house from us with most of our furniture, and they would be willing to pay handsomely for the lease. I can employ Trumbull to speak to Plymdale about it."

Rosamond left her husband's knee and walked slowly to the other end of the room; when she turned round and walked toward him it was evident that the tears had come, and that she was biting her under-lip and clasping her hands to keep herself from crying. Lydgate was wretched—shaken with anger, and yet feeling that it would be unmanly to vent the anger just now.

"I am very sorry, Rosamond; I know this is painful."

"I thought, at least, when I had borne to send the plate back and have that man taking an inventory of the furniture —I should have thought *that* would suffice."

"I explained it to you at the time, dear. That was only a security, and behind that security there is a debt. And that debt must be paid within the next few months, else we shall have our furniture sold. If young Plymdale will take our house and most of our furniture, we shall be able to pay that debt, and some others, too, and we shall be quit of a place too expensive for us. We might take a smaller house: Trumbull, I know, has a very decent one to let at thirty pounds a year, and this is ninety." Lydgate uttered this speech in the curt hammering way with which we usually try to nail down a vague mind to imperative facts. Tears rolled silently down Rosamond's cheeks; she just pressed her handkerchief against them, and stood looking at the large vase on the mantelpiece. It was a moment of more intense bitterness than she had ever felt before. At last she said, without hurry and with careful emphasis:

"I never could have believed that you would like to act in that way."

"Like it?" burst out Lydgate, rising from his chair, thrusting his hands in his pockets, and stalking away from the hearth; "it's not a question of liking. Of course I don't like it; it's the only thing I can do." He wheeled round there, and turned toward her.

"I should have thought there were many other means than that," said Rosamond. "Let us have a sale and leave Middlemarch altogether."

"To do what? What is the use of my leaving my work in Middlemarch to go where I have none? We should be just as penniless elsewhere as we are here," said Lydgate, still more angrily.

"If we are to be in that position it will be entirely your own doing, Tertius," said Rosamond, turning round to speak with the fullest conviction. "You will not behave as you ought to do to your own family. You offended Captain Lydgate. Sir Godwin was very kind to me when we were at Quallingham, and I am sure if you showed proper regard to him and told him your affairs he would do anything for you. But rather than that you like giving up our house and furniture to Mr. Ned Plymdale."

There was something like fierceness in Lydgate's eyes, as he answered with new violence: "Well, then, if you will have it so, I do like it. I admit that I like it better than making a fool of myself by going to beg where it's of no use. Understand then, that it is what *I like to do.*"

There was a tone in the last sentence which was equivalent to the clutch of his strong hand on Rosamond's delicate arm. But for all that, his will was not a whit stronger than hers. She immediately walked out of the room in silence, but with an intense determination to hinder what Lydgate liked to do.

He went out of the house, but as his blood cooled he felt that the chief result of the discussion was a deposit of dread within him at the idea of opening with his wife, in future, subjects which might again urge him to violent speech. It was as if a fracture in delicate crystal had begun, and he was afraid of any movement that might make it fatal. His marriage would be a mere piece of bitter irony if they could not go on loving each other. He had long ago made up his mind to what he thought was her negative character—her want of sensibility, which showed itself in disregard both of his specific wishes and of his general aims. The first great disappointment had been borne: the tender devotedness and docile adoration of the ideal wife must be renounced, and life must be taken up on a lower stage of expectation, as it is by men who have lost their limbs. But the real wife had not only her claims, she had still a hold on his heart, and it was his intense desire that the hold should remain strong. In marriage, the certainty, "She will never love me much," is easier to bear than the fear, "I shall love her no more." Hence, after that outburst, his inward effort was entirely to excuse her, and to blame the hard circumstances which were partly his fault. He tried that evening, by petting her, to heal the wound he had made in the morning, and it was not in Rosamond's nature to be repellent or sulky; indeed, she welcomed the signs that her husband loved her and was under

control. But this was something quite distinct from loving
him.

Lydgate would not have chosen soon to recur to the plan of
parting with the house; he was resolved to carry it out, and
say as little more about it as possible. But Rosamond herself
touched on it at breakfast by saying, mildly :

"Have you spoken to Trumbull yet? "

"No," said Lydgate, " but I shall call on him as I go by
this morning. No time must be lost." He took Rosamond's
question as a sign that she withdrew her inward opposition,
and kissed her head caressingly when he got up to go away.

As soon as it was late enough to make a call, Rosamond went
to Mrs. Plymdale, Mr. Ned's mother, and entered with pretty
congratulations into the subject of the coming marriage. Mrs.
Plymdale's maternal view was, that Rosamond might possibly
now have retrospective glimpses of her own folly; and feeling
the advantages to be at present all on the side of her son, was
too kind a woman not to behave graciously.

"Yes, Ned is most happy, I must say. And Sophy Toller
is all I could desire in a daughter-in-law. Of course her
father is able to do something handsome for her—that is only
what would be expected with a brewery like his. And the
connection is everything we should desire. But that is not
what I look at. She is such a very nice girl—no airs, no pre-
tensions, though on a level with the first. I don't mean with
the titled aristocracy. I see very little good in people aiming
out of their own sphere. I mean that Sophy is equal to the
best in the town, and she is contented with that."

"I have always thought her very agreeable," said Rosamond.

"I look upon it as a reward for Ned, who never held his
head too high, that he should have got into the very best
connection," continued Mrs. Plymdale, her native sharpness
softened by a fervid sense that she was taking a correct view.
"And such particular people as the Tollers are, they might
have objected because some of our friends are not theirs. It
is well known that your aunt Bulstrode and I have been intimate from our youth, and Mr. Plymdale has been always on
Mr. Bulstrode's side. And I myself prefer serious opinions.
But the Tollers have welcomed Ned all the same."

42

"I am sure he is a very deserving, well-principled young man," said Rosamond, with a neat air of patronage, in return for Mrs. Plymdale's wholesome corrections.

"Oh, he has not the style of a captain in the army, or that sort of carriage as if everybody was beneath him, or that showy kind of talking, and singing, and intellectual talent. But I am thankful he has not. It is a poor preparation both for here and Hereafter."

"Oh, dear yes; appearances have very little to do with happiness," said Rosamond. "I think there is every prospect of their being a happy couple. What house will they take?"

"Oh, as for that, they must put up with what they can get. They have been looking at the house in St. Peter's Place, next to Mr. Hackbutt's; it belongs to him, and he is putting it nicely in repair. I suppose they are not likely to hear of a better. Indeed, I think Ned will decide the matter to-day."

"I should think it is a nice house; I like St. Peter's Place."

"Well, it is near the church, and a genteel situation. But the windows are narrow, and it is all ups and downs. You don't happen to know of any other that would be at liberty?" said Mrs. Plymdale, fixing her round black eyes on Rosamond with the animation of a sudden thought in them.

"Oh, no; I hear so little of those things."

Rosamond had not foreseen that question and answer in setting out to pay her visit; she had simply meant to gather any information which would help her to avert the parting with her own house under circumstances thoroughly disagreeable to her. As to the untruth in her reply, she no more reflected on it than she did on the untruth there was in her saying that appearances had very little to do with happiness. Her object, she was convinced, was thoroughly justifiable: it was Lydgate whose intention was inexcusable; and there was a plan in her mind which, when she had carried it out fully, would prove how very false a step it would have been for him to have descended from his position.

She returned home by Mr. Borthrop Trumbull's office, meaning to call there. It was the first time in her life that Rosamond had thought of doing anything in the form of business, but she felt equal to the occasion. That she should be obliged

" ' I am, then, to consider the commission
withdrawn ? ' "

MIDDLEMARCH, *Page* 659

to do what she intensely disliked, was an idea which turned her quiet tenacity into active invention. Here was a case in which it could not be enough simply to disobey and be serenely, placidly obstinate: she must act according to her judgment, and she said to herself that her judgment was right—"indeed, if it had not been, she would not have wished to act on it."

Mr. Trumbull was in the back room of his office, and received Rosamond with his finest manners, not only because he had much sensibility to her charms, but because the good-natured fibre in him was stirred by his certainty that Lydgate was in difficulties, and that this uncommonly pretty woman— this young lady with the highest personal attractions—was likely to feel the pinch of trouble—to find herself involved in circumstances beyond her control. He begged her to do him the honor to take a seat, and stood before her trimming and comporting himself with an eager solicitude, which was chiefly benevolent. Rosamond's first question was, whether her husband had called on Mr. Trumbull that morning, to speak about disposing of their house.

"Yes, ma'am, yes, he did, he did so," said the good auctioneer, trying to throw something soothing into his iteration. "I was about to fulfil his order, if possible, this afternoon. He wished me not to procrastinate."

"I called to tell you not to go any further, Mr. Trumbull; and I beg of you not to mention what has been said on the subject. Will you oblige me?"

"Certainly I will, Mrs. Lydgate, certainly. Confidence is sacred with me on business or any other topic. I am then to consider the commission withdrawn?" said Mr. Trumbull, adjusting the long ends of his blue cravat with both hands, and looking at Rosamond deferentially.

"Yes, if you please. I find that Mr. Ned Plymdale has taken a house—the one in St. Peter's Place next to Mr. Hackbutt's. Mr. Lydgate would be annoyed that his orders should be fulfilled uselessly. And besides that, there are other circumstances which render the proposal unnecessary."

"Very good, Mrs. Lydgate, very good. I am at your command, whenever you require any service of me," said Mr. Trumbull, who felt pleasure in conjecturing that some new resources had been opened. "Rely on me, I beg. The affair shall go no further."

That evening Lydgate was a little comforted by observing that Rosamond was more lively than she had usually been of late, and even seemed interested in doing what would please him without being asked. He thought: "If she will be happy, and I can rub through, what does it all signify? It is only a narrow swamp that we have to pass in a long journey. If I can get my mind clear again, I shall do."

He was so much cheered that he began to search for an account of experiments which he had long ago meant to look up, and had neglected out of that creeping self-despair which comes in the train of petty anxieties. He felt again some of the old delightful absorption in a far-reaching inquiry, while Rosamond played the quiet music which was as helpful to his meditation as the plash of an oar on the evening lake. It was rather late; he had pushed away all the books, and was looking at the fire with his hands clasped behind his head in forgetfulness of everything except the construction of a new controlling experiment, when Rosamond, who had left the piano and was leaning back in her chair watching him, said:

"Mr. Ned Plymdale has taken a house already."

Lydgate, startled and jarred, looked up in silence for a moment, like a man who has been disturbed in his sleep. Then flushing with an unpleasant consciousness, he asked:

"How do you know?"

"I called at Mrs. Plymdale's this morning, and she told me that he had taken the house in St. Peter's Place, next to Mr. Hackbutt's."

Lydgate was silent. He drew his hands from behind his head and pressed them against the hair which was hanging, as it was apt to do, in a mass on his forehead, while he rested his elbows on his knees. He was feeling bitter disappointment, as if he had opened a door out of a suffocating place and had found it walled up; but he also felt sure that Rosamond was pleased with the cause of his disappointment. He preferred not looking at her and not speaking, until he had got over the first spasm of vexation. After all, he said in his bitterness, what can a woman care about so much as house and furniture? a husband without them is an absurdity. When he looked up and pushed his hair aside, his dark eyes had a miserable blank non-expectance of sympathy in them, but he only said, coolly:

"Perhaps some one else may turn up. I told Trumbull to be on the lookout if he failed with Plymdale."

Rosamond made no remark. She trusted to the chance that nothing more would pass between her husband and the auctioneer until some issue should have justified her interference; at any rate, she had hindered the event which she immediately dreaded. After a pause, she said:

"How much money is it that those disagreeable people want?"

"What disagreeable people?"

"Those who took the list—and the others. I mean, how much money would satisfy them so that you need not be troubled any more?"

Lydgate surveyed her for a moment, as if he were looking for symptoms, and then said: "Oh, if I could have got six hundred from Plymdale for furniture and as premium, I might have managed. I could have paid off Dover, and given enough on account to the others to make them wait patiently, if we contracted our expenses."

"But I mean how much should you want if we stayed in this house?"

"More than I am likely to get anywhere," said Lydgate, with rather a grating sarcasm in his tone. It angered him to perceive that Rosamond's mind was wandering over impracticable wishes instead of facing possible efforts.

"Why should you not mention the sum?" said Rosamond, with a mild indication that she did not like his manners.

"Well," said Lydgate in a guessing tone, "it would take at least a thousand to set me at ease. But," he added, incisively, "I have to consider what I shall do without it, not with it."

Rosamond said no more.

But the next day she carried out her plan of writing to Sir Godwin Lydgate. Since the Captain's visit, she had received a letter from him, and also one from Mrs. Mengan, his married sister, condoling with her on the loss of her baby, and express-

ing vaguely the hope that they should see her again at Quallingham. Lydgate had told her that this politeness meant
nothing; but she was secretly convinced that any backward-
ness in Lydgate's family toward him was due to his cold and
contemptuous behavior, and she had answered the letters in
her most charming manner, feeling some confidence that a
specific invitation would follow. But there had been total
silence. The Captain evidently was not a great penman, and
Rosamond reflected that the sisters might have been abroad.
However, the season was come for thinking of friends at
home, and at any rate Sir Godwin, who had chucked her under
the chin, and pronounced her to be like the celebrated beauty,
Mrs. Croly, who had made a conquest of him in 1790, would
be touched by an appeal from her, and would find it pleasant
for her sake to behave as he ought to do toward his nephew.
Rosamond was naïvely convinced of what an old gentleman
ought to do to prevent her from suffering annoyance. And
she wrote what she considered the most judicious letter possible—one which would strike Sir Godwin as a proof of her
excellent sense—pointing out how desirable it was that Tertius
should quit such a place as Middlemarch for one more fitted
to his talents, how the unpleasant character of the inhabitants
had hindered his professional success, and how in consequence
he was in money difficulties from which it would require a
thousand pounds thoroughly to extricate him. She did not
say that Tertius was unaware of her intention to write; for
she had the idea that his supposed sanction of her letter would
be in accordance with what she did say of his great regard for
his uncle Godwin as the relative who had always been his best
friend. Such was the force of poor Rosamond's tactics now
she applied them to affairs.

This had happened before the party on New Year's Day,
and no answer had yet come from Sir Godwin. But on the
morning of that day Lydgate had to learn that Rosamond had
revoked his order to Borthrop Trumbull. Feeling it necessary
that she should be gradually accustomed to the idea of their
quitting the house in Lowick Gate, he overcame his reluctance
to speak to her again on the subject, and when they were
breakfasting said:

"I shall try to see Trumbull this morning, and tell him to advertise the house in the *Pioneer* and the *Trumpet*. If the thing were advertised, some one might be inclined to take it who would not otherwise have thought of a change. In these country places many people go on in their old houses when their families are too large for them, for want of knowing where they can find another. And Trumbull seems to have got no bite at all."

Rosamond knew that the inevitable moment was come. "I ordered Trumbull not to inquire further," she said, with a careful calmness that was evidently defensive.

Lydgate stared at her in mute amazement. Only half an hour before he had been fastening up her plaits for her and talking the "little language" of affection, which Rosamond, though not returning it, accepted as if she had been a serene and lovely image, now and then miraculously dimpling toward her votary. With such fibres still astir in him, the shock he received could not at once be distinctly anger; it was confused pain. He laid down the knife and fork with which he was carving, and throwing himself back in his chair, said at last, with a cool irony in his tone:

"May I ask when and why you did so?"

"When I knew that the Plymdales had taken a house, I called to tell him not to mention ours to them, and at the same time I told him not to let the affair go on any further. I know that it would be very injurious to you if it were known that you wished to part with your house and furniture, and I had a very strong objection to it. I think that was reason enough."

"It was of no consequence, then, that I had told you imperative reasons of another kind; of no consequence that I had come to a different conclusion, and given an order accordingly?" said Lydgate, bitingly, the thunder and lightning gathering about his brow and eyes.

The effect of any one's anger on Rosamond had always been to make her shrink in cold dislike, and to become all the more calmly correct in the conviction that she was not the person to misbehave, whatever others might do. She replied:

"I think I had a perfect right to speak on a subject which concerns me at least as much as you."

"Clearly, you had a right to speak, but only to me. You had no right to contradict my orders secretly, and treat me as if I were a fool," said Lydgate, in the same tone as before. Then, with some added scorn, "Is it possible to make you understand what the consequences will be? Is it of any use for me to tell you again why we *must* try to part with the house?"

"It is not necessary for you to tell me again," said Rosamond, in a voice that fell and trickled like cold water-drops. "I remembered what you said. You spoke just as violently as you do now. But that does not alter my opinion that you ought to try every other means rather than take a step which is so painful to me. And as to advertising the house, I think it would be perfectly degrading to you."

"And suppose I disregard your opinion as you disregard mine?"

"You can do so, of course. But I think you ought to have told me before we were married that you would place me in the worst position rather than give up your own will."

Lydgate did not speak, but tossed his head on one side, and twitched the corners of his mouth in despair. Rosamond, seeing that he was not looking at her, rose and set his cup of coffee before him; but he took no notice of it, and went on with an inward drama and argument, occasionally moving in his seat, resting one arm on the table, and rubbing his hand against his hair. There was a conflux of emotions and thoughts in him that would not let him either give thorough way to his anger or persevere with simple rigidity of resolve. Rosamond took advantage of his silence.

"When we were married every one felt that your position was very high. I could not have imagined then that you would want to sell our furniture and take a house in Bride Street, where the rooms are like cages. If we are to live in that way, let us at least leave Middlemarch."

"These would be very strong considerations," said Lydgate, half ironically—still there was a withered paleness about his lips as he looked at his coffee and did not drink—"these would be very strong considerations if I did not happen to be in debt."

"Many persons must have been in debt in the same way,

but if they are respectable, people trust them. I am sure I
have heard papa say that the Torbits were in debt, and they
went on very well. It cannot be good to act rashly," said
Rosamond, with serene wisdom.

Lydgate sat paralyzed by opposing impulses. Since no
reasoning he could apply to Rosamond seemed likely to conquer her assent, he wanted to smash and grind some object on
which he could at least produce an impression, or else to tell
her brutally that he was master, and she must obey. But he
not only dreaded the effect of such extremities on their mutual
life—he had a growing dread of Rosamond's quiet elusive obstinacy, which would not allow any assertion of power to be
final; and again, she had touched him in a spot of keenest
feeling by implying that she had been deluded with a false
vision of happiness in marrying him. As to saying that he
was master, it was not the fact. The very resolution to which
he had wrought himself by dint of logic and honorable pride
was beginning to relax under her torpedo contact. He swallowed half his cup of coffee, and then rose to go.

"I may at least request that you will not go to Trumbull at
present—until it has been seen that there are no other means,"
said Rosamond. Although she was not subject to much fear,
she felt it safer not to betray that she had written to Sir
Godwin. "Promise me that you will not go to him for a few
weeks, or without telling me."

Lydgate gave a short laugh. "I think it is I who should
exact a promise that you will do nothing without telling me,"
he said, turning his eyes sharply upon her, and then moving
to the door.

"You remember that we are going to dine at papa's," said
Rosamond, wishing that he should turn and make a more
thorough concession to her. But he only said, "Oh, yes,"
impatiently, and went away. She held it to be very odious
in him that he did not think the painful propositions he had
had to make to her were enough, without showing so unpleasant a temper. And when she put the moderate request that he
would defer going to Trumbull again, it was cruel in him not
to assure her of what he meant to do. She was convinced of
her having acted in every way for the best; and each grating

or angry speech of Lydgate's served only as an addition to the register of offences in her mind. Poor Rosamond for months had begun to associate her husband with feelings of disappointment, and the terribly inflexible relation of marriage had lost its charm of encouraging delightful dreams. It had freed her from the disagreeables of her father's house, but it had not given her everything that she had wished and hoped. The Lydgate with whom she had been in love had been a group of airy conditions for her, most of which had disappeared, while their place had been taken by every-day details which must be lived through slowly from hour to hour, not floated through with a rapid selection of favorable aspects. The habits of Lydgate's profession, his home preoccupation with scientific subjects, which seemed to her almost like a morbid vampire's taste, his peculiar views of things which had never entered into the dialogue of courtship—all these continually alienating influences, even without the fact of his having placed himself at a disadvantage in the town, and without the first shock of revelation about Dover's debt, would have made his presence dull to her. There was another presence which ever since the early days of her marriage, until four months ago, had been an agreeable excitement, but that was gone: Rosamond would not confess to herself how much the consequent blank had to do with her utter *ennui;* and it seemed to her (perhaps she was right) that an invitation to Quallingham, and an opening for Lydgate to settle elsewhere than in Middlemarch—in London, or somewhere likely to be free from unpleasantness—would satisfy her quite well, and make her indifferent to the absence of Will Ladislaw, toward whom she felt some resentment for his exaltation of Mrs. Casaubon.

That was the state of things with Lydgate and Rosamond on the New Year's Day when they dined at her father's, she looking mildly neutral toward him in remembrance of his ill-tempered behavior at breakfast, and he carrying a much deeper effect from the inward conflict in which that morning scene was only one of many epochs. His flushed effort while talking to Mr. Farebrother—his effort after the cynical pretense that all ways of getting money are essentially the same, and that chance has an empire which reduces choice to a fool's illusion—was but the symptom of a wavering resolve, a benumbed response to the old stimuli of enthusiasm.

What was he to do? He saw even more keenly than Rosamond did the dreariness of taking her into the small house in Bride Street, where she would have scanty furniture around her and discontent within; a life of privation and life with Rosamond were two images which had become more and more irreconcilable ever since the threat of privation had disclosed itself. But even if his resolves had forced the two images into combination, the useful preliminaries to that hard change were not visibly within reach. And though he had not given the promise which his wife had asked for, he did not go again to Trumbull. He even began to think of taking a rapid journey to the North and seeing Sir Godwin. He had once believed that nothing would urge him into making an application for money to his uncle, but he had not then known the full pressure of alternatives yet more disagreeable. He could not depend on the effect of a letter; it was only in an interview, however disagreeable this might be to himself, that he could give a thorough explanation and could test the effectiveness of kinship. No sooner had Lydgate begun to represent this step to himself as the easiest than there was a reaction of anger that he—he who had long ago determined to live aloof from such abject calculations, such self-interested anxiety about the inclinations and the pockets of men with whom he had been proud to have no aims in common—should have fallen not simply to their level, but to the level of soliciting them.

CHAPTER LXV.

"One of us two must bowen douteless,
And, sith a man is more reasonable
Than woman is, ye [men] moste be suffrable."
—CHAUCER: *Canterbury Tales.*

THE bias of human nature to be slow in correspondence triumphs even over the present quickening in the general pace of things: what wonder then that in 1832 old Sir Godwin

Lydgate was slow to write a letter which was of consequence to others rather than to himself? Nearly three weeks of the new year were gone, and Rosamond, awaiting an answer to her winning appeal, was every day disappointed. Lydgate, in total ignorance of her expectations, was seeing the bills come in, and feeling that Dover's use of his advantage over other creditors was imminent. He had never mentioned to Rosamond his brooding purpose of going to Quallingham: he did not want to admit what would appear to her a concession to her wishes after indignant refusal, until the last moment; but he was really expecting to set off soon. A slice of the railway would enable him to manage the whole journey and back in four days.

But one morning after Lydgate had gone out, a letter came addressed to him, which Rosamond saw clearly to be from Sir Godwin. She was full of hope. Perhaps there might be a particular note to her enclosed; but Lydgate was naturally addressed on the question of money or other aid, and the fact that he was written to, nay, the very delay in writing at all, seemed to certify that the answer was thoroughly compliant. She was too much excited by these thoughts to do anything but light stitching in a warm corner of the dining-room with the outside of this momentous letter lying on the table before her. About twelve she heard her husband's step in the passage, and tripping to open the door, she said in her lightest tones, "Tertius, come in here—here is a letter for you."

"Ah?" he said, not taking off his hat, but just turning her round within his arm to walk toward the spot where the letter lay. "My uncle Godwin!" he exclaimed, while Rosamond reseated herself, and watched him as he opened the letter. She had expected him to be surprised.

While Lydgate's eyes glanced rapidly over the brief letter, she saw his face, usually of a pale brown, taking on a dry whiteness; with nostrils and lips quivering he tossed down the letter before her, and said violently:

"It will be impossible to endure life with you, if you will always be acting secretly—acting in opposition to me and hiding your actions."

He checked his speech and turned his back on her—then

wheeled round and walked about, sat down, and got up again restlessly, grasping hard the objects deep down in his pockets. He was afraid of saying something irremediably cruel.

Rosamond too had changed color as she read. The letter ran in this way:

DEAR TERTIUS:—Don't set your wife to write to me when you have anything to ask. It is a roundabout, wheedling sort of thing which I should not have credited you with. I never choose to write to a woman on matters of business. As to my supplying you with a thousand pounds, or only half that sum, I can do nothing of the sort. My own family drains me to the last penny. With two younger sons and three daughters, I am not likely to have cash to spare. You seem to have got through your own money pretty quickly, and to have made a mess where you are; the sooner you go somewhere else the better. But I have nothing to do with men of your profession, and can't help you there. I did the best I could for you as guardian, and let you have your own way in taking to medicine. You might have gone into the army or the Church. Your money would have held out for that, and there would have been a surer ladder before you. Your uncle Charles has had a grudge against you for not going into his profession, but not I. I have always wished you well, but you must consider yourself on your own legs entirely now.
                          Your affectionate uncle,
                                  GODWIN LYDGATE.

When Rosamond had finished reading the letter she sat quite still, with her hands folded before her, restraining any show of her keen disappointment, and intrenching herself in quiet passivity under her husband's wrath. Lydgate paused in his movements, looked at her again, and said with biting severity—

"Will this be enough to convince you of the harm you may do by secret meddling? Have you sense enough to recognize now your incompetence to judge and act for me—to interfere with your ignorance in affairs which it belongs to me to decide on?"

The words were hard; but this was not the first time that Lydgate had been frustrated by her. She did not look at him, and made no reply.

"I had nearly resolved on going to Quallingham. It would have cost me pain enough to do it, yet it might have been of some use. But it has been of no use for me to think of anything. You have always been counteracting me secretly. You delude me with a false assent, and then I am at the mercy of your devices. If you mean to resist every wish I express, say so and defy me. I shall at least know what I am doing then."

It is a terrible moment in young lives when the closeness of love's bond has turned to this power of galling. In spite of Rosamond's self-control, a tear fell silently and rolled over her lips. She still said nothing; but under that quietude was hidden an intense effect; she was in such entire disgust with her husband that she wished she had never seen him. Sir Godwin's rudeness toward her and utter want of feeling ranged him with Dover and all other creditors—disagreeable people who only thought of themselves, and did not mind how annoying they were to her. Even her father was unkind, and might have done more for them. In fact there was but one person in Rosamond's world whom she did not regard as blameworthy, and that was the graceful creature with blonde plaits and with little hands crossed before her, who had never expressed herself unbecomingly, and had always acted for the best—the best naturally being what she best liked.

Lydgate pausing and looking at her began to feel that half-maddening sense of helplessness which comes over passionate people when their passion is met by an innocent-looking silence whose meek victimized air seems to put them in the wrong, and at last infects even the justest indignation with a doubt of its justice. He needed to recover the full sense that he was in the right by moderating his words.

"Can you not see, Rosamond," he began again, trying to be simply grave and not bitter, "that nothing can be so fatal as a want of openness and confidence between us? It has happened again and again that I have expressed a decided wish, and you have seemed to assent, yet after that you have secretly disobeyed my wish. In that way I can never know what I have to trust to. There would be some hope for us if you would admit this. Am I such an unreasonable, furious brute? Why should you not be open with me?"

Still silence.

"Will you only say that you have been mistaken, and that I may depend on your not acting secretly in future?" said Lydgate, urgently, but with something of request in his tone which Rosamond was quick to perceive. She spoke with coolness.

"I cannot possibly make admissions or promises in answer to such words as you have used toward me. I have not been accustomed to language of that kind. You have spoken of my ' secret meddling,' and my ' interfering ignorance,' and my ' false assent.' I have never expressed myself in that way to you, and I think that you ought to apologize. You spoke of it being impossible to live with me. Certainly you have not made my life pleasant to me of late. I think it was to be expected that I should try to avert some of the hardships which our marriage has brought on me." Another tear fell as Rosamond ceased speaking, and she pressed it away as quietly as the first.

Lydgate flung himself into a chair, feeling checkmated. What place was there in her mind for a remonstrance to lodge in? He laid down his hat, flung one arm over the back of his chair, and looked down for some moments without speaking. Rosamond had the double purchase over him of insensibility to the point of justice in his reproach, and of sensibility to the undeniable hardships now present in her married life. Although her duplicity in the affair of the house had exceeded what he knew, and had really hindered the Plymdales from knowing of it, she had no consciousness that her action could rightly be called false. We are not obliged to identify our own acts according to a strict classification, any more than the materials of our grocery and clothes. Rosamond felt that she was aggrieved, and this was what Lydgate had to recognize.

As for him, the need of accommodating himself to her nature, which was inflexible in proportion to its negations, held him as with pincers. He had begun to have an alarmed foresight of her irrevocable loss of love for him, and the consequent dreariness of their life. The ready fulness of his emotions made this dread alternate quickly with the first violent movements of his anger. It would assuredly have been a vain boast in him to say that he was her master.

"You have not made my life pleasant to me of late "—" the hardships which our marriage has brought on me "—these words were stinging his imagination as a pain makes an ex-

aggerated dream.   If he were not only to sink from his highest resolve, but to sink into the hideous fettering of domestic
hate?

"Rosamond," he said, turning his eyes on her with a melancholy look, "you should allow for a man's words when he is
disappointed and provoked.   You and I cannot have opposite
interests.   I cannot part my happiness from yours.   If I am
angry with you, it is that you seem not to see how any concealment divides us.   How could I wish to make anything
hard to you either by my words or conduct?   When I hurt
you, I hurt part of my own life.   I should never be angry
with you if you would be quite open with me."

"I have only wished to prevent you from hurrying us into
wretchedness without any necessity," said Rosamond, the
tears coming again from a softened feeling now that her husband had softened.   "It is so very hard to be disgraced here
among all the people we know, and to live in such a miserable
way.   I wish I had died with the baby."

She spoke and wept with that gentleness which makes such
words and tears omnipotent over a loving-hearted man.   Lydgate drew his chair near to hers and pressed her delicate head
against his cheek with his powerful tender hand.   He only
caressed her; he did not say anything; for what was there to
say?   He could not promise to shield her from the dreaded
wretchedness, for he could see no sure means of doing so.
When he left her to go out again, he told himself that it was
ten times harder for her than for him: he had a life away
from home, and constant appeals to his activity on behalf of
others.   He wished to excuse everything in her if he could—
but it was inevitable that in that excusing mood he should
think of her as if she were an animal of another and feebler
species.   Nevertheless she had mastered him.

CHAPTER LXVI.

" 'Tis one thing to be tempted, Escalus,
Another thing to fall."
—*Measure for Measure.*

LYDGATE certainly had good reason to reflect on the service
his practice did him in counteracting his personal cares. He
had no longer free energy enough for spontaneous research and
speculative thinking, but by the bedside of patients the direct
external calls on his judgment and sympathies brought the
added impulse needed to draw him out of himself. It was
not simply that beneficent harness of routine which enables
silly men to live respectably and unhappy men to live calmly
—it was a perpetual claim on the immediate fresh application
of thought, and on the consideration of another's need and
trial. Many of us looking back through life would say that the
kindest man we have ever known has been a medical man, or
perhaps that surgeon whose fine tact, directed by deeply informed perception, has come to us in our need with a more
sublime beneficence than that of miracle workers. Some of
that twice-blessed mercy was always with Lydgate in his
work at the hospital or in private houses, serving better than
any opiate to quiet and sustain him under his anxieties and
his sense of mental degeneracy.

Mr. Farebrother's suspicion as to the opiate was true, however. Under the first galling pressure of foreseen difficulties,
and the first perception that his marriage, if it were not to be
a yoked loneliness, must be a state of effort to go on loving
without too much care about being loved, he had once or twice
tried a dose of opium. But he had no hereditary constitu-
tional craving after such transient escapes from the hauntings
of misery. He was strong, could drink a great deal of wine,
but did not care about it; and when the men round him were
drinking spirits, he took sugar and water, having a contemptuous pity even for the earliest stages of excitement from drink.
It was the same with gambling. He had looked on at a great
deal of gambling in Paris, watching it as if it had been a dis-
43

ease. He was no more tempted by such winning than he was
by drink. He had said to himself that the only winning he
cared for must be attained by a conscious process of high,
difficult combination tending toward a beneficent result. The
power he longed for could not be represented by agitated
fingers clutching a heap of coin, or by the half-barbarous,
half-idiotic triumph in the eyes of a man who sweeps within
his arms the ventures of twenty chapfallen companions.

But just as he had tried opium, so his thought now began
to turn upon gambling—not with appetite for its excitement,
but with a sort of wistful inward gaze after that easy way of
getting money, which implied no asking and brought no responsibility. If he had been in London or Paris at that time,
it is probable that such thoughts, seconded by opportunity,
would have taken him into a gambling-house, no longer to
watch the gamblers, but to watch with them in kindred eagerness. Repugnance would have been surmounted by the immense need to win, if chance would be kind enough to let him.
An incident which happened not very long after that airy
notion of getting aid from his uncle had been excluded, was a
strong sign of the effect that might have followed any extant
opportunity of gambling.

The billiard-room at the Green Dragon was the constant
resort of a certain set, most of whom, like our acquaintance
Mr. Bambridge, were regarded as men of pleasure. It was
here that poor Fred Vincy had made part of his memorable
debt, having lost money in betting, and been obliged to borrow
of that gay companion. It was generally known in Middlemarch that a good deal of money was lost and won in this
way; and the consequent repute of the Green Dragon as a
place of dissipation naturally heightened in some quarters the
temptation to go there. Probably its regular visitants, like the
initiates of freemasonry, wished that there were something a
little more tremendous to keep to themselves concerning it;
but they were not a closed community, and many decent seniors as well as juniors occasionally turned into the billiard-
room to see what was going on. Lydgate, who had the
muscular aptitude for billiards, and was fond of the game, had
once or twice in the early days after his arrival in Middle-

march taken his turn with the cue at the Green Dragon; but afterward he had no leisure for the game, and no inclination for the socialities there. One evening, however, he had occasion to seek Mr. Bambridge at that resort. The horse-dealer had engaged to get him a customer for his remaining good horse, for which Lydgate had determined to substitute a cheap hack, hoping by this reduction of style to get perhaps twenty pounds; and he cared now for every small sum, as a help toward feeding the patience of his tradesmen. To run up to the billiard-room, as he was passing, would save time.

Mr. Bambridge was not yet come, but would be sure to arrive by and by, said his friend Mr. Horrock; and Lydgate stayed, playing a game for the sake of passing the time. That evening he had the peculiar light in the eyes and the unusual vivacity which had been once noticed in him by Mr. Farebrother. The exceptional fact of his presence was much noticed in the room, where there was a good deal of Middlemarch company; and several lookers-on, as well as some of the players, were betting with animation. Lydgate was playing well, and felt confident; the bets were dropping round him, and with a swift glancing thought of the probable gain which might double the sum he was saving from his horse, he began to bet on his own play, and won again and again. Mr. Bambridge had come in, but Lydgate did not notice him. He was not only excited with his play, but visions were gleaming on him of going the next day to Brassing, where there was gambling on a grander scale to be had, and where, by one powerful snatch at the devil's bait, he might carry it off without the hook, and buy his rescue from his daily solicitings.

He was still winning when two new visitors entered. One of them was young Hawley, just come from his law studies in town, and the other was Fred Vincy, who had spent several evenings of late at this old haunt of his. Young Hawley, an accomplished billiard-player, brought a cool fresh hand to the cue. But Fred Vincy, startled at seeing Lydgate, and astonished to see him betting with an excited air, stood aside, and kept out of the circle round the table.

Fred had been rewarding resolution by a little laxity of late. He had been working heartily for six months at all out-

door occupations under Mr. Garth, and by dint of severe practice had nearly mastered the defects of his handwriting, this
practice being, perhaps, a little less severe that it was often
carried on in the evening at Mr. Garth's under the eyes of
Mary. But the last fortnight Mary had been staying at
Lowick Parsonage with the ladies there, during Mr. Farebrother's residence at Middlemarch, where he was carrying out
some parochial plans; and Fred, not seeing anything more
agreeable to do, had turned into the Green Dragon, partly to
play at billiards, partly to taste the old flavor of discourse
about horses, sport, and things in general, considered from a
point of view which was not strenuously correct. He had not
been out hunting once this season, had had no horse of his
own to ride, and had gone from place to place chiefly with
Mr. Garth in his gig, or on the sober cob which Mr. Garth
could lend him. It was a little too bad, Fred began to think,
that he should be kept in the traces with more severity than
if he had been a clergyman. "I will tell you what, Mistress
Mary—it will be rather harder work to learn surveying and
drawing plans than it would have been to write sermons," he
had said, wishing her to appreciate what he went through
for her sake; "and as to Hercules and Theseus, they were
nothing to me. They had sport, and never learned to write a
book-keeping hand." And now Mary being out of the way
for a little while, Fred, like any other strong dog who cannot
slip his collar, had pulled up the staple of his chain and made
a small escape, not of course meaning to go fast or far. There
could be no reason why he should not play at billiards, but he
was determined not to bet. As to money just now, Fred had
in his mind the heroic project of saving almost all of the eighty
pounds that Mr. Garth offered him, and returning it, which
he could easily do by giving up all futile money-spending,
since he had a superfluous stock of clothes, and no expense in
his board. In that way, he could, in one year, go a good
way toward repaying the ninety pounds of which he had de-
prived Mrs. Garth, unhappily at a time when she needed that
sum more than she did now. Nevertheless, it must be acknowledged that on this evening, which was the fifth of his
recent visits to the billiard-room, Fred had, not in his pocket,

but in his mind, the ten pounds which he meant to reserve for
himself from his half year's salary (having before him the
pleasure of carrying thirty to Mrs. Garth when Mary was
likely to be come home again)—he had those ten pounds in
his mind as a fund from which he might risk something, if
there were a chance of a good bet.   Why?   Well, when
sovereigns were flying about, why shouldn't he catch a few?
He would never go far along that road again; but a man likes
to assure himself, and men of pleasure generally, what he
could do in the way of mischief if he chose, and that if he ab-
stains from making himself ill, or beggaring himself, or talking with the utmost looseness which the narrow limits of the
human capacity will allow, it is not because he is a spooney.
Fred did not enter into formal reasons, which are a very
artificial, inexact way of representing the tingling returns of
old habit, and the caprices of young blood: but there was
lurking in him a prophetic sense that evening, that when he
began to play he should also begin to bet—that he should enjoy some punch-drinking, and in general prepare himself for
feeling " rather seedy " in the morning.   It is in such indefin-
able movements that action often begins.

But the last thing likely to have entered Fred's expectation
was that he should see his brother-in-law, Lydgate—of whom
he had never quite dropped the old opinion that he was a prig,
and tremendously conscious of his superiority—looking excited and betting, just as he himself might have done.   Fred
felt a shock greater than he could quite account for by the
vague knowledge that Lydgate was in debt, and that his father
had refused to help him; and his own inclination to enter the
play was suddenly checked.   It was a strange reversal of at-
titudes: Fred's blonde face and blue eyes, usually bright and
careless, ready to give attention to anything that held out a
promise of amusement, looking involuntarily grave and almost
embarrassed as if by the sight of something unfitting; while
Lydgate, who had habitually an air of self-possessed strength,
and a certain meditativeness that seemed to lie behind his
most observant attention, was acting, watching, speaking with
that excited narrow consciousness which reminds one of an
animal with fierce eyes and retractile claws.

Lydgate, by betting on his own strokes, had won sixteen pounds; but young Hawley's arrival had changed the poise of things. He made first-rate strokes himself, and began to bet against Lydgate's strokes, the strain of whose nerves was thus changed from simple confidence in his own movements to defying another person's doubt in them. The defiance was more exciting than the confidence, but it was less sure. He continued to bet on his own play, but began often to fail. Still he went on, for his mind was as utterly narrowed into that precipitous crevice of play as if he had been the most ignorant lounger there. Fred observed that Lydgate was losing fast, and found himself in the new situation of puzzling his brains to think of some device by which, without being offensive, he could withdraw Lydgate's attention, and perhaps suggest to him a reason for quitting the room. He saw that others were observing Lydgate's strange unlikeness to himself, and it occurred to him that merely to touch his elbow and call him aside for a moment might rouse him from his absorption. He could think of nothing cleverer than the daring improbability of saying that he wanted to see Rosy, and wished to know if she were at home this evening; and he was going desperately to carry out this weak device, when a waiter came up to him with a message, saying that Mr. Farebrother was below, and begged to speak with him.

Fred was surprised, not quite comfortably, but sending word that he would be down immediately, he went with a new impulse up to Lydgate, said, "Can I speak to you a moment?" and drew him aside.

"Farebrother has just sent up a message to say that he wants to speak to me. He is below. I thought you might like to know he was there, if you had anything to say to him."

Fred had simply snatched up this pretext for speaking, because he could not say, "You are losing confoundedly, and are making everybody stare at you; you had better come away." But inspiration could hardly have served him better. Lydgate had not before seen that Fred was present, and his sudden appearance with an announcement of Mr. Farebrother had the effect of a sharp concussion.

"No, no," said Lydgate; "I have nothing particular to say

to him. But—the game is up—I must be going—I came in
just to see Bambridge."

"Bambridge is over there, but he is making a row—I don't
think he's ready for business. Come down with me to Farebrother. I expect he is going to blow me up, and you will
shield me," said Fred, with some adroitness.

Lydgate felt shame, but could not bear to act as if he felt
it, by refusing to see Mr. Farebrother; and he went down.
They merely shook hands, however, and spoke of the frost;
and when all three had turned into the street, the vicar seemed
quite willing to say good-bye to Lydgate. His present purpose was clearly to talk with Fred alone, and he said, kindly,
"I disturbed you, young gentleman, because I have some
pressing business with you. Walk with me to St. Botolph's,
will you?"

It was a fine night, the sky thick with stars, and Mr. Farebrother proposed that they should make a circuit to the old
church by the London road. The next thing he said was:

"I thought Lydgate never went to the Green Dragon?"

"So did I," said Fred. "But he said that he went to see
Bambridge."

"He was not playing, then?"

Fred had not meant to tell this, but he was obliged now to
say, "Yes, he was. But I suppose it was an accidental thing.
I have never seen him there before."

"You have been going often yourself, then, lately?"

"Oh, about five or six times."

"I think you had some good reason for giving up the habit
of going there?"

"Yes. You know all about it," said Fred, not liking to be
catechised in this way. "I made a clean breast to you."

"I suppose that gives me a warrant to speak about the
matter now. It is understood between us, is it not?—that we
are on a footing of open friendship: I have listened to you,
and you will be willing to listen to me. I may take my turn
in talking a little about myself?"

"I am under the deepest obligation to you, Mr. Farebrother,"
said Fred, in a state of uncomfortable surmise.

"I will not affect to deny that you are under some obliga-

tion to me. But I am going to confess to you, Fred, that I
have been tempted to reverse all that by keeping silence with
you just now. When somebody said to me, 'Young Vincy has
taken to being at the billiard-table every night again—he
won't bear the curb long,' I was tempted to do the opposite
of what I am doing—to hold my tongue and wait while you
went down the ladder again, betting first and then——"

"I have not made any bets," said Fred, hastily.

"Glad to hear it. But I say, my prompting was to look
on and see you take the wrong turning, wear out Garth's
patience, and lose the best opportunity of your life—the opportunity which you made some rather difficult effort to secure.
You can guess the feeling which raised that temptation in me
—I am sure you know it. I am sure you know that the satisfaction of your affection stands in the way of mine."

There was a pause. Mr. Farebrother seemed to wait for a
recognition of the fact; and the emotion perceptible in the
tones of his fine voice gave solemnity to his words. But no
feeling could quell Fred's alarm.

"I could not be expected to give her up," he said, after a
moment's hesitation: it was not a case for any pretence of
generosity.

"Clearly not, when her affection met yours. But relations
of this sort, even when they are of long standing, are always
liable to change. I can easily conceive that you might act in
a way to loosen the tie she feels toward you—it must be remembered that she is only conditionally bound to you—and
that in that case, another man, who may flatter himself that
he has a hold on her regard, might succeeed in winning that
firm place in her love as well as respect which you had let
slip. I can easily conceive such a result," repeated Mr. Farebrother, emphatically. "There is a companionship of ready
sympathy, which might get the advantage even over the long-
est associations."

It seemed to Fred that if Mr. Farebrother had had a beak
and talons instead of his very capable tongue, his mode of
attack could hardly be more cruel. He had a horrible conviction that behind all this hypothetic statement there was a
knowledge of some actual change in Mary's feeling.

"Of course I know it might easily be all up with me," he said in a troubled voice. "If she is beginning to compare——" He broke off, not liking to betray all he felt, and then said, by the help of a little bitterness, "But I thought you were friendly to me."

"So I am; that is why we are here. But I have had a strong disposition to be otherwise. I have said to myself, 'If there is a likelihood of that youngster doing himself harm, why should you interfere? Aren't you worth as much as he is, and don't your sixteen years over and above his, in which you have gone rather hungry, give you more right to satisfaction than he has? If there's a chance of his going to the dogs, let him—perhaps you could nohow hinder it—and do you take the benefit.'"

There was a pause, in which Fred was seized by a most uncomfortable chill. What was coming next? He dreaded to hear that something had been said to Mary—he felt as if he were listening to a threat rather than a warning. When the vicar began again there was a change in his tone like the encouraging transition to a major key.

"But I had once meant better than that, and I am come back to my old intention. I thought that I could hardly *secure myself* in it better, Fred, than by telling you just what had gone on in me. And now, do you understand me? I want you to make the happiness of her life and your own, and if there is any chance that a word of warning from me may turn aside any risk to the contrary—well, I have uttered it."

There was a drop in the vicar's voice when he spoke the last words. He paused—they were standing on a patch of green where the road diverged toward St. Botolph's, and he put out his hand, as if to imply that the conversation was closed. Fred was moved quite newly. Some one highly susceptible to the contemplation of a fine act has said, that it produces a sort of regenerating shudder through the frame, and makes one feel ready to begin a new life. A good degree of that effect was just then present in Fred Vincy.

"I will try to be worthy," he said, breaking off before he could say "of you as well as of her." And meanwhile Mr. Farebrother had gathered the impulse to say something more.

"You must not imagine that I believe there is at present any decline in her preference of you, Fred. Set your heart at rest, that if you keep right, other things will keep right."

"I shall never forget what you have done," Fred answered. "I can't say anything that seems worth saying—only I will try that your goodness shall not be thrown away."

"That's enough. Good-bye, and God bless you."

In that way they parted. But both of them walked about a long while before they went out of the starlight. Much of Fred's rumination might be summed up in the words, "It certainly would have been a fine thing for her to marry Fare-brother—but if she loves me best and I am a good husband?"

Perhaps Mr. Farebrother's might be concentrated into a single shrug and one little speech. "To think of the part one little woman can play in the life of a man, so that to re-nounce her may be a very good imitation of heroism, and to win her may be a discipline!"

CHAPTER LXVII.

Now is there civil war within the soul:
Resolve is thrust from off the sacred throne
By clamorous Needs, and Pride the grand-vizier
Makes humble compact, plays the supple part
Of envoy and deft-tongued apologist
For hungry rebels.

HAPPILY Lydgate had ended by losing in the billiard-room, and brought away no encouragement to make a raid on luck. On the contrary, he felt unmixed disgust with himself the next day when he had to pay four or five pounds over and above his gains, and he carried about with him a most unpleasant vision of the figure he had made, not only rubbing elbows with the men at the Green Dragon, but behaving just as they did. A philoso-pher fallen to betting is hardly distinguishable from a Philis-tine under the same circumstances: the difference will chiefly be found in his subsequent reflections, and Lydgate chewed a very disagreeable cud in that way. His reason told him how the affair might have been magnified into ruin by a slight change of scenery—if it had been a gambling-house that he had turned into, where chance could be clutched with both hands instead of being picked up with thumb and forefinger. Nevertheless, though reason strangled the desire to gamble, there remained the feeling that, with an assurance of luck to the needful amount, he would have liked to gamble, rather than take the alternative which was beginning to urge itself as inevitable.

That alternative was to apply to Mr. Bulstrode. Lydgate had so many times boasted both to himself and others that he was totally independent of Bulstrode, to whose plans he had lent himself solely because they enabled him to carry out his own ideas of professional work and public benefit—he had so constantly in their personal intercourse had his pride sustained by the sense that he was making a good social use of this predominating banker, whose opinions he thought contemptible and whose motives often seemed to him an absurd mixture of contradictory impressions—that he had been creating for himself strong ideal obstacles to the proffering of any considerable request to him on his own account.

Still, early in March his affairs were at that pass in which men begin to say that their oaths were delivered in ignorance, and to perceive that the act which they had called impossible to them is becoming manifestly possible. With Dover's ugly security soon to be put in force, with the proceeds of his practice immediately absorbed in paying back debts, and with the chance, if the worst were known, of daily supplies being refused on credit, above all with the vision of Rosamond's hopeless discontent continually haunting him, Lydgate had begun to see that he should inevitably bend himself to ask help from somebody or other. At first he had considered whether he should write to Mr. Vincy; but on questioning Rosamond he found that, as he had suspected, she had already applied twice to her father, the last time being since the disappointment from Sir Godwin; and papa had said that Lydgate must look out for himself. "Papa said he had come, with one bad year after another, to trade more and more on borrowed capital, and had had to give up many indulgences; he could not spare a single hundred from the charges of his family." He said, "Let Lydgate ask Bulstrode: they have always been hand and glove."

Indeed, Lydgate himself had come to the conclusion that if he must end by asking for a free loan, his relations with Bulstrode, more at least than with any other man, might take the shape of a claim which was not purely personal. Bulstrode had indirectly helped to cause the failure of his practice, and had also been highly gratified by getting a medical partner in his plans:—but who among us ever reduced himself to the sort of dependence in which Lydgate now stood, without trying to believe that he had claims which diminished the humiliation of asking? It was true that of late there had seemed to be a new languor of interest in Bulstrode about the hospital; but his health had got worse, and showed signs of a deep-seated nervous affection. In other respects he did not appear to be changed: he had always been highly polite, but Lydgate had observed in him, from the first, a marked coldness about his marriage and other private circumstances, a coldness which he had hitherto preferred to any warmth of familiarity between them. He deferred the intention from day to day, his habit of acting on his conclusions being made infirm by his repugnance to every possible conclusion and its consequent act. He saw Mr. Bulstrode often, but he did not try to use any occasion for his private purpose. At one moment he thought, "I will write a letter: I prefer that to any circuitous talk"; at another he thought, "No; if I were talking to him, I could make a retreat before any signs of disinclination."

Still the days passed, and no letter was written, no special interview sought. In his shrinking from the humiliation of a dependent attitude toward Bulstrode, he began to familiarize his imagination with another step even more unlike his remembered self. He began spontaneously to consider whether it would be possible to carry out that puerile notion of Rosamond's which had often made him angry, namely, that they should quit Middlemarch without seeing anything beyond that preface. The question came—"Would any man buy the practice of me even now, for as little as it is worth? Then the sale might happen as a necessary preparation for going away."

But against his taking this step, which he still felt to be a contemptible relinquishment of present work, a guilty turning aside from what was a real and might be a widening channel

for worthy activity, to start again without any justified desti-
nation, there was this obstacle, that the purchaser, if procur-
able at all, might not be quickly forthcoming.   And afterward?
Rosamond in a poor lodging, though in the largest city or
most distant town, would not find the life that could save her
from gloom, and save him from the reproach of having plunged
her into it.   For when a man is at the foot of the hill in his
fortunes, he may stay a long while there in spite of professional accomplishment.   In the British climate there is no
incompatibility between scientific insight and furnished lodg-
ings : the incompatibility is chiefly between scientific ambition
and a wife who objects to that kind of residence.

But in the midst of his hesitation, opportunity came to decide him.   A note from Mr. Bulstrode requested Lydgate to
call on him at the bank.   A hypochondriacal tendency had
shown itself in the banker's constitution of late; and a lack
of sleep, which was really only a slight exaggeration of an
habitual dyspeptic symptom, had been dwelt on by him as a
sign of threatening insanity.   He wanted to consult Lydgate
without delay on that particular morning, although he had
nothing to tell beyond what he had told before.   He listened
eagerly to what Lydgate had to say in dissipation of his fears,
though this too was only repetition; and this moment in
which Bulstrode was receiving a medical opinion with a sense
of comfort, seemed to make the communication of a personal
need to him easier than it had been in Lydgate's contemplation
beforehand.   He had been insisting that it would be well for
Mr. Bulstrode to relax his attention to business.

"One sees how any mental strain, however slight, may affect
a delicate frame," said Lydgate, at that stage of the consultation when the remarks tend to pass from the personal to the
general, "by the deep stamp which anxiety will make for a
time even on the young and vigorous.   I am naturally very
strong; yet I have been thoroughly shaken lately by an ac-
cumulation of trouble."

"I presume that a constitution in the susceptible state in
which mine at present is, would be especially liable to fall a
victim to cholera, if it visited our district.   And since its appearance near London, we may well besiege the Mercy-seat

for our protection," said Mr. Bulstrode, not intending to evade Lydgate's allusion, but really preoccupied with alarms about himself.

"You have at all events taken your share in using good practical precautions for the town, and that is the best mode of asking for protection," said Lydgate, with a strong distaste for the broken metaphor and bad logic of the banker's religion, somewhat increased by the apparent deafness of his sympathy. But his mind had taken up its long-prepared movement toward getting help, and was not yet arrested. He added, "The town has done well in the way of cleansing, and finding appliances; and I think that if the cholera should come, even our enemies will admit that the arrangements in the hospital are a public good."

"Truly," said Mr. Bulstrode, with some coldness. "With regard to what you say, Mr. Lydgate, about the relaxation of my mental labor, I have for some time been entertaining a purpose to that effect—a purpose of a very decided character. I contemplate at least a temporary withdrawal from the management of much business, whether benevolent or commercial. Also I think of changing my residence for a time: probably I shall close or let 'The Shrubs,' and take some place near the coast—under advice, of course, as to salubrity. That would be a measure which you would recommend?"

"Oh, yes," said Lydgate, falling backward in his chair, with ill-repressed impatience under the banker's pale earnest eyes and intense preoccupation with himself.

"I have for some time felt that I should open this subject with you in relation to our hospital," continued Bulstrode. "Under the circumstances I have indicated, of course I must cease to have any personal share in the management, and it is contrary to my views of responsibility to continue a large application of means to an institution which I cannot watch over and to some extent regulate. I shall therefore, in case of my ultimate decision to leave Middlemarch, consider that I withdraw other support to the New Hospital than that which will subsist in the fact that I chiefly supplied the expenses of building it, and have contributed further large sums to its successful working."

Lydgate's thought, when Bulstrode paused according to his wont, was, "He has perhaps been losing a good deal of money." This was the most plausible explanation of a speech which had caused rather a startling change in his expectations. He said in reply—

"The loss to the hospital can hardly be made up, I fear."

"Hardly," returned Bulstrode, in the same deliberate, silvery tone; "except by some changes of plan. The only person who may be certainly counted on as willing to increase her contributions is Mrs. Casaubon. I have had an interview with her on the subject, and I have pointed out to her, as I am about to do to you, that it will be desirable to win a more general support to the New Hospital by a change of system."

Another pause, but Lydgate did not speak.

"The change I mean is an amalgamation with the Infirmary, so that the New Hospital shall be regarded as a special addition to the elder institution, having the same directing board. It will be necessary, also, that the medical management of the two shall be combined. In this way any difficulty as to the adequate maintenance of our new establishment will be removed; the benevolent interests of the town will cease to be divided."

Mr. Bulstrode had lowered his eyes from Lydgate's face to the buttons of his coat as he again paused.

"No doubt that is a good device as to ways and means," said Lydgate, with an edge of ivory in his tone. "But I can't be expected to rejoice in it at once, since one of the first results will be that the other medical men will upset or interrupt my methods, if it were only because they are mine."

"I myself, as you know, Mr. Lydgate, highly valued the opportunity of new and independent procedure which you have diligently employed: the original plan, I confess, was one which I had much at heart, under submission to the Divine Will. But since providential indications demand a renunciation from me, I renounce."

Bulstrode showed a rather exasperating ability in this conversation. The broken metaphor and bad logic of motive which had stirred his hearer's contempt were quite consistent with a mode of putting the facts which made it difficult for

Lydgate to vent his own indignation and disappointment. After some rapid reflection, he only asked—

"What did Mrs. Casaubon say?"

"That was the further statement which I wished to make to you," said Bulstrode, who had thoroughly prepared his ministerial explanation. "She is, you are aware, a woman of most munificent disposition, and happily in possession—not I presume of great wealth, but of funds which she can well spare. She has informed me that though she has destined the chief part of those funds to another purpose, she is willing to consider whether she cannot fully take my place in relation to the hospital. But she wishes for ample time to mature her thoughts on the subject, and I have told her that there is no need for haste—that, in fact, my own plans are not yet absolute."

Lydgate was ready to say, "If Mrs. Casaubon would take your place, there would be gain instead of loss." But there was still a weight on his mind which arrested this cheerful candor. He replied, "I suppose, then, that I may enter into the subject with Mrs. Casaubon."

"Precisely; that is what she expressly desires. Her decision, she says, will much depend on what you can tell her. But not at present; she is, I believe, just setting out on a journey. I have her letter here," said Mr. Bulstrode, drawing it out and reading from it. "'I am immediately otherwise engaged,' she says. 'I am going into Yorkshire with Sir James and Lady Chettam; and the conclusions I come to about some land which I am to see there may affect my power of contributing to the hospital.' Thus, Mr. Lydgate, there is no haste necessary in this matter; but I wished to apprise you beforehand of what may possibly occur."

Mr. Bulstrode returned the letter to his side pocket, and changed his attitude as if his business were closed. Lydgate, whose renewed hope about the hospital only made him more conscious of the facts which poisoned his hope, felt that his effort after help, if made at all, must be made now and vigorously.

"I am much obliged to you for giving me full notice," he said, with a firm intention in his tone, yet with an interruptedness in his delivery which showed that he spoke unwillingly. "The highest object to me is my profession, and I had identified the hospital with the best use I can at present make of my profession. But the best use is not always the same with monetary success. Everything which has made the hospital unpopular has helped with other causes—I think they are all connected with my professional zeal—to make me unpopular as a practitioner. I get chiefly patients who can't pay me. I should like them best, if I had nobody to pay on my own side." Lydgate waited a little, but Bulstrode only bowed, looking at him fixedly, and he went on with the same interrupted enunciation—as if he were biting an objectional leek.

"I have slipped into money difficulties which I can see no way out of, unless some one who trusts me and my future will advance me a sum without other security. I had very little fortune left when I came here. I have no prospects of money from my own family. My expenses, in consequence of my marriage, have been very much greater than I had expected. The result at this moment is that it would take a thousand pounds to clear me. I mean, to free me from the risk of having all my goods sold in security of my largest debt—as well as to pay my other debts—and leave anything to keep us a little beforehand with our small income. I find that it is out of the question that my wife's father should make such an advance. That is why I mention my position to—to the only other man who may be held to have some personal connection with my prosperity or ruin."

Lydgate hated to hear himself. But he had spoken now, and had spoken with unmistakable directness. Mr. Bulstrode replied without haste, but also without hesitation.

"I am grieved, though, I confess, not surprised by this information, Mr. Lydgate. For my own part, I regretted your alliance with my brother-in-law's family, which has always been of prodigal habits, and which has already been much indebted to me for sustainment in its present position. My advice to you, Mr. Lydgate, would be, that instead of involving yourself in further obligations, and continuing a doubtful struggle, you should simply become a bankrupt."

"That would not improve my prospect," said Lydgate, ris-

44

ing and speaking bitterly, "even if it were a more agreeable thing in itself."

"It is always a trial," said Mr. Bulstrode; "but trial, my dear sir, is our portion here, and is a needed corrective. I recommend you to weigh the advice I have given."

"Thank you," said Lydgate, not quite knowing what he said. "I have occupied you too long. Good-day."

CHAPTER LXVIII.

"What suit of grace hath Virtue to put on
If Vice shall wear as good and do as well?
If Wrong, if Craft, if Indiscretion
Act as fair parts with ends as laudable?
Which all this mighty volume of events
The world, the universal map of deeds,
Strongly controls, and proves from all descents,
That the directed course still best succeeds.
For should not grave and learn'd Experience
That looks with the eyes of all the world beside,
And with all ages holds intelligence,
Go safer than Deceit without a guide!"

DANIEL: *Musophilus.*

THAT change of plan and shifting of interest which Bulstrode stated or betrayed in his conversation with Lydgate, had been determined in him by some severe experience which he had gone through since the epoch of Mr. Larcher's sale, when Raffles had recognized Will Ladislaw, and when the banker had in vain attempted an act of restitution which might move Divine Providence to arrest painful consequences.

His certainty that Raffles, unless he were dead, would return to Middlemarch before long, had been justified. On Christmas eve he had reappeared at The Shrubs. Bulstrode was at home to receive him and hinder his communication with the rest of the family, but he could not altogether hinder the circumstances of the visit from compromising himself and alarming his wife. Raffles proved more unmanageable than he had shown himself to be in his former appearances, his chronic state of mental restlessness, the growing effect of habitual intemperance, quickly shaking off every impression from what was said to him. He insisted on staying in the house, and Bulstrode, weighing two sets of evils, felt that this was at least not a worse alternative than his going into the town. He kept him in his own room for the evening and saw him to bed, Raffles all the while amusing himself with the annoyance he was causing this decent and highly prosperous fellow-sinner, an amusement which he facetiously expressed as sympathy with his friend's pleasure in entertaining a man who had been serviceable to him, and who had not had all his earnings. There was a cunning calculation under his noisy joking—a cool resolve to extract something the handsomer from Bulstrode as payment for release from this new application of torture. But his cunning had a little overcast its mark.

Bulstrode was indeed more tortured than the coarse fibre of Raffles could enable him to imagine. He had told his wife that he was simply taking care of this wretched creature, the victim of vice, who might otherwise injure himself; he implied, without the direct form of falsehood, that there was a family tie which bound him to this care, and that there were signs of mental alienation in Raffles which urged caution. He would himself drive the unfortunate being away the next morning. In these hints he felt that he was supplying Mrs. Bulstrode with precautionary information for his daughters and servants, and accounting for his allowing no one but himself to enter the room even with food and drink. But he sat in an agony of fear lest Raffles should be overheard in his loud and plain references to past facts—lest Mrs. Bulstrode should be even tempted to listen at the door. How could he hinder her? how betray his terror by opening the door to detect her? She was a woman of honest direct habits, and little likely to take so low a course in order to arrive at a painful knowledge; but fear was stronger than the calculation of probabilities.

In this way Raffles had pushed the torture too far, and produced an effect which had not been in his plan. By showing himself hopelessly unmanageable he had made Bulstrode feel that a strong defiance was the only resource left. After taking Raffles to bed that night, the banker ordered his closed carriage to be ready at half-past seven the next morning. At six o'clock he had already been long dressed, and had spent some of his wretchedness in prayer, pleading his motives for averting the worst evil, if in anything he had used falsity and spoken what was not true before God. For Bulstrode shrank from a direct lie with an intensity disproportionate to the number of his more indirect misdeeds. But many of these misdeeds were like the subtle muscular movements which are not taken account of in the consciousness, though they bring about the end that we fix our mind on and desire. And it is only what we are vividly conscious of that we can vividly imagine to be seen by Omniscience.

Bulstrode carried his candle to the bedside of Raffles, who was apparently in a painful dream. He stood silent, hoping that the presence of the light would serve to waken the sleeper gradually and gently, for he feared some noise as the consequence of a too sudden awakening. He had watched, for a couple of minutes or more, the shudderings and pantings which seemed likely to end in waking, when Raffles, with a long, half-stifled moan, started up and stared around him in terror, trembling and gasping. But he made no further noise, and Bulstrode, setting down the candle, awaited his recovery.

It was a quarter of an hour later before Bulstrode, with a cold peremptoriness of manner which he had not before shown, said, "I came to call you thus early, Mr. Raffles, because I have ordered the carriage to be ready at half-past seven, and intend myself to conduct you as far as Ilsely, where you can either take the railway or await a coach."

Raffles was about to speak, but Bulstrode anticipated him imperiously, with the words: "Be silent, sir, and hear what I have to say. I shall supply you with money now, and I will furnish you with a reasonable sum from time to time, on your application to me by letter; but if you choose to present yourself here again, if you return to Middlemarch, if you use your tongue in a manner injurious to me, you will have to live on such fruits as your malice can bring you, without help from me. Nobody will pay you well for blasting my name. I know the worst you can do against me, and I shall brave it if you dare to thrust yourself upon me again. Get up, sir, and do as I order you, without noise, or I will send for a policeman to take you off my premises, and you may carry your stories

into every pothouse in the town, but you shall have no six-
pence from me to pay your expenses there."

Bulstrode had rarely in his life spoken with such nervous
energy: he had been deliberating on this speech and its probable effects through a large part of the night; and although
he did not trust to its ultimately saving him from any return
of Raffles, he had concluded that it was the best throw he
could make. It succeeded in enforcing submission from the
jaded man this morning: his empoisoned system at this moment quailed before Bulstrode's cold, resolute bearing, and he
was taken off quietly in the carriage before the family break-
fast-time. The servants imagined him to be a poor relation,
and were not surprised that a strict man like their master,
who held his head high in the world, should be ashamed of
such a cousin and want to get rid of him. The banker's drive
of ten miles with his hated companion was a dreary beginning
of the Christmas day; but at the end of the drive, Raffles had
recovered his spirits, and parted in a contentment for which
there was the good reason that the banker had given him a
hundred pounds. Various motives urged Bulstrode to this
open-handedness, but he did not himself inquire closely into
all of them. As he had stood watching Raffles in his uneasy
sleep, it had certainly entered his mind that the man had been
much shattered since the first gift of two hundred pounds.

He had taken care to repeat the incisive statement of his
resolve not to be played on any more; and had tried to pene-
trate Raffles with the fact that he had shown the risks of brib-
ing him to be quite equal to the risks of defying him. But
when, freed from his repulsive presence, Bulstrode returned
to his quiet home, he brought with him no confidence that he
had secured more than a respite. It was as if he had had a
loathsome dream, and could not shake off its images with their
hateful kindred of sensations—as if on all the pleasant sur-
roundings of his life a dangerous reptile had left his slimy
traces.

Who can know how much of his most inward life is made
up of the thoughts he believes other men to have about him,
until that fabric of opinion is threatened with ruin?

Bulstrode was only the more conscious that there was a de-

posit of uneasy presentiment in his wife's mind, because she
carefully avoided any allusion to it.   He had been used every
day to taste the flavor of supremacy and the tribute of complete deference: and the certainty that he was watched or
measured, with a hidden suspicion of his having some dis-
creditable secret, made his voice totter when he was speaking
to edification.   Foreseeing, to men of Bulstrode's anxious
temperament, is often worse than seeing; and his imagination
continually heightened the anguish of an imminent disgrace.
Yes, imminent; for if his defiance of Raffles did not keep the
man away—and though he prayed for this result he hardly
hoped for it—the disgrace was certain.   In vain he said to
himself that, if permitted, it would be a divine visitation, a
chastisement, a preparation; he recoiled from the imagined
burning; and he judged that it must be more for the Divine
glory that he should escape dishonor.   That recoil had at last
urged him to make preparations for quitting Middlemarch.
If evil truth must be reported of him, he would then be at a
less scorching distance from the contempt of his old neighbors;
and in a new scene, where his life would not have gathered
the same wide sensibility, the tormentor, if he pursued him,
would be less formidable.   To leave the place finally would,
he knew, be extremely painful to his wife, and on other
grounds he would have preferred to stay where he had struck
root.   Hence he made his preparations at first in a condi-
tional way, wishing to leave on all sides an opening for his
return after brief absence, if any favorable intervention of
Providence should dissipate his fears.   He was preparing to
transfer his management of the bank, and to give up any
active control of other commercial affairs in the neighborhood,
on the ground of his failing health, but without excluding his
future resumption of such work.   The measure would cause
him some added expense, and some diminution of income, beyond what he had already undergone from the general depression of trade; and the hospital presented itself as a principal
object of outlay on which he could fairly economize.
   This was the experience which had determined his conversation with Lydgate.   But at this time his arrangements
had most of them gone no further than a stage at which he ,

could recall them, if they proved to be unnecessary. He continually deferred the final steps; in the midst of his fears, like many a man who is in danger of shipwreck or of being dashed from his carriage by runaway horses, he had a clinging impression that something would happen to hinder the worst, and that to spoil his life by a late transplantation might be over-hasty—especially since it was difficult to account satisfactorily to his wife for the project of their indefinite exile from the only place where she would like to live.

Among the affairs Bulstrode had to care for, was the management of the farm at Stone Court in case of his absence; and on this, as well as on all other matters connected with any houses and land he possessed in or about Middlemarch, he had consulted Caleb Garth. Like every one else who had business of that sort, he wanted to get the agent who was more anxious for his employer's interests than his own. With regard to Stone Court, since Bulstrode wished to retain his hold on the stock, and to have an arrangement by which he himself could, if he chose, resume his favorite recreation of superintendence, Caleb had advised him not to trust to a mere bailiff, but to let the land, stock, and implements yearly, and take a proportionate share of the proceeds.

"May I trust you to find me a tenant on these terms, Mr. Garth?" said Bulstrode. "And will you mention to me the yearly sum which would repay you for managing these affairs which we have discussed together?"

"I'll think about it," said Caleb, in his blunt way. "I'll see how I can make it out."

If it had not been that he had to consider Fred Vincy's future, Mr. Garth would not probably have been glad of any addition to his work, of which his wife was always fearing an excess for him as he grew older. But on quitting Bulstrode after that conversation, a very alluring idea occurred to him about this said letting of Stone Court. What if Bulstrode would agree to his placing Fred Vincy there, on the understanding that he, Caleb Garth, should be responsible for the management? It would be an excellent schooling for Fred; he might make a modest income there, and still have time left to get knowledge by helping in other business. He mentioned his notion to Mrs. Garth with such evident delight that she could not bear to chill his pleasure by expressing her constant fear of his undertaking too much.

"The lad would be as happy as two," he said, throwing himself back in his chair, and looking radiant, "if I could tell him it was all settled. Think, Susan! His mind had been running on that place for years before old Featherstone died. And it would be as pretty a turn of things as could be, that he should hold the place in a good industrious way, after all—by his taking to business. For it's likely enough Bulstrode might let him go on, and gradually buy the stock. He hasn't made up his mind, I can see, whether or not he shall settle somewhere else, as a lasting thing. I never was better pleased with a notion in my life. And then the children might be married by and by, Susan."

"You will not give any hint of the plan to Fred, until you are sure that Bulstrode would agree to the plan?" said Mrs. Garth, in a tone of gentle caution. "And as to marriage, Caleb, we old people need not help to hasten it."

"Oh, I don't know," said Caleb, swinging his head aside. "Marriage is a taming thing. Fred would want less of my bit and bridle. However, I shall say nothing till I know the ground I'm treading on. I shall speak to Bulstrode again."

He took his earliest opportunity of doing so. Bulstrode had anything but a warm interest in his nephew, Fred Vincy, but he had a strong wish to secure Mr. Garth's services on many scattered points of business, at which he was sure to be a considerable loser, if they were under less conscientious management. On that ground he made no objection to Mr. Garth's proposal; and there was also another reason why he was not sorry to give a consent which was to benefit one of the Vincy family. It was that Mrs. Bulstrode, having heard of Lydgate's debts, had been anxious to know whether her husband could not do something for poor Rosamond, and had been much troubled on learning from him that Lydgate's affairs were not easily remediable, and that the wisest plan was to let them "take their course." Mrs. Bulstrode had then said for the first time, "I think you are always a little hard toward my family, Nicholas. And I am sure I have no reason to deny any of my relatives. Too worldly they may be, but no one ever had to say they were not respectable."

"My dear Harriet," said Mr. Bulstrode, wincing under his wife's eyes, which were filling with tears, "I have supplied your brother with a great deal of capital. I cannot be expected to take care of his married children." ·

That seemed to be true, and Mrs. Bulstrode's remonstrance subsided into pity for poor Rosamond, whose extravagant education she had always foreseen the fruits of.

But remembering that dialogue, Mr. Bulstrode felt that when he had to talk to his wife fully about his plan of quitting Middlemarch, he should be glad to tell her that he had made an arrangement which might be for the good of her nephew, Fred. At present he had merely mentioned to her that he thought of shutting up The Shrubs for a few months, and taking a house on the Southern Coast.

Hence Mr. Garth got the assurance he desired, namely, that in case of Bulstrode's departure from Middlemarch for an indefinite time, Fred Vincy should be allowed to have the tenancy of Stone Court on the terms proposed.

Caleb was so elated with his hope of this "neat turn" being given to things, that if his self-control had not been braced by a little affectionate wifely scolding, he would have betrayed everything to Mary, wanting "to give the child comfort." However, he restrained himself, and kept in strict privacy from Fred certain visits which he was making to Stone Court, in order to look more thoroughly into the state of the land and stock, and take a preliminary estimate. He was certainly more eager in these visits than the probable speed of events required him to be; but he was stimulated by a fatherly delight in occupying his mind with this bit of probable happiness, which he held in store, like a hidden birthday gift, for Fred and Mary.

"But suppose the whole scheme should turn out to be a castle in the air?" said Mrs. Garth.

"Well, well," replied Caleb; "the castle will tumble about nobody's head."

CHAPTER LXIX.

" If thou hast heard a word, let it die with thee."
—*Ecclesiasticus.*

MR. BULSTRODE was still seated in his manager's room at the bank, about three o'clock of the same day on which he had received Lydgate there, when the clerk entered to say that his horse was waiting, and also that Mr. Garth was outside and begged to speak with him.

"By all means," said Bulstrode; and Caleb entered. "Pray sit down, Mr. Garth," continued the banker, in his suavest tone. "I am glad that you arrived just in time to find me here. I know you count your minutes."

"Oh," said Caleb, gently, with a slow swing of his head on one side, as he seated himself and laid his hat on the floor. He looked at the ground, leaning forward and letting his long fingers droop between his legs, while each finger moved in succession, as if it were sharing some thought which filled his large, quiet brow.

Mr. Bulstrode, like every one else who knew Caleb, was used to his slowness in beginning to speak on any topic which he felt to be important, and rather expected that he was about to recur to the buying of some houses in Blindman's Court, for the sake of pulling them down, as a sacrifice of property which would be well repaid by the influx of air and light on that spot. It was by propositions of this kind that Caleb was sometimes troublesome to his employers; but he had usually found Bulstrode ready to meet him in projects of improvement, and they had got on well together. When he spoke again, however, it was to say, in rather a subdued voice:

"I have just come away from Stone Court, Mr. Bulstrode."

"You found nothing wrong there, I hope," said the banker; "I was there myself yesterday. Abel has done well with the lambs this year."

"Why, yes," said Caleb, looking up gravely, "there *is* something wrong—a stranger, who is very ill, I think. He wants a doctor, and I came to tell you of that. His name is Raffles."

He saw the shock of his words passing through Bulstrode's frame. On this subject the banker had thought that his fears were too constantly on the watch to be taken by surprise; but he had been mistaken.

"Poor wretch!" he said, in a compassionate tone, though his lips trembled a little. "Do you know how he came there?"

"I took him myself," said Caleb, quietly—"took him up in my gig. He had got down from the coach, and was walking a little beyond the turning from the toll-house, and I overtook him. He remembered seeing me with you once before, at Stone Court, and he asked me to take him on. I saw he was ill: it seemed to me the right thing to do, to carry him under shelter. And now I think you should lose no time in getting advice for him." Caleb took up his hat from the floor as he ended, and rose slowly from his seat.

"Certainly," said Bulstrode, whose mind was very active at this moment. "Perhaps you will yourself oblige me, Mr. Garth, by calling at Mr. Lydgate's as you pass—or stay! he may at this hour probably be at the hospital. I will first send my man on the horse there with a note this instant, and then I will myself ride to Stone Court."

Bulstrode quickly wrote a note, and went out himself to give the commission to his man. When he returned, Caleb was standing, as before, with one hand on the back of the chair, holding his hat with the other. In Bulstrode's mind the dominant thought was: "Perhaps Raffles only spoke to Garth of his illness. Garth may wonder, as he must have done before, at this disreputable fellow's claiming intimacy with me; but he will know nothing. He is friendly to me—I can be of use to him."

He longed for some confirmation of this hopeful conjecture, but to have asked any question as to what Raffles had said or done would have been to betray fear.

"I am exceedingly obliged to you, Mr. Garth," he said, in his usual tone of politeness. "My servant will be back in a few minutes, and I shall then go myself to see what can be done for this unfortunate man. Perhaps you had some other business with me? If so, pray be seated."

"Thank you," said Caleb, making a slight gesture with his

right hand to waive the invitation. "I wish to say, Mr. Bulstrode, that I must request you to put your business into some other hands than mine. I am obliged to you for your handsome way of meeting me—about the letting of Stone Court, and all other business. But I must give it up."

A sharp certainty entered like a stab into Bulstrode's soul.

"This is sudden, Mr. Garth," was all he could say at first.

"It is," said Caleb; "but it is quite fixed. I must give it up."

He spoke with a firmness which was very gentle, and yet he could see that Bulstrode seemed to cower under that gentleness, his face looking dried and his eyes swerving away from the glance which rested on him. Caleb felt a deep pity for him, but he could have used no pretexts to account for his resolve, even if they would have been of any use.

"You have been led to this, I apprehend, by some slanders concerning me uttered by that unhappy creature," said Bulstrode, anxious now to know the utmost.

"That is true. I can't deny that I act upon what I heard from him."

"You are a conscientious man, Mr. Garth—a man, I trust, who feels himself accountable to God. You would not wish to injure me by being too ready to believe a slander," said Bulstrode, casting about for pleas that might be adapted to his hearer's mind. "That is a poor reason for giving up a connection which, I think I may say, will be mutually beneficial."

"I would injure no man if I could help it," said Caleb; "even if I thought God winked at it. I hope I should have a feeling for my fellow-creature. But, sir—I am obliged to believe that this Raffles has told me the truth. And I can't be happy in working with you, or profiting by you. It hurts my mind. I must beg you to seek another agent."

"Very well, Mr. Garth. But I must at least claim to know the worst that he has told you. I must know what is the foul speech that I am liable to be the victim of," said Bulstrode, a certain amount of anger beginning to mingle with his humiliation before this quiet man who renounced his benefits.

"That's needless," said Caleb, waving his hand, bowing his head slightly, and not swerving from the tone which had in it the merciful intention to spare this pitiable man. "What he has said to me will never pass from my lips, unless something now unknown forces it from me. If you led a harmful life for gain, and kept others out of their rights by deceit, to get the more for yourself, I dare say you repent—you would like to go back, and can't: that must be a bitter thing"—Caleb paused a moment, and shook his head—"it is not for me to make your life harder to you."

"But you do—you do make it harder to me," said Bulstrode, constrained into a genuine, pleading cry. "You make it harder to me by turning your back on me."

"That I'm forced to do," said Caleb, still more gently, lifting up his hand. "I am sorry. I don't judge you and say, he is wicked, and I am righteous. God forbid. I don't know everything. A man may do wrong, and his will may rise clear out of it, though he can't get his life clear. That's a bad punishment. If it is so with you,—well, I'm very sorry for you. But I have that feeling inside me, that I can't go on working with you. That's all, Mr. Bulstrode. Everything else is buried, so far as my will goes. And I wish you good-day."

"One moment, Mr. Garth!" said Bustrode, hurriedly. "I may trust, then, to your solemn assurance that you will not repeat either to man or woman what—even if it have any degree of truth in it—is yet a malicious representation?"

Caleb's wrath was stirred, and he said, indignantly:

"Why should I have said it if I didn't mean it? I am in no fear of you. Such tales as that will never tempt my tongue."

"Excuse me—I am agitated—I am the victim of this abandoned man."

"Stop a bit! You have got to consider whether you didn't help to make him worse, when you profited by his vices."

"You are wronging me by too readily believing him," said Bulstrode, oppressed, as by a nightmare, with the inability to deny flatly what Raffles might have said; and yet feeling it an escape that Caleb had not so stated it to him as to ask for that flat denial.

"No," said Caleb, lifting his hand deprecatingly; "I am ready to believe better, when better is proved. I rob you of no good chance. As to speaking, I hold it a crime to expose a man's sin unless I'm clear it must be done to save the innocent. That is my way of thinking, Mr. Bulstrode, and what I say, I've no need to swear. I wish you good-day."

Some hours later, when he was at home, Caleb said to his wife, incidentally, that he had had some little differences with Bulstrode, and that, in consequence, he had given up all notion of taking Stone Court, and indeed had resigned doing further business for him.

"He was disposed to interfere too much, was he?" said Mrs. Garth, imagining that her husband had been touched on his sensitive point, and not been allowed to do what he thought right as to materials and modes of work.

"Oh," said Caleb, bowing his head, and waving his hand gravely. And Mrs. Garth knew that this was a sign of his not intending to speak further on the subject.

As for Bulstrode, he had almost immediately mounted his horse and set off for Stone Court, being anxious to arrive there before Lydgate.

His mind was crowded with images and conjectures, which were a language to his hopes and fears, just as we hear tones from the vibrations which shake our whole system. The deep humiliation with which he had winced under Caleb Garth's knowledge of his past, and rejection of his patronage, alternated with and almost gave way to the sense of safety in the fact that Garth, and no other, had been the man to whom Raffles had spoken. It seemed to him a sort of earnest that Providence intended his rescue from worse consequences; the way being thus left open for the hope of secrecy. That Raffles should be afflicted with illness, that he should have been led to Stone Court rather than elsewhere—Bulstrode's heart fluttered at the vision of probabilities which these events conjured up. If it should turn out that he was freed from all danger of disgrace—if he could breathe in perfect liberty —his life should be more consecrated than it had ever been before. He mentally lifted up this vow as if it would urge the result he longed for—he tried to believe in the potency of that prayerful resolution—its potency to determine death. He knew that he ought to say, "Thy will be done"; and he said it often.　But the intense desire remained, that the will of God might be the death of that hated man.

Yet when he arrived at Stone Court he could not see the change in Raffles without a shock.　But for his pallor and feebleness, Bulstrode would have called the change in him entirely mental.　Instead of his loud tormenting mood, he showed an intense, vague terror, and seemed to deprecate Bulstrode's anger, because the money was all gone—he had been robbed—it had, half of it, been taken from him.　He had only come here because he was ill and somebody was hunting him—somebody was after him: he had told nobody anything; he had kept his mouth shut.　Bulstrode, not knowing the significance of these symptoms, interpreted this new nervous susceptibility into a means of alarming Raffles into true confessions, and taxed him with falsehood in saying that he had not told anything, since he had just told the man who took him up in his gig and brought him to Stone Court.　Raffles denied this with solemn adjurations; the fact being that the links of consciousness were interrupted in him, and that his minute terror-stricken narrative to Caleb Garth had been delivered under a set of visionary impulses which had dropped back into darkness.

Bulstrode's heart sank again at this sign that he could get no grasp over the wretched man's mind, and that no word of Raffles could be trusted as to the fact which he most wanted to know—namely, whether or not he had really kept silence to every one in the neighborhood except Caleb Garth.　The housekeeper had told him, without the least constraint of manner, that since Mr. Garth left, Raffles had asked her for beer, and after that had not spoken, seeming very ill.　On that side it might be concluded that there had been no betrayal. Mrs. Abel thought, like the servants at The Shrubs, that the strange man belonged to the unpleasant "kin" who are among the troubles of the rich; she had at first referred the kinship to Mr. Rigg, and where there was property left, the buzzing presence of such large blue-bottles seemed natural enough. How he could be "kin" to Bulstrode as well was not so clear, but Mrs. Abel agreed with her husband that there was "no knowing"—a proposition which had a great deal of mental food for her, so that she shook her head over it without further speculation.

In less than an hour Lydgate arrived. Bulstrode met him outside the wainscoted parlor, where Raffles was, and said:

"I have called you in, Mr. Lydgate, to an unfortunate man who was once in my employment, many years ago. Afterward he went to America, and returned, I fear, to an idle, dissolute life. Being destitute, he has a claim on me. He was slightly connected with Rigg, the former owner of this place, and in consequence found his way here. I believe he is seriously ill: apparently his mind is affected. I feel bound to do the utmost for him."

Lydgate, who had the remembrance of his last conversation with Bulstrode strongly upon him, was not disposed to say an unnecessary word to him, and bowed slightly in answer to this account; but just before entering the room he turned automatically and said, "What is his name?"—to know names being as much a part of the medical man's accomplishments as of the practical politician's.

"Raffles, John Raffles," said Bulstrode, who hoped that, whatever became of Raffles, Lydgate would never know any more of him.

When he had thoroughly examined and considered the patient, Lydgate ordered that he should go to bed, and be kept there in as complete quiet as possible, and then went with Bulstrode into another room.

"It is a serious case, I apprehend," said the banker, before Lydgate began to speak.

"No—and yes," said Lydgate, half dubiously. "It is difficult to decide as to the possible effect of long-standing complications; but the man had a robust constitution to begin with. I should not expect this attack to be fatal, though of course the system is in a ticklish state. He should be well watched and attended to."

"I will remain here myself," said Bulstrode. "Mrs. Abel and her husband are inexperienced. I can easily remain here for the night, if you will oblige me by taking a note for Mrs. Bulstrode."

"I should think that is hardly necessary," said Lydgate.

"He seems tame and terrified enough. He might become more unmanageable. But there is a man here—is there not?"

"I have more than once stayed here a few nights, for the sake of seclusion," said Bulstrode, indifferently; "I am quite disposed to do so now. Mrs. Abel and her husband can relieve or aid me, if necessary."

"Very well. Then I need give my directions only to you," said Lydgate, not feeling surprised at a little peculiarity in Bulstrode.

"You think, then, that the case is hopeful?" said Bulstrode, when Lydgate had ended giving his orders.

"Unless there turn out to be further complications, such as I have not at present detected—yes," said Lydgate. "He may pass on to a worse stage; but I should not wonder if he got better in a few days, by adhering to the treatment I have prescribed. There must be firmness. Remember, if he calls for liquors of any sort, not to give them to him. In my opinion, men in his condition are oftener killed by treatment than by the disease. Still, new symptoms may arise. I shall come again to-morrow morning."

After waiting for the note to be carried to Mrs. Bulstrode, Lydgate rode away, forming no conjectures, in the first instance, about the history of Raffles, but rehearsing the whole argument, which had lately been much stirred by the publication of Dr. Ware's abundant experience in America, as to the right way of treating cases of alcoholic poisoning such as this. Lydgate, when abroad, had already been interested in this question: he was strongly convinced against the prevalent practice of allowing alcohol and persistently administering large doses of opium; and he had repeatedly acted on this conviction with a favorable result.

"The man is in a diseased state," he thought, "but there's a good deal of wear in him still. I suppose he is an object of charity to Bulstrode. It is curious what patches of hardness and tenderness lie side by side in men's dispositions. Bulstrode seems the most unsympathetic fellow I ever saw about some people, and yet he has taken no end of trouble, and spent a great deal of money, on benevolent objects. I suppose

45

he has some test by which he finds out whom Heaven cares for—he has made up his mind that it doesn't care for me."

This streak of bitterness came from a plenteous source, and kept widening in the current of his thought as he neared Lowick Gate. He had not been there since his first interview with Bulstrode in the morning, having been found at the hospital by the banker's messenger; and for the first time he was returning to his home without the vision of any expedient in the background which left him a hope of raising money enough to deliver him from the coming destitution of everything which made his married life tolerable—everything which saved him and Rosamond from that bare isolation in which they would be forced to recognize how little of a comfort they could be to each other. It was more bearable to do without tenderness for himself than to see that his own tenderness could make no amends for the lack of other things to her. The sufferings of his own pride from humiliations past and to come were keen enough, yet they were hardly distinguishable to himself from that more acute pain which dominated them—the pain of foreseeing that Rosamond would come to regard him chiefly as the cause of disappointment and unhappiness to her. He had never liked the makeshifts of poverty, and they had never before entered into his prospects for himself; but he was beginning now to imagine how two creatures who loved each other, and had a stock of thoughts in common, might laugh over their shabby furniture, and their calculations how far they could afford butter and eggs. But the glimpse of that poetry seemed as far off from him as the carelessness of the Golden Age; in poor Rosamond's mind there was not room enough for luxuries to look small in. He got down from his horse in a very sad mood, and went into the house, not expecting to be cheered except by his dinner, and reflecting that before the evening closed it would be wise to tell Rosamond of his application to Bulstrode and its failure. It would be well not to lose time in preparing her for the worst.

But his dinner waited long for him before he was able to eat it. For on entering he found that Dover's agent had already put a man in the house; and when he asked where Mrs. Lydgate was, he was told that she was in her bedroom.

He went up and found her stretched on the bed, pale and silent, without an answer even in her face to any word or look of his. He sat down by the bed and, leaning over her, said, with almost a cry of prayer:

"Forgive me for this misery, my poor Rosamond! Let us only love one another."

She looked at him silently, still with the blank despair on her face; but then the tears began to fill her blue eyes, and her lip trembled. The strong man had had too much to bear that day. He let his head fall beside hers, and sobbed.

He did not hinder her from going to her father early in the morning—it seemed now that he ought not to hinder her from doing as she pleased. In half an hour she came back, and said that papa and mamma wished her to go and stay with them while things were in this miserable state. Papa said he could do nothing about the debt—if he paid this, there would be half a dozen more. She had better come back home again till Lydgate had got a comfortable home for her. "Do you object, Tertius?"

"Do as you like," said Lydgate. "But things are not coming to a crisis immediately. There is no hurry."

"I should not go till to-morrow," said Rosamond; "I shall want to pack my clothes."

"Oh, I would wait a little longer than to-morrow—there is no knowing what may happen," said Lydgate, with bitter irony. "I may get my neck broken, and that may make things easier to you."

It was Lydgate's misfortune, and Rosamond's, too, that his tenderness toward her, which was both an emotional prompting and a well-considered resolve, was inevitably interrupted by these outbursts of indignation, either ironical or remonstrant. She thought them totally unwarranted, and the repulsion which this exceptional severity excited in her was in danger of making the more persistent tenderness unacceptable.

"I see you do not wish me to go," she said, with chill mildness; "why can you not say so, without that kind of violence? I shall stay until you request me to do otherwise."

Lydgate said no more, but went out on his rounds. He felt bruised and shattered, and there was a dark line under his eyes which Rosamond had not seen before. She could not bear to look at him. Tertius had a way of taking things which made them a great deal worse for her.

----•----

CHAPTER LXX.

"Our deeds still travel with us from afar,
And what we have been makes us what we are."

BULSTRODE's first object after Lydgate had left Stone Court was to examine Raffles's pockets, which he imagined were sure to carry signs in the shape of hotel-bills of the places he had stopped in, if he had not told the truth in saying that he had come straight from Liverpool because he was ill and had no money. There were various bills crammed into his pocket-book, but none of a later date than Christmas at any other place, except one, which bore date that morning. This was crumpled up with a hand-bill about a horse-fair in one of his tail-pockets, and represented the cost of three days' stay at an inn at Bilkley, where the fair was held—a town at least forty miles from Middlemarch. The bill was heavy; and since Raffles had no luggage with him, it seemed probable that he had left his portmanteau behind in payment, in order to save money for his travelling fare; for his purse was empty, and he had only a couple of sixpences and some loose pence in his pockets.

Bulstrode gathered a sense of safety from these indications that Raffles had really kept at a distance from Middlemarch since his memorable visit at Christmas. At a distance, and among people who were strangers to Bulstrode, what satisfaction could there be to Raffles's tormenting, self-magnifying vein in telling old, scandalous stories about a Middlemarch banker? And what harm if he did talk? The chief point now was to keep watch over him as long as there was any danger of that intelligible raving, that unaccountable impulse to tell, which seemed to have acted toward Caleb Garth; and Bulstrode felt much anxiety lest some such impulse should

come over him at the sight of Lydgate. He sat up alone with
him through the night, only ordering the housekeeper to lie
down in her clothes, so as to be ready when he called her,
alleging his own indisposition to sleep, and his anxiety to carry
out the doctor's orders. He did carry them out faithfully,
although Raffles was incessantly asking for brandy, and declaring that he was sinking away—that the earth was sinking away from under him. He was restless and sleepless,
but still quailing and manageable. On the offer of the food
ordered by Lydgate, which he refused, and the denial of other
things which he demanded, he seemed to concentrate all his
terror on Bulstrode, imploringly deprecating his anger, his
revenge on him by starvation, and declaring with strong oaths
that he had never told any mortal a word against him. Even
this Bulstrode felt that he would not have liked Lydgate to
hear; but a more alarming sign of fitful alternation in his
delirium was, that in the morning twilight Raffles suddenly
seemed to imagine a doctor present addressing him, and declaring that Bulstrode wanted to starve him to death out of revenge for telling, when he never had told.

Bulstrode's native imperiousness and strength of determination served him well. This delicate-looking man, himself
nervously perturbed, found the needed stimulus in his strenu-
ous circumstances, and through that difficult night and morning, while he had the air of an animated corpse returned to
movement without warmth, holding the mastery by its chill
impassibility, his mind was intensely at work thinking of what
he had to guard against, and what would win him security.
Whatever prayers he might lift up, whatever statements he
might inwardly make of this man's wretched spiritual condition, and the duty he himself was under to submit to the punishment divinely appointed for him, rather than to wish for
evil to another—through all this effort to condense words into
a solid mental state, there pierced and spread with irresistible
vividness the images of the events he desired. And in the
train of those images came their apology. He could not but
see the death of Raffles, and see in it his own deliverance.
What was the removal of this wretched creature? He was
impenitent; but were not public criminals impenitent?—yet

the law decided on their fate. Should Providence in this case award death, there was no sin in contemplating death as the desirable issue—if he kept his hands from hastening it—if he scrupulously did what was prescribed. Even here there might be a mistake: human prescriptions were fallible things: Lydgate had said that treatment had hastened death—why not his own method of treatment? But, of course, intention was everything in the question of right and wrong.

And Bulstrode set himself to keep his intention separate from his desire. He inwardly declared that he intended to obey orders. Why should he have got into any argument about the validity of these orders? It was only the common trick of desire—which avails itself of any irrelevant skepticism, finding larger room for itself in all uncertainty about effects, in every obscurity that looks like the absence of law. Still, he did obey the orders.

His anxieties continually glanced toward Lydgate, and his remembrance of what had taken place between them the morning before was accompanied with sensibilities which had not been roused at all during the actual scene. He had then cared but little about Lydgate's painful impressions with regard to the suggested change in the hospital, or about the disposition toward himself which what he held to be his justifiable refusal of a rather exorbitant request might call forth. He recurred to the scene now with a perception that he had probably made Lydgate his enemy, and with an awakened desire to propitiate him, or rather to create in him a strong sense of personal obligation. He regretted that he had not at once made even an unreasonable money sacrifice. For in case of unpleasant suspicions, or even knowledge, gathered from the raving of Raffles, Bulstrode would have felt that he had a defence in Lydgate's mind by having conferred a momentous benefit on him. But the regret had, perhaps, come too late.

Strange, piteous conflict in the soul of this unhappy man, who had longed for years to be better than he was—who had taken his selfish passions into discipline and clad them in severe robes, so that he had walked with them as a devout choir, till now that a terror had risen among them, and they could chant no longer, but threw out their common cries for safety.

It was nearly the middle of the day before Lydgate arrived. He had meant to come earlier, but had been detained, he said; and his shattered looks were noticed by Bulstrode. But he immediately threw himself into the consideration of the patient, and inquired strictly into all that had occurred. Raffles was worse, would take hardly any food, was persistently wakeful and restlessly raving, but still not violent. Contrary to Bulstrode's alarmed expectation, he took little notice of Lydgate's presence, and continued to talk or murmur incoherently.

"What do you think of him?" said Bulstrode, in private.

"The symptoms are worse."

"You are less hopeful?"

"No; I still think he may come round. Are you going to stay here yourself?" said Lydgate, looking at Bulstrode with an abrupt question, which made him uneasy, though in reality it was not due to any suspicious conjecture.

"Yes, I think so," said Bulstrode, governing himself and speaking with deliberation. "Mrs. Bulstrode is advised of the reasons which detain me. Mrs. Abel and her husband are not experienced enough to be left quite alone, and this kind of responsibility is scarcely included in their service of me. You have some fresh instructions, I presume."

The chief new instruction that Lydgate had to give was on the administration of extremely moderate doses of opium, in case of the sleeplessness continuing after several hours. He had taken the precaution of bringing opium in his pocket, and he gave minute directions to Bulstrode as to the doses, and the point at which they should cease. He insisted on the risk of not ceasing; and repeated his order that no alcohol should be given.

"From what I see of the case," he ended, "narcotism is the only thing I should be much afraid of. He may wear through, even without much food. There's a good deal of strength in him."

"You look ill yourself, Mr. Lydgate—a most unusual, I may say unprecedented, thing in my knowledge of you," said

Bulstrode, showing a solicitude as unlike his indifference the day before as his present recklessness about his own fatigue was unlike his habitual self-cherishing anxiety. "I fear you are harassed."

"Yes, I am," said Lydgate, brusquely, holding his hat, and ready to go.

"Something new, I fear," said Bulstrode, inquiringly. "Pray be seated."

"No, thank you," said Lydgate, with some *hauteur*. "I mentioned to you yesterday what was the state of my affairs. There is nothing to add, except that the execution has since then been actually put into my house. One can tell a good deal of trouble in a short sentence. I will say good-morning."

"Stay, Mr. Lydgate, stay," said Bulstrode; "I have been reconsidering this subject. I was yesterday taken by surprise, and saw it superficially. Mrs. Bulstrode is anxious for her niece, and I myself should grieve at a calamitous change in your position. Claims on me are numerous, but, on reconsideration, I esteem it right that I should incur a small sacrifice rather than leave you unaided. You said, I think, that a thousand pounds would suffice entirely to free you from your burdens, and enable you to recover a firm stand?"

"Yes," said Lydgate, a great leap of joy within him surmounting every other feeling; "that would pay all my debts, and leave me a little on hand. I could set about economizing in our way of living. And by and by my practice might look up."

"If you will wait a moment, Mr. Lydgate, I will draw a check to that amount. I am aware that help, to be effectual in these cases, should be thorough."

While Bulstrode wrote, Lydgate turned to the window thinking of his home—thinking of his life with its good start saved from frustration, its good purposes still unbroken.

"You can give me a note of hand for this, Mr. Lydgate," said the banker, advancing toward him with the check. "And by and by, I hope, you may be in circumstances gradually to repay me. Meanwhile, I have pleasure in thinking that you will be released from further difficulty."

"I am deeply obliged to you," said Lydgate. "You have restored to me the prospect of working with some happiness and some chance of good."

It appeared to him a very natural movement in Bulstrode that he should have reconsidered his refusal: it corresponded with the more munificent side of his character. But as he put his hack into a canter, that he might get the sooner home and tell the good news to Rosamond, and get cash at the bank to pay over to Dover's agent, there crossed his mind, with an unpleasant impression, as from a dark-winged flight of evil augury across his vision, the thought of that contrast in himself which a few months had brought—that he should be overjoyed at being under a strong personal obligation—that he should be overjoyed at getting money for himself from Bulstrode.

The banker felt that he had done something to nullify one cause of uneasiness, and yet he was scarcely the easier. He did not measure the quantity of diseased motive which had made him wish for Lydgate's good-will, but the quantity was none the less actively there, like an irritating agent in his blood. A man vows, and yet will not cast away the means of breaking his vow. Is it that he distinctly means to break it? Not at all. But the desires which tend to break it are at work in him dimly, and make their way into his imagination, and relax his muscles in the very moments when he is telling himself over again the reasons for his vow. Raffles, recovering quickly, returning to the free use of his odious powers—how could Bulstrode wish for that? Raffles dead was the image that brought release, and indirectly he prayed for that way of release, beseeching that, if it were possible, the rest of his days here below might be freed from the threat of an ignominy which would break him utterly as an instrument of God's service. Lydgate's opinion was not on the side of promise that this prayer would be fulfilled; and as the day advanced, Bulstrode felt himself getting irritated at the persistent life in this man, whom he would fain have seen sinking into the silence of death; imperious will stirred murderous impulses toward this brute life, over which will, by itself, had no power. He said inwardly that he was getting too much worn; he

would not sit up with the patient to-night, but leave him to
Mrs. Abel, who, if necessary, could call her husband.

At six o'clock, Raffles having had only fitful, perturbed
snatches of sleep, from which he waked with fresh restlessness and perpetual cries that he was sinking away, Bulstrode
began to administer the opium according to Lydgate's directions. At the end of half an hour or more he called Mrs.
Abel, and told her that he found himself unfit for further
watching. He must now consign the patient to her care; and
he proceeded to repeat to her Lydgate's directions as to the
quantity of each dose. Mrs. Abel had not before known anything of Lydgate's prescriptions : she had simply prepared and
brought whatever Bulstrode ordered, and had done what he
pointed out to her. She began now to ask what else she
should do besides administering the opium.

"Nothing at present, except the offer of the soup or the
soda-water : you can come to me for further directions. Unless there is any important change, I shall not come into the
room again to-night. You will ask your husband for help, if
necessary. I must go to bed early."

"You've much need, sir, I'm sure," said Mrs. Abel, "and
to take something more strengthening than what you've done."

Bulstrode went away now without anxiety as to what Raffles
might say in his raving, which had taken on a muttering in-
coherence not likely to create any dangerous belief. At any
rate, he must risk this. He went down into the wainscoted
parlor first, and began to consider whether he would not
have his horse saddled and go home by the moonlight, and
give up caring for earthly consequences. Then, he wished
that he had begged Lydgate to come again that evening. Perhaps he might deliver a different opinion, and think that
Raffles was getting into a less hopeful state. Should he send
for Lydgate? If Raffles were really getting worse, and slowly
dying, Bulstrode felt that he could go to bed and sleep in
gratitude to Providence. But was he worse ? Lydgate might
come and simply say that he was going on as he expected, and
predict that he would by and by fall into a good sleep, and
get well. What was the use of sending for him? Bulstrode
shrank from that result. No ideas or opinions could hinder

him from seeing the one probability to be, that Raffles recovered would be just the same man as before, with his strength as a tormentor renewed, obliging him to drag away his wife to spend her years apart from her friends and native place, carrying an alienating suspicion against him in her heart.

He had sat an hour and a half in this conflict by the firelight only, when a sudden thought made him rise and light the bed-candle, which he had brought down with him. The thought was, that he had not told Mrs. Abel when the doses of opium must cease.

He took hold of the candlestick, but stood motionless for a long while. She might already have given him more than Lydgate had prescribed. But it was excusable in him, that he should forget part of an order, in his present wearied condition. He walked upstairs, candle in hand, not knowing whether he should straightway enter his own room and go to bed, or turn to the patient's room and rectify his omission. He paused in the passage, with his face turned toward Raffles's room, and he could hear him moaning and murmuring. He was not asleep, then. Who could know that Lydgate's prescription would not be better disobeyed than followed, since there was still no sleep?

He turned into his own room. Before he had quite undressed, Mrs. Abel rapped at the door; he opened it an inch, so that he could hear her speak low.

"If you please, sir, should I have no brandy nor nothing to give the poor creetur? He feels sinking away, and nothing else will he swaller—and but little strength in it, if he did—only the opium. And he says more and more he's sinking down through the earth."

To her surprise, Mr. Bulstrode did not answer. A struggle was going on within him.

"I think he must die for want o' support, if he goes on in that way. When I nursed my poor master, Mr. Robisson, I had to give him port-wine and brandy constant, and a big glass at a time," added Mrs. Abel, with a touch of remonstrance in her tone.

But again Mr. Bulstrode did not answer immediately, and she continued: "It's not a time to spare when people are at death's door, nor would you wish it, sir, I'm sure. Else I should give him our own bottle o' rum as we keep by us. But a sitter-up so as you've been, and doing everything as laid in your power——"

Here a key was thrust through the inch of doorway, and Mr. Bulstrode said, huskily: "That is the key of the wine-cooler. You will find plenty of brandy there."

Early in the morning—about six—Mr. Bulstrode rose and spent some time in prayer. Does any one suppose that private prayer is necessarily candid—necessarily goes to the roots of action? Private prayer is inaudible speech, and speech is representative; who can represent himself just as he is, even in his own reflections? Bulstrode had not yet unravelled in his thought the confused promptings of the last four-and-twenty hours.

He listened in the passage, and could hear hard stertorous breathing. Then he walked out in the garden, and looked at the early rime on the grass and fresh spring leaves. When he re-entered the house, he felt startled at the sight of Mrs. Abel.

"How is your patient—asleep, I think?" he said, with an attempt at cheerfulness in his tone.

"He's gone very deep, sir," said Mrs. Abel. "He went off gradual between three and four o'clock. Would you please to go and look at him? I thought it no harm to leave him. My man's gone afield, and the little girl's seeing to the kettles."

Bulstrode went up. At a glance he knew that Raffles was not in the sleep which brings revival, but in the sleep which streams deeper and deeper into the gulf of death.

He looked round the room and saw a bottle with some brandy in it, and the almost empty opium phial. He put the phial out of sight, and carried the brandy-bottle downstairs with him, locking it again in the wine-cooler.

While breakfasting, he considered whether he should ride to Middlemarch at once, or wait for Lydgate's arrival. He decided to wait, and told Mrs. Abel that she might go about her work—he could watch in the bed-chamber.

As he sat there and beheld the enemy of his peace going irrevocably into silence, he felt more at rest than he had done for many months. His conscience was soothed by the enfolding wing of secrecy, which seemed just then like an angel sent down for his relief. He drew out his pocket-book to review various memoranda there as to the arrangements he had projected, and partly carried out, in the prospect of quitting Middlemarch, and considered how far he would let them stand or recall them, now that his absence would be brief. Some economies which he felt desirable might still find a suitable occasion in his temporary withdrawal from management, and he hoped still that Mrs. Casaubon would take a large share in the expenses of the hospital. In that way the moments passed, until a change in the stertorous breathing was marked enough to draw his attention wholly to the bed, and forced him to think of the departing life, which had once been subservient to his own—which he had once been glad to find base enough for him to act on as he would. It was his gladness then which impelled him now to be glad that the life was at an end.

And who could say that the death of Raffles had been hastened? Who knew what would have saved him?

Lydgate arrived at half-past ten, in time to witness the final pause of the breath. When he entered the room, Bulstrode observed a sudden expression in his face, which was not so much surprise as a recognition that he had not judged correctly. He stood by the bed in silence for some time, with his eyes turned on the dying man, but with that subdued activity of expression which showed that he was carrying on an inward debate.

"When did this change begin?" said he, looking at Bulstrode.

"I did not watch by him last night," said Bulstrode. "I was over-worn, and left him under Mrs. Abel's care. She said that he sank into sleep between three and four o'clock. When I came in before eight he was nearly in this condition."

Lydgate did not ask another question, but watched in silence until he said: "It's all over."

This morning Lydgate was in a state of recovered hope and freedom. He had set out on his work with all his old animation, and felt himself strong enough to bear all the deficiencies of his married life. And he was conscious that Bulstrode had been a benefactor to him. But he was uneasy about this case. He had not expected it to terminate as it had done. Yet he hardly knew how to put a question on the subject to Bulstrode without appearing to insult him; and if he examined the housekeeper—why, the man was dead. There seemed to be no use in implying that somebody's ignorance or imprudence had killed him. And after all, he himself might be wrong.

He and Bulstrode rode back to Middlemarch together, talking of many things—chiefly cholera, and the chances of the Reform Bill in the House of Lords, and the firm resolve of the political Unions. Nothing was said about Raffles, except that Bulstrode mentioned the necessity of having a grave for him in Lowick churchyard, and observed that, so far as he knew, the poor man had no connections, except Rigg, whom he had stated to be unfriendly toward him.

On returning home, Lydgate had a visit from Mr. Farebrother. The vicar had not been in the town the day before, but the news that there was an execution in Lydgate's house had got to Lowick by the evening, having been carried by Mr. Spicer, shoemaker and parish-clerk, who had it from his brother, the respectable bell-hanger in Lowick Gate. Since that evening when Lydgate had come down from the billiard-room with Fred Vincy, Mr. Farebrother's thoughts about him had been rather gloomy. Playing at the Green Dragon once or oftener might have been a trifle in another man; but in Lydgate it was one of several signs that he was getting unlike his former self. He was beginning to do things for which he had formerly even an excessive scorn. Whatever certain dissatisfactions in marriage—which some silly tinklings of gossip had given him hints of—might have to do with this change, Mr. Farebrother felt sure that it was chiefly connected with the debts which were being more and more distinctly reported, and he began to fear that any notion of Lydgate's having resources or friends in the background must be quite illusory. The rebuff he had met with in his first attempt to win Lydgate's confidence disinclined him to a second; but this news of the execution being actually in the house, determined the vicar to overcome his reluctance.

Lydgate had just dismissed a poor patient, in whom he was much interested, and he came forward to put out his hand with an open cheerfulness which surprised Mr. Farebrother. Could this, too, be a proud rejection of sympathy and help? Never mind; the sympathy and help should be offered.

"How are you, Lydgate? I came to see you because I had heard something which made me anxious about you," said the vicar, in the tone of a good brother, only that there was no reproach in it. They were both seated by this time, and Lydgate answered immediately:

"I think I know what you mean. You had heard that there was an execution in the house?"

"Yes; is it true?"

"It was true," said Lydgate, with an air of freedom, as if he did not mind talking about the affair now. "But the danger is over; the debt is paid. I am out of my difficulties now: I shall be freed from debts, and able, I hope, to start afresh on a better plan."

"I am very thankful to hear it," said the vicar, falling back in his chair, and speaking with that low-toned quickness which often follows the removal of a load. "I like that better than all the news in the *Times*. I confess I came to you with a heavy heart."

"Thank you for coming," said Lydgate, cordially. "I can enjoy the kindness all the more because I am happier. I have certainly been a good deal crushed. I'm afraid I shall find the bruises still painful by and by," he added, smiling rather sadly; "but just now I can only feel that the torture-screw is off."

Mr. Farebrother was silent for a moment, and then said, earnestly, "My dear fellow, let me ask you one question. Forgive me if I take a liberty."

"I don't believe you will ask anything that ought to offend me."

"Then—this is necessary to set my heart quite at rest—you have not—have you?—in order to pay your debts, incurred another debt which may harass you worse hereafter?"

"No," said Lydgate, coloring slightly. "There is no reason why I should not tell you—since the fact is so—that the person to whom I am indebted is Bulstrode. He has made me a very handsome advance—a thousand pounds—and he can afford to wait for repayment."

" Well, that is generous," said Mr. Farebrother, compelling himself to approve of the man whom he disliked. His delicate feeling shrank from dwelling, even in his thought, on the fact that he had always urged Lydgate to avoid any personal entanglement with Bulstrode. He added immediately: " And Bulstrode must naturally feel an interest in your welfare, after you have worked with him in a way which has probably reduced your income instead of adding to it. I am glad to think that he has acted accordingly."

Lydgate felt uncomfortable under these kindly suppositions. They made more distinct within him the uneasy consciousness which had shown its first dim stirrings only a few hours before, that Bulstrode's motives for his sudden beneficence, following close upon the chillest indifference, might be merely selfish. He let the kindly suppositions pass. He could not tell the history of the loan, but it was more vividly present with him than ever, as well as the fact which the vicar delicately ignored—that this relation of personal indebtedness to Bulstrode was what he had once been most resolved to avoid.

He began, instead of answering, to speak of his projected economies, and of his having come to look at his life from a different point of view.

"I shall set up a surgery," he said. "I really think I made a mistaken effort in that respect. And if Rosamond will not mind, I shall take an apprentice. I don't like these things, but if one carries them out faithfully they are not really lowering. I have had a severe galling to begin with: that will make the small rubs seem easy."

Poor Lydgate! the "if Rosamond will not mind," which had fallen from him involuntarily as a part of his thought, was a significant mark of the yoke he bore. But Mr. Farebrother, whose hopes entered strongly into the same current with Lydgate's, and who knew nothing about him that could now raise a melancholy presentiment, left him with affectionate congratulation.

CHAPTER LXXI.

"*Clown.* * * * 'Twas in the Bunch of Grapes, where, indeed, you have a delight to sit, have you not?
"*Froth.* I have so; because it is an open room, and good for winter.
"*Clo.* Why, very well, then: I hope here be truths."

—*Measure for Measure.*

FIVE days after the death of Raffles, Mr. Bambridge was standing at his leisure under the large archway leading into the yard of the Green Dragon. He was not fond of solitary contemplation, but he had only just come out of the house, and any human figure standing at ease under the archway in the early afternoon was as certain to attract companionship as a pigeon which has found something worth pecking at. In this case there was no material object to feed upon, but the eye of reason saw a probability of mental sustenance in the shape of gossip. Mr. Hopkins, the meek-mannered draper opposite, was the first to act on this inward vision, being the more ambitious of a little masculine talk because his customers were chiefly women. Mr. Bambridge was rather curt to the draper, feeling that Hopkins was of course glad to talk to *him*, but that he was not going to waste much of his talk on Hopkins. Soon, however, there was a small cluster of more important listeners, who were either deposited from the passers-by, or had sauntered to the spot expressly to see if there were anything going on at the Green Dragon; and Mr. Bambridge was finding it worth his while to say many impressive things about the fine studs he had been seeing, and the purchases he had made, on a journey in the north from which he had just returned. Gentlemen present were assured that when they could show him anything to cut out a blood mare, a bay, rising four, which was to be seen at Doncaster if they chose to go and look at it, Mr. Bambridge would gratify them by being shot "from here to Hereford." Also, a pair of blacks which he was going to put into the break recalled vividly to his mind a pair which he had sold to Faulkner in '19, for a hundred guineas, and which Faulkner had sold for a hundred and sixty two months later—any gent who could disprove this

46

statement being offered the privilege of calling Mr. Bambridge by a very ugly name until the exercise made his throat dry.

When the discourse was at this point of animation, came up Mr. Frank Hawley. He was not a man to compromise his dignity by lounging at the Green Dragon, but happening to pass along the High Street and seeing Bambridge on the other side, he took some of his long strides across to ask the horse-dealer whether he had found the first-rate gig-horse which he had engaged to look for. Mr. Hawley was requested to wait until he had seen a gray selected at Bilkley: if that did not meet his wishes to a hair, Bambridge did not know a horse when he saw it, which seemed to be the highest conceivable unlikelihood. Mr. Hawley, standing with his back to the street, was fixing a time for looking at the gray and seeing it tried, when a horseman passed slowly by.

"Bulstrode!" said two or three voices at once in a low tone, one of them, which was the draper's, respectfully prefixing the "Mr."; but nobody having more intention in this inter-jectural naming than if they had said "the Riverston coach" when that vehicle appeared in the distance. Mr. Hawley gave a careless glance round at Bulstrode's back, but as Bam-bridge's eyes followed it he made a sarcastic grimace.

"By Jingo! that reminds me," he began, lowering his voice a little, "I picked up something else at Bilkley besides your gig-horse, Mr. Hawley. I picked up a fine story about Bul-strode. Do you know how he came by his fortune? Any gentleman wanting a bit of curious information, I can give it him free of expense. If everybody got their deserts, Bul-strode might have had to say his prayers at Botany Bay."

"What do you mean?" said Mr. Hawley, thrusting his hands into his pockets, and pushing a little forward under the archway. If Bulstrode should turn out to be a rascal, Frank Hawley had a prophetic soul.

"I had it from a party who was an old chum of Bulstrode's. I'll tell you where I first picked him up," said Bambridge, with a sudden gesture of his forefinger. "He was at Larcher's sale, but I knew nothing of him then—he slipped through my fingers—was after Bulstrode, no doubt. He tells me he can tap Bulstrode to any amount, knows all his secrets. However, he blabbed to me at Bilkley: he takes a stiff glass. Damme if I think he meant to turn king's evidence; but he's that sort of bragging fellow, the bragging runs over hedge and ditch with him, till he'd brag of a spavin as if it 'ud fetch money. A man should know when to pull up." Mr. Bambridge made this remark with an air of disgust, satisfied that his own bragging showed a fine sense of the marketable.

"What's the man's name? Where can he be found?" said Mr. Hawley.

"As to where he is to be found, I left him to it at the Saracen's Head; but his name is Raffles."

"Raffles!" exclaimed Mr. Hopkins. "I furnished his funeral yesterday. He was buried at Lowick. Mr. Bulstrode followed him. A very decent funeral."

There was a strong sensation among the listeners. Mr. Bambridge gave an ejaculation in which "brimstone" was the mildest word, and Mr. Hawley, knitting his brows and bending his head forward, exclaimed: "What?—where did the man die?"

"At Stone Court," said the draper. "The housekeeper said he was a relation of the master's. He came there ill on Friday."

"Why it was on Wednesday I took a glass with him," interposed Bambridge.

"Did any doctor attend him?" said Mr. Hawley.

"Yes, Mr. Lydgate. Mr. Bulstrode sat up with him one night. He died the third morning."

"Go on, Bambridge," said Mr. Hawley, insistently. "What did this fellow say about Bulstrode?"

The group had already become larger, the town clerk's presence being a guarantee that something worth listening to was going on there: and Mr. Bambridge delivered his narrative in the hearing of seven. It was mainly what we know, including the fact about Will Ladislaw, with some local color and circumstances added: it was what Bulstrode had dreaded the betrayal of—and hoped to have buried forever with the corpse of Raffles—it was that haunting ghost of his earlier life which, as he rode past the archway of the Green Dragon, he was trusting that Providence had delivered him from. Yes,

Providence.   He had not confessed to himself yet that he had
done anything in the way of contrivance to this end; he had
accepted what seemed to have been offered.   It was impossible to prove that he had done anything which hastened the
departure of that man's soul.

But this gossip about Bulstrode spread through Middlemarch
like the smell of fire.   Mr. Frank Hawley followed up his
information by sending a clerk whom he could trust to Stone
Court on a pretext of inquiring about hay, but really to gather
all that could be learned about Raffles and his illness from
Mrs. Abel.   In this way it came to his knowledge that Mr.
Garth had carried the man to Stone Court in his gig; and Mr.
Hawley, in consequence, took an opportunity of seeing Caleb,
calling at his office to ask whether he had time to undertake
an arbitration if it were required, and then asking him incidentally about Raffles.   Caleb was betrayed into no word
injurious to Bulstrode beyond the fact that he was forced to
admit that he had given up acting for him within the last week.
Mr. Hawley drew his inferences, and feeling convinced that
Raffles had told his story to Garth, and that Garth had given
up Bulstrode's affairs in consequence, said so a few hours later
to Mr. Toller.   The statement was passed on until it had
quite lost the stamp of an inference, and was taken as information coming straight from Garth, so that even a diligent
historian might have concluded Caleb to be the chief publisher
of Bulstrode's misdemeanors.

Mr. Hawley was not slow to perceive that there was no
handle for the law either in the revelations made by Raffles or
in the circumstances of his death.   He had himself ridden to
Lowick village that he might look at the register and talk over
the matter with Mr. Farebrother, who was not more surprised
than the lawyer that an ugly secret should have come to light
about Bulstrode, though he had always had justice enough in
him to hinder his antipathy from turning into conclusions.
But, while they were talking, another combination was silently
going forward in Mr. Farebrother's mind, which foreshadowed
what was soon to be loudly spoken of in Middlemarch as a
necessary "putting of two and two together."   With the
reasons which kept Bulstrode in dread of Raffles there flashed

the thought that the dread might have something to do with his munificence toward his medical man: and though he resisted the suggestion that it had been consciously accepted in any way as a bribe, he had a foreboding that this complication of things might be of malignant effect on Lydgate's reputation. He perceived that Mr. Hawley knew nothing at present of the sudden relief from debt, and he himself was careful to glide away from all approaches toward the subject.

"Well," he said, with a deep breath, wanting to wind up the illimitable discussion of what might have been, though nothing could be legally proven, "it is a strange story. So our mercurial Ladislaw has a queer genealogy! A high-spirited young lady and a musical Polish patriot make a likely enough stock for him to spring from, but I should never have suspected a grafting of the Jew pawnbroker. However, there's no knowing what a mixture will turn out beforehand. Some sorts of dirt serve to clarify." '

"It's just what I should have expected," said Mr. Hawley, mounting his horse. "Any cursed alien blood, Jew, Corsican, or Gypsy."

"I know he's one of your black sheep, Hawley. But he is really a disinterested, unworldly fellow," said Mr. Farebrother, smiling.

"Ay, ay, that is your Whiggish twist," said Mr. Hawley, who had been in the habit of saying apologetically that Farebrother was such a d——d pleasant good-hearted fellow you would mistake him for a Tory.

Mr. Hawley rode home without thinking of Lydgate's attendance on Raffles in any other light than as a piece of evidence on the side of Bulstrode. But the news that Lydgate had all at once become able not only to get rid of the execution in his house, but to pay all his debts in Middlemarch, was spreading fast, gathering round it conjectures and comments which gave it new body and impetus, and soon filling the ears of other people besides Mr. Hawley, who were not slow to see a significant relation between this sudden command of money and Bulstrode's desire to stifle the scandal of Raffles. That the money came from Bulstrode would infallibly have been guessed, even if there had been no direct evidence of it; for it

had beforehand entered into the gossip about Lydgate's affairs,
that neither his father-in-law nor his own family would do
anything for him, and direct evidence was furnished not only
by a clerk at the bank, but by innocent Mrs. Bulstrode herself, who mentioned the loan to Mrs. Plymdale, who mentioned it to her daughter-in-law of the house of Toller, who
mentioned it generally.   The business was felt to be so public
and important that it required dinners to feed it, and many
invitations were just then issued and accepted on the strength
of this scandal concerning Bulstrode and Lydgate; wives,
widows, and single ladies took their work and went out to tea
oftener than usual; and all public conviviality, from the Green
Dragon to Dollop's, gathered a zest which could not be won
from the question whether the Lords would throw out the
Reform Bill.

For hardly anybody doubted that some scandalous reason or
other was at the bottom of Bulstrode's liberality to Lydgate.
Mr. Hawley indeed, in the first instance, invited a select
party, including the two physicians, with Mr. Toller and Mr.
Wrench, expressly to hold a close discussion as to the probabilities of Raffles' illness, reciting to them all the particulars
which had been gathered from Mrs. Abel in connection with
Lydgate's certificate, that the death was due to *delirium tre-
mens;* and the medical gentlemen, who all stood undisturbedly
on the old paths in relation to this disease, declared that they
could see nothing in these particulars which could be trans-
formed into a positive ground of suspicion.   But the moral
grounds of suspicion remained: the strong motives Bulstrode
clearly had for wishing to be rid of Raffles, and the fact that
at this critical moment he had given Lydgate the help which
he must for some time have known the need for; the disposition, moreover, to believe that Bulstrode would be unscrupu-
lous, and the absence of any indisposition to believe that
Lydgate might be as easily bribed as other haughty-minded
men when they have found themselves in want of money.
Even if the money had been given merely to make him hold
his tongue about the scandal of Bulstrode's earlier life, the
fact threw an odious light on Lydgate, who had long been
sneered at as making himself subservient to the banker for the

sake of working himself into predominance, and discrediting
the elder members of his profession.   Hence, in spite of the
negative as to any direct sign of guilt in relation to the death
at Stone Court, Mr. Hawley's select party broke up with the
sense that the affair had "an ugly look."

But this vague conviction of indeterminable guilt, which
was enough to keep up much head-shaking and biting innuendo
even among substantial professional seniors, had for the general mind all the superior power of mystery over fact.
Everybody liked better to conjecture how the thing was, than
simply to know it; for conjecture soon became more confident
than knowledge, and had a more liberal allowance for the
incompatible.   Even the more definite scandal concerning Bulstrode's earlier life was, for some minds, melted into the mass
of mystery, as so much lively metal to be poured out in dialogue, and to take such fantastic shapes as heaven pleased.

This was the tone of thought chiefly sanctioned by Mrs.
Dollop, the spirited landlady of the Tankard in Slaughter
Lane, who had often to resist the shallow pragmatism of customers disposed to think that their reports from the outer
world were of equal force with what had "come up" in her
mind.   How it had been brought to her she didn't know, but
it was there before her as if it had been scored with the chalk
on the chimney-board—"as Bulstrode should say, his inside
was *that black* as if the hairs of his head knowed the thoughts
of his heart, he'd tear 'em up by the roots."

"That's odd," said Mr. Limp, a meditative shoemaker,
with weak eyes and a piping voice.   "Why, I read in the
Trumpet that was what the Duke of Wellington said when he
turned his coat and went over to the Romans."

"Very like," said Mrs. Dollop.   "If one raskill said it, it's
more reason why another should.   But hypo*crite* as he's been,
and holding things with that high hand, as there was no parson
i' the country good enough for him, he was forced to take Old
Harry into his counsel, and Old Harry's been too many for
him."

"Ay, ay, he's a 'complice you can't send out o' the country," said Mr. Crabbe, the glazier, who gathered much news
and groped among it dimly.   "But by what I can make out,

there's them says Bulstrode was for running away, for fear o' being found out before now."

"He'll be drove away, whether or no," said Mr. Dill, the barber, who had just dropped in. "I shaved Fletcher, Hawley's clerk. this morning—he's got a bad finger—and he says they're all of one mind to get rid of Bulstrode. Mr. Thesiger is turned against him, and wants him out o' the parish. And there's gentlemen in this town says they'd as soon dine with a fellow from the hulks. 'And a deal sooner I would,' says Fletcher; 'for what's more against one's stomach than a man coming and making himself bad company with his religion, and giving out as the Ten Commandments are not enough for him, and all the while he's worse than half the men at the tread-mill?' Fletcher said so himself."

"It'll be a bad thing for the town, though, if Bulstrode's money goes out of it," said Mr. Limp, quaveringly.

"Ah, there's better folks spend their money worse," said a firm-voiced dyer, whose crimson hands looked out of keeping with his good-natured face.

"But he won't keep his money, by what I can make out," said the glazier. "Don't they say as there's somebody can strip it off him? By what I can understan', they could take every penny off him, if they went to lawing."

"No such thing!" said the barber, who felt himself a little above his company at Dollop's, but liked it none the worse. "Fletcher says it's no such thing. He says they might prove over and over again whose child this young Ladislaw was, and they'd do no more than if they proved I came out of the Fens —he couldn't touch a penny."

"Look you there now!" said Mrs. Dollop, indignantly. "I thank the Lord he took my children to Himself, if that's all the law can do for the motherless. Then by that, it's o' no use who your father and mother is. But as to listening to what one lawyer says without asking another—I wonder at a man o' your cleverness, Mr. Dill. It's well known there's always two sides, if no more; else who'd go to law, I should like to know? It's a poor tale with all the law as there is up and down, if it's no use proving whose child you are. Fletcher may say that if he likes, but I say, don't Fletcher *me !*"

Mr. Dill affected to laugh in a complimentary way at Mrs. Dollop, as a woman who was more than a match for the lawyers; being disposed to submit to much twitting from a landlady who had a long score against him.

"If they come to lawing, and it's all true as folks say, there's more to be looked for nor money," said the glazier. "There's this poor creeter as is dead and gone: by what I can make out, he'd seen the day when he was a deal finer gentleman nor Bulstrode."

"Finer gentleman! I'll warrant him," said Mrs. Dollop; "and a far personabler man, by what I can hear. As I said when Mr. Baldwin, the tax-gatherer, comes in, a-standing where you sit, and says, ' Bulstrode got all his money as he brought into this town by thieving and swindling,'—I said: ' You don't make me no wiser, Mr. Baldwin: it's set my blood a-creeping to look at him ever sin' here he came into Slaughter Lane a-wanting to buy the house over my head: folks don't look the color o' the dough-tub and stare at you as if they wanted to see into your backbone for nothingk.' That was what I said, and Mr. Baldwin can bear me witness."

"And in the rights of it, too," said Mr. Crabbe. "For by what I can make out, this Raffles, as they call him, was a lusty, fresh-colored man as you'd wish to see, and the best o' company—though dead he lies in Lowick church-yard sure enough; and by what I can understan', there's them knows more than they *should* know about how he got there."

"I'll believe you!" said Mrs. Dollop with a touch of scorn at Mr. Crabbe's apparent dimness. "When a man's been 'ticed to a lone house, and there's them can pay for hospitals and nurses for half the country-side choose to be sitters-up night and day, and nobody to come near but a doctor as is known to stick at nothingk, and as poor as he can hang together, and after that so flush o' money as he can pay off Mr. Byles the butcher as his bill has been running on for the best o' joints since last Michaelmas was a twelvemonth—I don't want anybody to come and tell me as there's been more going on nor the Prayer-book's got a service for—I don't want to stand winking and blinking and thinking."

Mrs. Dollop looked round with the air of a landlady accustomed to dominate her company. There was a chorus of adhesion from the more courageous; but Mr. Limp, after taking a draught, placed his flat hands together and pressed them hard between his knees, looking down at them with blear-eyed contemplation, as if the scorching power of Mrs. Dollop's speech had quite dried up and nullified his wits until they could be brought round again by further moisture.

"Why shouldn't they dig the man up and have the Crowner?" said the dyer. "It's been done many an' many's the time. If there's been foul play, they might find it out."

"Not they, Mr. Jonas!" said Mrs. Dollop, emphatically. "I know what doctors are. They're a deal too cunning to be found out. And this Doctor Lydgate that's been for cutting up everybody before the breath was well out o' their body—it's plain enough what use he wanted to make o' looking into respectable people's insides. He knows drugs, you may be sure, as you can neither smell nor see, neither before they're swallowed nor after. Why, I've seen drops myself ordered by Doctor Gambit, as is our club doctor and a good charikter, and has brought more live children into the world nor ever another i' Middlemarch—I say I've seen drops myself made no difference whether they was in the glass or out, and yet have griped you the next day. So I'll leave your own sense to judge. Don't tell me! All I say is, it's a mercy they didn't take this Doctor Lydgate on to our club. There's many a mother's child might ha' rued it."

The heads of this discussion at "Dollop's" had been the common theme among all classes in the town, had been carried to Lowick Parsonage on one side and to Tipton Grange on the other, and come fully to the ears of the Vincy family, and had been discussed with sad reference to "poor Harriet" by all Mrs. Bulstrode's friends, before Lydgate knew distinctly why people were looking strangely at him, and before Bulstrode himself suspected the betrayal of his secrets. He had not been accustomed to very cordial relations with his neighbors, and hence he could not miss the signs of cordiality; moreover, he had been taking journeys on business of various kinds, having now made up his mind that he need not quit

Middlemarch, and feeling able consequently to determine on matters which he had before left in suspense.

"We will make a journey to Cheltenham in the course of a month or two," he had said to his wife. "There are great spiritual advantages to be had in that town along with the air and the waters, and six weeks there will be eminently refreshing to us."

He really believed in the spiritual advantages, and meant that his life henceforth should be more devoted because of those later sins which he represented to himself as hypothetic, praying hypothetically for their pardon—"if I have herein transgressed."

As to the hospital, he avoided saying anything further to Lydgate, fearing to manifest a too sudden change of plans immediately on the death of Raffles. In his secret soul he believed that Lydgate suspected his orders to have been intentionally disobeyed, and suspecting this, he must also suspect a motive. But nothing had been betrayed to him as to the history of Raffles, and Bulstrode was anxious not to do anything which should give emphasis to his undefined suspicions. As to any certainty that a particular method of treatment would either save or kill, Lydgate himself was constantly arguing against such dogmatism; he had no right to speak, and he had every motive for being silent. Hence Bulstrode felt himself providentially secured. The only incident he had strongly winced under had been an occasional encounter with Caleb Garth, who, however, had raised his hat with mild gravity.

Meanwhile, on the part of the principal townsmen a strong determination was growing against him.

A meeting was to be held in the Town Hall on a sanitary question which had risen into pressing importance by the occurrence of a cholera case in the town. Since the act of Parliament, which had been hurriedly passed, authorizing assessments for sanitary measures, there had been a Board for the superintendence of such measures appointed in Middlemarch, and much cleansing and preparation had been concurred in by Whigs and Tories. The question now was, whether a piece of ground outside the town should be secured as a burial-ground by means of assessment or by private subscription.

The meeting was to be open, and almost everybody of impor
tance in the town was expected to be there.

Mr. Bulstrode was a member of the Board, and just before
twelve o'clock he started from the bank with the intention of
urging the plan of private subscription. Under the hesitation
of his projects, he had for some time kept himself in the
background, and he felt that he should this morning resume
his old position as a man of action and influence in the public
affairs of the town where he expected to end his days. Among
the various persons going in the same direction, he saw Lydgate: they joined, talked over the object of the meeting, and
entered it together.

It seemed that everybody of mark had been earlier than
they. But there were still spaces left near the head of the
large central table, and they made their way thither. Mr.
Farebrother sat opposite, not far from Mr. Hawley; all the
medical men were there; Mr. Thesiger was in the chair, and
Mr. Brooke of Tipton was on his right hand.

Lydgate noticed a peculiar interchange of glances when he
and Bulstrode took their seats.

After the business had been fully opened by the chairman,
who pointed out the advantages of purchasing by subscription
a piece of ground large enough to be ultimately used as a general cemetery, Mr. Bulstrode, whose rather high-pitched but
subdued and fluent voice the town was used to at meetings of
this sort, rose and asked leave to deliver his opinion. Lydgate could see again the peculiar interchange of glances before
Mr. Hawley started up, and said in his firm, resonant voice:
"Mr. Chairman, I request that before any one delivers his
opinion on this point I may be permitted to speak on a question of public feeling, which, not only by myself, but by many
gentlemen present, is regarded as preliminary."

Mr. Hawley's mode of speech, even when public decorum
repressed his "awful language," was formidable in its curt-
ness and self-possession. Mr. Thesiger sanctioned the request,
Mr. Bulstrode sat down, and Mr. Hawley continued.

"In what I have to say, Mr. Chairman, I am not speaking
simply on my own behalf: I am speaking with the concurrence
and at the express request of no fewer than eight of my fel-

low-townsmen, who are immediately around us. It is our
united sentiment that Mr. Bulstrode should be called upon—
and I do now call upon him—to resign public positions which
he holds, not simply as a tax-payer, but as a gentleman
among gentlemen. There are practices and there are arts
which, owing to circumstances, the law cannot visit, though
they may be worse than many things which are legally punish-
able. Honest men and gentlemen, if they don't want the
company of people who perpetrate such acts, have got to defend themselves as they best can, and that is what I and the
friends whom I may call my clients in this affair are determined to do. I don't say that Mr. Bulstrode has been guilty
of shameful acts, but I call upon him either publicly to deny
and confute the scandalous statements made against him by a
man now dead, and who died in his house,—the statement
that he was for many years engaged in nefarious practices,
and that he won his fortune by dishonest procedures—or else
to withdraw from positions which could only have been allowed
him as a gentleman among gentlemen."

All eyes in the room were turned on Mr. Bulstrode, who,
since the first mention of his name, had been going through a
crisis of feeling almost too violent for his delicate ‘frame to
support. Lydgate, who himself was undergoing a shock, as
from the terrible practical interpretation of some faint augury,
felt, nevertheless, that his own movement of resentful hatred
was checked by that instinct of the Healer which thinks first
of bringing rescue or relief to the sufferer, when he looked at
the shrunken misery of Bulstrode's livid face.

The quick vision that his life was after all a failure, that
he was a dishonored man, and must quail before the glance of
those toward whom he had habitually assumed the attitude
of a reprover—that God had disowned him before men, and left
him unscreened to the triumphant scorn of those who were
glad to have their hatred justified—the sense of utter futility
in that equivocation with his conscience in dealing with the
life of his accomplice, an equivocation which now turned
venomously upon him with the full-grown fang of a discovered
lie:—all this rushed through him like the agony of terror
which fails to kill, and leaves the ears still open to the return·

ing wave of execration. The sudden sense of exposure, after the re-established sense of safety, came not to the coarse organization of a criminal, but to the susceptible nerve of a man whose intensest being lay in such mastery and predominance as the conditions of his life had shaped for him.

But in that intense being lay the strength of reaction. Through all his bodily infirmity there ran a tenacious nerve of ambitious self-preserving will, which had continually leaped out like a flame, scattering all doctrinal fears, and which, even while he sat an object of compassion for the merciful, was beginning to stir and glow under his ashy paleness. Before the last words were out of Mr. Hawley's mouth, Bulstrode felt that he should answer, and that his answer would be a retort. He dared not get up and say, "I am not guilty; the whole story is false "—even if he had dared this, it would have seemed to him, under his present keen sense of betrayal, as vain as to pull, for covering to his nakedness, a frail rag which would rend at every little strain.

For a few moments there was total silence, while every man in the room was looking at Bulstrode. He sat perfectly still, leaning hard against the back of his chair; he could not venture to rise, and when he began to speak he pressed his hands upon the seat on each side of him. But his voice was perfectly audible, though hoarser than usual, and his words were distinctly pronounced, though he paused between each sentence as if short of breath. He said, turning first toward Mr. Thesiger and then looking at Mr. Hawley:

"I protest before you, sir, as a Christian minister, against the sanction of proceedings toward me which are dictated by virulent hatred. Those who are hostile to me are glad to believe any libel uttered by a loose tongue against me. And their consciences become strict against me. Say that the evil-speaking of which I am to be made the victim accuses me of malpractices "—here Bulstrode's voice rose and took on a more biting accent, till it seemed a low cry—" who shall be my accuser? Not men whose lives are unchristian, nay, scandalous—not men who themselves use low instruments to carry out their ends—whose profession is a tissue of chicanery—who have been spending their income on their own sensual enjoyments, while I have been devoting mine to advance the best objects with regard to this life and the next."

After the word chicanery there was a growing noise, half of murmurs and half of hisses, while four persons started up at once—Mr. Hawley, Mr. Toller, Mr. Chichely, and Mr. Hackbutt; but Mr. Hawley's outburst was instantaneous, and left the others behind in silence.

"If you mean me, sir, I call you and every one else to the inspection of my professional life. As to Christian or unchristian, I repudiate your canting, palavering Christianity; and as to the way in which I spend my income, it is not my principle to maintain thieves and cheat offspring of their due inheritance in order to support religion and set myself up as a saintly Kill-joy. I affect no niceness of conscience—I have not found any nice standards necessary yet to measure your actions by, sir. And I again call upon you to enter into satisfactory explanations concerning the scandals against you, or else to withdraw from posts in which we at any rate decline you as a colleague. I say, sir, we decline to coöperate with a man whose character is not cleared from infamous lights cast upon it, not only by reports, but by recent actions."

"Allow me, Mr. Hawley," said the chairman; and Mr. Hawley, still fuming, bowed half impatiently, and sat down with his hands thrust deep in his pockets.

"Mr. Bulstrode, it is not desirable, I think, to prolong the present discussion," said Mr. Thesiger, turning to the pallid, trembling man; "I must so far concur with what has fallen from Mr. Hawley in expression of a general feeling, as to think it due to your Christian profession that you should clear yourself, if possible, from unhappy aspersions. I for my part should be willing to give you full opportunity and hearing. But I must say that your present attitude is painfully inconsistent with those principles which you have sought to identify yourself with, and for the honor of which I am bound to care. I recommend you at present, as your clergyman, and one who hopes for your reinstatement in respect, to quit the room, and avoid futher hindrance to business."

Bulstrode, after a moment's hesitation, took his hat from the floor and slowly rose, but he grasped the corner of the

chair so totteringly that Lydgate felt sure there was not
strength enough in him to walk away without support.   What
could he do?   He could not see a man sink close to him for
want of help.   He rose and gave his arm to Bulstrode, and in
that way led him out of the room; yet this act, which might
have been one of gentle duty and pure compassion, was at this
moment unspeakably bitter to him.   It seemed as if he were
putting his sign-manual to that association of himself with
Bulstrode, of which he now saw the full meaning as it must
have presented itself to other minds.   He now felt the conviction that this man who was leaning tremblingly on his arm,
had given him the thousand pounds as a bribe, and that somehow the treatment of Raffles had been tampered with from an
evil motive.   The inferences were closely linked enough ; the
town knew of the loan, believed it to be a bribe, and believed
that he took it as a bribe.

Poor Lydgate, his mind struggling under the terrible clutch
of this revelation, was all the while morally forced to take
Mr. Bulstrode to the bank, send a man off for his carriage, and
wait to accompany him home.

Meanwhile the business of the meeting was dispatched, and
fringed off into eager discussion among various groups concerning this affair of Bulstrode—and Lydgate.

Mr. Brooke, who had before heard only imperfect hints of
it, and was very uneasy that he had "gone a little too far " in
countenancing Bulstrode, now got himself fully informed, and
felt some benevolent sadness in talking to Mr. Farebrother
about the ugly light in which Lydgate had come to be regarded.
Mr. Farebrother was going to walk back to Lowick.

"Step into my carriage," said Mr. Brooke.   "I am going
round to see Mrs. Casaubon.   She was to come back from
Yorkshire last night.   She will like to see me, you know."

So they drove along, Mr. Brooke chatting with good-natured
hope that there had not really been anything black in Lydgate's behavior—a young fellow whom he had seen to be quite
above the common mark, when he brought a letter from his
uncle, Sir Godwin.   Mr. Farebrother said little: he was
deeply mournful : with a keen perception of human weakness.
he could not be confident that under the pressure of humiliating
needs Lydgate had not fallen below himself.

When the carriage drove up to the gate of the manor, Dorothea was out on the gravel, and came to greet them.

"Well, my dear," said Mr. Brooke, "we have just come from a meeting—a sanitary meeting, you know."

"Was Mr. Lydgate there?" said Dorothea, who looked full of health and animation, and stood with her head bare under the gleaming April lights. "I want to see him and have a great consultation with him about the hospital. I have engaged with Mr. Bulstrode to do so."

"Oh, my dear," said Mr. Brooke, "we have been hearing bad news—bad news, you know."

They walked through the garden toward the churchyard gate, Mr. Farebrother wanting to go on to the parsonage; and Dorothea heard the whole sad story.

She listened with deep interest, and begged to hear twice over the facts and impressions concerning Lydgate. After a short silence, pausing at the churchyard gate, and addressing Mr. Farebrother, she said energetically:

"You don't believe that Mr. Lydgate is guilty of anything base? I will not believe it. Let us find out the truth and clear him!"

47

BOOK VIII.—SUNSET AND SUNRISE.

CHAPTER LXXII.

"Full souls are double mirrors, making still
An endless vista of fair things before
Repeating things behind."

DOROTHEA'S impetuous generosity, which would have leaped at once to the vindication of Lydgate from the suspicion of having accepted money as a bribe, underwent a melancholy check when she came to consider all the circumstances of the case by the light of Mr. Farebrother's experience.

"It is a delicate matter to touch," he said. "How can we begin to inquire into it? It must be either publicly by setting the magistrate and coroner to work, or privately by questioning Lydgate. As to the first proceeding, there is no solid ground to go upon, else Hawley would have adopted it; and as to opening the subject with Lydgate, I confess I should shrink from it. He would probably take it as a deadly insult. I have more than once experienced the difficulty of speaking to him on personal matters. And one should know the truth about his conduct beforehand, to feel very confident of a good result."

"I feel convinced that his conduct has not been guilty: I believe that people are almost always better than their neighbors think they are," said Dorothea. Some of her intensest experience in the last two years had set her mind strongly in opposition to any unfavorable construction of others; and for the first time she felt rather discontented with Mr. Farebrother. She disliked this cautious weighing of consequences, instead of an ardent faith in efforts of justice and mercy, which would conquer by their emotional force. Two days afterward, he was dining at the manor with her uncle and the Chettams, and when the dessert was standing uneaten, the servants were out of the room, and Mr. Brooke was nodding in a nap, she returned to the subject with renewed vivacity.

"Mr. Lydgate would understand that if his friends hear a calumny about him their first wish must be to justify him. What do we live for, if it is not to make life less difficult to each other? I cannot be indifferent to the troubles of a man who advised me in *my* trouble, and attended me in my illness."

Dorothea's tone and manner were not more energetic than they had been when she was at the head of her uncle's table nearly three years before, and her experience since had given her more right to express a decided opinion. But Sir James Chettam was no longer the diffident and acquiescent suitor: he was the anxious brother-in-law, with a devout admiration for his sister, but with a constant alarm lest she should fall under some new illusion almost as bad as marrying Casaubon. He smiled much less; when he said "Exactly," it was more often an introduction to a dissentient opinion than in those submissive bachelor days; and Dorothea found to her surprise that she had to resolve not to be afraid of him—all the more because he was really her best friend. He disagreed with her now.

"But, Dorothea," he said, remonstrantly, "you can't undertake to manage a man's life for him in that way. Lydgate must know—at least he will soon come to know—how he stands. If he can clear himself, he will. He must act for himself."

"I think his friends must wait till they find an opportunity," added Mr. Farebrother. "It is possible—I have often felt so much weakness in myself that I can conceive even a man of honorable disposition, such as I have always believed Lydgate to be, succumbing to such a temptation as that of accepting money which was offered more or less indirectly as a bribe to insure his silence about scandalous facts long gone by. I say, I can conceive this, if he were under the pressure of hard circumstances—if he had been harassed as I feel sure Lydgate has been. I would not believe anything worse of him except under stringent proof. But there is the terrible Nemesis following on some errors, that it is always possible for those who like it to interpret them into a crime: there is no proof in favor of the man outside his own consciousness and assertion."

"Oh, how cruel!" said Dorothea, clasping her hands. "And would you not like to be the one person who believed in that man's innocence, if the rest of the world belied him? Besides, there is a man's character beforehand to speak for him."

"But, my dear Mrs. Casaubon," said Mr. Farebrother, smiling gently at her ardor, "character is not cut in marble—it is not something solid and unalterable. It is something living and changing, and may become diseased as our bodies do."

"Then it may be rescued and healed," said Dorothea. "I should not be afraid of asking Mr. Lydgate to tell me the truth, that I might help him. Why should I be afraid? Now that I am not to have the land, James, I might do as Mr. Bulstrode proposed, and take his place in providing for the hospital; and I have to consult Mr. Lydgate, to know thoroughly what are the prospects of doing good by keeping up the present plans. There is the best opportunity in the world for me to ask for his confidence; and he would be able to tell me things which might make all the circumstances clear. Then we would all stand by him and bring him out of his trouble. People glorify all sorts of bravery except the bravery they might show on behalf of their nearest neighbors." Dorothea's eyes had a moist brightness in them, and the changed tones of her voice roused her uncle, who began to listen.

"It is true that a woman may venture on some efforts of sympathy which would hardly succeed if we men undertook them," said Mr. Farebrother, almost converted by Dorothea's ardor.

"Surely, a woman is bound to be cautious and listen to those who know the world better than she does," said Sir James, with his little frown. "Whatever you do in the end, Dorothea, you should really keep back at present, and not volunteer any meddling with this Bulstrode business. We don't know yet what may turn up. You must agree with me?" he ended, looking at Mr. Farebrother.

"I do think it would be better to wait," said the latter.

"Yes, yes, my dear," said Mr. Brooke, not quite knowing

at what point the discussion had arrived, but coming up to it
with a contribution which was generally appropriate. "It is
easy to go too far, you know. You must not let your ideas
run away with you. And as to being in a hurry to put money
into schemes—it won't do, you know. Garth has drawn me
in uncommonly with repairs, draining, that sort of thing: I'm
uncommonly out of pocket with one thing or another. I must
pull up. As for you, Chettam, you are spending a fortune on
those oak fences round your demesne."

Dorothea, submitting uneasily to this discouragement, went
with Celia into the library, which was her usual drawing-room.

"Now, Dodo, do listen to what James says," said Celia, "else
you will be getting into a scrape. You always did, and you
always will, when you set about doing as you please. And I
think it is a mercy now after all that you have got James to
think for you. He lets you have your plans, only he hinders
you from being taken in. And that is the good of having a
brother instead of a husband. A husband would not let you
have your plans."

"As if I wanted a husband!" said Dorothea. "I only want
not to have my feelings checked at every turn." Mrs. Casaubon was still undisciplined enough to burst into angry tears.

"Now, really, Dodo," said Celia, with rather a deeper guttural than usual, "you *are* contradictory: first one thing and
then another. You used to submit to Mr. Casaubon quite
shamefully: I think you would have given up ever coming to
see me if he had asked you."

"Of course I submitted to him, because it was my duty; it
was my feeling for him," said Dorothea, looking through the
prism of her tears.

"Then why can't you think it is your duty to submit a little to what James wishes?" said Celia, with a sense of strin-
gency in her argument. "Because he only wishes what is for
your own good, and, of course, men know best about everything, except what women know better."

Dorothea laughed and forgot her tears.

"Well, I mean about babies and those things," explained
Celia. "I should not give up to James when I knew he was
wrong, as you used to do to Mr. Casaubon."

CHAPTER LXXIII.

" Pity the laden one ; this wandering woe
May visit you and me."

WHEN Lydgate had allayed Mrs. Bulstrode's anxiety by telling her that her husband had been seized with faintness at the
meeting, but that he trusted soon to see him better, and would
call again the next day, unless she sent for him earlier, he
went directly home, got on his horse, and rode three miles out
of the town for the sake of being out of reach.

He felt himself becoming violent and unreasonable as if rag-
ing under the pain of stings. He was ready to curse the day
on which he had come to Middlemarch. Everything that had
happened to him there seemed a mere preparation for this
hateful fatality, which had come as a blight on his honorable
ambition, and must make even people who had only vulgar
standards regard his reputation as irrevocably damaged. In
such moments a man can hardly escape being unloving. Lydgate thought of himself as being the sufferer, and of others as
the agents who had injured his lot. He had meant everything
to turn out differently, and others had thrust themselves into
his life and thwarted his purposes. His marriage seemed an
unmitigated calamity; and he was afraid of going to Rosamond
before he had vented himself in this solitary rage, lest the
mere sight of her should exasperate him and make him behave
unwarrantably. There are episodes in most men's lives in
which their highest qualities can only cast a deterring shadow
over the objects that fill their inward vision. Lydgate's ten-
der-heartedness was present just then only as a dread lest he
should offend against it, not as an emotion that swayed him
to tenderness; for he was very miserable. Only those who
know the supremacy of the intellectual life—the life which
has a seed of ennobling thought and purpose within it—can understand the grief of one who falls from that serene activity in
the absorbing, soul-wasting struggle with worldly annoyances.

How was he to live on without vindicating himself among
people who suspected him of baseness? How could he go

silently away from Middlemarch as if he were retreating before a just condemnation?   And yet, how was he to set about vindicating himself?

For that scene at the meeting, which he had just witnessed, although it had told him no particulars, had been enough to make his own situation thoroughly clear to him.   Bulstrode had been in dread of scandalous disclosures on the part of Raffles.   Lydgate could now construct all the probabilities of the case.   "He was afraid of some betrayal in my hearing: all he wanted was to bind me to him by a strong obligation: that was why he passed on a sudden from hardness to liberality. And he may have tampered with the patient—he may have disobeyed my orders.   I fear he did.   But whether he did or not, the world believes that he somehow or other poisoned the man, and that I winked at the crime, if I didn't help in it. And yet—and yet he may not be guilty of the last offence; and it is just possible that the change toward me may have been a genuine relenting—the effect of second thoughts, such as he alleged.   What we call the ' just possible ' is sometimes true, and the thing we find it easier to believe is grossly false. In his last dealings with this man, Bulstrode may have kept his hands pure, in spite of my suspicions to the contrary."

There was a benumbing cruelty in his position.   Even if he renounced every other consideration than that of justifying himself—if he met shrugs, cold glances, and avoidance as an accusation, and made a public statement of all the facts as he knew them—who would be convinced?   It would be playing the part of a fool to offer his own testimony on behalf of himself, and say, "I did not take the money as a bribe."   The circumstances would always be stronger than his assertion. And besides, to come forward and tell everything about himself must include declarations about Bulstrode which would darken the suspicions of others against him.   He must tell that he had not known of Raffles' existence when he first mentioned his pressing need of money to Bulstrode, and that he took the money innocently as a result of that communication, not knowing that a new motive for the loan might have arisen on his being called in to this man.   And, after all, the suspicion of Bulstrode's motives might be unjust.

But then came the question whether he should have acted
in precisely the same way if he had not taken the money?
Certainly, if Raffles had continued alive and susceptible of
further treatment when he arrived, and he had then imagined
any disobedience to his orders on the part of Bulstrode, he
would have made a strict inquiry, and if his conjecture had
been verified he would have thrown up the case, in spite of his
recent heavy obligation.   But if he had not received any
money—if Bulstrode had never revoked his cold recommendation of bankruptcy—would he, Lydgate, have abstained from
all inquiry even on finding the man dead?—would the shrinking from an insult to Bulstrode—would the dubiousness of all
medical treatment and the argument that his own treatment
would pass for the wrong with most members of his profession
—have had just the same force or significance with him?

That was the uneasy corner of Lydgate's consciousness
while he was reviewing the facts and resisting all reproach.
If he had been independent, this matter of a patient's treatment and the distinct rule that he must do or see done that
which he believed best for the life committed to him, would
have been the point on which he would have been the sturdiest.
As it was, he had rested in the consideration that disobedience
to his orders, however it might have arisen, could not be considered a crime; that in the dominant opinion obedience to his
orders was just as likely to be fatal, and that the affair was
simply one of etiquette.   Whereas, again and again, in his
time of freedom, he had denounced the perversion of patholog-
ical doubt into moral doubt, and had said "the purest experiment in treatment may still be conscientious; my business is
to take care of life, and do the best I can think of for it.
Science is properly more scrupulous than dogma. Dogma
gives a charter to mistake, but the very breath of science is a
contest with mistake, and must keep the conscience alive."
Alas! the scientific conscience had got into the debasing company of money obligation and selfish respects.

"Is there a medical man of them all in Middlemarch who
would question himself as I do?" said poor Lydgate, with a
renewed outburst of rebellion against the oppression of his lot!
"And yet they will all feel warranted in making a wide space

between me and them, as if I were a leper! My practice and my reputation are utterly damned—I can see that. Even if I could be cleared by valid evidence, it would make little difference to the blessed world here. I have been set down as tainted, and should be cheapened to them all the same."

Already there had been abundant signs which had hitherto puzzled him, that just when he had been paying off his debts and getting cheerfully on his feet, the townsmen were avoiding him or looking strangely at him, and in two instances it came to his knowledge that patients of his had called in another practitioner. The reasons were too plain now. The general black-balling had begun.

No wonder that in Lydgate's energetic nature the sense of a hopeless misconstruction easily turned into a dogged resistance. The scowl which occasionally showed itself on his square brow was not a meaningless accident. Already when he was re-entering the town after that ride taken in the first hours of stinging pain, he was setting his mind on remaining in Middlemarch in spite of the worst that could be done against him. He would not retreat before calumny, as if he submitted to it. He would face it to the utmost, and no act of his should show that he was afraid. It belonged to the generosity as well as defiant force of his nature that he resolved not to shrink from showing to the full his sense of obligation to Bulstrode. It was true that the association with this man had been fatal to him— true that if he had had the thousand pounds still in his hands with all his debts unpaid he would have returned the money to Bulstrode, and taken beggary rather than the rescue which had been sullied with the suspicion of a bribe (for remember he was one of the proudest among the sons of men)—nevertheless, he would not turn away from this crushed fellow-mortal whose aid he had used, and make a pitiful effort to get acquittal for himself by howling against another. "I shall do as I think right, and explain to nobody. They will try to starve me out, but——" He was going on with an obstinate resolve, but he was getting near home, and the thought of Rosamond urged itself again into that chief place from which it had been thrust by the agonized struggles of wounded honor and pride.

How would Rosamond take it all? Here was another weight of chain to drag, and poor Lydgate was in a bad mood for bearing her dumb mastery. He had no impulse to tell her the trouble which must soon be common to them both. He preferred waiting for the incidental disclosure which events must soon bring about.

CHAPTER LXXIV.

"Mercifully grant that we may grow aged together."
—BOOK OF TOBIT: *Marriage Prayer.*

IN Middlemarch a wife could not long remain ignorant that the town held a bad opinion of her husband. No feminine intimate might carry her friendship so far as to make a plain statement to the wife of the unpleasant fact known or believed about her husband; but when a woman with her thoughts much at leisure got them suddenly employed on something grievously disadvantageous to her neighbors, various moral impulses were called into play which tended to stimulate utterance. Candor was one. To be candid, in Middlemarch phraseology, meant to use an early opportunity of letting your friends know that you did not take a cheerful view of their capacity, their conduct, or their position; and a robust candor never waited to be asked for its opinion. Then, again, there was the love of truth—a wide phrase, but meaning in this relation a lively objection to seeing a wife look happier than her husband's character warranted, or manifest too much satisfaction in her lot: the poor thing should have some hint given her that if she knew the truth she would have less complacency in her bonnet, and in light dishes for a supper party. Stronger than all, there was the regard for a friend's moral improvement, sometimes called her soul, which was likely to be benefited by remarks tending to gloom, uttered with the accompaniment of pensive staring at the furniture and a manner implying that the speaker would not tell what was on her mind, from regard to the feelings of her hearer. On the whole, one might say that an ardent charity was at work setting the virtuous mind to make a neighbor unhappy for her good.

There were hardly any wives in Middlemarch whose matrimonial misfortunes would in different ways be likely to call forth more of this moral activity than Rosamond and her aunt Bulstrode. Mrs. Bulstrode was not an object of dislike, and had never consciously injured any human being. Men had always thought her a handsome, comfortable woman, and had reckoned it among the signs of Bulstrode's hypocrisy that he had chosen a red-blooded Vincy, instead of a ghastly and melancholy person suited to his low esteem for earthly pleasure. When the scandal about her husband was disclosed, they remarked of her: "Ah, poor woman! She's as honest as the day—*she* never suspected anything wrong in him, you may depend on it." Women who were intimate with her talked together much of "poor Harriet," imagined what her feelings must be when she came to know everything, and conjectured how much she had already come to know. There was no spiteful disposition toward her; rather, there was a busy benevolence anxious to ascertain what it would be well for her to feel and do under the circumstances, which of course kept the imagination occupied with her character and history from the times when she was Harriet Vincy till now. With the review of Mrs. Bulstrode and her position it was inevitable to associate Rosamond, whose prospects were under the same blight with her aunt's. Rosamond was more severely criticised and less pitied, though she too, as one of the good old Vincy family who had always been known in Middlemarch, was regarded as a victim to marriage with an interloper. The Vincys had their weaknesses, but then they lay on the surface: there was never anything bad to be "found out" concerning them. Mrs. Bulstrode was vindicated from any resemblance to her husband. Harriet's faults were her own.

"She has always been showy," said Mrs. Hackbutt, making tea for a small party, "though she has got into the way of putting her religion forward, to conform to her husband; she has tried to hold her head up above Middlemarch by making it known that she invites clergymen and heaven-knows-who from Riverston and those places."

"We can hardly blame her for that," said Mrs. Sprague; 'because few of the best people in the town cared to associate with Bulstrode, and she must have somebody to sit down at her table."

"Mr. Thesiger has always countenanced him," said Mrs. Hackbutt. "I think he must be sorry now."

"But he was never fond of him in his heart—that every one knows," said Mrs. Tom Toller. "Mr. Thesiger never goes into extremes. He keeps to the truth in what is evangelical. It is only clergymen like Mr. Tyke, who want to use Dissenting hymn-books and that low kind of religion, who ever found Bulstrode to their taste."

"I understand Mr. Tyke is in great distress about him," said Mr. Hackbutt. "And well he may be: they say the Bulstrodes have half kept the Tyke family."

"And of course it is a discredit to his doctrines," said Mrs. Sprague, who was elderly, and old-fashioned in her opinions. "People will not make a boast of being methodistical in Middlemarch for a good while to come."

"I think we must not set down people's bad actions to their religion," said falcon-faced Mrs. Plymdale, who had been listening hitherto.

"Oh, my dear, we are forgetting," said Mrs. Sprague. "We ought not to be talking of this before you."

"I am sure I have no reason to be partial," said Mrs. Plymdale, coloring. "It's true Mr. Plymdale has always been on good terms with Mr. Bulstrode, and Harriet Vincy was my friend long before she married him. But I have always kept my own opinions and told her where she was wrong, poor thing. Still, in point of religion, I must say, Mr. Bulstrode might have done what he has, and worse, and yet have been a man of no religion. I don't say that there has not been a little too much of that—I like moderation myself. But truth is truth. The men tried at the assizes are not all overreligious, I suppose."

"Well," said Mrs. Hackbutt, wheeling adroitly, "all I can say is, that I think she ought to separate from him."

"I can't say that," said Mrs. Sprague. "She took him for better or worse, you know."

"But 'worse' can never mean finding out that your husband is fit for Newgate," said Mrs. Hackbutt. "Fancy living with such a man! I should expect to be poisoned."

"Yes, I think myself it is an encouragement to crime if such men are to be taken care of and waited on by good wives," said Mrs. Tom Toller.

"And a good wife poor Harriet has been," said Mrs. Plymdale. "She thinks her husband the first of men. It's true, he has never denied her anything."

"Well, we shall see what she will do," said Mrs. Hackbutt. "I suppose she knows nothing yet, poor creature. I do hope and trust I shall not see her, for I should be frightened to death lest I should say anything about her husband. Do you think any hint has reached her?"

"I should hardly think so," said Mrs. Tom Toller. "We hear that *he* is ill, and has never stirred out of the house since the meeting on Thursday; but she was with her girls at church yesterday, and they had new Tuscan bonnets. Her own had a feather in it. I have never seen that her religion made any difference in her dress."

"She wears very neat patterns always," said Mrs. Plymdale, a little stung. "And that feather, I know, she got dyed a pale lavender on purpose to be consistent. I must say it of Harriet that she wishes to do right."

"As to her knowing what has happened, it can't be kept from her long," said Mrs. Hackbutt. "The Vincys know, for Mr. Vincy was at the meeting. It will be a great blow to him. There is his daughter as well as his sister."

"Yes, indeed," said Mrs. Sprague. "Nobody supposes that Mr. Lydgate can go on holding up his head in Middlemarch, things look so black about the thousand pounds he took just at that man's death. It really makes one shudder."

"Pride must have a fall," said Mrs. Hackbutt.

"I am not so sorry for Rosamond Vincy that was, as I am for her aunt," said Mrs. Plymdale. "She needed a lesson."

"I suppose the Bulstrodes will go and live abroad somewhere," said Mrs. Sprague. "That is what is generally done when there is anything disgraceful in a family."

"And a most deadly blow it will be to Harriet," said Mrs.

Plymdale. "If ever a woman was crushed, she will be. I
pity her from my heart. And with all her faults, few women
are better. From a girl she had the neatest ways, and was
always good-hearted, and as open as the day. You might
look into her drawers when you would—always the same.
And so she has brought up Kate and Ellen. You may think
how hard it will be for her to go among foreigners."

"The doctor says that is what he should recommend the
Lydgates to do," said Mrs. Sprague. "He says Lydgate
ought to have kept among the French."

"That would suit *her* well enough, I dare say," said Mrs.
Plymdale; "there is that kind of lightness about her. But
she got that from her mother; she never got it from her aunt
Bulstrode, who always gave her good advice, and to my knowledge would rather have had her marry elsewhere."

Mrs. Plymdale was in a situation which caused her some
complication of feeling. There had been not only her intimacy with Mrs. Bulstrode, but also a profitable business relation of the great Plymdale dyeing house with Mr. Bulstrode,
which on the one hand would have inclined her to desire that
the mildest view of his character should be the true one, but
on the other, made her the more afraid of seeming to palliate
his culpability. Again, the late alliance of her family with
the Tollers had brought her in connection with the best circle,
which gratified her in every direction except in the inclination
to those serious views which she believed to be the best in
another sense. The sharp little woman's conscience was somewhat troubled in the adjustment of these opposing "bests,"
and of her griefs and satisfactions under late events, which
were likely to humble those who needed humbling, but also
to fall heavily on her old friend, whose faults she would have
preferred seeing on a background of prosperity.

Poor Mrs. Bulstrode, meanwhile, had been no further shaken
by the oncoming tread of calamity than in the busier stirring
of that secret uneasiness which had always been present in
her since the last visit of Raffles to The Shrubs. That the
hateful man had come ill to Stone Court, and that her husband
had chosen to remain there and watch over him, she allowed
to be explained by the fact that Raffles had been employed

and aided in earlier days, and that this made a tie of benevolence toward him in his degraded helplessness; and she had
been since then innocently cheered by her husband's more hopeful speech about his own health and ability to continue his attention to business.   The calm was disturbed when Lydgate had
brought him home ill from the meeting, and, in spite of comforting assurances during the next few days, she cried in private from the conviction that her husband was not suffering
from bodily illness merely, but from something that afflicted
his mind.   He would not allow her to read to him, and scarcely
to sit with him, alleging nervous susceptibility to sounds and
movements; yet she suspected that, in shutting himself up
in his private room, he wanted to be busy with his papers.
Something, she felt sure, had happened.   Perhaps it was some
great loss of money; and she was kept in the dark.   Not daring to question her husband, she said to Lydgate, on the fifth
day after the meeting, when she had not left home except to
go to church:

"Mr. Lydgate, pray be open with me: I like to know the
truth.   Has anything happened to Mr. Bulstrode?"

"Some little nervous shock," said Lydgate, evasively.   He
felt that it was not for him to make the painful revelation.

"But what brought it on?" said Mrs. Bulstrode, looking
directly at him with her large dark eyes.

"There is often something poisonous in the air of public
rooms," said Lydgate.   "Strong men can stand it, but it tells
on people in proportion to the delicacy of their systems.   It
is often impossible to account for the precise moment of an
attack—or rather, to say why the strength gives way at a
particular moment."

Mrs. Bulstrode was not satisfied with this answer.   There
remained in her a belief that some calamity had befallen her
husband, of which she was to be kept in ignorance; and it was
in her nature strongly to object to such concealment.   She
begged leave for her daughters to sit with their father, and
drove into the town to pay some visits, conjecturing that if
anything were known to have gone wrong in Mr. Bulstrode's
affairs, she should see or hear some sign of it.

She called on Mrs. Thesiger, who was not at home, and

then drove to Mrs. Hackbutt's, on the other side of the church-yard. Mrs. Hackbutt saw her coming from an upstairs win-dow, and, remembering her former alarm lest she should meet Mrs. Bulstrode, felt almost bound in consistency to send word that she was not at home; but against that there was a sud-den strong desire within her for the excitement of an inter-view, in which she was quite determined not to make the slightest allusion to what was in her mind.

Hence Mrs. Bulstrode was shown into the drawing-room, and Mrs. Hackbutt went to her with more tightness of lip and rubbing of her hands than was usually observable in her, these being precautions adopted against freedom of speech. She was resolved not to ask how Mr. Bulstrode was.

"I have not been anywhere except to church for nearly a week," said Mrs. Bulstrode, after a few introductory remarks. "But Mr. Bulstrode was taken so ill at the meeting on Thurs-day that I have not liked to leave the house."

Mrs. Hackbutt rubbed the back of one hand with the palm of the other held against her chest, and let her eyes ramble over the pattern on the rug.

"Was Mr. Hackbutt at the meeting?" persevered Mrs. Bul-strode.

"Yes, he was," said Mrs. Hackbutt, with the same attitude. "The land is to be bought by subscription, I believe."

"Let us hope that there will be no more cases of cholera to be buried in it," said Mrs. Bulstrode. "It is an awful visita-tion. But I always think Middlemarch a very healthy spot. I suppose it is being used to it from a child; but I never saw the town I should like to live at better, and especially our end."

"I am sure I should be glad that you always should live at Middlemarch, Mrs. Bulstrode," said Mrs. Hackbutt, with a slight sigh. "Still, we must learn to resign ourselves, wher-ever our lot may be cast. Though I am sure there will always be people in this town who will wish you well."

Mrs. Hackbutt longed to say, "If you take my advice you will part from your husband," but it seemed clear to her that the poor woman knew nothing of the thunder ready to bolt on her head, and she herself could do no more than prepare her a little. Mrs. Bulstrode felt suddenly rather chill and trembling: there was evidently something unusual behind this speech of Mrs. Hackbutt's; but though she had set out with the desire to be fully informed, she found herself unable now to pursue her brave purpose, and turning the conversation by an inquiry about the young Hackbutts, she soon took her leave, saying that she was going to see Mrs. Plymdale. On her way thither she tried to imagine that there might have been some unusually warm sparring at the meeting between Mr. Bulstrode and some of his frequent opponents—perhaps Mr. Hackbutt might have been one of them. That would account for everything.

But when she was in conversation with Mrs. Plymdale that comforting explanation seemed no longer tenable. "Selina" received her with a pathetic affectionateness and a disposition to give edifying answers on the commonest topics, which could hardly have reference to an ordinary quarrel of which the most important consequence was a perturbation of Mr. Bulstrode's health. Beforehand Mrs. Bulstrode had thought that she would sooner question Mrs. Plymdale than any one else; but she found to her surprise that an old friend is not always the person whom it is easiest to make a confidant of: there was the barrier of remembered communication under other circumstances—there was the dislike of being pitied and informed by one who had been long wont to allow her the superiority. For certain words of mysterious appropriateness that Mrs. Plymdale let fall about her resolution never to turn her back on her friends, convinced Mrs. Bulstrode that what had happened must be some kind of misfortune, and instead of being able to say with her native directness, "What is it that you have in your mind?" she found herself anxious to get away before she had heard anything more explicit. She began to have an agitating certainty that the misfortune was something more than the mere loss of money, being keenly sensitive to the fact that Selina now, just as Mrs. Hackbutt had done before, avoided noticing what she said about her husband, as they would have avoided noticing a personal blemish.

She said good-by with nervous haste, and told the coachman to drive to Mr. Vincy's warehouse. In that short drive her dread gathered so much force from the sense of darkness.

48

that when she entered the private counting-house, where her brother sat at his desk, her knees trembled, and her usually florid face was deathly pale. Something of the same effect was produced in him by the sight of her: he rose from his seat to meet her, took her by the hand, and said, with his impulsive rashness:

"God help you, Harriet! you know all."

That moment was perhaps worse than any which came after. It contained that concentrated experience which in great crises of emotion reveals the bias of a nature, and is prophetic of the ultimate act which will end an intermediate struggle. Without that memory of Raffles she might still have thought only of monetary ruin; but now, along with her brother's look and words, there darted into her mind the idea of some guilt in her husband—then, under the working of terror came the image of her husband exposed to disgrace—and then, after an instant of scorching shame, in which she felt only the eyes of the world, with one leap of her heart she was at his side in mournful but unreproaching fellowship with shame and isolation. All this went on within her in a mere flash of time—while she sank into the chair, and raised her eyes to her brother, who stood over her. "I know nothing, Walter. What is it?" she said, faintly.

He told her everything, very inartificially, in slow fragments, making her aware that the scandal went much beyond proof, especially as to the end of Raffles.

"People will talk," he said. "Even if a man has been acquitted by a jury, they'll talk, and nod and wink—and as far as the world goes, a man might often as well be guilty as not. It's a breakdown blow, and it damages Lydgate as much as Bulstrode. I don't pretend to say what is the truth. I only wish we had never heard the name of either Bulstrode or Lydgate. You'd better have been a Vincy all your life, and so had Rosamond."

Mrs. Bulstrode made no reply.

"But you must bear up as well as you can, Harriet. People don't blame *you*. And I'll stand by you whatever you make up your mind to do," said the brother, with rough but well-meaning affectionateness.

"Give me your arm to the carriage, Walter," said Mrs. Bulstrode. "I feel very weak."

And when she got home she was obliged to say to her daughter: "I am not well, my dear; I must go and lie down. Attend to your papa. Leave me in quiet. I shall take no dinner."

She locked herself in her room. She needed time to get used to her maimed consciousness, her poor lopped life, before she could walk steadily to the place allotted her. A new searching light had fallen on her husband's character, and she could not judge him leniently; the twenty years in which she had believed in him and venerated him, by virtue of his concealments, came back with particulars that made them seem an odious deceit. He had married her with that bad past life hidden behind him, and she had no faith left to protest his innocence of the worst that was imputed to him. Her honest ostentatious nature made the sharing of a merited dishonor as bitter as it could be to any mortal.

But this imperfectly taught woman, whose phrases and habits were an odd patchwork, had a loyal spirit within her. The man whose prosperity she had shared through nearly half a life, and who had unvaryingly cherished her—now that punishment had befallen him, it was not possible to her in any sense to forsake him. There is a forsaking which still sits at the same board and lies on the same couch with the forsaken soul, withering it the more by unloving proximity. She knew, when she locked her door, that she should unlock it ready to go down to her unhappy husband and espouse his sorrow, and say of his guilt, I will mourn and not reproach. But she needed time to gather up her strength; she needed to sob out her farewell to all the gladness and pride of her life. When she had resolved to go down, she prepared herself by some little acts which might seem mere folly to a hard onlooker; they were her way of expressing to all spectators, visible or invisible, that she had begun a new life in which she embraced humiliation. She took off all her ornaments and put on a plain black gown, and instead of wearing her much-adorned cap and large bows of hair, she brushed her hair down and put on a plain bonnet-cap, which made her look suddenly like an early Methodist.

Bulstrode, who knew that his wife had been out, and had
come in saying that she was not well, had spent the time in
an agitation equal to hers. He had looked forward to her
learning the truth from others, and had acquiesced in that
probability, as something easier to him than any confession.
But now that he imagined the moment of her knowledge
come, he awaited the result in anguish. His daughters had
been obliged to consent to leave him, and though he had
allowed some food to be brought to him, he had not touched
it. He felt himself perishing slowly in unpitied misery.
Perhaps he should never see his wife's face with affection in
it again. And if he turned to God there seemed to be no
answer but the pressure of retribution.

It was eight o'clock in the evening before the door opened
and his wife entered. He dared not look up at her. He sat
with his eyes bent down; and as she went toward him she
thought he looked smaller—he seemed so withered and
shrunken. A movement of new compassion and old tenderness went through her like a great wave, and putting one hand
on his which rested on the arm of the chair, and the other on
his shoulder, she said, solemnly but kindly:

"Look up, Nicholas."

He raised his eyes with a little start and looked at her half
amazed for a moment. Her pale face, her changed, mourning
dress, the trembling about her mouth, all said, "I know";
and her hands and eyes rested gently on him. He burst out
crying, and they cried together, she sitting at his side. They
could not yet speak to each other of the shame which she was
bearing with him, or of the acts which had brought it down
on them. His confession was silent, and her promise of faithfulness was silent. Open-minded as she was, she nevertheless
shrank from the words which would have expressed their
mutual consciousness, as she would have shrunk from flakes
of fire. She could not say, "How much is only slander and
false suspicion?" and he did not say, "I am innocent."

CHAPTER LXXV.

"Le sentiment de la fausseté des plaisirs présents, et l'ignorance de la vanité des plaisirs absents, causent l'inconstance." — PASCAL.

ROSAMOND had a gleam of returning cheerfulness when the house was freed from the threatening figure, and when all the disagreeable creditors were paid. But she was not joyous; her married life had fulfilled none of her hopes, and had been quite spoiled for her imagination. In this brief interval of calm, Lydgate, remembering that he had often been stormy in his hours of perturbation, and mindful of the pain Rosamond had had to bear, was carefully gentle toward her; but he, too, had lost some of his old spirit, and he still felt it necessary to refer to an economical change in their way of living as a matter of course, trying to reconcile her to it gradually, and repressing his anger when she answered by wishing that he would go to live in London. When she did not make this answer she listened languidly, and wondered what she had that was worth living for. The hard and contemptuous words which had fallen from her husband in his anger had deeply offended that vanity which he had at first called into active enjoyment; and what she regarded as his perverse way of looking at things, kept up a secret repulsion, which made her receive all his tenderness as a poor substitute for the happiness he had failed to give her. They were at a disadvantage with their neighbors, and there was no longer any outlook toward Quallingham— there was no outlook anywhere except in an occasional letter from Will Ladislaw. She had felt stung and disappointed by Will's resolution to quit Middlemarch; for, in spite of what she knew and guessed about his admiration for Dorothea, she secretly cherished the belief that he had, or would necessarily come to have, much more admiration for herself—Rosamond being one of those women who live much in the idea that each man they meet would have preferred them if the preference had not been hopeless. Mrs. Casaubon was all very well; but Will's interest in her dated before he knew Mrs. Lydgate. Rosamond took his way of talking to herself which was a mixture

of playful faultfinding and hyperbolical gallantry, as the disguise of a deeper feeling; and in his presence she felt that
agreeable titillation of vanity and sense of romantic drama
which Lydgate's presence had no longer the magic to create.
She even fancied—what will not men and women fancy in
these matters?—that Will exaggerated his admiration for Mrs.
Casaubon in order to pique herself. In this way poor Rosamond's brain had been busy before Will's departure. He
would have made, she thought, a much more suitable husband
for her than she had found in Lydgate. No notion could have
been falser than this, for Rosamond's discontent in her marriage was due to the conditions of marriage itself, to its demand for self-suppression and tolerance, and not to the nature of her husband; but the easy conception of an unreal
Better had a sentimental charm which diverted her ennui.
She constructed a little romance which was to vary the flat-
ness of her life: Will Ladislaw was always to be a bachelor
and live near her, always to be at her command, and have an
understood though never fully expressed passion for her, which
would be sending out lambent flames every now and then in
interesting scenes. His departure had been a proportionate disappointment, and had sadly increased her weariness of Middlemarch; but at first she had the alternative dream of pleasures
in store from her intercourse with the family at Quallingham.
Since then the troubles of her married life had deepened,
and the absence of other relief encouraged her regretful rumination over that thin romance which she had once fed on.
Men and women make sad mistakes about their own symptoms,
taking their vague uneasy longings sometimes for genius, sometimes for religion, and oftener still for a mighty love. Will
Ladislaw had written chatty letters, half to her and half to
Lydgate, and she had replied: their separation, she felt, was
not likely to be final, and the change she now most longed for
was that Lydgate should go to live in London; everything
would be agreeable in London; and she had set to work with
quiet determination to win this result, when there came a sudden, delightful promise which inspirited her.

It came shortly before the memorable meeting at the town-
hall, and was nothing less than a letter from Will Ladislaw

to Lydgate, which turned indeed chiefly on his new interest
in plans of colonization, but mentioned, incidentally, that he
might find it necessary to pay a visit to Middlemarch within
the next few weeks—a very pleasant necessity, he said, almost
as good as holidays to a schoolboy. He hoped there was his
old place on the rug, and a great deal of music in store for
him. But he was quite uncertain as to the time. While Lydgate was reading the letter to Rosamond her face looked like a
reviving flower—it grew prettier and more blooming. There
was nothing unendurable now; the debts were paid, Mr. Ladislaw was coming, and Lydgate would be persuaded to leave
Middlemarch and settle in London, which was "so different
from a provincial town."

That was a bright bit of a morning. But soon the sky
became black over poor Rosamond. The presence of a new
gloom in her husband, about which he was entirely reserved
toward her—for he dreaded to expose his lacerated feeling to
her neutrality and misconception—soon received a painfully
strange explanation, alien to all her previous notions of what
could affect her happiness. In the new gayety of her spirits,
thinking that Lydgate had merely a worse fit of moodiness
than usual, causing him to leave her remarks unanswered, and
evidently to keep out of her way as much as possible, she
chose, a few days after the meeting, and without speaking to
him on the subject, to send out notes of invitation for a small
evening party, feeling convinced that this was a judicious step,
since people seemed to have been keeping aloof from them, and
wanted restoring to the old habit of intercourse. When the
invitations had been accepted, she would tell Lydgate, and
give him a wise admonition as to how a medical man should
behave to his neighbors; for Rosamond had the gravest little
airs possible about other people's duties. But all the invitations were declined, and the last answer came into Lydgate's
hands.

"This is Chichely's scratch. What is he writing to you
about?" said Lydgate, wonderingly, as he handed the note to
her. She was obliged to let him see it, and, looking at her
severely, he said:

"Why on earth have you been sending out invitations without telling me, Rosamond? I beg, I insist, that you will not invite any one to this house. I suppose you have been inviting others, and they have refused, too."

She said nothing.

"Do you hear me?" thundered Lydgate.

"Yes, certainly I hear you," said Rosamond, turning her head aside with the movement of a graceful, long-necked bird.

Lydgate tossed his head without any grace, and walked out of the room, feeling himself dangerous. Rosamond's thought was, that he was getting more and more unbearable—not that there was any new special reason for this peremptoriness. His indisposition to tell her anything in which he was sure beforehand that she would not be interested was growing into an unreflecting habit, and she was in ignorance of everything connected with the thousand pounds except that the loan had come from her uncle Bulstrode. Lydgate's odious humors and their neighbors' apparent avoidance of them had an unaccountable date for her in their relief from money difficulties. If the invitations had been accepted, she would have gone to invite her mamma and the rest, whom she had seen nothing of for several days; and she now put on her bonnet to go and inquire what had become of them all, suddenly feeling as if there were a conspiracy to leave her in isolation with a husband disposed to offend everybody. It was after the dinner hour, and she found her father and mother seated together alone in the drawing-room. They greeted her with sad looks, saying, "Well, my dear!" and no more. She had never seen her father look so downcast; and seating herself near him, she said:

"Is there anything the matter, papa?"

He did not answer, but Mrs. Vincy said: "Oh, my dear, have you heard nothing? It won't be long before it reaches you."

"Is it anything about Tertius?" said Rosamond, turning pale. The idea of trouble immediately connected itself with what had been unaccountable to her in him.

"Oh, my dear, yes. To think of your marrying into this trouble. Debt was bad enough, but this will be worse."

"Stay, stay, Lucy," said Mrs. Vincy. "Have you heard nothing about your uncle Bulstrode, Rosamond?"

"No, papa," said the poor thing, feeling as if trouble were not anything she had before experienced, but some invisible power with an iron grasp that made her soul faint within her.

Her father told her everything, saying at the end: "It's better for you to know, my dear. I think Lydgate must leave the town. Things have gone against him. I dare say he couldn't help it. I don't accuse him of any harm," said Mr. Vincy. He had always before been disposed to find the utmost fault with Lydgate.

The shock to Rosamond was terrible. It seemed to her that no lot could be so cruelly hard as hers—to have married a man who had become the centre of infamous suspicions. In many cases it is inevitable that the shame is felt to be the worst part of crime; and it would have required a great deal of disentangling reflection, such as had never entered into Rosamond's life, for her in these moments to feel that her trouble was less than if her husband had been certainly known to have done something criminal. All the shame seemed to be there. And she had innocently married this man with the belief that he and his family were a glory to her! She showed her usual reticence to her parents, and only said, that if Lydgate had done as she wished he would have left Middlemarch long ago.

"She bears it beyond anything," said her mother when she was gone.

"Ah, thank God!" said Mr. Vincy, who was much broken down.

But Rosamond went home with a sense of justified repugnance toward her husband. What had he really done—how had he really acted? She did not know. Why had he not told her everything? He did not speak to her on the subject, and of course she could not speak to him. It came into her mind once that she would ask her father to let her go home again; but dwelling on that prospect made it seem utter dreariness to her: a married woman gone back to live with her parents—life seemed to have no meaning for her in such a position: she could not contemplate herself in it.

The next two days Lydgate observed a change in her, and

believed that she had heard the bad news. Would she speak
to him about it, or would she go on forever in the silence
which seemed to imply that she believed him guilty? We
must remember that he was in a morbid state of mind, in
which almost all contact was pain. Certainly Rosamond in
this case had equal reason to complain of reserve and want of
confidence on his part; but in the bitterness of his soul he
excused himself;—was he not justified in shrinking from the
task of telling her, since now she knew the truth she had no
impulse to speak to him? But a deeper-lying consciousness
that he was in fault made him restless, and the silence between
them became intolerable to him; it was as if they were both
adrift on one piece of wreck and looked away from each other.

He thought: "I am a fool. Haven't I given up expecting
anything? I have married care, not help." And that evening he said:

"Rosamond, have you heard anything that distresses you?"

"Yes," she answered, laying down her work, which she had
been carrying on with a languid semi-consciousness, most unlike her usual self.

"What have you heard?"

"Everything, I suppose. Papa told me."

"That people think me disgraced?"

"Yes," said Rosamond, faintly, beginning to sew again automatically.

There was silence. Lydgate thought: "If she has any
trust in me—any notion of what I am, she ought to speak now
and say that she does not believe I have deserved disgrace."

But Rosamond on her side went on moving her fingers languidly. Whatever was to be said on the subject she expected
to come from Tertius. What did she know? And if he were
innocent of any wrong, why did he not do something to clear
himself?

This silence of hers brought a new rush of gall to that bitter mood in which Lydgate had been saying to himself that
nobody believed in him—even Farebrother had not come forward. He had begun to question her with the intent that
their conversation should disperse the chill fog which had
gathered between them, but he felt his resolution checked by

despairing resentment. Even this trouble, like the rest, she seemed to regard as if it were hers alone. He was always to her a being apart, doing what she objected to. He started from his chair with an angry impulse, and thrusting his hands in his pockets, walked up and down the room. There was an underlying consciousness all the while that he should have to master this anger, and tell her everything, and convince her of the facts. For he had almost learned the lesson that he must bend himself to her nature, and that because she came short in her sympathy, he must give the more. Soon he recurred to his intention of opening himself: the occasion must not be lost. If he could bring her to feel with some solemnity that here was a slander which must be met and not run away from, and that the whole trouble had come out of his desperate want of money, it would be a moment for urging powerfully on her that they should be one in the resolve to do with as little money as possible, so that they might weather the bad time and keep themselves independent. He would mention the definite measures which he desired to take, and win her to a willing spirit. He was bound to try this—and what else was there for him to do?

He did not know how long he had been walking uneasily backward and forward, but Rosamond felt that it was long, and wished that he would sit down. She too had begun to think this an opportunity for urging on Tertius what he ought to do. Whatever might be the truth about all this misery, there was one dread which asserted itself.

Lydgate at last seated himself, not in his usual chair, but in one nearer to Rosamond, leaning aside in it toward her and looking at her gravely before he reopened the sad subject. He had conquered himself so far, and was about to speak with a sense of solemnity, as on an occasion which was not to be repeated. He had even opened his lips, when Rosamond, letting her hands fall, looked at him and said:

"Surely, Tertius——"

"Well?"

"Surely now at last you have given up the idea of staying in Middlemarch. I cannot go on living here. Let us go to London. Papa, and every one else, say you had better go.

Whatever misery I have to put up with, it will be easier away from here."

Lydgate felt miserably jarred.   Instead of that critical out-pouring for which he had prepared himself with effort, here was the old round to be gone through again.   He could not bear it.   With a quick change of countenance he rose and went out of the room.

Perhaps if he had been strong enough to persist in his de-termination to be the more because she was less, that evening might have had a better issue.   If his energy could have borne down that check, he might still have wrought on Rosa-mond's vision and will.   We cannot be sure that any natures, however inflexible or peculiar, will resist this effect from a more massive being than their own.   They may be taken by storm and for the moment converted, becoming part of the soul which enwraps them in the ardor of its movements.   But poor Lydgate had a throbbing pain within him, and his energy had fallen short of its task.

The beginning of mutual understanding and resolve seemed as far off as ever; nay, it seemed blocked out by the sense of unsuccessful effort.   They lived on from day to day with their thoughts still apart, Lydgate going about what work he had in a mood of despair, and Rosamond feeling, with some jus-tification, that he was behaving cruelly.   It was of no use to say anything to Tertius; but when Will Ladislaw came, she was determined to tell him everything.   In spite of her gen-eral reticence, she needed some one who would recognize her wrongs.

CHAPTER LXXVI.

" To mercy, pity, peace, and love
All pray in their distress,
And to these virtues of delight,
Return their thankfulness.

 * * * * *

For Mercy has a human heart,
Pity a human face;
And Love the human form divine;
And Peace the human dress. "
            —WILLIAM BLAKE: *Songs of Innocence.*

SOME days later, Lydgate was riding to Lowick Manor, in consequence of a summons from Dorothea. The summons had not been unexpected, since it had followed a letter from Mr. Bulstrode, in which he stated that he had resumed his arrangements for quitting Middlemarch, and must remind Lydgate of his previous communications about the hospital, to the purport of which he still adhered. It had been his duty, before taking further steps, to reopen the subject with Mrs. Casaubon, who now wished, as before, to discuss the question with Lydgate. "Your views may possibly have undergone some change," wrote Mr. Bulstrode; "but, in that case also, it is desirable that you should lay them before her."

Dorothea awaited his arrival with eager interest. Though, in deference to her masculine advisers, she had refrained from what Sir James had called "interfering in this Bulstrode business," the hardship of Lydgate's position was continually in her mind, and when Bulstrode applied to her again about the hospital, she felt that the opportunity was come to her which she had been hindered from hastening. In her luxurious home, wandering under the boughs of her own great trees, her thought was going out over the lot of others, and her emotions were imprisoned. The idea of some active good within her reach "haunted her like a passion," and another's need having once come to her as a distinct image, preoccupied her desire with the yearning to give relief, and made her own ease tasteless. She was full of confident hope about this interview with Lydgate, never heeding what was said about his personal re-

serve; never heeding that she was a very young woman.
Nothing could have seemed more irrelevant to Dorothea than
insistence on her youth and sex when she was moved to show
her human fellowship.

As she sat waiting in the library, she could do nothing but
live through again all the past scenes which had brought Lydgate into her memories. They all owed their significance to
her marriage and its troubles—but no; there were two occasions in which the image of Lydgate had come painfully in
connection with his wife and some one else. The pain had
been allayed for Dorothea, but it had left in her an awakened
conjecture as to what Lydgate's marriage might be to him,
a susceptibility to the slightest hint about Mrs. Lydgate.
These thoughts were like a drama to her, and made her eyes
bright, and gave an attitude of suspense to her whole frame,
though she was only looking out from the brown library on to
the turf and the bright green buds which stood in relief against
the dark evergreens.

When Lydgate came in, she was almost shocked at the
change in his face, which was strikingly perceptible to her
who had not seen him for two months. It was not the change
of emaciation, but that effect which even young faces will very
soon show from the persistent presence of resentment and de-
spondency. Her cordial look, when she put out her hand to
him, softened his expression, but only with melancholy.

"I have wished very much to see you for a long while, Mr.
Lydgate," said Dorothea, when they were seated opposite each
other; "but I put off asking you to come until Mr. Bulstrode
applied to me again about the hospital. I know that the
advantage of keeping the management of it separate from that
of the Infirmary depends on you, or, at least, on the good
which you are encouraged to hope for from having it under
your control. And I am sure you will not refuse to tell me
exactly what you think."

"You want to decide whether you should give a generous
support to the hospital," said Lydgate. "I cannot conscien-
tiously advise you to do it in dependence on any activity of
mine. I may be obliged to leave the town."

He spoke curtly, feeling the ache of despair as to his being able to carry out any purpose that Rosamond had set her mind against.

"Not because there is no one to believe in you?" said Dorothea, pouring out her words in clearness from a full heart. "I know the unhappy mistakes about you. I knew them from the first moment to be mistakes. You have never done anything vile. You would not do anything dishonorable."

It was the first assurance of belief in him that had fallen on Lydgate's ears. He drew a deep breath, and said, "Thank you." He could say no more: it was something very new and strange in his life that these few words of trust from a woman should be so much to him.

"I beseech you to tell me how everything was," said Dorothea, fearlessly. "I am sure that the truth would clear you."

Lydgate started up from his chair and went toward the window, forgetting where he was. He had so often gone over in his mind the possibility of explaining everything without aggravating appearances that would tell, perhaps unfairly, against Bulstrode, and had so often decided against it—he had so often said to himself that his assertions would not change people's impressions—that Dorothea's words sounded like a temptation to do something which in his soberness he had pronounced to be unreasonable.

"Tell me, pray," said Dorothea, with simple earnestness; "then we can consult together. It is wicked to let people think evil of any one falsely, when it can be hindered."

Lydgate turned, remembering where he was, and saw Dorothea's face looking up at him with a sweet, trustful gravity. The presence of a noble nature, generous in its wishes, ardent in its charity, changes the light for us: we begin to see things again in their larger, quieter masses, and to believe that we too can be seen and judged in the wholeness of our character. That influence was beginning to act on Lydgate, who had for many days been seeing all life as one who is dragged and struggling amid the throng. He sat down again, and felt that he was recovering his old self in the consciousness that he was with one who believed in it.

"I don't want," he said, "to bear hard on Bulstrode, who has lent me money of which I was in need—though I would rather have gone without it now. He is hunted down and miserable, and has only a poor thread of life in him. But 1 should like to tell you everything. It will be a comfort to me to speak where belief has gone beforehand, and where I shall not seem to be offering assertions of my own honesty. You will feel what is fair to another, as you feel what is fair to me."

"Do trust me," said Dorothea; "I will not repeat anything without your leave. But at the very least, I could say that you have made all the circumstances clear to me, and that I know you are not in any way guilty. Mr. Farebrother would believe me, and my uncle, and Sir James Chettam. Nay, there are persons in Middlemarch to whom I could go; although they don't know much of me, they would believe me. They would know that I could have no other motive than truth and justice. I would take any pains to clear you. I have very little to do. There is nothing better that I can do in the world."

Dorothea's voice, as she made this childlike picture of what she would do, might have been almost taken as a proof that she could do it effectively. The searching tenderness of her woman's tones seemed made for a defence against ready accusers. Lydgate did not stay to think that she was Quixotic : he gave himself up, for the first time in his life, to the exquisite sense of leaning entirely on a generous sympathy, without any check of proud reserve ; and he told her everything, from the time when, under the pressure of his difficulties, he unwillingly made his first application to Bulstrode ; gradually, in the relief of speaking, getting into a more thorough utterance of what had gone on in his mind—entering fully into the fact that his treatment of the patient was opposed to the dominant practice, into his doubts at the last, his ideal of medical duty, and his uneasy consciousness that the acceptance of the money had made some difference in his private inclination and professional behavior, though not in his fulfilment of any publicly recognized obligation.

"It has come to my knowledge since," he added, "that Hawley sent some one to examine the housekeeper at Stone Court, and said that she gave the patient all the opium in the phial I left, as well as a good deal of brandy. But that would not have been opposed to ordinary prescriptions, even of first-rate men. The suspicions against me had no hold there: they are grounded on the knowledge that I took money, that Bulstrode had strong motives for wishing the man to die, and that he gave me the money as a bribe to concur in some malpractices or other against the patient—that in any case I accepted a bribe to hold my tongue. They are just the suspicions that cling the most obstinately, because they lie in people's inclination and can never be disapproved. How my orders came to be disobeyed is a question to which I don't know the answer. It is still possible that Bulstrode was innocent of any criminal intention—even possible that he had nothing to do with the disobedience, and merely abstained from mentioning it. But all that has nothing to do with the public belief. It is one of those cases on which a man is condemned on the ground of his character—it is believed that he has committed a crime in some undefined way, because he had the motive for doing it; and Bulstrode's character has enveloped me, because I took his money. I am simply blighted, like a damaged ear of corn—the business is done and can't be undone."

"Oh, it is hard!" said Dorothea. "I understand the difficulty there is in your vindicating yourself. And that all this should have come to you who had meant to lead a higher life than the common, and to find out better ways—I cannot bear to rest in this as unchangeable. I know you meant that. I remember what you said to me when you first spoke to me about the hospital. There is no sorrow I have thought more about than that—to love what is great, and try to reach it, and yet to fail."

"Yes," said Lydgate, feeling that here he had found room for the full meaning of his grief. "I had some ambition. I meant everything to be different with me. I thought I had more strength and mastery. But the most terrible obstacles are such as nobody can see except one's self."

"Suppose," said Dorothea, meditatively—"suppose we kept on the hospital according to the present plan, and you stayed here, though only with the friendship and support of a few, the evil feeling toward you would gradually die out; there

49

would come opportunities in which the people would be forced
to acknowledge that they had been unjust to you, because
they would see that your purposes were pure. You may still
win a great fame like the Louis and Laennec I have heard you
speak of, and we shall all be proud of you," she ended, with a
smile.

"That might do if I had my old trust in myself," said Lydgate, mournfully. "Nothing galls me more than the notion of
turning round and running away before this slander, leaving
it unchecked behind me. Still I can't ask any one to put a
great deal of money into a plan which depends on me."

"It would be quite worth my while," said Dorothea, simply. "Only think. I am very uncomfortable with my money,
because they tell me I have too little for any great scheme of
the sort I like best, and yet I have too much. I don't know
what to do. I have seven hundred a year of my own fortune,
and nineteen hundred a year that Mr. Casaubon left me, and
between three and four thousand of ready money in the bank.
I wished to raise money and pay it off gradually out of my
income which I don't want, to buy land with and found a village which should be a school of industry: but Sir James and
my uncle have convinced me that the risk would be too great.
So you see that what I should most rejoice at would be to have
something good to do with my money: I should like it to make
other people's lives better to them. It makes me very uneasy
—coming all to me who don't want it."

A smile broke through the gloom of Lydgate's face. The
childlike, grave-eyed earnestness with which Dorothea said all
this was irresistible—blent into an adorable whole with her
ready understanding of high experience. (Of lower experience such as plays a great part in the world, poor Mrs. Casaubon had a very blurred, short-sighted knowledge, little helped
by her imagination.) But she took the smile as encouragement of her plan.

"I think you see now that you spoke too scrupulously," she
said, in a tone of persuasion. "The hospital would be one
good; and making your life quite whole and well again would
be another."

Lydgate's smile had died away. "You have the goodness

as well as the money to do all that; if it could be done," he
said. "But——"

He hesitated a little while, looking vaguely toward the window; and she sat in silent expectation. At last he turned
toward her and said impetuously:

"Why should I not tell you?—you know what sort of bond
marriage is. You will understand everything."

Dorothea felt her heart beginning to beat faster. Had he
that sorrow too? But she feared to say any word, and he
went on immediately.

"It is impossible for me now to do anything—to take any
step, without considering my wife's happiness. The thing
that I might like to do if I were alone, is become impossible
to me. I can't see her miserable. She married me without
knowing what she was going into, and it might have been better for her if she had not married me."

"I know, I know—you could not give her pain, if you were
not obliged to do it," said Dorothea, with keen memory of her
own life.

"And she has set her mind against staying. She wishes to
go. The troubles she has had here have wearied her," said
Lydgate, breaking off again, lest he should say too much.

"But when she saw the good that might come of staying——" said Dorothea, remonstrantly, looking at Lydgate as
if he had forgotten the reasons which had just been considered.
He did not speak immediately.

"She would not see it," he said at last, curtly, feeling at
first that this statement must do without explanation. "And,
indeed, I have lost all spirit about carrying on my life here."
He paused a moment, and then, following the impulse to let
Dorothea see deeper into the difficulty of his life, he said:
"The fact is, this trouble has come upon her confusedly. We
have not been able to speak to each other about it. I am not
sure what is in her mind about it; she may fear that I have
really done something base. It is my fault; I ought to be
more open. But I have been suffering cruelly."

"May I go and see her?" said Dorothea, eagerly. "Would
she accept my sympathy? I would tell her that you have not
been blamable before any one's judgment but your own. I

would tell her that you shall be cleared, in every fair mind.
I would cheer her heart. Will you ask her if I may go to
see her ? I did see her once."

"I am sure you may," said Lydgate, seizing the proposition
with some hope. "She would feel honored—cheered, I think,
by the proof that you at least have some respect for me. I
will not speak to her about your coming—that she may not
connect it with my wishes at all. I know very well that I
ought not to have left anything to be told her by others,
but——"

He broke off, and there was a moment's silence. Dorothea
refrained from saying what was in her mind—how well she
knew that there might be invisible barriers to speech between
husband and wife. This was a point on which even sympathy might make a wound. She returned to the more outward
aspect of Lydgate's position, saying cheerfully :

"And if Mrs. Lydgate knew that there were friends who
would believe in you and support you, she might then be glad
that you should stay in your place and recover your hopes—
and do what you meant to do. Perhaps then you would see
that it was right to agree with what I proposed about your
continuing at the hospital. Surely you would, if you still
have faith in it as a means of making your knowledge useful?"

Lydgate did not answer, and she saw that he was debating
with himself.

"You need not decide immediately," she said gently. "A
few days hence it will be early enough for me to send my
answer to Mr. Bulstrode."

Lydgate still waited, but at last turned to speak in his most
decisive tones.

"No; I prefer that there should be no interval left for
wavering. I am no longer sure enough of myself—I mean of
what it would be possible for me to do under the changed circumstances of my life. It would be dishonorable to let others
engage themselves to anything serious in dependence on me.
I might be obliged to go away after all; I see little chance of
anything else. The whole thing is too problematic; I cannot
consent to be the cause of your goodness being wasted. No—
let the New Hospital be joined with the Old Infirmary, and

everything go on as it might have done if I had never come. I have kept a valuable register since I have been there; I shall send it to a man who will make use of it," he ended bitterly. "I can think of nothing for a long while but getting an income."

"It hurts me very much to hear you speak so hopelessly," said Dorothea. "It would be a happiness to your friends, who believe in your future, in your power to do great things, if you would let them save you from that. Think how much money I have; it would be like taking a burthen from me if you took some of it every year till you got free from this fettering want of income. Why should not people do these things? It is so difficult to make shares at all even. This is one way."

"God bless you, Mrs. Casaubon!" said Lydgate, rising as if with the same impulse that made his words energetic, and resting his arm on the back of the great leather chair he had been sitting in. "It is good that you should have such feelings. But I am not the man who ought to allow himself to benefit by them. I have not given guarantees enough. I must not at least sink into the degradation of being pensioned for work that I never achieved. It is very clear to me that I must not count on anything else than getting away from Middlemarch as soon as I can manage it. I should not be able for a long while, at the very best, to get an income here, and —and it is easier to make necessary changes in a new place. I must do as other men do, and think what will please the world and bring in money; look for a little opening in the London crowd, and push myself; set up in a watering-place, or go to some southern town where there are plenty of idle English, and get myself puffed,—that is the sort of shell I must creep into and try to keep my soul alive in."

"Now that is not brave," said Dorothea, "to give up the fight."

"No, it is not brave," said Lydgate; "but if a man is afraid of creeping paralysis?" Then, in another tone: "Yet you have made a great difference in my courage by believing in me. Everything seems more bearable since I have talked to you; and if you can clear me in a few other minds, especially in Farebrother's, I shall be deeply grateful. The point I wish you not to mention is the fact of disobedience to my orders. That would soon get distorted. After all, there is no evidence for me but people's opinion of me beforehand. You can only repeat my own report of myself."

"Mr. Farebrother will believe—others will believe," said Dorothea. "I can say of you what will make it stupidity to suppose that you would be bribed to do a wickedness."

"I don't know," said Lydgate, with something like a groan in his voice. "I have not taken a bribe yet. But there is a pale shade of bribery which is sometimes called prosperity. You will do me another great kindness, then, and come to see my wife?"

"Yes, I will. I remember how pretty she is," said Dorothea, into whose mind every impression about Rosamond had cut deep. "I hope she will like me."

As Lydgate rode away, he thought: "This young creature has a heart large enough for the Virgin Mary. She evidently thinks nothing of her own future, and would pledge away half her income at once, as if she wanted nothing for herself but a chair to sit in from which she can look down with those clear eyes at the poor mortals who pray to her. She seemed to have what I never saw in any woman before—a fountain of friendship toward men—a man can make a friend of her. Casaubon must have raised some heroic hallucination in her. I wonder if she could have any other sort of passion for a man? Ladislaw?—there was certainly an unusual feeling between them. And Casaubon must have had a notion of it. Well—her love might help a man more than her money."

Dorothea on her side had immediately formed a plan of relieving Lydgate from his obligation to Bulstrode, which she felt sure was a part, though small, of the galling pressure he had to bear. She sat down at once under the inspiration of their interview, and wrote a brief note, in which she pleaded that she had more claim than Mr. Bulstrode had to the satisfaction of providing the money which had been serviceable to Lydgate—that it would be unkind in Lydgate not to grant her the position of being his helper in this small matter, the favor being entirely to her who had so little that was plainly marked out for her to do with her superfluous money. He might call

her a creditor or by any other name if it did but imply that
he granted her request. She enclosed a check for a thousand
pounds, and determined to take the letter with her the next
day when she went to see Rosamond.

CHAPTER LXXVII.

And thus thy fall hath left a kind of blot,
To mark the full-fraught man and best indued
With some suspicion.

—*Henry V.*, Part I.

THE next day Lydgate had to go to Brassing, and told Rosamond that he should be away till the evening. Of late she
had never gone beyond her own house and garden, except to
church, and once to see her papa, to whom she said: "If
Tertius goes away you will help us to move, will you not,
papa? I suppose we shall have very little money. I am
sure I hope some one will help us." And Mr. Vincy had said:
"Yes, child, I don't mind a hundred or two. I can see the
end of that." With these exceptions she had sat at home in
languid melancholy and suspense, fixing her mind on Will
Ladislaw's coming as the one point of hope and interest, and
associating this with some new urgency on Lydgate to make
immediate arrangements for leaving Middlemarch and going
to London, till she felt assured that the coming would be a
potent cause of the going, without at all seeing how. This
way of establishing sequences is too common to be fairly regarded as a peculiar folly in Rosamond. And it is precisely
this sort of sequence which causes the greatest shock when it
is sundered: for to see how an effect may be produced is often
to see possible missings and checks; but to see nothing except
the desirable cause, and close upon it the desirable effect, rids
us of doubt and makes our minds strongly intuitive. That
was the process going on in poor Rosamond, while she arranged
all objects around her with the same nicety as ever, only with
more slowness—or sat down to the piano, meaning to play,
and then desisting, yet lingering on the music stool with her
white fingers suspended on the wooden front, and looking be-

fore her in dreamy ennui. Her melancholy had become so
marked that Lydgate felt a strange timidity before it, as a
perpetual silent reproach; and the strong man, mastered by
his keen sensibilities toward this fair, fragile creature whose
life he seemed somehow to have bruised, shrank from her look,
and sometimes started at her approach, fear of her and fear
for her rushing in only the more forcibly after it had been
momentarily expelled by exasperation.

But this morning Rosamond descended from her room upstairs—where she sometimes sat the whole day when Lydgate
was out—equipped for a walk in the town. She had a letter
to post—a letter addressed to Mr. Ladislaw, and written with
charming discretion, but intended to hasten his arrival by a
hint of trouble. The servant-maid, their sole house-servant
now, noticed her coming downstairs in her walking-dress,
and thought " there never did anybody look so pretty in a bonnet, poor thing."

Meanwhile Dorothea's mind was filled with her project of
going to Rosamond, and with the many thoughts, both of the
past and the probable future, which gathered round the idea of
that visit. Until yesterday, when Lydgate had opened to her
a glimpse of some trouble in his married life, the image of
Mrs. Lydgate had always been associated for her with that
of Will Ladislaw. Even in her most uneasy moments—even
when she had been agitated by Mrs. Cadwallader's painfully
graphic report of gossip—her effort, nay, her strongest impulsive prompting, had been toward the vindication of Will from
any sullying surmises; and when, in her meeting with him
afterward, she had at first interpreted his words as a probable
allusion to a feeling toward Mrs. Lydgate which he was determined to cut himself off from indulging, she had had a quick,
sad, excusing vision of the charm there might be in his constant opportunities of companionship with that fair creature,
who most likely shared his other tastes as she evidently did
his delight in music. But there had followed his parting words
—the few passionate words in which he had implied that she
herself was the object of whom his love held him in dread:
that it was his love for her only which he was resolved not to
declare, but to carry away into banishment. From the time of

that parting, Dorothea, believing in Will's love for her, believing with a proud delight in his delicate sense of honor and his determination that no one should impeach him justly, felt her heart quite at rest as to the regard he might have for Mrs. Lydgate. She was sure that the regard was blameless.

There are natures in which, if they love us, we are conscious of having a sort of baptism and consecration; they bind us over to rectitude and purity by their pure belief about us, and our sins become that worst kind of sacrilege which tears down the invisible altar of trust. "If you are not good, none is good——" Those little words may give a terrific meaning to responsibility, may hold a vitriolic intensity for remorse.

Dorothea's nature was of that kind. Her own passionate faults lay along the easily counted open channels of her ardent character; and while she was full of pity for the visible mistakes of others, she had not yet any material within her experience for subtle constructions and suspicions of hidden wrong. But that simplicity of hers, holding up an ideal for others in her believing conception of them, was one of the great powers of her womanhood. And it had from the first acted strongly on Will Ladislaw. He felt, when he parted from her, that the brief words by which he had tried to convey to her his feeling about herself and the division which her fortune made between them, would only profit by their brevity when Dorothea had to interpret them; he felt that in her mind he had found his highest estimate.

And he was right there. In the months since their parting Dorothea had felt a delicious though sad repose in their relation to each other, as one which was inwardly whole and without blemish. She had an active force of antagonism within her, when the antagonism turned on the defence either of plans or persons that she believed in; and the wrongs which she felt that Will had received from her husband, and the external conditions which to others were grounds for slighting him, only gave the more tenacity to her affection and admiring judgment. And now with the disclosures about Bulstrode had come another fact affecting Will's social position, which aroused afresh Dorothea's inward resistance to what was said about him in that part of her world which lay within park palings.

"Young Ladislaw, the grandson of a thieving Jew pawn-broker," was a phrase which had entered emphatically into the dialogues about the Bulstrode business, at Lowick, Tipton, and Freshitt, and was a worse kind of placard on poor Will's back than the "Italian with white mice." Upright Sir James Chettam was convinced that his own satisfaction was righteous when he thought with some complacency that here was an added league to that mountainous distance between Ladislaw and Dorothea, which enabled him to dismiss any anxiety in that direction as too absurd. And perhaps there had been some pleasure in pointing Mr. Brooke's attention to this ugly bit of Ladislaw's genealogy, as a fresh candle for him to see his own folly by. Dorothea had observed the animus with which Will's part in the painful story had been recalled more than once; but she uttered no word, being checked now, as she had not been formerly in speaking of Will, by the conscious-ness of a deeper relation between them which must always remain in consecrated secrecy. But her silence shrouded her resistant emotion into a more thorough glow; and this misfor-tune in Will's lot which, it seemed, others were wishing to fling at his back as an opprobrium, only gave something more of enthusiasm to her clinging thought.

She entertained no visions of their ever coming into nearer union, and yet she had taken no posture of renunciation. She had accepted her whole relation to Will very simply as part of her marriage sorrows, and would have thought it very sinful in her to keep up an inward wail because she was not com-pletely happy, being rather disposed to dwell on the superflu-ities of her lot. She could bear that the chief pleasures of her tenderness should lie in memory, and the idea of marriage came to her solely as a repulsive proposition from some suitor of whom she at present knew nothing, but whose merits, as seen by her friends, would be a source of torment to her: "somebody who will manage your property for you, my dear," was Mr. Brooke's attractive suggestion of suitable character-istics. "I should like to manage it myself, if I knew what to do with it," said Dorothea. No—she adhered to her declara-tion that she would never be married again; and in the long valley of her life which looked so flat and empty of way-marks, guidance would come as she walked along the road, and saw her fellow-passengers by the way.

This habitual state of feeling about Will Ladislaw had been strong in all her waking hours since she had proposed to pay a visit to Mrs. Lydgate, making a sort of background against which she saw Rosamond's figure presented to her without hindrances to her interests and compassion. There was evidently some mental separation, some barrier to complete confidence, which had arisen between this wife and the husband who had yet made her happiness a law to him. That was a trouble which no third person must directly touch. But Dorothea thought with deep pity of the loneliness which must have come upon Rosamond from the suspicions cast upon her husband; and there would surely be help in the manifestation of respect for Lydgate and sympathy with her.

"I shall talk to her about her husband," thought Dorothea, as she was being driven toward the town. The clear spring morning, the scent of the moist earth, the fresh leaves just showing their creased-up wealth of greenery from out their half-opened sheaths, seemed part of the cheerfulness she was feeling from a long conversation with Mr. Farebrother, who had joyfully accepted the justifying explanation of Lydgate's conduct. "I shall take Mrs. Lydgate good news, and perhaps she will like to talk to me and make a friend of me."

Dorothea had another errand in Lowick Gate: it was about a new fine-toned bell for the school-house, and as she had to get out of her carriage very near to Lydgate's, she walked thither across the street, having told the coachman to wait for some packages. The street door was open, and the servant was taking the opportunity of looking out at the carriage which was pausing within sight, when it became apparent to her that the lady who "belonged to it" was coming toward her.

"Is Mrs. Lydgate at home?" said Dorothea.

"I'm not sure, my lady; I'll see, if you'll please to walk in," said Martha, a little confused on the score of her kitchen apron, but collected enough to be sure that "mum" was not the right title for this queenly young widow with a carriage and pair. "Will you please to walk in, and I'll go and see."

"Say that I am Mrs. Casaubon," said Dorothea, as Martha moved forward, intending to show her into the drawing-room and then to go upstairs to see if Rosamond had returned from her walk.

They crossed the broader part of the entrance hall, and turned up the passage which led to the garden. The drawing-room door was unlatched, and Martha, pushing it without looking into the room, waited for Mrs. Casaubon to enter and then turned away, the door having swung open and swung back again without noise.

Dorothea had less of outward vision than usual this morning, being filled with images of things as they had been and were going to be. She found herself on the other side of the door without seeing anything remarkable, but immediately she heard a voice speaking in low tones which startled her as with a sense of dreaming in daylight; and advancing unconsciously a step or two beyond the projecting slab of a book-case, she saw, in the terrible illumination of a certainty which filled up all outlines, something which made her pause motionless, without self-possession enough to speak.

Seated with his back toward her on a sofa which stood against the wall on a line with the door by which she had entered, she saw Will Ladislaw: close by him and turned toward him with a flushed tearfulness which gave a new brilliancy to her face sat Rosamond, her bonnet hanging back, while Will leaning toward her clasped both her upraised hands in his and spoke with low-toned fervor.

Rosamond in her agitated absorption had not noticed the silently advancing figure; but when Dorothea, after the first immeasurable instant of this vision, moved confusedly backward and found herself impeded by some piece of furniture, Rosamond was suddenly aware of her presence, and with a spasmodic movement snatched away her hands and rose, looking at Dorothea, who was necessarily arrested. Will Ladislaw, starting up, looked round also, and meeting Dorothea's eyes with a new lightning in them, seemed changing to marble. But she immediately turned them away from him to Rosamond, and said in a firm voice:

"Excuse me, Mrs. Lydgate, the servant did not know that

you were here. I called to deliver an important letter for Mr. Lydgate, which I wished to put into your hands."

She laid down the letter on the small table which had checked her retreat, and then including Rosamond and Will in one distant glance and bow, she went quickly out of the room, meeting in the passage the surprised Martha, who said she was sorry the mistress was not at home, and then showed the strange lady out with an inward reflection that grand people were probably more impatient than others.

Dorothea walked across the street with her most elastic step, and was quickly in her carriage again.

"Drive on to Freshitt Hall," she said to the coachman, and any one looking at her might have thought that though she was paler than usual, she was never animated by a more self-possessed energy. And that was really her experience. It was as if she had drunk a great draught of scorn that stimulated her beyond the susceptibility to other feelings. She had seen something so far below her belief that her emotions rushed back from it and made an excited throng without an object. She needed something active to turn her excitement out upon. She felt power to walk and work for a day, without meat or drink. And she would carry out the purpose with which she had started in the morning, of going to Freshitt and Tipton to tell Sir James and her uncle all that she wished them to know about Lydgate, whose married loneliness under his trial now presented itself to her with new significance, and made her more ardent in readiness to be his champion. She had never felt anything like this triumphant power of indignation in the struggle of her married life, in which there had always been a quickly subduing pang; and she took it as a sign of new strength.

"Dodo, how very bright your eyes are!" said Celia, when Sir James was gone out of the room. "And you don't see anything you look at, Arthur or anything. You are going to do something uncomfortable, I know. Is it all about Mr. Lydgate, or has something else happened?" Celia had been used to watch her sister with expectation.

"Yes, dear, a great many things have happened," said Dodo, in her full tones.

"I wonder what," said Celia, folding her arms cozily and leaning forward upon them.

"Oh, all the troubles of all people on the face of the earth!" said Dorothea, lifting her arms to the back of her head.

"Dear me, Dodo, are you going to have a scheme for them?" said Celia, a little uneasy at this Hamlet-like raving.

But Sir James came in again, ready to accompany Dorothea to the Grange, and she finished her expedition well, not swerving in her resolution until she descended at her own door.

CHAPTER LXXVIII.

Would it were yesterday and I i' the grave,
With her sweet faith above for monument.

ROSAMOND and Will stood motionless—they did not know how long—he looking toward the spot where Dorothea had stood, and she looking toward him with doubt. It seemed an endless time to Rosamond, in whose inmost soul there was hardly so much annoyance as gratification from what had just happened. Shallow natures dream of an easy sway over the emotions of others, trusting implicitly in their own petty magic to turn the deepest streams, and confident, by pretty gestures and remarks, of making the thing that is not as though it were. She knew that Will had received a severe blow, but she had been little used to imagining other people's states of mind except as a material cut into shape by her own wishes; and she believed in her own power to soothe or subdue. Even Tertius, that most perverse of men, was always subdued in the long run: events had been obstinate, but still Rosamond would have said now, as she did before her marriage, that she never gave up what she had set her mind on.

She put out her arm and laid the tips of her fingers on Will's coat-sleeve.

"Don't touch me!" he said, with an utterance like the cut of a lash, darting from her, and changing from pink to white and back again, as if his whole frame were tingling with the pain of the sting. He wheeled around to the other side of the room and stood opposite to her, with the tips of his fingers in his pockets and his head thrown back, looking fiercely, not at Rosamond, but at a point a few inches away from her.

She was keenly offended, but the signs she made of this were such as only Lydgate was used to interpret. She became suddenly quiet, and seated herself, untying her hanging bonnet and laying it down with her shawl. Her little hands which she folded before her were very cold.

It would have been safer for Will in the first instance to have taken up his hat and gone away; but he had felt no impulse to do this; on the contrary, he had a horrible inclination to stay and shatter Rosamond with his anger. It seemed as impossible to bear the fatality she had drawn down on him without venting his fury, as it would be to a panther to bear the javelin-wound without springing and biting. And yet— how could he tell a woman that he was ready to curse her? He was fuming under a repressive law which he was forced to acknowledge: he was dangerously poised, and Rosamond's voice now brought the decisive vibration. In flute-like tones of sarcasm she said:

"You can easily go after Mrs. Casaubon and explain your preference."

"Go after her!" he burst out, with a sharp edge in his voice. "Do you think she would turn to look at me, or value any word I ever uttered to her again at more than a dirty feather? Explain! How can a man explain at the expense of a woman?"

"You can tell her what you please," said Rosamond, with more tremor.

"Do you suppose she would like me better for sacrificing you? She is not a woman to be flattered because I made myself despicable—to believe that I must be true to her because I was a dastard to you."

He began to move about with the restlessness of a wild animal that sees prey but cannot reach it. Presently he burst out again:

"I had no hope before—not much—of anything better to come. But I had one certainty—that she believed in me. Whatever people had said or done about me, she believed in me. That's gone! She'll never again think me anything but a paltry pretence—too nice to take heaven except upon flattering conditions, and yet selling myself for any devil's change by the sly. She'll think of me as an incarnate insult to her, from the first moment we——"

Will stopped as if he had found himself grasping something that must not be thrown and shattered. He found another vent for his rage by snatching up Rosamond's words again, as if they were reptiles to be throttled and flung off.

"Explain! Tell a man to explain how he dropped into hell! Explain my preference! I never had a *preference* for her, any more than I have a preference for breathing. No other woman exists by the side of her. I would rather touch her hand if it were dead, than I would touch any other woman's living."

Rosamond, while these poisoned weapons were being hurled at her, was almost losing the sense of her identity and seemed to be waking into some new terrible existence. She had no sense of chill resolute repulsion, of reticent self-justification, such as she had known under Lydgate's most stormy displeasure: all her sensibility was turned into a bewildering novelty of pain; she felt a new terrified recoil under a lash never experienced before. What another nature felt in opposition to her own was being burnt and bitten into her consciousness. When Will had ceased to speak, she had become an image of sickened misery: her lips were pale, and her eyes had a tearless dismay in them. If it had been Tertius who stood opposite to her, that look of misery would have been a pang to him, and he would have sunk by her side to comfort her, with that strong-armed comfort which she had often held very cheap.

Let it be forgiven to Will that he had no such movement of pity. He had felt no bond beforehand to this woman who had spoiled the ideal treasure of his life, and he held himself blameless. He knew that he was cruel, but had no relenting in him yet.

After he had done speaking, he still moved about, half in absence of mind, and Rosamond sat perfectly still. At length Will, seeming to bethink himself, took up his hat, yet stood some moments irresolute. He had spoken to her in a way that made a phrase of common politeness difficult to utter; and yet, now that he had come to the point of going away from her without further speech, he shrank from it as a brutality; he felt checked and stultified in his anger. He walked toward the mantelpiece and leaned his arm on it, and waited in silence for —he hardly knew what. The vindictive fire was still burning in him, and he could utter no word of retractation; but it was nevertheless in his mind that having come back to this hearth where he had enjoyed a caressing friendship, he had found calamity seated there—he had had suddenly revealed to him a trouble that lay outside the home as well as within it. And what seemed a foreboding was pressing upon him as with slow pincers: that his life might come to be enslaved by this helpless woman who had thrown herself upon him in the dreary sadness of her heart. But he was in gloomy rebellion against the fact that his quick apprehensiveness foreshadowed to him, and when his eyes fell on Rosamond's blighted face it seemed to him that he was the more pitiable of the two; for pain must enter into its glorified life of memory before it can turn into compassion.

And so they remained for many minutes, opposite each other, far apart, in silence: Will's face still possessed by a mute rage, and Rosamond's by a mute misery. The poor thing had no force to fling out any passion in return; the terrible collapse of the illusion toward which all her hope had been strained was a stroke which had too thoroughly shaken her: her little world was in ruins, and she felt herself tottering in the midst as a lonely bewildered consciousness.

Will wished that she would speak and bring some mitigating shadow across his own cruel speech, which seemed to stand staring at them both in mockery of any attempt at revived fellowship. But she said nothing, and at last, with a desperate effort over himself, he asked, "Shall I come in and see Lydgate this evening?"

"If you like," Rosamond answered, just audibly.

And then Will went out of the house, Martha never knowing that he had been in.

After he was gone, Rosamond tried to get up from her seat, but fell back fainting. When she came to herself again, she felt too ill to make the exertion of rising to ring the bell, and she remained helpless until the girl, surprised at her long absence, thought for the first time of looking for her in all the

downstairs rooms.   Rosamond said that she had felt suddenly
sick and faint, and wanted to be helped upstairs.   When there,
she threw herself on the bed with her clothes on, and lay in
apparent torpor, as she had done once before on a memorable
day of grief.

Lydgate came home earlier than he had expected, about
half-past five, and found her there.   The perception that she
was ill threw every other thought into the background.   When
he felt her pulse, her eyes rested on him with more persis-
tence than they had done for a long while, as if she felt some
content that he was there.   He perceived the difference in·
a moment, and, seating himself by her, put his arm gently
under her, and bending over her, said, " My poor Rosamond!
has something agitated you? "   Clinging to him, she fell into
hysterical sobbings and cries, and for the next hour he did
nothing but soothe and tend her.   He imagined that Dorothea
had been to see her, and that all this effect on her nervous
system, which evidently involved some new turning toward
himself, was due to the excitement of the new impressions
which that visit had raised.

CHAPTER LXXIX.

"Now, I saw in my dream, that just as they had ended their talk, they drew nigh
to a very miry slough, that was in the midst of the plain; and they, being heedless,
did both fall suddenly into the bog. The name of the slough was Despond."—
BUNYAN.

WHEN Rosamond was quiet, and Lydgate had left her, hoping that she might soon sleep under the effect of an anodyne,
he went into the drawing-room to fetch a book which he had
left there, meaning to spend the evening in his workroom, and
he saw on the table Dorothea's letter addressed to him.   He
had not ventured to ask Rosamond if Mrs. Casaubon had
called, but the reading of this letter assured him of the fact,
for Dorothea mentioned that it was to be carried by herself.

When Will Ladislaw came in a little later, Lydgate met him
with a surprise, which made it clear that he had not been told

of the earlier visit, and Will could not say, "Did not Mrs. Lydgate tell you that I came this morning?"

"Poor Rosamond is ill," Lydgate added immediately on his greeting.

"Not seriously, I hope," said Will.

"No—only a slight nervous shock—the effect of some agitation. She has been overwrought lately. The truth is, Ladislaw, I am an unlucky devil. We have gone through several rounds of purgatory since you left, and I have lately got on to a worse ledge of it than ever. I suppose you are only just come down—you look rather battered—you have not been long enough in the town to hear anything?"

"I travelled all night and got to the White Hart at eight o'clock this morning. I have been shutting myself up and resting," said Will, feeling himself a sneak, but seeing no alternative to this evasion.

And then he heard Lydgate's account of the troubles which Rosamond had already depicted to him in her way. She had not mentioned the fact of Will's name being connected with the public story—this detail not immediately affecting her—and he now heard it for the first time.

"I thought it better to tell you that your name is mixed up with the disclosures," said Lydgate, who could understand better than most men how Ladislaw might be stung by the revelation. "You will be sure to hear it as soon as you turn out into the town. I suppose it is true that Raffles spoke to you."

"Yes," said Will, sardonically. "I shall be fortunate if gossip does not make me the most disreputable person in the whole affair. I should think the latest version must be, that I plotted with Raffles to murder Bulstrode, and ran away from Middlemarch for the purpose."

He was thinking: "Here is a new ring in the sound of my name to recommend it in her hearing; however—what does it signify now?"

But he said nothing of Bulstrode's offer to him. Will was very open and careless about his personal affairs, but it was among the more exquisite touches in nature's modelling of him that he had a delicate generosity which warned him into reticence here. He shrank from saying that he had rejected Bulstrode's money, in the moment when he was learning that it was Lydgate's misfortune to have accepted it.

Lydgate too was reticent in the midst of his confidence. He made no allusion to Rosamond's feeling under their trouble, and of Dorothea he only said, "Mrs. Casaubon has been the one person to come forward and say that she had no belief in the suspicions against me." Observing a change in Will's face, he avoided any further mention of her, feeling himself too ignorant of their relation to each other not to fear that his words might have some hidden, painful bearing on it. And it occurred to him that Dorothea was the real cause of the present visit to Middlemarch.

The two men were pitying each other, but it was only Will who guessed the extent of his companion's trouble. When Lydgate spoke with desperate resignation of going to settle in London, and said with a faint smile, "We shall have you again, old fellow," Will felt inexpressibly mournful, and said nothing. Rosamond had that morning entreated him to urge this step on Lydgate; and it seemed to him as if he were beholding in a magic panorama a future where he himself was sliding into that pleasureless yielding to the small solicitations of circumstance, which is a commoner history of perdition than any single momentous bargain.

We are on a perilous margin when we begin to look passively at our future selves, and see our own figures led with dull consent into insipid misdoing and shabby achievement. Poor Lydgate was inwardly groaning on that margin, and Will was arriving at it. It seemed to him this evening as if the cruelty of his outburst to Rosamond had made an obligation for him, and he dreaded the obligation: he dreaded Lydgate's unsuspecting good-will: he dreaded his own distaste for his spoiled life, which would leave him in motiveless levity.

CHAPTER LXXX.

" Stern lawgiver ! yet thou dost wear
The Godhead's most benignant grace;
Nor know we anything so fair
As is the smile upon thy face;
Flowers laugh before thèe on their beds,
And fragrance in thy footing treads;
Thou dost preserve the Stars from wrong;
And the most ancient Heavens, through thee, are fresh and strong. "
—WORDSWORTH : *Ode to Duty.*

WHEN Dorothea had seen Mr. Farebrother in the morning, she had promised to go and dine at the parsonage on her return from Freshitt. There was a frequent interchange of visits between her and the Farebrother family, which enabled her to say that she was not at all lonely at the manor, and to resist for the present the severe prescription of a lady companion. When she reached home and remembered her engagement, she was glad of it; and finding that she had still an hour before she could dress for dinner, she walked straight to the schoolhouse and entered into a conversation with the master and mistress about the new bell, giving eager attention to their small details and repetitions, and getting up a dramatic sense that her life was very busy. She paused on her way back to talk to old Master Bunney who was putting in some garden-seeds, and discoursed wisely with that rural sage about the crops that would make the most return on a perch of ground, and the result of sixty years' experience as to soils—namely, that if your soil was pretty mellow it would do, but if there came wet, wet, wet to make it all of a mummy, why then——

Finding that the social spirit had beguiled her into being rather late, she dressed hastily and went over to the parsonage rather earlier than was necessary. That house was never dull, Mr. Farebrother, like another White of Selborne, having continually something new to tell of his inarticulate guests and *protégés*, whom he was teaching the boys not to torment; and he had just set up a pair of beautiful goats to be pets of the village in general, and to walk at large as sacred animals. The evening went by cheerfully till after tea, Dorothea talking more than usual and dilating with Mr. Farebrother on the pos-

sible histories of creatures that converse compendiously with
their antennæ, and for aught we know may hold reformed
parliaments; when suddenly some inarticulate little sounds
were heard which called everybody's attention.

"Henrietta Noble," said Mrs. Farebrother, seeing her small
sister moving about the furniture-legs distressfully, "what is
the matter?"

"I have lost my tortoise-shell lozenge-box. I fear the kitten has rolled it away," said the tiny old lady, involuntarily
continuing her beaver-like notes.

"Is it a great treasure, aunt?" said Mr. Farebrother, putting up his glasses and looking at the carpet.

"Mr. Ladislaw gave it me," said Miss Noble. "A German
box—very pretty; but if it falls it always spins away as far
as it can."

"Oh, if it is Ladislaw's present," said Mr. Farebrother, in
a deep tone of comprehension, getting up and hunting. The
box was found at last under a chiffonier, and Miss Noble
grasped it with delight, saying, "It was under a fender the
last time."

"That is an affair of the heart with my aunt," said Mr.
Farebrother, smiling at Dorothea, as he reseated himself.

"If Henrietta Noble forms an attachment to any one, Mrs.
Casaubon," said his mother, emphatically,—"she is like a dog
—she would take their shoes for a pillow and sleep the better."

"Mr. Ladislaw's shoes, I would," said Henrietta Noble.

Dorothea made an attempt at smiling in return. She was
surprised and annoyed to find that her heart was palpitating
violently, and that it was quite useless to try after a recovery
of her former animation. Alarmed at herself—fearing some
further betrayal of a change so marked in its occasion—she
rose and said in a low voice with undisguised anxiety: "I
must go; I have over-tired myself."

Mr. Farebrother, quick in perception, rose and said: "It
is true; you must have half-exhausted yourself in talking
about Lydgate. That sort of work tells upon one after the
excitement is over."

He gave her his arm back to the manor, but Dorothea did
not attempt to speak, even when he said good-night.

The limit of resistance was reached, and she had sunk back helpless within the clutch of inescapable anguish. Dismissing Tantripp with a few faint words, she locked her door, and turning away from it toward the vacant room, she pressed her hands hard on the top of her head and moaned out:

"Oh, I did love him!"

Then came the hour in which the waves of suffering shook her too thoroughly to leave any power of thought. She could only cry in loud whispers, between her sobs, after her lost belief which she had planted and kept alive from a very little seed since the days in Rome—after her lost joy of clinging with silent love and faith to one who, misprized by others, was worthy in her thought—after her lost woman's pride of reigning in his memory—after her sweet dim perspective of hope that along some pathway they should meet with unchanged recognition and take up the backward years as a yesterday.

In that hour she repeated what the merciful eyes of solitude have looked on for ages in the spiritual struggles of man—she besought hardness and coldness and aching weariness to bring her relief from the mysterious incorporeal might of her anguish: she lay on the bare floor and let the night grow cold around her; while her grand woman's frame was shaken by sobs as if she had been a despairing child.

There were two images—two living forms that tore her heart in two, as if it had been the heart of a mother who seems to see her child divided by the sword, and presses one bleeding half to her breast while her gaze goes forth in agony toward the half which is carried away by the lying woman that has never known the mother's pang.

Here, with the nearness of an answering smile, here within the vibrating bond of mutual speech, was the bright creature whom she had trusted—who had come to her like the spirit of morning visiting the dim vault where she sat as the bride of a worn-out life; and now, with a full consciousness which had never awakened before, she stretched out her arms toward him and cried with bitter cries that their nearness was a parting vision; she discovered her passion to herself in the unshrinking utterance of despair.

And there, aloof, yet persistently with her, moving wher-ever she moved, was the Will Ladislaw who was a changed belief exhausted of hope, a detected illusion—no, a living man toward whom there could not yet struggle any wail of regretful pity, from the midst of scorn and indignation and jealous offended pride.   The fire of Dorothea's anger was not easily spent, and it flamed out in fitful returns of spurning reproach. Why had he come obtruding his life into hers—hers that might have been whole enough without him?   Why had he brought his cheap regard and his lip-born words to her who had nothing paltry to give in exchange?   He knew that he was deluding her—wished, in the very moment of farewell, to make her believe that he gave her the whole price of her heart, and knew that he had spent it half before.   Why had he not stayed among the crowd of whom she asked nothing—but only prayed that they might be less contemptible?

But she lost energy at last even for her loud-whispered cries and moans: she subsided into helpless sobs, and on the cold floor she sobbed herself to sleep.

In the chill hours of the morning twilight, when all was dim around her, she awoke—not with any amazed wondering where she was or what had happened, but with the clearest consciousness that she was looking into the eyes of sorrow. She rose, and wrapped warm things around her, and seated herself in a great chair where she had often watched before. She was vigorous enough to have borne that hard night without feeling ill in body, beyond some aching and fatigue; but she had waked to a new condition: she felt as if her soul had been liberated from its terrible conflict; she was no longer wrestling with her grief, but could sit down with it as a lasting companion and make it a sharer in her thoughts.   For now the thoughts came thickly.   It was not in Dorothea's nature, for longer than the duration of a paroxysm, to sit in the narrow cell of her calamity, in the besotted misery of a consciousness that only sees another's lot as an accident of its own.

She began now to live through that yesterday morning deliberately again, forcing herself to dwell on every detail and its possible meaning.   Was she alone in that scene ?   Was it her event only?   She forced herself to think of it as bound up with another woman's life—a woman toward whom she had

set out with a longing to carry some clearness and comfort into
her beclouded youth. In her first outleap of jealous indignation and disgust, when quitting the hateful room, she had flung
away all the mercy with which she had undertaken that visit.
She had enveloped both Will and Rosamond in her burning
scorn, and it seemed to her as if Rosamond were burned out
of her sight forever. But that base prompting which makes a
woman more cruel to a rival than to a faithless lover, could
have no strength of recurrence in Dorothea when the dominant
spirit of justice within her had once overcome the tumult and
had once shown her the truer measure of things. All the active
thought with which she had before been representing to herself the trials of Lydgate's lot, and this young marriage union
which, like her own, seemed to have its hidden as well as evident troubles—all this vivid, sympathetic experience returned
to her now as a power: it asserted itself as acquired knowledge
asserts itself, and will not let us see as we saw in the day of
our ignorance. She said to her own irremediable grief, that it
should make her more helpful, instead of driving her back
from effort.

And what sort of crisis might not this be in three lives
whose contact with hers laid an obligation on her as if they
had been suppliants bearing the sacred branch? The objects
of her rescue were not to be sought out by her fancy: they
were chosen for her. She yearned toward the perfect right,
that it might make a throne within her, and rule her errant
will. "What should I do—how should I act now, this very
day, if I could clutch my own pain, and compel it to silence,
and think of those three?"

It had taken long for her to come to that question, and
there was light piercing into the room. She opened her cur-
tains, and looked out toward the bit of road that lay in view,
with fields beyond outside the entrance-gates. On the road
there was a man with a bundle on his back and a woman carrying her baby; in the field she could see figures moving—
perhaps the shepherd with his dog. Far off in the bending
sky was the pearly light; and she felt the largeness of the
world and the manifold wakings of men to labor and endurance.
She was a part of that involuntary, palpitating life, and could

neither look out on it from her luxurious shelter as a mere spectator, nor hide her eyes in selfish complaining.

What she would resolve to do that day did not yet seem quite clear, but something that she could achieve stirred her as with an approaching murmur which would soon gather distinctness. She took off the clothes which seemed to have some of the weariness of a hard watching in them, and began to make her toilet. Presently she rang for Tantripp, who came in her dressing-gown.

"Why, madam, you've never been in bed this blessed night," burst out Tantripp, looking first at the bed and then at Dorothea's face, which in spite of bathing had the pale cheeks and pink eyelids of a *mater dolorosa*. "You'll kill yourself, you *will*. Anybody might think now you had a right to give yourself a little comfort."

"Don't be alarmed, Tantripp," said Dorothea, smiling. "I have slept; I am not ill. I shall be glad of a cup of coffee as soon as possible. And I want you to bring me my new dress, and most likely I shall want my new bonnet to-day."

"They've lain there a month and more ready for you, madam, and most thankful I shall be to see you with a couple o' pounds' worth less of crape," said Tantripp, stooping to light the fire. "There's a reason in mourning, as I've always said; and three folds at the bottom of your skirt and a plain quilling in your bonnet—and if ever anybody looked like an angel, it's you in a net quilling—is what's consistent for a second year. At least, that's *my* thinking," ended Tantripp, looking anxiously at the fire; "and if anybody was to marry me flattering himself I should wear those hijeous weepers two years for him, he'd be deceived by his own vanity, that's all."

"The fire will do, my good Tan," said Dorothea, speaking as she used to do in the old Lausanne days, only with a very low voice; "get me the coffee."

She folded herself in the large chair, and leaned her head against it in fatigued quiescence, while Tantripp went away wondering at this strange contrariness in her young mistress —that just the morning when she had more of a widow's face than ever, she should have asked for her lighter mourning which she had waived before. Tantripp would never have found the clue to this mystery. Dorothea wished to acknowledge that she had not the less an active life before her because she had buried a private joy; and the tradition that fresh garments belonged to all initiation haunting her mind, made her grasp after even that slight outward hélp toward calm resolve; for the resolve was not easy.

Nevertheless, at eleven o'clock she was walking toward Middlemarch, having made up her mind that she would make as quietly and unnoticeably as possible her second attempt to see and save Rosamond.

CHAPTER LXXXI.

" Du Erde warst auch diese Nacht beständig,
Und athmest neu erquickt zu meinen Füssen,
Beginnest schon mit Lust mich zu umgeben,
Du regst und rührst ein kräftiges Beschliessen
Zum höcsten Dasein immerfort zu streben. "

—Faust : 2r Theil.

WHEN Dorothea was again at Lydgate's door speaking to Martha, he was in the room close by with the door ajar, preparing to go out. He heard her voice, and immediately came to her.

"Do you think that Mrs. Lydgate can receive me this morning?" she said, having reflected that it would be better to leave out all allusion to her previous visit.

"I have no doubt she will," said Lydgate, suppressing his thought about Dorothea's looks, which were as much changed as Rosamond's, "if you will be kind enough to come in and let me tell her that you are here. She has not been very well since you were here yesterday, but she is better this morning, and I think it is very likely that she will be cheered by seeing you again."

It was plain that Lydgate, as Dorothea had expected, knew nothing about the circumstances of her yesterday's visit; nay, he appeared to imagine that she had carried it out according to her intention. She had prepared a little note asking Rosamond to see her, which she would have given to the servant if he had not been in the way, but now she was in much anxiety as to the result of his announcement.

After leading her into the drawing-room, he paused to take a letter from his pocket and put it into her hands, saying: "I wrote this last night, and was going to carry it to Lowick in my ride.   When one is grateful for something too good for common thanks, writing is less unsatisfactory than speech— one does not at least *hear* how inadequate the words are."

Dorothea's face brightened.   "It is I who have most to thank for, since you have let me take that place.   You *have* consented?" she said, suddenly doubting.

"Yes, the check is going to Bulstrode to-day."

He said no more, but went upstairs to Rosamond, who had but lately finished dressing herself, and sat languidly wondering what she should do next, her habitual industry in small things, even in the days of her sadness, prompting her to begin some kind of occupation, which she dragged through slowly or paused in from lack of interest.   She looked ill, but had recovered her usual quietude of manner, and Lydgate had feared to disturb her by any questions.   He had told her of Dorothea's letter containing the check, and afterward he had said: "Ladislaw has come, Rosy; he sat with me last night; I dare say he will be here again to-day.   I thought he looked rather battered and depressed."   And Rosamond had made no reply.

Now, when he came up, he said to her very gently: "Rosy, dear, Mrs. Casaubon is come to see you again; you would like to see her, would you not?"   That she colored and gave rather a startled movement did not surprise him after the agitation produced by the interview yesterday—a beneficent agitation, he thought, since it seemed to have made her turn to him again.

Rosamond dared not say no.   She dared not with a tone of her voice touch the facts of yesterday.   Why had Mrs. Casaubon come again?   The answer was a blank which Rosamond could only fill up with dread, for Will Ladislaw's lacerating words had made every thought of Dorothea a fresh smart to her.   Nevertheless, in her new humiliating uncertainty she dared do nothing but comply.   She did not say yes, but she rose and let Lydgate put a light shawl over her shoulders, while he said, "I am going out immediately."   Then something crossed her mind which prompted her to say, "Pray tell Mar-

tha not to bring any one else into the drawing-room." And
Lydgate assented, thinking that he fully understood this wish.
He led her down to the drawing-room door, and then turned
away, observing to himself that he was rather a blundering
husband to be dependent for his wife's trust in him on the
influence of another woman.

Rosamond wrapping her soft shawl around her as she walked
toward Dorothea, was inwardly wrapping her soul in cold
reserve.   Had Mrs. Casaubon come to say anything to her
about Will?   If so, it was a liberty that Rosamond resented;
and she prepared herself to meet every word with polite impassibility.   Will had bruised her pride too sorely for her to
feel any compunction toward him and Dorothea: her own
injury seemed much the greater.   Dorothea was not only the
"preferred" woman, but had also a formidable advantage in
being Lydgate's benefactor; and to poor Rosamond's pained,
confused vision it seemed that this Mrs. Casaubon—this woman
who predominated in all things concerning her—must have
come now with the sense of having the advantage, and with
animosity prompting her to use it.   Indeed, not Rosamond
only, but any one else, knowing the outer facts of the case,
and not the simple inspiration on which Dorothea acted, might
well have wondered why she came.

Looking like the lovely ghost of herself, her graceful slim-
ness wrapped in her soft white shawl, the rounded infantine
mouth and cheek inevitably suggesting mildness and innocence,
Rosamond paused at three yards' distance from her visitor and
bowed.   But Dorothea, who had taken off her gloves, from an
impulse which she could never resist when she wanted a sense
of freedom, came forward, and, with her face full of sad yet
sweet openness, put out her hand.   Rosamond could not avoid
meeting her glance, could not avoid putting her small hand
into Dorothea's, which clasped it with gentle motherliness;
and immediately a doubt of her own prepossessions began to
stir within her.   Rosamond's eye was quick for faces; she saw
that Mrs. Casaubon's face looked pale and changed since yesterday, yet gentle, and like the firm softness of her hand.
But Dorothea had counted a little too much on her own
strength: the clearness and intensity of her mental action this

morning were the continuance of a nervous exaltation which made her frame as dangerously responsive as a bit of finest Venetian crystal; and in looking at Rosamond, she suddenly found her heart swelling, and was unable to speak—all her effort was required to keep back tears. She succeeded in that, and the emotion only passed over her face like the spirit of a sob; but it added to Rosamond's impression that Mrs. Casaubon's state of mind must be something quite different from what she had imagined.

So they sat down without a word of preface on the two chairs that happened to be nearest, and happened also to be close together; though Rosamond's notion when she first bowed was that she should stay a long way off from Mrs. Casaubon. But she ceased thinking how anything would turn out—merely wondering what would come. And Dorothea began to speak quite simply, gathering firmness as she went on.

"I had an errand yesterday which I did not finish; that is why I am here again so soon. You will not think me too troublesome when I tell you that I came to talk to you about the injustice that has been shown toward Mr. Lydgate. It will cheer you—will it not?—to know a great deal about him, that he may not like to speak about himself just because it is in his own vindication and to his own honor. You will like to know that your husband has warm friends, who have not left off believing in his high character? You will let me speak of this without thinking that I take a liberty?"

The cordial, pleading tones which seemed to flow with generous heedlessness above all the facts which had filled Rosamond's mind as grounds of obstruction and hatred between her and this woman, came as soothingly as a warm stream over her shrinking fears. Of course Mrs. Casaubon had the facts in her mind, but she was not going to speak of anything connected with them. That relief was too great for Rosamond to feel much else at the moment. She answered prettily, in the new ease of her soul—

"I know you have been very good. I shall like to hear anything you will say to me about Tertius."

"The day before yesterday," said Dorothea, "when I had asked him to come to Lowick to give me his opinion on the

affairs of the hospital, he told me everything about his conduct and feelings in this sad event which has made ignorant
people cast suspicions on him. The reason he told me was
because I was very bold and asked him. I believed that he
had never acted dishonorably, and I begged him to tell me the
history. He confessed to me that he had never told it before,
not even to you, because he had a great dislike to say, ' I was
not wrong,' as if that were proof, when there are guilty people
who will say so. The truth is, he knew nothing of this man
Raffles, or that there were any bad secrets about him; and he
thought that Mr. Bulstrode offered him the money because he
repented, out of kindness, of having refused it before.. All
his anxiety about his patient was to treat him rightly, and he
was a little uncomfortable that the case did not end as he had
expected; but he thought then and still thinks that there may
have been no wrong in it on any one's part. And I have told
Mr. Farebrother, and Mr. Brooke, and Sir James Chettam:
they all believe in your husband. That will cheer you, will it
not? That will give you courage?"

Dorothea's face had become animated, and as it beamed on
Rosamond very close to her, she felt something like bashful
timidity before a superior, in the presence of this self-forget-
ful ardor. She said, with blushing embarrassment: "Thank
you; you are very kind."

"And he felt that he had been so wrong not to pour out
everything about this to you. But you will forgive him. It
was because he feels so much more about your happiness than
anything else—he feels his life bound into one with yours,
and it hurts him more than anything that his misfortune must
hurt you. He could speak to me because I am an indifferent
person. And then I asked him if I might come to see you;
because I felt so much for his trouble and yours. That is why
I came yesterday, and why I am come to-day. Trouble is so
hard to bear, is it not?—How can we live and think that any
one has trouble—piercing trouble—and we could help them,
and never try?"

Dorothea, completely swayed by the feeling that she was
uttering, forgot everything but that she was speaking from
out the heart of her own trial to Rosamond's. The emotion

had wrought itself more and more into her utterance, till the tones might have gone to one's very marrow, like a low cry from some suffering creature in the darkness. And she had unconsciously laid her hand again on the little hand that she had pressed before.

Rosamond, with an overmastering pang, as if a wound within her had been probed, burst into hysterical crying as she had done the day before when she clung to her husband. Poor Dorothea was feeling a great wave of her own sorrow returning over her—her thought being drawn to the possible share that Will Ladislaw might have in Rosamond's mental tumult. She was beginning to fear that she should not be able to suppress herself enough to the end of this meeting; and while her hand was still resting on Rosamond's lap, though the hand underneath it was withdrawn, she was struggling against her own rising sobs. She tried to master herself with the thought that this might be a turning-point in three lives—not in her own; no, there the irrevocable had happened, but—in those three lives which were touching hers with the solemn neighborhood of danger and distress. The fragile creature who was crying close to her—there might still be time to rescue her from the misery of false incompatible bonds: and this moment was unlike any other: she and Rosamond could never be together again with the same thrilling consciousness of yesterday within them both. She felt the relation between them to be peculiar enough to give her a peculiar influence, though she had no conception that the way in which her own feelings were involved was fully known to Mrs. Lydgate.

It was a newer crisis in Rosamond's experience than even Dorothea could imagine: she was under the first great shock that had shattered her dream-world in which she had been easily confident of herself and critical of others; and this strange, unexpected manifestation of feeling in a woman whom she had approached with a shrinking aversion and dread, as one who must necessarily have a jealous hatred toward her, made her soul totter all the more with a sense that she had been walking in an unknown world which had just broken in upon her.

When Rosamond's convulsed throat was subsiding into calm, and she withdrew the handkerchief with which she had been hiding her face, her eyes met Dorothea's as helplessly as if they had been blue flowers. What was the use of thinking about behavior after this crying? And Dorothea looked almost as childish, with the neglected trace of a silent tear. Pride was broken down between these two.

"We were talking about your husband," Dorothea said, with some timidity. "I thought his looks were sadly changed with suffering the other day. I had not seen him for many weeks before. He said he had been feeling very lonely in his trial; but I think he would have borne it all better if he had been able to be quite open with you."

"Tertius is so angry and impatient if I say anything," said Rosamond, imagining that he had been complaining of her to Dorothea. "He ought not to wonder that I object to speak to him on painful subjects."

"It was himself he blamed for not speaking," said Dorothea. "What he said of you was that he could not be happy in doing anything which made you unhappy—that his marriage was of course a bond which must affect his choice about everything; and for that reason he refused my proposal that he should keep his position at the hospital, because that would bind him to stay in Middlemarch, and he would not undertake to do anything which would be painful to you. He could say that to me, because he knows that I had much trial in my marriage, from my husband's illness, which hindered his plans and saddened him; and he knows that I have felt how hard it is to walk always in fear of hurting another who is tied to us."

Dorothea waited a little; she had discerned a faint pleasure stealing over Rosamond's face. But there was no answer, and she went on, with a gathering tremor: "Marriage is so unlike everything else. There is something even awful in the nearness which it brings. Even if we loved some one else better than—than those we were married to, it would be of no use"—poor Dorothea, in her palpitating anxiety, could only seize her language brokenly—"I mean, marriage drinks up all our power of giving or getting any blessedness in that sort of love. I know it may be very dear—but it murders our marriage—and
51

then the marriage stays with us like a murder—and everything
else is gone.　And then our husband—if he loved and trusted
us, and we have not helped him, but made a curse in his
life——"

Her voice had sunk very low: there was a dread upon her
of presuming too far, and of speaking as if she herself were
perfection addressing error.　She was too much preoccupied
with her own anxiety, to be aware that Rosamond was trembling too; and filled with the need to express pitying fellowship rather than rebuke, she put her hands on Rosamond's and
said with more agitated rapidity: "I know, I know that the
feeling may be very dear—it has taken hold of us unawares—
it is so hard, it may seem like death to part with it, and we
are weak—I am weak——"

The waves of her own sorrow, from out of which she was
struggling to save another, rushed over Dorothea with con-
quering force.　She stopped in speechless agitation, not crying, but feeling as if she were being inwardly grappled.　Her
face had become of a deathlier paleness, her lips trembled,
and she pressed her hands helplessly on the hands that lay
under them.

Rosamond, taken hold of by an emotion stronger than her
own—hurried along in a new movement which gave all things
some new, awful, undefined aspect—could find no words, but
involuntarily she put her lips to Dorothea's forehead, which
was very near her, and then for a minute the two women
clasped each other as if they had been in a shipwreck.

"You are thinking what is not true," said Rosamond, in an
eager half-whisper, while she was still feeling Dorothea's arms
round her—urged by a mysterious necessity to free herself
from something that oppressed her as if it were blood-guiltiness.

They moved apart, looking at each other.

"When you came in yesterday—it was not as you thought,"
said Rosamond in the same tone.

There was a movement of surprised attention in Dorothea.
She expected a vindication of Rosamond herself.

"He was telling me how he loved another woman, that I
might know he could never love me," said Rosamond, getting
more and more hurried as she went on.　"And now I think

he hates me because—because you mistook him yesterday. He says it is through me that you will think ill of him—think that he is a false person. But it shall not be through me. He has never had any love for me—I know he has not—he has always thought slightly of me. He said yesterday that no other woman existed for him beside you. The blame of what happened is entirely mine. He said he could never explain to you—because of me. He said you could never think well of him again. But now I have told you, and he cannot reproach me any more."

Rosamond had delivered her soul under impulses which she had not known before. She had begun her confession under the subduing influence of Dorothea's emotion; and as she went on she had gathered the sense that she was repelling Will's reproaches, which were still like a knife-wound within her.

The revulsion of feeling in Dorothea was too strong to be called joy. It was a tumult in which the terrible strain of the night and morning made a resistant pain: she could only perceive that this would be joy when she had recovered her power of feeling it. Her immediate consciousness was one of immense sympathy without check; she cared for Rosamond without struggle now, and responded earnestly to her last words—

"No, he cannot reproach you any more."

With her usual tendency to over-estimate the good in others, she felt a great outgoing of her heart toward Rosamond, for the generous effort which had redeemed her from suffering, not counting that the effort was a reflex of her own energy.

After they had been silent a little, she said:

"You are not sorry that I came this morning?"

"No, you have been very good to me," said Rosamond. "I did not think that you would be so good. I was very unhappy. I am not happy now. Everything is so sad."

"But better days will come. Your husband will be rightly valued. And he depends on you for comfort. He loves you best. The worst loss would be to lose that—and you have not lost it," said Dorothea.

She tried to thrust away the too overpowering thought of her own relief, lest she should fail to win some sign that Rosamond's affection was yearning back toward her husband.

" Tertius did not find fault with me, then? " said Rosamond, understanding now that Lydgate might have said anything to Mrs. Casaubon, and that she certainly was different from other women. Perhaps there was a faint taste of jealousy in the question. A smile began to play over Dorothea's face as she said:

" No, indeed! How could you imagine it? " But here the door opened, and Lydgate entered.

" I am come back in my quality of doctor," he said. "After I went away, I was haunted by two pale faces: Mrs. Casaubon looked as much in need of care as you, Rosy. And I thought that I had not done my duty in leaving you together; so when I had been to Coleman's I came home again. I noticed that you were walking, Mrs. Casaubon, and the sky has changed— I think we may have rain. May I send some one to order your carriage to come for you? "

"Oh, no! I am strong. I need the walk," said Dorothea, rising with animation in her face. "Mrs. Lydgate and I have chatted a great deal, and it is time for me to go. I have always been accused of being immoderate and saying too much."

She put out her hand to Rosamond, and they said an earnest, quiet good-by without kiss or other show of effusion. There had been between them too much serious emotion for them to use the signs of it superficially.

As Lydgate took her to the door she said nothing of Rosamond, but told him of Mr. Farebrother and the other friends who had listened with belief to his story.

When he came back to Rosamond, she had already thrown herself on the sofa, in resigned fatigue.

" Well, Rosy," he said, standing over her, and touching her hair, " what do you think of Mrs. Casaubon now you have seen so much of her? "

" I think she must be better than any one," said Rosamond, " and she is very beautiful. If you go to talk to her so often, you will be more discontented with me than ever! "

Lydgate laughed at the "so often." "But has she made you any less discontented with me? "

" I think she has," said Rosamond, looking up in his face. " How heavy your eyes are, Tertius—and do push your hair

back." He lifted up his large white hand to obey her, and
felt thankful for this little mark of interest in him.   Poor
Rosamond's vagrant fancy had come back terribly scourged—
meek enough to nestle under the old despised shelter.   And
the shelter was still there.   Lydgate had accepted his narrowed
lot with sad resignation.   He had chosen this fragile creature,
and had taken the burthen of her life upon his arms.   He
must walk as he could, carrying that burthen pitifully.

CHAPTER LXXXII.

" My grief lies onward and my joy behind. "
                              SHAKESPEARE : *Sonnets.*

EXILES notoriously feed much on hopes, and are unlikely to
stay in banishment unless they are obliged.   When Will Ladislaw exiled himself from Middlemarch he had placed no
stronger obstacle to his return than his own resolve, which
was by no means an iron barrier, but simply a state of mind
liable to melt into a minuet with other states of mind, and to
find itself bowing, smiling, and giving place with polite facil-
ity.   As the months went on it had seemed more and more
difficult to him to say why he should not run down to Middlemarch—merely for the sake of hearing something about Dorothea: and if on such a flying visit he should chance by some
strange coincidence to meet with her, there was no reason for
him to be ashamed of having taken an innocent journey which
he had beforehand supposed that he should not take.   Since
he was hopelessly divided from her, he might surely venture
into her neighborhood; and as to the suspicious friends who
kept a dragon watch over her—their opinion seemed less and
less important with time and change of air.

And there had come a reason quite irrespective of Dorothea,
which seemed to make a journey to Middlemarch a sort of
philanthropic duty.   Will had given a disinterested attention
to an intended settlement on a new plan in the Far West, and
the need for funds in order to carry out a good design had set
him on debating with himself whether it would not be a laud-

able use to make of his claim on Bulstrode, to urge the application of that money which had been offered to himself as a means of carrying out a scheme likely to be largely beneficial. The question seemed a very dubious one to Will, and his repugnance to again entering into any relation with the banker might have made him dismiss it quickly, if there had not arisen in his imagination the probability that his judgment might be more safely determined by a visit to Middlemarch.

That was the object which Will stated to himself as a reason for coming down. He had meant to confide in Lydgate, and discuss the money question with him, and he had meant to amuse himself for the few evenings of his stay by having a great deal of music and badinage with fair Rosamond without neglecting his friends at Lowick Parsonage—if the parsonage was close to the manor, that was no fault of his. He had neglected the Farebrothers before his departure, from a proud resistance to the possible accusation of indirectly seeking interviews with Dorothea; but hunger tames us, and Will had become very hungry for the vision of a certain form and the sound of a certain voice. Nothing had done instead—not the opera, nor the converse of zealous politicians, nor the flattering reception (in dim corners) of his new hand in leading articles.

Thus he had come down, foreseeing with confidence how almst everything would be in his familiar little world; fearing, indeed, that there would be no surprises in his visit. But he had found that humdrum world in a terribly dynamic condition, in which even badinage and lyrism had turned explosive; and the first day of this visit had become the most fatal epoch of his life. The next morning he felt so harassed with the nightmare of consequences—he dreaded so much the immediate issues before him—that seeing while he breakfasted the arrival of the Riverston coach, he went out hurriedly and took his place on it, that he might be relieved, at least for a day, from the necessity of doing or saying anything in Middlemarch. Will Ladislaw was in one of those tangled crises which are commoner in experience than one might imagine, from the shallow absoluteness of men's judgments. He had found Lydgate, for whom he had the sincerest respect, under circumstances which claimed his thorough and frankly declared sym-

pathy; and the reason why, in spite of that claim, it would
have been better for Will to have avoided all further intimacy,
or even contact, with Lydgate, was precisely of the kind to
make such a course appear impossible.   To a creature of Will's
susceptible temperament—without any neutral region of indifference in his nature, ready to turn everything that befell him
into the collisions of a passionate drama—the revelation that
Rosamond had made her happiness in any way dependent on
him was a difficulty which his outburst of rage toward her
had immeasurably increased for him.   He hated his own cruelty, and yet he dreaded to show the fulness of his relenting;
he must go to her again; the friendship could not be put to a
sudden end; and her unhappiness was a power which he
dreaded.   And all the while there was no more foretaste of
enjoyment in the life before him than if his limbs had been
lopped off and he was making his fresh start on crutches.   In
the night he had debated whether he should not get on the
coach, not for Riverston, but for London, leaving a note to
Lydgate which would give a makeshift reason for his retreat.
But there were strong cords pulling him back from that abrupt
departure; the blight on his happiness in thinking of Dorothea, the crushing of that chief hope which had remained in
spite of the acknowledged necessity for renunciation, was too
fresh a misery for him to resign himself to it and go straightway into a distance which was also despair.

Thus he did nothing more decided than taking the Riverston
coach.   He came back again by it while it was still daylight,
having made up his mind that he must go to Lydgate's that
evening.   The Rubicon, we know, was a very insignificant
stream to look at; its significance lay entirely in certain invisible conditions.   Will felt as if he were forced to cross his
small boundary ditch, and what he saw beyond it was not empire, but discontented subjection.

But it is given to us sometimes even in our every-day life
to witness the saving influence of a noble nature, the divine
efficacy of rescue that may lie in a self-subduing act of fellowship.   If Dorothea, after her night's anguish, had not taken
that walk to Rosamond—why, she perhaps would have been
a woman who gained a higher character for discretion, but it

would certainly not have been as well for those three who were
on one hearth in Lydgate's house at half-past seven that
evening.

Rosamond had been prepared for Will's visit, and she
received him with a languid coldness which Lydgate accounted
for by her nervous exhaustion, of which he could not suppose
that it had any relation to Will. And when she sat in silence
bending over a bit of work, he innocently apologized for her in
an indirect way by begging her to lean backward and rest.
Will was miserable in the necessity for playing the part of a
friend who was making his first appearance and greeting to
Rosamond, while his thoughts were busy about her feeling
since that scene of yesterday, which seemed still inexorably to
enclose them both, like the painful vision of a double madness.
It happened that nothing called Lydgate out of the room; but
when Rosamond poured out the tea and Will came near to
fetch it, she placed a tiny bit of folded paper in his saucer.
He saw it and secured it quickly, but as he went back to his
inn he had no eagerness to unfold the paper. What Rosamond
had written to him would probably deepen the painful impressions of the evening. Still, he opened and read it by his bed
candle. There were only these few words in her neatly flow-
ing hand:

"I have told Mrs. Casaubon. She is not under any mistake about you, I told her because she came to see me and was very kind. You will have nothing to reproach me
with now. I shall not have made any difference to you."

The effect of these words was not quite all gladness. As
Will dwelt on them with excited imagination, he felt his
cheeks and ears burning at the thought of what had occurred
between Dorothea and Rosamond—at the uncertainty how far
Dorothea might still feel her dignity wounded in having an
explanation of his conduct offered to her. There might still
remain in her mind a changed association with him which
made an irremediable difference—a lasting flaw. With active
fancy he wrought himself into a state of doubt little more easy
than that of the man who has escaped from wreck by night
and stands on unknown ground in the darkness. Until that
wretched yesterday—except the moment of vexation long ago
in the very same room and in the very same presence—all their

vision, all their thought of each other, had been as in a world apart, where the sunshine fell on tall white lilies, where no evil lurked, and no other soul entered. But now—would Dorothea meet him in that world again?

------◆------

CHAPTER LXXXIII.

" And now good-morrow to our waking souls
Which watch not one another out of fear;
For love all love of other sights controls,
And makes one little room, an everywhere. "
—DR. DONNE.

ON the second morning after Dorothea's visit to Rosamond, she had had two nights of sound sleep, and had not only lost all traces of fatigue, but felt as if she had a great deal of superfluous strength—that is to say, more strength than she could manage to concentrate on any occupation. The day before, she had taken long walks outside the grounds, and had paid two visits to the parsonage; but she never in her life told any one the reason why she spent her time in that fruitless manner, and this morning she was rather angry with herself for her childish restlessness. To-day was to be spent quite differently. What was there to be done in the village? Oh, dear! nothing. Everybody was well and had flannel; nobody's pig had died; and it was Saturday morning, when there was a general scrubbing of floors and door-stones, and when it was useless to go into the school. But there were various subjects that Dorothea was trying to get clear upon, and she resolved to throw herself energetically into the gravest of all. She sat down in the library before her particular little heap of books on political economy and kindred matters, out of which she was trying to get light as to the best way of spending money so as not to injure one's neighbors, or—what comes to the same thing—so as to .do them the most good. Here was a weighty subject which, if she could but lay hold of it, would certainly keep her mind steady. Unhappily her mind slipped off it for a whole hour; and at the end she found herself reading sentences twice over with an intense consciousness of many things, but not of any one thing contained in the text. This was hopeless. Should she order the carriage and drive to Tipton? No; for some reason or other she preferred staying at Lowick. But her vagrant mind must be reduced to order: there was an art in self-discipline; and she walked round and round the brown library, considering by what sort of manœuvre she could arrest her wandering thoughts. Perhaps a mere task was the best means—something to which she must go doggedly. Was there not the geography of Asia Minor, in which her slackness had often been rebuked by Mr. Casaubon? She went to the cabinet of maps and unrolled one: this morning she might make herself finally sure that Paphlagonia was not on the Levantine coast, and fix her total darkness about the Chalybes firmly on the shores of the Euxine. A map was a fine thing to study when you were disposed to think of something else, being made up of names that would turn into a chime if you went back upon them. Dorothea set earnestly to work, bending close to her map, and uttering the names in an audible, subdued tone, which often got into a chime. She looked amusingly girlish after all her deep experience—nodding her head and marking the names off on her fingers, with a little pursing of her lip, and now and then breaking off to put her hands on each side of her face and say, "Oh, dear! oh, dear!"

There was no reason why this should end any more than a merry-go-round; but it was at last interrupted by the opening of the door and the announcement of Miss Noble.

The little old lady, whose bonnet hardly reached Dorothea's shoulder, was warmly welcomed, but while her hand was being pressed she made many of her beaver-like noises, as if she had something difficult to say.

"Do sit down," said Dorothea, rolling a chair forward. "Am I wanted for anything? I shall be so glad if I can do anything."

"I will not stay," said Miss Noble, putting her hand into her small basket, and holding some article inside it nervously; "I have left a friend in the churchyard." She lapsed into her inarticulate sounds, and unconsciously drew forth the article which she was fingering. It was the tortoise-shell lozenge-box, and Dorothea felt the color mounting to her cheeks.

"Mr. Ladislaw," continued the timid little woman. "He fears he has offended you, and has begged me to ask if you will see him for a few minutes."

Dorothea did not answer on the instant: it was crossing her mind that she could not receive him in this library, where her husband's prohibition seemed to dwell. She looked toward the window. Could she go out and meet him in the grounds? The sky was heavy, and the trees had begun to shiver as at a coming storm. Besides, she shrank from going out to him.

"Do see him, Mrs. Casaubon," said Miss Noble, pathetically; "else I must go back and say No, and that will hurt him."

"Yes, I will see him," said Dorothea. "Pray tell him to come."

What else was there to be done? There was nothing that she longed for at that moment except to see Will: the possibility of seeing him had thrust itself insistently between her and every other object; and yet she had a throbbing excitement like an alarm upon her—a sense that she was doing something daringly defiant for his sake.

When the little lady had trotted away on her mission, Dorothea stood in the middle of the library with her hands falling clasped before her, making no attempt to compose herself in an attitude of dignified unconsciousness. What she was least conscious of just then was her own body: she was thinking of what was likely to be in Will's mind, and of the hard feelings that others had had about him. How could any duty bind her to hardness? Resistance to unjust dispraise had mingled with her feeling for him from the very first, and now in the rebound of her heart after her anguish the resistance was stronger than ever.

"If I love him too much it is because he has been used so ill:"—there was a voice within her saying this to some imagined audience in the library, when the door was opened, and she saw Will before her.

She did not move, and he came toward her with more doubt and timidity in his face than she had ever seen before. He was in a state of uncertainty which made him afraid lest some look or word of his should condemn him to a new distance from her· and Dorothea was afraid of her own emotion. She looked as if there were a spell upon her, keeping her motion-less and hindering her from unclasping her hands, while some intense, grave yearning was imprisoned within her eyes. See-ing that she did not put out her hand as usual, Will paused a yard from her and said with embarrassment, "I am so grate-ful to you for seeing me."

"I wanted to see you," said Dorothea, having no other words at command. It did not occur to her to sit down, and Will did not give a cheerful interpretation to this queenly way of receiving him; but he went on to say what he had made up his mind to say:

"I fear you think me foolish and perhaps wrong for coming back so soon. I have been punished for my impatience. You know—every one knows now—a painful story about my parentage. I knew of it before I went away, and I always meant to tell you of it if—if we ever met again."

There was a slight movement in Dorothea, and she unclasped her hands, but immediately folded them over each other.

"But the affair is matter of gossip now," Will continued. "I wished you to know that something connected with it—something which happened before I went away—helped to bring me down here again. At least I thought it excused my coming. It was the idea of getting Bulstrode to apply some money to a public purpose—some money which he had thought of giving me. Perhaps it is rather to Bulstrode's credit that he privately offered me compensation for an old injury; he offered to give me a good income to make amends, but I sup-pose you know the disagreeable story?"

Will looked doubtfully at Dorothea, but his manner was gathering some of the defiant courage with which he always thought of this fact in his destiny. He added: "You know that it must be altogether painful to me."

"Yes—yes—I know," said Dorothea, hastily.

"I did not choose to accept an income from such a source. I was sure that you would not think well of me if I did so," said Will. Why should he mind saying anything of that sort to her now? She knew that he had avowed his love for her. "I felt that——" he broke off, nevertheless.

"You acted as I should have expected you to act," said

Dorothea, her face brightening, and her head becoming a little more erect on its beautiful stem.

"I did not believe that you would let any circumstance of my birth create a prejudice in you against me, though it was sure to do so in others," said Will, shaking his head backward in his old way, and looking with a grave appeal into her eyes.

"If it were a new hardship it would be a new reason for me to cling to you," said Dorothea, fervidly. "Nothing could have changed me but——" her heart was swelling, and it was difficult to go on; she made a great effort over herself to say, in a low tremulous voice, "but thinking that you were different—not so good as I had believed you to be."

"You are sure to believe me better than I am in everything but one," said Will, giving way to his own feeling in the evidence of hers. "I mean in my truth to you. When I thought you doubted of that, I didn't care about anything that was left. I thought it was all over with me, and there was nothing to try for—only things to endure."

"I don't doubt you any longer," said Dorothea, putting out her hand, a vague fear for him impelling her unutterable affection.

He took her hand and raised it to his lips with something like a sob. But he stood with his hat and gloves in the other hand, and might have done for the portrait of a Royalist. Still it was difficult to loose the hand, and Dorothea, withdrawing it in a confusion that distressed her, looked and moved away.

"See how dark the clouds have become, and how the trees are tossed," she said, walking toward the window, yet speaking and moving with only a dim sense of what she was doing.

Will followed her a little distance, and leaned against the tall back of a leather chair on which he ventured now to lay his hat and gloves, and free himself from the intolerable durance of formality to which he had been for the first time condemned in Dorothea's presence. It must be confessed that he felt very happy at that moment leaning on the chair. He was not much afraid of anything that she might feel now.

They stood silent, not looking at each other, but looking at the evergreens which were being tossed, and were showing the

pale underside of their leaves against the blackening sky.
Will never enjoyed the prospect of a storm so much: it delivered him from the necessity of going away.   Leaves and little
branches were hurled about, and the thunder was getting
nearer.   The light was more and more sombre, but there came
a flash of lightning which made them start and look at each
other and then smile.   Dorothea began to say what she had
been thinking of:

"That was a wrong thing for you to say, that you would
have nothing to try for.   If we had lost our own chief good,
other people's good would remain, and that is worth trying
for.   Some can be happy.   I seemed to see that more clearly
than ever, when I was the most wretched.   I can hardly think
how I could have borne the trouble, if that feeling had not
come to me to make strength."

"You have never felt the sort of misery I felt," said Will;
"the misery of knowing that you must despise me."

"But I have felt worse—it was worse to think ill——"
Dorothea had begun impetuously, but broke off.

Will colored.   He had the sense that whatever she said was
uttered in the vision of a fatality that kept them apart.   He
was silent a moment, and then said passionately:

"We may at least have the comfort of speaking to each other
without disguise.   Since I must go away—since we must always be divided—you may think of me as one on the brink of
the grave."

While he was speaking there came a vivid flash of lightning
which lit each of them up for the other—and the light seemed
to be the terror of a hopeless love.   Dorothea darted instantaneously from the window; Will followed her, seizing her hand
with a spasmodic movement; and so they stood, with their
hands clasped, like two children, looking out on the storm,
while the thunder gave a tremendous crack and roll above
them, and the rain began to pour down.   Then they turned
their faces toward each other, with the memory of his last
words in them, and they did not loose each other's hands.

"There is no hope for me," said Will.   "Even if you loved
me as well as I love you—even if I were everything to you—I
shall most likely always be very poor: on a sober calculation

one can count on nothing but a creeping lot. It is impossible
for us ever to belong to each other. It is perhaps base of me to
have asked for a word from you. I meant to go away into
silence, but I have not been able to do what I meant."

"Don't be sorry," said Dorothea, in her clear, tender tones.
"I would rather share all the trouble of our parting."

Her lips trembled, and so did his. It was never known
which lips were the first to move toward the other lips; but
they kissed tremblingly, and then they moved apart.

The rain was dashing against the window-panes as if an
angry spirit were within it, and behind it was the great swoop
of the wind; it was one of those moments in which both the
busy and the idle pause with a certain awe.

Dorothea sat down on the seat nearest to her, a long low
ottoman in the middle of the room, and with her hands folded
over each other on her lap, looked at the drear outer world.
Will stood still an instant looking at her, then seated himself
beside her, and laid his hand on hers, which turned itself
upward to be clasped. They sat in that way without looking
at each other, until the rain abated and began to fall in still-
ness. Each had been full of thoughts which neither of them
could begin to utter.

But when the rain was quiet, Dorothea turned to look at Will.
With passionate exclamation, as if some torture screw were
threatening him, he started up and said, "It is impossible!"

He went and leaned on the back of the chair again, and
seemed to be battling with his own anger, while she looked
toward him sadly.

"It is as fatal as a murder or any other horror that divides
people," he burst out again; "it is more intolerable—to have
our life maimed by petty accidents."

"No—don't say that—your life need not be maimed," said
Dorothea, gently.

"Yes, it must," said Will, angrily. "It is cruel of you to
speak in that way—as if there were any comfort. You may
see beyond the misery of it, but I don't. It is unkind—it is
throwing back my love for you as if it were a trifle, to speak
in that way in the face of the fact. We can never be married."

"Some time—we might," said Dorothea, in a trembling voice.

"When?" said Will, bitterly. "What is the use of counting on any success of mine? It is a mere toss up whether I shall ever do more than keep myself decently, unless I choose to sell myself as a mere pen and a mouthpiece. I can see that clearly enough. I could not offer myself to any woman, even if she had no luxuries to renounce."

There was silence. Dorothea's heart was full of something that she wanted to say, and yet the words were too difficult. She was wholly possessed by them; at that moment debate was mute within her. And it was very hard that she could not say what she wanted to say. Will was looking out of the window angrily. If he would have looked at her and not gone away from her side, she thought everything would have been easier. At last he turned, still resting against the chair, and stretching his hand automatically toward his hat, said with a sort of exasperation, "Good-by."

"Oh, I cannot bear it—my heart will break," said Dorothea, starting from her seat, the flood of her young passion bearing down all the obstructions which had kept her silent—the great tears rising and falling in an instant: "I don't mind about poverty—I hate my wealth."

In an instant Will was close to her and had his arms round her, but she drew her head back and held his away gently that she might go on speaking, her large, tear-filled eyes looking at his very simply, while she said, in a sobbing, child-like way: "We could live quite well on my own fortune—it is too much—seven hundred a year—I want so little—no new clothes—and I will learn what everything costs."

CHAPTER LXXXIV.

"Though it be songe of old and younge,
That I sholde be to blame.
Theyrs be the charge, that spoke so large
In hurtynge of my name."
—*The Not-browne Mayde.*

IT was just after the Lords had thrown out the Reform Bill; that explains how Mr. Cadwallader came to be walking on the slope of the lawn near the great conservatory at Freshitt

Hall, holding the *Times* in his hands behind him, while he talked with a trout-fisher's dispassionateness about the prospects of the country to Sir James Chettam.   Mrs. Cadwallader, the Dowager Lady Chettam, and Celia were sometimes seated on garden chairs, sometimes walking to meet little Arthur, who was being drawn in his chariot, and, as became the infantine Bouddha, was sheltered by his sacred umbrella with handsome silken fringe.

The ladies also talked politics, though more fitfully.   Mrs. Cadwallader was strong on the intended creation of peers: she had it for certain from her cousin that Truberry had gone over to the other side entirely at the instigation of his wife, who had scented peerages in the air from the very first introduction of the Reform question, and would sign her soul away to take precedence of her younger sister, who had married a baronet. Lady Chettam thought that such conduct was very reprehensible, and remembered that Mrs. Truberry's mother was a Miss Walsingham, of Melspring.   Celia confessed it was nicer to be " Lady " than " Mrs.," and that Dodo never minded about precedence if she could have her own way.   Mrs. Cadwallader held that it was a poor satisfaction to take precedence when everybody about you knew that you had not a drop of good blood in your veins; and Celia, again stopping to look at Arthur, said, " It would be very nice, though, if he were a Viscount—and his lordship's little tooth coming through!   He might have been, if James had been an Earl."

" My dear Celia," said the Dowager, " James's title is worth far more than any new earldom.   I never wished his father to be anything else than Sir James."

" Oh, I only meant about Arthur's little tooth," said Celia, comfortably.   " But see, here is my uncle coming."

She tripped off to meet her uncle, while Sir James and Mr. Cadwallader came forward to make one group with the ladies. Celia had slipped her arm through her uncle's, and he patted her hand with a rather melancholy " Well, my dear! "   As they approached, it was evident that Mr. Brooke was looking dejected, but this was fully accounted for by the state of politics; and as he was shaking hands all round without more greeting than a " Well, you're all here, you know," the rector said, laughingly:

52

"Don't take the throwing out of the Bill so much to heart, Brooke; you've got all the riff-raff of the country on your side."

"The Bill, eh? ah!" said Mr. Brooke, with a mild distractedness of manner. "Thrown out, you know, eh? The Lords are going too far, though. They'll have to pull up. Sad news, you know. I mean, here at home—sad news. But you must not blame me, Chettam."

"What is the matter?" said Sir James. "Not another gamekeeper shot, I hope? It's what I should expect, when a fellow like Trapping Bass is let off so easily."

"Gamekeeper? No. Let us go in; I can tell you all in the house, you know," said Mr. Brooke, nodding at the Cadwalladers, to show that he included them in his confidence. "As to poachers like Trapping Bass, you know, Chettam," he continued, as they were entering, "when you are a magistrate, you'll not find it so easy to commit. Severity is all very well, but it's a great deal easier when you've got somebody to do it for you. You have a soft place in your heart yourself, you know—you're not a Draco, a Jeffreys, that sort of thing."

Mr. Brooke was evidently in a state of nervous perturbation. When he had something painful to tell, it was usually his way to introduce it among a number of disjointed particulars, as if it were a medicine that would get a milder flavor by mixing. He continued his chat with Sir James about the poachers until they were all seated, and Mrs. Cadwallader, impatient of this drivelling, said:

"I'm dying to know the sad news. The gamekeeper is not shot: that is settled. What is it, then?"

"Well, it's a very trying thing, you know," said Mr. Brooke. "I'm glad you and the rector are here; it's a family matter— but you will help us all to bear it, Cadwallader. I've got to break it to you, my dear." Here Mr. Brooke looked at Celia —"You've no notion what it is, you know. And, Chettam, it will annoy you uncommonly—but, you see, you have not been able to hinder it, any more than I have. There's something singular in things: they come round, you know."

"It must be about Dodo," said Celia, who had been used to think of her sister as the dangerous part of the family machinery. She had seated herself on a low stool against her husband's knee.

"For God's sake let us hear what it is!" said Sir James.

"Well, you know, Chettam, I couldn't help Casaubon's will: it was a sort of will to make things worse."

"Exactly," said Sir James, hastily. "But *what* is worse?"

"Dorothea is going to be married again, you know," said Mr. Brooke, nodding toward Celia, who immediately looked up at her husband with a frightened glance, and put her hand on his knee.

Sir James was almost white with anger, but he did not speak.

"Merciful heaven!" said Mrs. Cadwallader. "Not to young Ladislaw?"

Mr. Brooke nodded, saying, "Yes; to Ladislaw," and then fell into a prudential silence.

"You see, Humphrey!" said Mrs. Cadwallader, waving her arm toward her husband. "Another time you will admit that I have some foresight: or rather you will contradict me and be just as blind as ever. *You* supposed that the young gentleman was gone out of the country."

"So he might be, and yet come back," said the rector, quietly.

"When did you learn this?" said Sir James, not liking to hear any one else speak, though finding it difficult to speak himself.

"Yesterday," said Mr. Brooke, meekly. "I went to Lowick. Dorothea sent for me, you know. It had come about quite suddenly—neither of them had any idea two days ago—not any idea, you know. There's something singular in things. But Dorothea is quite determined—it is no use opposing. I put it strongly to her. I did my duty, Chettam. But she can act as she likes, you know."

"It would have been better if I had called him out and shot him a year ago," said Sir James, not from bloody-mindedness, but because he needed something strong to say.

"Really, James, that would have been very disagreeable," said Celia.

"Be reasonable, Chettam. Look at the affair more quietly," said Mr. Cadwallader, sorry to see his good-natured friend so overmastered by anger.

"That is not so very easy for a man of any dignity—with any sense of right—when the affair happens to be in his own family," said Sir James, still in his white indignation. "It is perfectly scandalous. If Ladislaw had had a spark of honor he would have gone out of the country at once, and never shown his face in it again. However, I am not surprised. The day after Casaubon's funeral I said what ought to be done. But I was not listened to."

"You wanted what was impossible, you know, Chettam," said Mr. Brooke. "You wanted him shipped off. I told you Ladislaw was not to be done as we liked with, he had his ideas. He was a remarkable fellow—I always said he was a remarkable fellow."

"Yes," said Sir James, unable to repress a retort, "it is rather a pity you formed that high opinion of him. We are indebted to that for his being lodged in this neighborhood. We are indebted to that for seeing a woman like Dorothea degrading herself by marrying him." Sir James made little stoppages between his clauses, the words not coming easily. "A man so marked out by her husband's will, that delicacy ought to have forbidden her from seeing him again—who takes her out of her proper rank—into poverty—has the meanness to accept such a sacrifice—has always had an objectionable position—a bad origin—and, *I believe*, is a man of little principle and light character. That is my opinion," Sir James ended emphatically, turning aside and crossing his leg.

"I pointed everything out to her," said Mr. Brooke, apologetically—"I mean the poverty, and abandoning her position. I said, 'My dear, you don't know what it is to live on seven hundred a year, and have no carriage, and that kind of thing, and go amongst people who don't know who you are.' I put it strongly to her. But I advise you to talk to Dorothea herself. The fact is, she has a dislike to Casaubon's property. You will hear what she says, you know."

"No—excuse me—I shall not," said Sir James, with more coolness. "I cannot bear to see her again; it is too painful. It hurts me too much that a woman like Dorothea should have done what is wrong."

"Be just, Chettam," said the easy, large-lipped rector, who

objected to all this unnecessary discomfort. "Mrs. Casaubon may be acting imprudently : she is giving up a fortune for the sake of a man, and we men have so poor an opinion of each other that we can hardly call a woman wise who does that. But I think you should not condemn it as a wrong action, in the strict sense of the word."

"Yes, I do," answered Sir James. "I think that Dorothea commits a wrong action in marrying Ladislaw."

"My dear fellow, we are rather apt to consider an act wrong because it is unpleasant to us," said the rector, quietly. Like many men who take life easily, he had the knack of saying a home truth occasionally to those who felt themselves virtuously out of temper. Sir James took out his handkerchief and began to bite the corner.

"It is very dreadful of Dodo, though," said Celia, wishing to justify her husband. "She said she *never would* marry again—not anybody at all."

"I heard her say the same thing myself," said Lady Chettam, majestically, as if this were royal evidence.

"Oh, there is usually a silent exception in such cases," said Mrs. Cadwallader. "The only wonder to me is, that any of you are surprised. You did nothing to hinder it. If you would have had Lord Triton down here to woo her with his philanthropy, he might have carried her off before the year was over. There was no safety in anything else. Mr. Casaubon had prepared all this as beautifully as possible. He made himself disagreeable—or it pleased God to make him so—and then he dared her to contradict him. It's the way to make any trumpery tempting, to ticket it at a high price in that way."

"I don't know what you mean by wrong, Cadwallader," said Sir James, still feeling a little stung, and turning round in his chair toward the rector. "He's not a man we can take into the family. At least, I must speak for myself," he continued, carefully keeping his eyes off Mr. Brooke. "I suppose others will find his society too pleasant to care about the propriety of the thing."

"Well, you know, Chettam," said Mr. Brooke, good-humoredly, nursing his leg, "I can't turn my back on Dorothea.

I must be a father to her up to a certain point. I said, ' My
dear, I won't refuse to give you away.' I had spoken strongly
before.   But I can cut off the entail, you know.   It will cost
money and be troublesome; but I can do it, you know."

Mr. Brooke nodded at Sir James, and felt that he was both
showing his own force of resolution and propitiating what was
just in the baronet's vexation.   He had hit on a more ingenious mode of parrying than he was aware of.   He had touched
a motive of which Sir James was ashamed.   The mass of his
feeling about Dorothea's marriage to Ladislaw was due partly
to excusable prejudice, or even justifiable opinion, partly to a
jealous repugnance hardly less in Ladislaw's case than in
Casaubon's.   He was convinced that the marriage was a fatal
one for Dorothea.   But amid that mass ran a vein of which he
was too good and honorable a man to like the avowal even to
himself: it was undeniable that the union of the two estates—
Tipton and Freshitt—lying charmingly within a ring-fence,
was a prospect that flattered him for his son and heir.   Hence
when Mr. Brooke noddingly appealed to that motive, Sir James
felt a sudden embarrassment; there was a stoppage in his
throat; he even blushed.   He had found more words than
usual in the first jet of his anger, but Mr. Brooke's propitiation was more clogging to his tongue than Mr. Cadwallader's
caustic hint.

But Celia was glad to have room for speech after her uncle's
suggestion of the marriage ceremony, and she said, though
with as little eagerness of manner as if the question had turned
on an invitation to dinner, " Do you mean that Dodo is going
to be married directly, uncle? "

" In three weeks, you know," said Mr. Brooke, helplessly.
" I can do nothing to hinder it, Cadwallader," he added, turning for a little countenance toward the rector, who said:

" *I* should not make any fuss about it.   If she likes to be
poor, that is her affair.   Nobody would have said anything if
she married the young fellow because he was rich.   Plenty of
beneficed clergy are poorer than they will be.   Here is Elinor,"
continued the provoking husband; " she vexed her friends by
marrying me: I had hardly a thousand a year—I was a lout—
nobody could see anything in me—my shoes were not the right

cut—all the men wondered how a woman could like me. Upon my word, I must take Ladislaw's part until I hear more harm of him."

"Humphrey, that is all sophistry, and you know it," said his wife. "Everything is all one—that is the beginning and end with you. As if you had not been a Cadwallader! Does any one suppose that I would have taken such a monster as you by any other name?"

"And a clergyman, too," observed Lady Chettam, with approbation. "Elinor cannot be said to have descended below her rank. It is difficult to say what Mr. Ladislaw is, eh, James?"

Sir James gave a small grunt, which was less respectful than his usual mode of answering his mother. Celia looked up at him like a thoughtful kitten.

"It must be admitted that his blood is a frightful mixture," said Mrs. Cadwallader. "The Casaubon cuttlefish fluid to begin with, and then a rebellious Polish fiddler or dancing-master, was it?—and then an old clo——"

"Nonsense, Elinor," said the rector, rising. "It is time for us to go."

"After all, he is a pretty sprig," said Mrs. Cadwallader, rising, too, and wishing to make amends. "He is like the fine old Crichley portraits before the idiots came in."

"I'll go with you," said Mr. Brooke, starting up with alacrity. "You must all come and dine with me to-morrow, you know—eh, Celia, my dear?"

"You will, James—won't you?" said Celia, taking her husband's hand.

"Oh, of course, if you like," said Sir James, pulling down his waistcoat, but unable yet to adjust his face good-humoredly. "That is to say, if it is not to meet anybody else."

"No, no, no," said Mr. Brooke, understanding the condition. "Dorothea would not come, you know, unless you had been to see her."

When Sir James and Celia were alone, she said, "Do you mind about my having the carriage to go to Lowick, James?"

"What, now, directly?" he answered, with some surprise.

"Yes, it is very important," said Celia.

"Remember, Celia, I cannot see her," said Sir James.

"Not if she gave up marrying?"

"What is the use of saying that?—however, I'm going to the stables. I'll tell Briggs to bring the carriage round."

Celia thought it was of great use, if not to say that, at least to take a journey to Lowick in order to influence Dorothea's mind. All through their girlhood she had felt that she could act on her sister by a word judiciously placed—by opening a little window for the daylight of her own understanding to enter among the strange colored lamps by which Dodo habitually saw. And Celia the matron naturally felt more able to advise her childless sister. How could any one understand Dodo so well as Celia did, or love her so tenderly?

Dorothea, busy in her boudoir, felt a glow of pleasure at the sight of her sister so soon after the revelation of her intended marriage. She had prefigured to herself, even with exaggeration, the disgust of her friends, and she had even feared that Celia might be kept aloof from her.

"O Kitty, I am delighted to see you!" said Dorothea, putting her hands on Celia's shoulders, and beaming on her. "I almost thought you would not come to me."

"I have not brought Arthur, because I was in a hurry," said Celia, and they sat down on two small chairs opposite each other, with their knees touching.

"You know, Dodo, it is very bad," said Celia, in her placid guttural, looking as prettily free from humorous as possible. "You have disappointed us all so. And I can't think that it ever *will* be—you never can go and live in that way. And then there are all your plans! You never can have thought of that. James would have taken any trouble for you, and you might have gone on all your life doing what you liked."

"On the contrary, dear," said Dorothea, "I never could do anything that I liked. I have never carried out any plan yet."

"Because you always wanted things that wouldn't do. But other plans would have come. And how *can* you marry Mr. Ladislaw, that we none of us ever thought you *could* marry? It shocks James so dreadfully. And then it is all so different from what you have always been. You would have Mr. Casaubon because he had such a great soul, and was so old and dismal and learned; and now, to think of marrying Mr. Ladislaw, who has got no estate or anything. I suppose it is because you must be making yourself uncomfortable in some way or other."

Dorothea laughed.

"Well, it is very serious, Dodo," said Celia, becoming more impressive. "How will you live? and you will go away among queer people. And I shall never see you—and you won't mind about little Arthur—and I thought you always would——"

Celia's rare tears had got into her eyes, and the corners of her mouth were agitated.

"Dear Celia," said Dorothea, with tender gravity, "if you don't ever see me, it will not be my fault."

"Yes, it will," said Celia, with the same touching distortion of her small features. "How can I come to you or have you with me when James can't bear it?—that is because he thinks it is not right—he thinks you are so wrong, Dodo. But you always were wrong: only I can't help loving you. And nobody can think where you will live: where can you go?"

"I am going to London," said Dorothea.

"How can you always live in a street? And you will be so poor. I could give you half of my things, only how can I, when I never see you?"

"Bless you, Kitty," said Dorothea, with gentle warmth. "Take comfort: perhaps James will forgive me some time."

"But it would be much better if you would not be married," said Celia, drying her eyes, and returning to her argument; "then there would be nothing uncomfortable. And you would not do what nobody thought you could do. James always said you ought to be a queen; but this is not at all being like a queen. You know what mistakes you have always been making, Dodo, and this is another. Nobody thinks Mr. Ladislaw a proper husband for you. And you *said* you would never be married again."

"It is quite true that I might be a wiser person, Celia," said Dorothea, "and that I might have done something better, if I had been better. But this is what I am going to do. I have promised to marry Mr. Ladislaw; and I am going to marry him."

The tone in which Dorothea said this was a note that Celia had long learned to recognize. She was silent a few moments, and then said, as if she had dismissed all contest, "Is he very fond of you, Dodo?"

"I hope so. I am very fond of him."

"That is nice," said Celia, comfortably. "Only I would rather you had such a sort of husband as James is, with a place very near, that I could drive to."

Dorothea smiled, and Celia looked rather meditative. Presently she said, "I cannot think how it all came about." Celia thought it would be pleasant to hear the story.

"I dare say not," said Dorothea, pinching her sister's chin. "If you knew how it came about, it would not seem wonderful to you."

"Can't you tell me?" said Celia, settling her arms cozily.

"No, dear, you would have to feel with me, else you would never know."

CHAPTER LXXXV.

"Then went the jury out, whose names were Mr. Blindman, Mr. Nogood, Mr. Malice, Mr. Love-lust, Mr. Live-loose, Mr. Heady, Mr. High-mind, Mr. Enmity, Mr. Liar, Mr. Cruelty, Mr. Hate-light, Mr. Implacable, who every one gave in his private verdict against him among themselves, and afterward unanimously concluded to bring him in guilty before the judge. And first among themselves, Mr. Blindman, the foreman, said, I see clearly that this man is a heretic. Then said Mr. Nogood, Away with such a fellow from the earth! Ay, said Mr. Malice, for I hate the very look of him. Then said Mr. Love-lust, I could never endure him. Nor I, said Mr. Live-loose; for he would be always condemning my way. Hang him, hang him, said Mr. Heady. A sorry scrub, said Mr. High-mind. My heart riseth against him, said Mr. Enmity. He is a rogue, said Mr. Liar. Hanging is too good for him, said Mr. Cruelty. Let us dispatch him out of the way, said Mr. Hate-light. Then said Mr. Implacable. Might I have all the world given me, I could not be reconciled to him; therefore let us forthwith bring him in guilty of death."—*Pilgrim's Progress.*

WHEN immortal Bunyan makes his picture of the persecuting passions bringing in their verdict of guilty, who pities Faithful? That is a rare and blessed lot which some greatest men have not attained, to know ourselves guiltless before a condemning crowd—to be sure that what we are denounced for is solely the good in us. The pitiable lot is that of the man who could not call himself a martyr even though he were to persuade himself that the men who stoned him were but ugly passions incarnate—who knows that he is stoned, not for

professing the Right, but for not being the man he professed
to be.

This was the consciousness that Bulstrode was withering
under while he made his preparations for departing from Middlemarch, and going to end his stricken life in that sad refuge,
the indifference of new faces. The duteous, merciful constancy of his wife had delivered him from one dread, but it
could not hinder her presence from being still a tribunal before
which he shrank from confession and desired advocacy. His
equivocations with himself about the death of Raffles had sustained the conception of an Omniscience whom he prayed to,
yet he had a terror upon him which would not let him expose
them to judgment by a full confession to his wife: the acts
which he had washed and diluted with inward argument and
motive, and for which it seemed comparatively easy to win
invisible pardon—what name would she call them by? That
she should ever silently call his acts murder was what he could
not bear. He felt shrouded by her doubt: he got strength to
face her from the sense that she could not yet feel warranted
in pronouncing that worst condemnation on him. Some time,
perhaps—when he was dying—he would tell all: in the deep
shadow of that time, when she held his hand in the gathering
darkness, she might listen without recoiling from his touch.
Perhaps: but concealment had been the habit of his life, and
the impulse to confession had no power against the dread of a
deeper humiliation.

He was full of timid care for his wife, not only because he
deprecated any harshness of judgment from her, but because
he felt a deep distress at the sight of her suffering. She had
sent her daughters away to board at a school on the coast, that
this crisis might be hidden from them as far as possible. Set
free by their absence from the intolerable necessity of accounting for her grief or of beholding their frightened wonder, she
could live unconstrainedly, with the sorrow that was every day
streaking her hair with whiteness and making her eyelids
languid.

"Tell me anything that you would like to have me do, Harriet," Bulstrode had said to her; "I mean with regard to
arrangements of property. It is my intention not to sell the

land I possess in this neighborhood, but to leave it to you as
a safe provision.   If you have any wish on such subjects, do
not conceal it from me."

A few days afterward, when she had returned from a visit
to her brother's, she began to speak to her husband on a
subject which had for some time been in her mind.

"I *should* like to do something for my brother's family,
Nicholas; and I think we are bound to make some amends to
Rosamond and her husband.   Walter says that Mr. Lydgate
must leave town, and his practice is almost good for nothing,
and they have very little left to settle anywhere with.   I
would rather do without something for ourselves to make some
amends to my poor brother's family."

Mrs. Bulstrode did not wish to go nearer to the facts than
in the phrase "make some amends"; knowing that her husband must understand her.   He had a particular reason, which
she was not aware of, for wincing under her suggestion.   He
hesitated before he said:

"It is not possible to carry out your wish in the way you
propose, my dear.   Mr. Lydgate has virtually rejected any
further service from me.   He has returned the thousand
pounds which I lent him.   Mrs. Casaubon advanced him the
sum for that purpose.   Here is his letter."

The letter seemed to cut Mrs. Bulstrode severely.   The
mention of Mrs. Casaubon's loan seemed a reflection of that
public feeling which held it a matter of course that every one
should avoid a connection with her husband.   She was silent
for some time; and the tears fell one after the other, her chin
trembling as she wiped them away.   Bulstrode, sitting opposite to her, ached at the sight of that grief-worn face, which
two months before had been bright and blooming.   It had aged
to keep sad company with his own withered features.   Urged
into some effort at comforting her, he said:

"There is another means, Harriet, by which I might do a
service to your brother's family, if you like to act in it.   And
it would, I think, be beneficial to you; it would be an advan-
tageous way of managing the land which I mean to be yours."

She looked attentive.

"Garth once thought of undertaking the management of

Stone Court in order to place your nephew Fred there. The stock was to remain as it is, and they were to pay a certain share of the profits instead of an ordinary rent. That would be a desirable beginning for the young man, in conjunction with his employment under Garth. Would it be a satisfaction to you?"

"Yes, it would," said Mrs. Bulstrode, with some return of energy. "Poor Walter is so cast down; I would try anything in my power to do him some good before I go away. We have always been brother and sister."

"You must make the proposal to Garth yourself, Harriet," said Mr. Bulstrode, not liking what he had to say, but desiring the end he had in view, for other reasons besides the consolation of his wife. "You must state to him that the land is virtually yours, and that he need have no transactions with me. Communications can be made through Standish. I mention this, because Garth gave up being my agent. I can put into your hands a paper which he himself drew up, stating conditions; and you can propose his renewed acceptance of them. I think it is not unlikely that he will accept when you propose the thing for the sake of your nephew."

CHAPTER LXXXVI.

"Le cœur se sature d'amour comme d'un sel divin qui le conserve; de là l'incorruptible abherence de ceux qui se sont aimés dès l'aube de la vie, et la fraîcheur des vieilles amours prolongée. Il existe un embaumement d'amour. C'est de Daphnis et Chlöe que sont faits Philemon et Baucis. Cette vieillesse là, ressemblance du soir avec l'aurore."

—VICTOR HUGO: *L'homme qui rit.*

MRS. GARTH, hearing Caleb enter the passage about tea-time, opened the parlor door and said: "There you are, Caleb. Have you had your dinner?" (Mr. Garth's meals were much subordinated to "business.")

"Oh, yes, a good dinner—cold mutton and I don't know what. Where is Mary?"

"In the garden with Letty, I think."

"Fred is not come yet?"

"No. Are you going out again without taking tea, Caleb?"

said Mrs. Garth, seeing that her absent-minded husband was
putting on again the hat which he had just taken off.

"No, no; I'm only going to Mary a minute."

Mary was in a grassy corner of the garden, where there was
a swing loftily hung between two pear trees.   She had a pink
kerchief tied over her head, making a little poke to shade her
eyes from the level sunbeams, while she was giving a glorious
swing to Letty, who laughed and screamed wildly.

Seeing her father, Mary left the swing and went to meet
him, pushing back the pink kerchief and smiling afar off at
him with the involuntary smile of loving pleasure.

"I came to look for you, Mary," said Mr. Garth.   "Let us
walk about a bit."

Mary knew quite well that her father had something particular to say: his eyebrows made their pathetic angle, and
there was a tender gravity in his voice: these things had been
signs to her when she was Letty's age.   She put her arm
within his, and they turned by the row of nut trees.

"It will be a sad while before you can be married, Mary,"
said her father, not looking at her, but at the end of the stick
which he held in his other hand.

"Not a sad while, father—I mean to be merry," said Mary,
laughingly.   "I have been single and merry for four-and-
twenty years and more: I suppose it will not be quite as long
again as that."   Then, after a little pause, she said, more
gravely, bending her face before her father's, "If you are contented with Fred?"

Caleb screwed up his mouth and turned his head aside wisely.

"Now, father, you did praise him last Wednesday.   You
said he had an uncommon notion of stock and a good eye for
things."

"Did I?" said Caleb, rather slyly.

"Yes, I put it all down, and the date, *anno Domini*, and
everything," said Mary.   "You like things to be neatly
booked.   And then his behavior to you, father, is really good;
he has a deep respect for you; and it is impossible to have a
better temper than Fred has."

"Ay, ay; you want to coax me into thinking him a fine
match."

"No, indeed, father. I don't love him because he is a fine match."

"What for, then?"

"Oh, dear, because I have always loved him. I should never like scolding any one else so well; and that is a point to be thought of in a husband."

"Your mind is quite settled, then, Mary?" said Caleb, returning to his first tone. "There's no other wish come into it since things have been going on as they have been of late?" (Caleb meant a great deal in that vague phrase); "because, better late than never. A woman must not force her heart— she'll do a man no good by that."

"My feelings have not changed, father," said Mary, calmly. "I shall be constant to Fred as long as he is constant to me. I don't think either of us could spare the other, or like any one else better, however much we might admire them. It would make too great a difference to us—like seeing all the old places altered, and changing the name for everything. We must wait for each other a long while; but Fred knows that."

Instead of speaking immediately, Caleb stood still and screwed his stick on the grassy walk. Then he said, with emotion in his voice: "Well, I've got a bit of news. What do you think of Fred going to live at Stone Court, and managing the land there?"

"How can that ever be, father?" said Mary, wonderingly.

"He could manage it for his aunt Bulstrode. The poor woman has been to me begging and praying. She wants to do the lad good, and it might be a fine thing for him. With saving, he might gradually buy the stock, and he has a turn for farming."

"Oh, Fred would be so happy! It is too good to believe."

"Ah, but mind you," said Caleb, turning his head warningly, "I must take it on *my* shoulders, and be responsible, and see after everything; and that will grieve your mother a bit, though she mayn't say so. Fred had need be careful."

"Perhaps it is too much, father," said Mary, checked in her joy. "There would be no happiness in bringing you any fresh trouble."

"Nay, nay, work is my delight, child, when it doesn't vex your mother. And then, if you and Fred get married," here Caleb's voice shook just perceptibly, "he'll be steady and saving; and you've got your mother's cleverness, and mine, too, in a woman's sort of a way; and you'll keep him in order. He'll be coming by and by, so I wanted to tell you first, because I think you'd like to tell *him* by yourselves. After that, I could talk it well over with him, and we could go into business and the nature of things."

"Oh, you dear good father!" cried Mary, putting her hands round her father's neck, while he bent his head placidly, willing to be caressed. "I wonder if any other girl thinks her father the best man in the world!"

"Nonsense, child; you'll think your husband better."

"Impossible," said Mary, relapsing into her usual tone; "husbands are an inferior class of men, who require keeping in order."

When they were entering the house with Letty, who had run to join them, Mary saw Fred at the orchard-gate, and went to meet him.

"What fine clothes you wear, you extravagant youth!" said Mary, as Fred stood still and raised his hat to her with playful formality. "You are not learning economy."

"Now that is too bad, Mary," said Fred. "Just look at the edges of these coat-cuffs! It is only by dint of good brushing that I look respectable. I am saving up three suits —one for a wedding suit."

"How very droll you will look!—like a gentleman in an old fashion-book."

"Oh, no, they will keep two years."

"Two years! be reasonable, Fred," said Mary, turning to walk. "Don't encourage flattering expectations."

"Why not? One lives on them better than on unflattering ones. If we can't be married in two years, the truth will be quite bad enough when it comes."

"I have heard a story of a young gentleman who once encouraged flattering expectations, and they did him harm."

"Mary, if you've got something discouraging to tell me I shall bolt; I shall go into the house to Mr. Garth. I am out of spirits. My father is so cut up—home is not like itself. I can't bear any more bad news."

"Should you call it bad news to be told that you were to live at Stone Court, and manage the farm, and be remarkably prudent, and save money every year till all the stock and furniture were your own, and you were a distinguished agricultural character, as Mr. Borthrop Trumbull says—rather stout, I fear, and with the Greek and Latin sadly weather-worn?"

"You don't mean anything except nonsense, Mary?" said Fred, coloring slightly, nevertheless.

"That is what my father has just told me of as what may happen, and he never talks nonsense," said Mary, looking up at Fred now, while he grasped her hand as they walked, till it rather hurt her, but she would not complain.

"Oh, I could be a tremendously good fellow, then, Mary, and we could be married directly."

"Not so fast, sir; how do you know that I would not rather defer our marriage for some years? That would leave you time to misbehave, and then if I liked some one else better I should have an excuse for jilting you."

"Pray don't joke, Mary," said Fred, with strong feeling. "Tell me seriously that all this is true, and that you are happy because of it—because you love me best."

"It is all true, Fred, and I am happy because of it—because I love you best," said Mary, in a tone of obedient recitation.

They lingered on the door-step under the steep-roofed porch, and Fred, almost in a whisper, said:

"When we were first engaged with the umbrella-ring, Mary, you used to——"

The spirit of joy began to laugh more decidedly in Mary's eyes, but the fatal Ben came running to the door with Brownie yapping behind him, and bouncing against them, said:

"Fred and Mary! are you ever coming in?—or may I eat your cake?"

53

FINALE.

EVERY limit is a beginning as well as an ending. Who can quit young lives after being long in company with them, and not desire to know what befell them in their after-years? For the fragment of a life, however typical, is not the sample of an even web: promises may not be kept, and an ardent outset may be followed by declension; latent powers may find their long-waited opportunity; a past error may urge a grand retrieval.

Marriage, which has been the bourne of so many narratives, is still a great beginning, as it was to Adam and Eve, who kept their honeymoon in Eden, but had their first little one among the thorns and thistles of the wilderness. It is still the beginning of the home epic—the gradual conquest or irremediable loss of that complete union which makes the advancing years a climax, and age the harvest of sweet memories in common.

Some set out, like Crusaders of old, with a glorious equipment of hope and enthusiasm, and get broken by the way, wanting patience with each other and the world.

All who have cared for Fred Vincy and Mary Garth will like to know that these two made no such failure, but achieved a solid mutual happiness. Fred surprised his neighbors in various ways. He became rather distinguished in his side of the county as a theoretic and practical farmer, and produced a work on the "Cultivation of Green Crops and and the Economy of Cattle-Feeding" which won him high congratulations at agricultural meetings. In Middlemarch admiration was more reserved; most persons there were inclined to believe that the merit of Fred's authorship was due to his wife, since they had never expected Fred Vincy to write on turnips and mangel-wurzel.

But when Mary wrote a little book for her boys, called "Stories of Great Men, taken from Plutarch," and had it printed and published by Gripp & Co., Middlemarch, every one in the town was willing to give the credit of this work to

Fred, observing that he had been to the university, "where the ancients were studied," and might have been a clergyman if he had chosen.

In this way it was made clear that Middlemarch had never been deceived, and that there was no need to praise anybody for writing a book, since it was always done by somebody else.

Moreover, Fred remained unswervingly steady. Some years after his marriage he told Mary that his happiness was half owing to Farebrother, who gave him a strong pull-up at the right moment. I cannot say that he was never again misled by his hopefulness: the yield of crops or the profits of a cattle sale usually fell below his estimate; and he was always prone to believe that he could make money by the purchase of a horse which turned out badly—though this, Mary observed, was, of course, the fault of the horse, not of Fred's judgment. He kept his love of horsemanship, but he rarely allowed himself a day's hunting; and when he did so, it was remarkable that he submitted to be laughed at for cowardliness at the fences, seeming to see Mary and the boys sitting on the five-barred gate, or showing their curly heads between hedge and ditch.

There were three boys: Mary was not discontented that she brought forth men-children only; and when Fred wished to have a girl like her, she said, laughingly, "That would be too great a trial to your mother." Mrs. Vincy in her declining years, and in the diminished lustre of her housekeeping, was much comforted by her perception that two at least of Fred's boys were real Vincys, and did not "feature the Garths." But Mary secretly rejoiced that the youngest of the three was very much what her father must have been when he wore a round jacket, and showed a marvellous nicety of aim in playing at marbles, or in throwing stones to bring down the mellow pears.

Ben and Letty Garth, who were uncle and aunt before they were well in their teens, disputed much as to whether nephews or nieces were more desirable; Ben contending that it was clear girls were good for less than boys, else they would not be always in petticoats, which showed how little they were meant for; whereupon Letty, who argued much from books,

got angry in replying that God made coats of skins for Adam
and Eve alike—also it occurred to her that in the East the
men, too, wore petticoats. But this latter argument, obscur-
ing the majesty of the former, was one too many, for Ben
answered contemptuously, "The more spooneys they!" and
immediately appealed to his mother whether boys were not
better than girls. Mrs. Garth pronounced that both were
alike naughty, ·but that boys were undoubtedly stronger,
could run faster, and throw with more precision to a greater
distance. With this oracular sentence Ben was well satisfied,
not minding the naughtiness; but Letty took it ill, her feeling
of superiority being stronger than her muscles.

Fred never became rich—his hopefulness had not led him
to expect that; but he gradually saved enough to become owner
of the stock and furniture at Stone Court, and the work which
Mr. Garth put into his hands carried him in plenty through
those "bad times" which are always present with farmers.
Mary, in her matronly days, became as solid in figure as her
mother; but, unlike her, gave the boys little formal teaching,
so that Mrs. Garth was alarmed lest they should never be
well grounded in grammar and geography. Nevertheless, they
were found quite forward enough when they went to school;
perhaps, because they had liked nothing so well as being with
their mother. When Fred was riding home on winter evenings he had a pleasant vision beforehand of the bright hearth
in the wainscoted parlor, and was sorry for other men who
could not have Mary for their wife, especially for Mr. Farebrother. "He was ten times worthier of you than I was,"
Fred could now say to her, magnanimously. "To be sure he
was," Mary answered; "and for that reason he could do better without me. But you—I shudder to think what you
would have been—a curate in debt for horse-hire and cambric
pocket-handkerchiefs!"

On inquiry it might possibly be found that Fred and Mary
still inhabit Stone Court—that the creeping plants still cast
the foam of their blossoms over the fine stone wall into the
field where the walnut trees stand in stately row—and that on
sunny days the two lovers who were first engaged with the
umbrella-ring may be seen in white-haired placidity at the

open window from which Mary Garth, in the days of old
Peter Featherstone, had often been ordered to look out for
Mr. Lydgate.

Lydgate's hair never became white. He died when he
was only fifty, leaving his wife and children provided for by
a heavy insurance on his life. He had gained an excellent
practice, alternating, according to the season, between London
and a Continental bathing-place; having written a treatise on
gout, a disease which has a good deal of wealth on its side.
His skill was relied on by many paying patients, but he
always regarded himself as a failure: he had not done what
he had once meant to do. His acquaintances thought him
enviable to have so charming a wife, and nothing happened
to shake their opinion. Rosamond never committed a second
compromising indiscretion. She simply continued to be mild
in her temper, inflexible in her judgment, disposed to admon-
ish her husband, and able to frustrate him by stratagem. As
the years went on he opposed her less and less, whence Rosamond concluded that he had learned the value of her opinion;
on the other hand, she had a more thorough conviction of his
talents now that he had gained a good income, and instead of
the threatened cage in Bride Street, provided one all flowers
and gilding, fit for the bird of Paradise that she resembled.
In brief, Lydgate was what is called a successful man. But
he died prematurely of diphtheria, and Rosamond afterward
married an elderly and wealthy physician, who took kindly to
her four children. She made a very pretty show with her
daughters, driving out in her carriage, and often spoke of her
happiness as " a reward "—she did not say for what, but probably she meant that it was a reward for her patience with
Tertius, whose temper never became faultless, and to the last
occasionally let slip a bitter speech which was more memorable than the signs he made of his repentance. He once called
her his basil plant; and when she asked for an explanation,
said that basil was a plant which had flourished wonderfully
on a murdered man's brains. Rosamond had a placid but
strong answer to such speeches. Why, then, had he chosen
her? It was a pity he had not had Mrs. Ladislaw, whom he
was always praising and placing above her. And thus the

conversation ended with the advantage on Rosamond's side. But it would be unjust not to tell, that she never uttered a word in depreciation of Dorothea, keeping in religious remembrance the generosity which had come to her aid in the sharpest crisis of her life.

Dorothea herself had no dreams of being praised above other women, feeling that there was always something better which she might have done, if she had only been better and known better. Still, she never repented that she had given up position and fortune to marry Will Ladislaw, and he would have held it the greatest shame as well as sorrow to him if she had repented. They were bound to each other by a love stronger than any impulses which could have marred it. No life would have been possible to Dorothea which was not filled with emotion, and she had now a life filled also with a beneficent activity which she had not the doubtful pains of discovering and marking out for herself. Will became an ardent public man, working well in those times when reforms were begun with a young hopefulness of immediate good which has been much checked in our days, and getting at last returned to Parliament by a constituency who paid his expenses. Dorothea could have liked nothing better, since wrongs existed, than that her husband should be in the thick of the struggle against them, and that she should give him wifely help. Many who knew her thought it a pity that so substantive and rare a creature should have been absorbed into the life of another, and be only known in a certain circle as wife and mother. But no one stated exactly what else that was in her power she ought rather to have done—not even Sir James Chettam, who went no further than the negative prescription that she ought not to have married Will Ladislaw.

But this opinion of his did not cause a lasting alienation; and the way in which the family was made whole again was characteristic of all concerned. Mr. Brooke could not resist the pleasure of corresponding with Will and Dorothea; and one morning when his pen had been remarkably fluent on the prospects of municipal reform, it ran off into an invitation to the Grange, which, once written, could not be done away with at less cost than the sacrifice (hardly to be conceived) of the whole valuable letter. During the months of this correspondence, Mr. Brooke had continually, in his talk with Sir James Chettam, been presupposing or hinting that the intention of cutting off the entail was still maintained; and the day on which his pen gave the daring invitation, he went to Freshitt expressly to intimate that he had a stronger sense than ever of the reasons for taking that energetic step as a precaution against any mixture of low blood in the heir of the Brookes.

But that morning something exciting had happened at the Hall. A letter had come to Celia which made her cry silently as she read it; and when Sir James, unused to see her in tears, asked anxiously what was the matter, she burst out in a wail such as he had never heard from her before.

"Dorothea has a little boy. And you will not let me go and see her. And I am sure she wants to see me. And she will not know what to do with the baby—she will do wrong things with it. And they thought she would die. It is very dreadful! Suppose it had been me and little Arthur, and Dodo had been hindered from coming to see me! I wish you would be less unkind, James!"

"Good heavens, Celia!" said Sir James, much wrought upon, "what do you wish? I will do anything you like. I will take you to town to-morrow if you wish it." And Celia did wish it.

It was after this that Mr. Brooke came, and, meeting the Baronet in the grounds, began to chat with him in ignorance of the news, which Sir James for some reason did not care to tell him immediately. But when the entail was touched on in the usual way, he said: "My dear sir, it is not for me to dictate to you, but for my part I would let that alone. I would let things remain as they are."

Mr. Brooke felt so much surprise that he did not at once find out how much he was relieved by the sense that he was not expected to do anything in particular.

Such being the bent of Celia's heart, it was inevitable that Sir James should consent to a reconciliation with Dorothea and her husband. Where women love each other, men learn to smother their mutual dislike. Sir James never liked Lad-

islaw, and Will always preferred to have Sir James's company mixed with another kind: they were on a footing of
reciprocal tolerance which was made quite easy only when
Dorothea and Celia were present.

It became an understood thing that Mr. and Mrs. Ladislaw
should pay at least two visits during the year to the Grange,
and there came gradually a small row of cousins at Freshitt
who enjoyed playing with the two cousins visiting Tipton
as much as if the blood of these cousins had been less
dubiously mixed.

Mr. Brooke lived to a good old age, and his estate was
inherited by Dorothea's son, who might have represented
Middlemarch, but declined, thinking that his opinions had less
chance of being stifled if he remained out-of-doors.

Sir James never ceased to regard Dorothea's second marriage as a mistake; and indeed this remained the tradition
concerning it in Middlemarch, where she was spoken of to a
younger generation as a fine girl who married a sickly clergyman, old enough to be her father, and in little more than a
year after his death gave up her estate to marry his cousin—
young enough to have been his son, with no property, and not
well born. Those who had not seen anything of Dorothea
usually observed that she could not have been "a nice woman,"
else she would not have married either the one or the other.

Certainly those determining acts of her life were not ideally
beautiful. They were the mixed result of young and noble
impulse struggling amidst the conditions of an imperfect social
state, in which great feelings will often take the aspect of
error, and great faith the aspect of illusion. For there is no
creature whose inward being is so strong that it is not greatly
determined by what lies outside it. A new Theresa will hardly
have the opportunity of reforming a conventual life, any more
than a new Antigone will spend her heroic piety in daring all
for the sake of a brother's burial: the medium in which their
ardent deeds took shape is forever gone. But we insignificant
people with our daily words and acts are preparing the lives
of many Dorotheas, some of which may present a far sadder
sacrifice than that of the Dorothea whose story we know.

Her finely touched spirit had still its fine issues, though

they were not widely visible. Her full nature, like that river of which Cyrus broke the strength, spent itself in channels which had no great name on earth. But the effect of her being on those around her was incalculably diffusive: for the growing good of the world is partly dependent on unhistoric acts; and that things are not so ill with you and me as they might have been, is half owing to the number who lived faithfully a hidden life, and the rest in unvisited tombs.

THE END.

Ingram Content Group UK Ltd.
Milton Keynes UK
UKHW022209240723
425713UK00005B/153